DEADLY FANTASY:

A BASEBALL STORY

ANDREW WOLFENSON

BALDING LEGAL PUBLISHING

Deadly Fantasy: A Baseball Story

© 2014

Balding Legal Publishing

2414 Morris Avenue, Suite 104

Union, NJ 07083

WWW.BALDINGLEGAL.COM

ISBN-13:   978-0615971636

ISBN-10:   0615971636

For the Wolfenson ladies:

Jennifer, Sara, Danielle, and Alina

PRAISE FOR *DEADLY FANTASY: A BASEBALL STORY*

"As a sports attorney I work regularly with athletes who are passionate about their sport. Jeff Goldstein takes this passion to a whole new and disturbing level. If there really were a fantasy league player like Jeff, then I would fear for the safety of my clients."

Jordan S. Solomon, Esq.

"Who would ever think a game amongst friends would turn to deception and murder? It would if there were a large cash payoff at the end of the season... and if one particular person was bent on winning it, no matter the cost to others. Author Andrew Wolfenson takes loyalty and America's National Pastime where they've never been before by playing Fantasy League Baseball with a life and death scoreboard, unquestionably making this book a home run."

Jon D'Amore – Author of the true mob story, The Boss *Always* Sits In The Back

"Deadly Fantasy has baseball, suspense, murder, gambling, and a tinge of dark humor. What more does one need? With the behind the scenes knowledge of a grizzled baseball reporter, Andrew Wolfenson paints an exciting page-turner of a story. It's a fun, informative read. Outside of catching a major league ball game on a balmy summer evening, I can't think of a better way of spending my time than reading this excellent book. Just like when former slugger Dave Kingman got a hold of a fastball, Deadly Fantasy is a solid hit over the fence, into the upper deck."

John Hartmann – Author of Jacket: The Trials of a New Jersey Defense Attorney

PRAISE FOR *DEADLY FANTASY: A BASEBALL STORY*

"Andrew Wolfenson's <u>Deadly Fantasy</u> combines the fixations of Coover's <u>Universal Baseball Association</u> with the suspense of Alfred Hitchcock in a taut tale of obsession and insanity."

Ron Kaplan – Author of <u>501 Baseball Books Fans Must Read Before They Die</u>

"I really enjoyed it. Your dialogue is awesome – very realistic, and easy to follow. You are also amazingly good at 'girl talk' scenes. Your descriptive paragraphs are terrific, and there was more than enough in this story to keep me well entertained, and I am not even a baseball fan!"

Holly Foley – Educator/Blogger

"<u>Deadly Fantasy</u> takes us deep into uncharted territory, the possible 'dark side' of fantasy baseball, and intricately describes one fan's struggle between reality and fantasy. I thoroughly enjoyed the book and its comparisons of different baseball eras and, also, the battle between fantasy players' loyalties to specific players as opposed to teams."

Anthony "Tony" DeMarco, Vice President, Lancaster Barnstormers

TABLE OF CONTENTS

TABLE OF CONTENTS

ACKNOWLEDGMENTS

The writing and re-writing of this book has been a twenty-year process. Not consecutive, thankfully, but it has been a long road and, as always, I have been blessed with the help of others. I want to thank the men who acted as editors for me at different parts of the process – one of whom first introduced me to baseball, and the other who stokes the fires of my love for the game on an almost daily basis – my father, Gil Wolfenson, and my friend, George Fiszer. Your input, especially your "constructive criticism," was invaluable. I also want to thank Diana Ani Stokely for her cover artwork, once again demonstrating that she can take my rudimentary concept and bring it to life in such an amazing manner.

Special thanks also goes to those who took the time from their otherwise hectic lives to write the blurbs that appear both on the "Praise" page and on the covers of the book – your kind words are, of course, greatly appreciated.

Lastly, I want to thank the members of my current fantasy baseball league, the league where I rule, with an iron fist, as Commissioner. My role as Commissioner provides me with a welcome diversion from work, and I am blessed to be involved in a league with such a great group of guys. I must add that none of the members of my league served, in any way, as models for any of the characters in this book. Any resemblance to any of you, as the disclaimer goes, is purely unintentional and coincidental.

FOREWARD

The copyright on the first page may read 2014, but in reality, I began to write this book in 1994, when my wife was pregnant with my first daughter. No company was willing to take a chance on the book back then, however, and my last printed copy of the manuscript, encased in a black binder, eventually found its way to an upper shelf in my office. While cleaning the office's conference room in 2012, I found the printed copy, covered in dust, and decided to give it another try – after first writing and publishing my legal thriller, *In His Own Defense*. I also located a 1990's–style floppy disk which contained much of the novel, and, fortunately, still had such antiquated computer systems in my office that I was able to upload the pages to my laptop and network. Recreating the originally-written novel, therefore, was not an overly onerous task.

Its content, however, was circa 1994. That means no internet, no cell phones, no texting, and no e-mails. To put things in perspective from a baseball standpoint, the terms "steroids" and "PED's" had not yet even entered the sport's vernacular – the epic home run battle between Mark McGwire and Sammy Sosa, the race that would eventually serve as the benchmark for steroid usage, was still four years away. The Yankees had not been to the World Series for over a decade, and it would still be two more years before they returned to their rightful position as World Champions. Meanwhile, their arch-rivals, the Red Sox, had not won the World Series since 1918, a span of 76 years.

A little more perspective - The Yankee Captain, Derek Jeter, has recently announced his retirement, effective at the end of the 2014 season. When this book was originally written, he had not yet made his first appearance in a major league game.

And on a more global sports level, the infamous OJ Simpson "Bronco chase" took place in the summer of 1994. Olympic skater Nancy Kerrigan was brutally attacked following a practice session by a man acting at the behest of Tonya Harding's husband in January of 1994. The New York Rangers won their first Stanley Cup championship in 54 years (they have not won another since).

For the non-sports fans, January 1994 brought a verdict of not guilty, by reason of insanity, for husband-mutilator Lorena Bobbitt. "Schindler's List" won seven Academy Awards. George W. Bush was elected ... Governor of Texas. Justin Bieber was ... born.

Yes, the original version of this book was written that long ago.

As such, I was forced to rewrite much of the novel in order to make it compatible with 2014. The basic story is the same, but it has been updated to reflect modern technology. Even twenty years later, I should note, I have yet to come across any other book which deals with a fictional fantasy baseball league player – in that respect, this book remains, in my mind, fresh and original. The issues discussed in the book with respect to both baseball and life in general, I believe, still exist today. I hope that you agree.

CHAPTER 1

"There are some people who live in a dream world, and there are some who face reality; and then there are those who turn one into the other."

- Douglas H. Everett

"To have long term success as a coach or in any position of leadership, you have to be obsessed in some way."

- Pat Riley, Former NBA coach (winner of five NBA titles) and current President of the Miami Heat

There are 30 teams in Major League Baseball. Each of those teams has one General Manager and one Manager. The former is responsible for drafting, trading for, and signing the men who will comprise each team's full active roster. The latter is responsible for day-to-day field operations, most importantly which of those players will see action in the teams' games. What this means is that there are 60 people who are essentially responsible for selecting the players who are privileged enough to don a major league baseball uniform at any given time, as well as which of those select few will actually see playing time.

At the same time, there are untold millions of "armchair" managers and General Managers, those who sit at home and watch and read about baseball, often second-guessing the decisions made by that select 60. Sports-themed radio shows are dominated by callers who propose what they would do in order to improve their favorite major league team, and there are countless blogs penned on a daily basis by observers, ranging from casual to rabid, regarding the same topics.

13

To allow those observers and students of the game (and those who dare say how they would do things not only differently, but better) the chance to prove their baseball-related acumen, the game of "fantasy baseball" was invented several decades ago. This game, originally devised by writer Daniel Okrent, allows fans to gather with their friends and others, or even on the internet, to form their own "leagues" – each person selects the names of real baseball players to create a structured "fantasy team." Depending on the size of the teams in the league, each owner is to select a specified number of pitchers and position players in order to populate his roster, either through an auction system (each "owner/manager" is provided with a pre-determined amount of "money" to spend in the draft) or through a straight draft system (meaning players are merely selected, in a pre-determined order, by the league owners.)

In one version of such a league, the statistics amassed by the selected players in various categories (such as home runs, runs batted in, and batting average for hitters, as well as wins, saves, and earned run average for pitchers) are then compared against those of the players who have been selected for the other teams. One other pitching category used in such leagues is "WHIP", an acronym for "walks plus hits over innings pitched," and is a statistic that was created by Okrent for use in the fantasy game.

The teams are then ranked in each of the categories, highest to lowest, and points are awarded to the teams based on their relative positions to the others. The team with the best aggregate statistics, and therefore the most points earned based on the statistical rankings, emerges as champion of the "fantasy league."

Another form of such leagues is termed "head-to-head" – in this format, two different "fantasy" teams square off against each other on a weekly basis, and only the statistics of those two teams, in the various categories, are compared against each other. Whichever of the two teams emerges ahead in the majority of the statistical categories earns a "win" for that week, and then each of the teams is ranked against the remainder of the league according to their weekly wins and losses (or ties), just like "real" teams are in the major leagues. The top-ranking teams then advance to a playoff system and, eventually, one wins the final battle and emerges as league champion.

According to one recent study, over 33 million people in the United States alone participated in a fantasy baseball or football league in 2013. Reports also estimate that approximately 20 percent of males aged 18 to 49 participate. The overall number represents approximately ten percent of the country's population, and is higher than the population of any state in the country, with the exception of California. In fact, if one were to add the populations of the 20 least populous states in the U.S., their total population, as of 2012, would be less than the number of people who currently play fantasy baseball and/or football. The economic impact of fantasy sports has been estimated to be $2 billion per year, including players' entry fees and advertising on fantasy internet pages.

There is even a fantasy league devoted to the United States Supreme Court. According to published reports, more than 20,000 people have signed up to a website on which they each try to predict how the Supreme Court Justices will vote on the cases heard by the court during that specific term.

Many of these individuals who participate in the sports-related fantasy leagues are no doubt casual fans, who participate simply in order to enjoy a social outlet with their friends. Others enjoy the managerial aspect of participating in the league, intending to create and "manage" a team to their respective championships while pretending to be a real major league General Manager or Manager. Hence the moniker "fantasy" to describe the leagues.

Some, however, take their participation in a fantasy baseball league much more seriously than others. This is the story of one such individual.

*****

The stadium's immaculately-groomed green grass sparkled, providing a stark study in contrast as a bright sun hung lazily over the otherwise decaying urban landscape. From the seats behind home plate, the brilliant yellow orb seemed to rest atop the blindingly-white frieze which dangled over the center field stands. Looking for all the world like an airport postcard, the climbing, horseshoe-shaped rows of blue seats provided a sharp contrast to the glittering metal of the stadium, which bore a remarkable likeness to the home of the New York Yankees from the mid-1970's until 2008, the cathedral which had been razed in 2009 in favor of a larger, more opulent edifice, constructed of limestone and granite, and which was built solely for monetary purposes, to allow for installation of more corporate-friendly luxury boxes.

The capacity crowd of 57,000 roared, half of the assemblage standing and the other half sitting precariously on the edge of their seats. Those in the first-row seats furiously pounded the walls in front of them, the red, white and blue bunting which adorned the facades fluttering wildly with each impact. The center field scoreboard told the story of a thrilling game - it was the bottom of the ninth inning, and there were two outs. The home team, down to its final out, was trailing by a 4-2 count. The scoreboard did show one seemingly disassociated fact to the otherwise familiar sight, however, as the listed home team was not the Yankees, but rather a team identified as the "Golds."

16

Impatient base runners nervously paced the infield dirt adjacent to second and third bases, their cleats burrowing ever-widening indentations in the base paths as they circled. Each knew that they would have to score in order to prevent the Golds from losing the game, and knew that even a slight hesitation could make the difference between scoring a run and making the last out. The next-scheduled batter, seldom-used but powerful Pete Nicks, had just finished taking heavy-handed practice swings in the on-deck circle and was beginning to make his way, hesitantly, to home plate, clearly bearing the weight of the game's importance on his broad shoulders.

Suddenly, Nicks saw the third-base coach waving him away and turned around; he then saw the manager beckoning him back to the dugout. The reserve outfielder, in a twist of events, would not be getting the chance to end the game, either with a big hit or an out. He turned, sheepishly, shrugged his shoulders and walked slowly off of the field as he quietly, almost imperceptibly, exhaled a sigh of relief. As he trudged back to the waiting handshakes of his teammates in the dugout, his fear of being the man who made the last out of the game alleviated, the unmistakable voice of legendary field announcer Bob Sheppard, once described as the "voice of God," began to introduce a pinch hitter. His deep tones reverberated throughout the various sections of the stadium as the crowd noise again swelled to a roar. "Now batting for Mercedes," the venerable announcer intoned as his words echoed throughout the stadium, "number 48, the player-manager of the Golds, Jeff Goldstein, number 48." Jeff Goldstein, the back of his pinstriped uniform bearing the emblazoned navy-colored number 48, grabbed a bat, bounded out of the dugout, and strode confidently to the plate, the announcer's introduction ringing in his ears as the originally-scheduled batter took a seat on the dugout bench.

The familiar opening guitar lick of the Rolling Stones' *"Start Me Up"* rang from the stadium's speakers, shaking the structure of the decaying building, and the remainder of the capacity crowd now rose to its feet, the sound of more than a hundred thousand hands rhythmically clapping as the hitter took his place in the batter's box. Several rows behind the first-base dugout, a petite brunette, her long brown hair flowing over the shoulders of her off-white blouse, cheered wildly. "Let's go, honey," she cried, her voice seeming to rise above the music and the shouts of others and filling the batter's ears with inspiration as he looked to her seat, gazed into her almond-colored eyes, and nodded before turning his attention back to the pitcher's mound.

The pitcher, seemingly oblivious to the noise of the raucous crowd and its sustained clapping and cheering, focused all of his attention on his catcher's fingers, the backstop's index finger extended downward to signal that he wanted the hurler to start this new batter off with a fastball. The pitcher nodded his approval of the pitch selection, began his windup, and delivered his first pitch. The batter did not move as the ball flew 90 feet to the catcher. The sound of the ball passing by him and striking the catcher's mitt echoed through the batter's ears, as his bat continued to rest on his shoulder. The umpire quickly thrust his arm into the air to signal that the pitch was a strike, barely clipping the left side of home plate, although to the hitter the pitch seemed to be outside of the strike zone. Goldstein lifted the bat off of his shoulder and looked back to the umpire with disdain, a look which was matched by the umpire, and dug in for the second pitch. Apparently Goldstein's glare had its intended effect on the official, however, because even though the ball crossed by the plate in approximately the same place as the first, this time, the pitch was much less theatrically termed a ball by the umpire.

18

Hall of Fame announcer Mel Allen was broadcasting the game for the nationwide television audience. The folksy drawl of his voice straining to be heard above the crowd, he began to describe the action as the pitcher delivered the third pitch to the Golds' player-manager. "How about that? The umpire has called the same pitch two different ways, leaving the count on Goldstein at one ball and one strike. There are two outs, the Golds losing by two. Runners at second and third, representing the tying runs. Williams checks the runners, rocks, and delivers the ball plateward."

The center field camera captured the scene perfectly - the hitter's eyes widened, watching the spinning white ball with the red laces grow larger and larger as it approached him. This time, the ball was aimed directly over the middle of the plate, a location which made swinging at it desirable, if not required. When it was within striking distance, time seemed to slow, so much so that Jeff Goldstein, his body coiled next to home plate, was able to make out the imprinted signature of the baseball commissioner which sat between the rows of laces. He strode forward and whipped his borrowed 33 ounce-bat around in a fluid semi-circle, and the crack of polished ash colliding with the spinning white ball reverberated up to the top of the bleachers, its thunderous impact rising above the chanting crowd. The projectile rocketed skyward in an arc-like motion, carried approximately 400 feet from home plate, and eventually came to rest in the outstretched arms of a young boy in the left field stands.

Up in the broadcast booth, Allen's broadcast partner, Russ Hodges, leapt from his seat and threw off his headset, yelling, "The Golds won the pennant, the Golds won the pennant" into his microphone as Allen thrust his arms triumphantly in the air. Down on the field, Jeff Goldstein circled the bases triumphantly, holding his left arm up, thumb extended skyward, and stomping deliberately and authoritatively on each of the three canvas squares with his right foot. He watched both of the base-runners cross home plate, knotting the score at 4-4, and his gait slowed to a trot as he approached the five-cornered home base, where a crowd of players and fans stood waiting to greet him. Before he touched home plate, he slowed further, almost to a walk, and looked over his left shoulder at the scoreboard, which now, presciently for the home team fans, but perhaps seeming presumptuous to the away fans, showed the Golds ahead by a 5-4 final score.

He touched the front of his right cleat to the triangular point of home plate, and the throng of fans and players engulfed him. The brunette woman from behind the dugout ran down the aisle and leapt over the railing onto the playing field, ducking under the delirious players and fans to reach home plate at the same time as the game's hero. The two embraced and locked lips, his arms lifting her off of the ground. "You did it," she yelled in his ear between kisses, "I knew that you could." He kissed her again, and then slowly lowered her to the ground. Three of the players then lifted him above the crowd, where he remained, thrusting his arms skyward, as television cameras captured the spectacle for all eternity.

From his perch on the shoulders of his players, Jeff Goldstein could hear the crowd roar and chant his name. Fireworks exploded in the distance, giant clouds of smoke billowing from beyond the center field stands from where the pyrotechnic displays emanated. The opening words of Queen's classic *"We Are the Champions"* rose above the din of the crowd cheers, tears filling the new hero's eyes as he continued to survey the scene which was unfolding before him. Soon, however, the sounds of adulation and fireworks disappeared, and were replaced by the sound of his ringing cell phone.

CHAPTER 2

Flickers of sunlight entered the Upper West Side apartment from breaks in the horizontal blinds, as the Saturday morning sun rose to breathe new life into another New York City day. Under side-by-side framed pictures of the 1978 and 1996 World Champion New York Yankees lay Jeff Goldstein, an accountant by trade, soundly sleeping under his flimsy blanket as his Yankees wristwatch ticked softly but steadily on the night table next to his bed. The quiet ticking of the watch made the only noise in the apartment aside from Jeff's allergy-wracked breathing, and the streets were unusually quiet, the hustle and bustle of city life still a couple of hours from kicking into high gear.

Jeff's curly hair was matted to one side as his head weighed heavily on his pillow, and his 177-pound body was clad only in Yankee boxer shorts. Another pillow lay on the floor next to his bed, resting alongside three days' worth of dirty clothes. Three of the drawers of the dresser which sat to his left were opened, rumpled clothes spilling out from each. In the kitchen, two empty glasses and a beer bottle sat in the sink, and a half-eaten slice of pizza was adhering itself to a plate on the counter. A cardboard box which contained another slice of pizza and several unattached strands of cheese lay wedged into a nearby garbage can. Two more empty beer bottles sat on the table in the room between the bedroom and kitchen, standing silent sentinel to a half-empty bowl of peanuts which rested in the table's center next to a television remote control.

The silence of the apartment, however, like the chanting crowd, was interrupted by the ringing of Jeff's cell phone. Jeff slowly lifted his head from its pillow, and reached up with his tingling left hand in a feeble attempt to lift

21

the phone from the other side of the bed. He coughed up some phlegm, which was somewhat of a morning ritual, and attempted to clear his throat before speaking.

"Hello?" he croaked, his barely-audible voice still filled with phlegm and coming out as little more than a hoarse whisper.

"Hey man, did you see the Yankees' game last night?" asked the voice on the other end of the telephone line, a voice that had obviously been awake for some time. Jeff immediately recognized the voice as belonging to Chris Perrine. The two had been friends since high school, and both were rabid baseball and Yankees' fans.

Jeff slowly but successfully managed to open his eyes and glanced over at the red illumination of his alarm clock, all the while struggling to maintain his grip on the phone. Through blurred vision and teary, reddened eyes, he could barely make out the numbers - 7:30. He vaguely remembered going to bed the night before at about 2:00 and then tossing and turning for some time before drifting off into slumber, meaning that he had slept for a little more than five hours at most. "It's fucking seven thirty on a Saturday, you asshole," he barked, his voice gaining strength with each word. "Why the hell are you calling me? You know that I'm working like a dog and need all the sleep I can get. I spend two nights a week in my own bed. Let me enjoy the morning a little."

"What do you mean why am I calling you?" asked the voice on the other end of the telephone, "and don't blame me for where you sleep at night, stud man." Chris rambled on; in what Jeff thought was little more than an attempt at annoying him further. "I thought for sure that you'd know why I was calling. I expected you to call me earlier this morning." He paused. "So don't try

22

to shit me and tell me that you don't know why I'm calling, because I can't believe that you haven't called me yet."

Jeff groaned audibly. "Chris," he whined, "It's too early to play Abbott and Costello, O.K.?" referring to the classic *"Who's on First?"* sketch. He coughed, and his voice cleared as he continued. "I really don't know why the fuck you are calling me so early. What the hell do you want?"

"You're joking, right?" asked Chris. "Don't tell me you didn't watch the game last night."

"What, the Yankee game?" Jeff asked, scratching his head as he tried to recall what would have taken place last night to make the game so memorable, so important, that his friend would call him and wake him at such an ungodly early hour. He had no answer. "The last I saw was when the game was scoreless in the third inning. Then I had to go out," he paused, "and I ... uh, I couldn't pay attention anymore."

Chris answered with mock horror. "What do you mean that you couldn't pay attention?" he asked, stressing the word "mean" as he laughed.

Jeff sighed. "I really don't feel like talking about it, but last night I was having dinner with Michelle. All of a sudden, things went completely to shit, like out of nowhere. Trust me, Chris, it was a bad scene." He paused and sighed before continuing. "And believe it or not, with all of her crap raining down on me, at that point watching the game was the last thing on my mind."

"Sounds bad, Jeff. What happened?" Chris asked, his voice now showing concern.

Jeff sat up, propping two pillows behind his back for support with his left hand. "To be honest, this probably won't surprise you all that much. We were sitting and having a nice dinner, and suddenly, from left field, and don't ask me why, she started with the commitment thing again," he said, folding one of the pillows in half so that he had more back support, "and it just went downhill from there. I gotta tell you, no matter how old I get, I still can't figure out women. Especially her, even though we've been together so long."

"Where did this all happen?"

"We were eating in an Italian restaurant on West 76th Street. She started with me in a restaurant. It was like in the fucking movies or television, when people do the break-up thing when they're out eating so that the other person doesn't make a scene. Well, last night Michelle was a one-woman scene. I couldn't believe it. In fact, I still don't believe it, even as I am telling you the story now." He paused, rubbing his right eye with his left hand before resuming the conversation. "I was sitting there, eating my linguine and clam sauce, and trying to watch the game on a little TV that was hanging over the bar on the other side of the room. It wasn't easy, believe me, trying to pay attention to the game and also talk to her."

"I don't like where this is going," Chris interjected. "I've seen this movie before, you know. We have both lived this movie before."

"Shut up." Jeff barked. He paused, before continuing his explanation. "Like a gunshot, all of a sudden she launched into me. Like I said, it was quite a scene she put on, all by herself as I sat there. She started to talk, and for whatever reason began to cry before she even finished one sentence. She did a little more yelling at me, and then she ran outside. Realizing that she wasn't planning on coming back after a couple of minutes passed, I had to follow to see what was wrong. She said I wasn't paying enough attention to her." He paused again. "Get this, she said I watched too much baseball, and it took up too much of my time."

"Your time?" asked Chris.

"Yeah, my time," answered Jeff. "What a load of shit."

"Well, you do spend a lot of time watching baseball. What did you say to her?"

"What did I say to her? As you can probably guess, obviously not the right thing," Jeff replied, his sigh of exasperation evident through the phone. "What the hell could I say to her? I swear, I just don't understand women. At first I told her that she was crazy."

"Oh, that sounds like a good move," Chris interrupted, a hint of laughter betraying his sarcasm.

"No shit, Jeff replied, coldly. "You ain't kidding, but it's not funny," he added. "After that, honestly, I don't even know what I said to her. It was all a blur. And besides, she wasn't going to listen to what I had to say anyway. Look at it this way -- we are officially broken up now. At least I think we are. But, as is usually the case, everything will probably be back to normal in a few days."

"Days?" Chris asked. "Are you sure? From what you're telling me, it sounds like she was pretty mad."

Jeff thought for a moment before answering. She was mad, but she had been angry at him before and, somehow, things always turned out fine. This was just, hopefully, just another step forward in strengthening their relationship. He realized that he key word in that thought was, of course, hopefully. "Yeah, days," he answered. He paused after a moment of further reflection. "Well, maybe not days. But give me a couple of weeks, or, worst case scenario, a few months. It will work out."

"Do you really think so?" Chris asked, concerned. "I mean, it sounds like she was really mad. I hope that you're right."

Again, Jeff paused and thought before answering. Maybe he was being overly optimistic, but only time would bear out whether or not he was correct. "To be honest with you, I don't know," he said, rubbing his eyes again and focusing his gaze on the photograph of Michelle that sat in a wooden frame on his nightstand. The photo was taken almost two years ago, during a weekend trip to Washington, D.C. Dressed in a white sweater and navy blue shorts, Michelle stood on the top steps of the Lincoln Memorial. Her dark hair was slightly askew, as several locks were being blown to the left side by a gust of wind. Her legs were crossed, left in front of right, and her left hand was placed provocatively on the top of her left thigh. She was leaning forward, her lips were puckered in an imaginary kiss. Her sensuality provided the perfect contrast to the cold marble feet of Abraham Lincoln that framed the picture's background. "Maybe not. But I certainly hope so," he added, wishfully.

He turned, looking over at another picture of Michelle, taken during a sojourn to the Baseball Hall of Fame in Cooperstown several years earlier, which hung from a metal frame over his bed. He stared at her almond-shaped eyes, which beamed out hypnotically from beneath a Yankees cap as she stood

26

in front of a display celebrating the New York glory days of the 1950's, and repeated, "I hope so."

"Well, at least you'll have more time for her after the last week in October," Chris joked, referring to the end of the World Series and, therefore, the end of baseball season.

"Very funny, you dick," Jeff's voice was rising at his friend's insensitivity. "Why the hell are you calling me this early in the morning? What happened, did something so unbelievably amazing happen in the Yankee game last night that it couldn't wait until a more reasonable hour?"

"As a matter of fact," Chris said, "I thought you would have made sure to watch the game, Mr. Baseball fanatic. Because something amazing, or important, did happen. The Yankees won, dude, they're back in first place."

Jeff's eyes widened, his attention level rising. "Did they really? That's right, I totally forgot that they could move into first with a win." To put it nicely, the past couple of years had not been kind to the Yankees or their fans. A few years without a World Series appearance and a clearly aging, if not geriatric roster, had been enough to put Yankee nation in a state of panic, which was why having them return to first place in their division was something to celebrate. "That is awesome." He paused.

"Worth calling?" Chris asked, mockingly.

His voice now at a more normal level, Jeff calmly answered, "yes and no. It was worth calling me, but I wish you had waited until later in the morning, or even early afternoon." He paused, his mind suddenly whirring with a different set of thoughts about last night's contest. "Tell me," he asked, "if I remember correctly Taylor started for them. Did he get the win? And how did Jamison do?"

There was a noticeable pause. "I don't remember," Chris finally said, coldly. Now it was Chris' turn to get mad at Jeff due to this new line of inquiry. "Who gives a shit?" he shot back.

"I just want to know," Jeff protested, more than a little surprised by the sudden change in the tone of his friend's response.

"You just want to know?" Chris said, mimicking his friend's voice. "What the hell is your problem? We're back in first place, maybe ready to make a run at the pennant for the first time in years, and all that you care about is whether that shit Jamison got a single or two? And whether Taylor got the win?" His voice grew louder with each word. "This is about that stupid fantasy league, isn't it? Well, sorry, but it doesn't matter who got the win, amigo. It matters only that the Yankees got the win. Right?"

"Hey, calm down man, you know that I'm psyched." He paused, allowing his friend time to cool off and completely ignoring the comment about his fantasy baseball league; as if by omitting any further mention of it Chris would think that his reasons for asking were unrelated. "It's not all that I care about. I just want to know. So Taylor, did he get the win? If so, no doubt it will help the team stay in first with him regaining his confidence."

Jeff immediately knew that he should have waited longer before asking the question, as Chris' voice rose even higher. Clearly he was not buying into Jeff's contrived statement about the team's hurler. "What the fuck is your problem, man? No wonder Michelle was giving you hell. But it's not even that you watch too much baseball. It's too much of that fucking fantasy league. Fuck Taylor. Get your priorities straight. The Yankees are in first place." Chris paused and thought about the hypocrisy of his last two sentences. "And yes, I know how stupid that sounds. I realize that there are more important things in life. But if you want so badly to see who got the win, you lazy shit, turn on the damned television. This is the information age, you know, so you can look on your phone. I'm not going to tell you. And you know what; you should worry more about what the fuck your girlfriend is doing now instead of asking me stupid-ass questions about whether some piece of shit guy got a hit or a win!"

Jeff tried in vain to speak over Chris' voice, which was, incredibly, still becoming increasingly louder with each word. "Alright, chill out," he interrupted, "forget that I even asked. I'm happy, OK? We'll have to get together later for a couple of beers to celebrate. We can meet at the sports bar, and see if they can win again tonight. Maybe even stay in first for a couple of days."

"Don't mess with me, Jeff." Chris yelled in response, his voice still too high for Jeff's comfort. "Why, is another of your pitchers on your little team throwing tonight, so you want to watch the game to see how they do? The only way that you'll be happy is if the losers on your fantasy team get that extra hit or lower their stupid hits-to-innings ratio." He paused and then added, with obvious disdain, "you know something, Jeff, you used to be a real baseball fan, not just a stats monger." The silence which followed that last word confirmed that Chris had clicked off his phone in anger.

29

"Can't get a break," Jeff muttered to himself, as he lay back down, closed his eyes, and pulled the blanket over his head, "first Michelle and now Chris. But at least I can work stuff out with him easily enough." He would call Chris later, and make arrangements for them to meet that evening at the sports bar with some of their other friends. They could watch a game together, and all would be forgotten. A couple of drinks and everything would be fine. Dealing with guys was so much easier than dealing with women. Fixing the problems with Michelle, he knew would take a great deal more effort. He lay in bed, the sunlight blocked by his blanket, and drifted back to sleep for a little while, a welcome respite from his suddenly acrimonious life.

Two hours later, Jeff struggled to his feet, his eyes still squinting at the morning sun, which was now streaming in through the blinds in his bedroom. He put on a pair of gym shorts and a faded Yankees' t-shirt, and shuffled slowly, deliberately, to the front door. Opening the door, he gingerly bent down to pick up the morning edition of the *New York Times*. Eschewing modern technology such as smart phones, the internet, and 24-hour score tickers on the bottom of ESPN and other sports stations, Jeff preferred to get his initial baseball information and game recaps from the print media.

The newspaper, folded neatly into thirds, beckoned to him from atop his baseball-diamond shaped welcome mat. The sound of his creaking bones echoed through the empty, dimly-lit hallway, providing the only sound on what appeared to be an otherwise silent weekend morning. He closed the door behind him, and, once inside his apartment, sat down on his couch, in front of the empty bottles and peanuts, and opened the paper to the sports section.

"YANKS WIN - BACK IN FIRST PLACE" blared the headline which stretched from end to end across the top of the sports section's first page. The

headline was irrelevant to Jeff, however, who intently scoured the accompanying article looking for any mention of the winning pitcher's identity or of the hitting performance of center fielder Rob Jamison. "Shit, why do they make it so hard to find the stats?" he cried, still looking for the elusive statistics as he literally tore the paper in half with his newsprint-covered hands as he flipped the pages before reaching page 10 for the continuation of the article. There, on the third column of the page, was the box score of the previous night's game.

Jeff's stare immediately went to the New York hitters, with Jamison's numbers appearing in their familiar sixth spot in the batting order. These results, unfortunately, were anything but good for Jeff and his "Golds" fantasy baseball team. For the third consecutive game, Jamison had, in baseball parlance, "taken the collar." This time, he had no hits to show for his four at-bats, making him hitless in his last 14 at-bats and dropping his season's batting average to an unsavory .229. Even worse, he was in a prolonged slump and his average over the past several weeks stood at a pathetic .196.

To further compound the problem, the Yankees' pitching line was no more beneficial to Jeff. Starter Bobby Taylor, whose numbers over the past four weeks had proven much more of a hindrance than benefit to both the Yankees and fantasy owners across the country, had again suffered through a bad outing.

In his haste, Jeff had failed to notice the opening paragraph to the newspaper article, which indicated that the Yankees had staged a late rally, coming from behind to capture a heart-stopping, ninth-inning, 6-5 victory over their rivals, the hated Red Sox. A three-run home run by third baseman Johnny Velazquez had provided the difference, making a winner out of second-year reliever Billy Martin. Martin, born to two Yankees' fanatics and named after the

31

late Yankee second baseman and five-time manager, won his fifth consecutive game, putting to rest any concerns about the sophomore jinx that he had seemingly endured in the season's first three months. He was gaining strength with each appearance, and was looking more and more like the 11-3 rookie pitching phenom of the year before.

Taylor, meanwhile, one of the starting pitchers on Jeff's fantasy league team, left the game in the fifth inning with only one out and runners on first and second. The Yankees trailed by a 4-2 score, but Martin got two quick outs, stranding the runners, and keeping the game within reach. It was Taylor's fourth consecutive rough outing. In fact, things were going so badly for the veteran right-hander that the Yankee manager commented after the game that the team was contemplating sending him to the minor leagues to re-learn his mechanics, to determine if there was a flaw in his pitching motion which could be easily repaired. Against a lesser caliber of players, team officials felt, he might be able to regain the confidence that appeared to be lacking in his last few starts.

Jeff had thought of doing the same thing on several occasions, that is, drop Taylor into the minor leagues or bench of his own team. That way, his statistics wouldn't count towards the team's totals. He knew that keeping Taylor on his major-league roster could prove fatal to his chances of winning the title, but wavered on whether or not to make a roster move. His fear was that Taylor would turn the corner, and that he would not get the benefit of a positive start if and when it happened. Also, with the Yankees winning at a ferocious clip, the likelihood of a win for Taylor, even with a middling outing, remained. At least in theory, that is. The realities of his last few starts had been, as Jeff was acutely aware, quite the opposite.

The account of the game from the *Times* and the latest copy of *The Baseball News*, however, provided little solace. The same was true for the various on-line sites which devoted countless pages to analyzing everything baseball and everything fantasy baseball. Jeff had finished reading the *Times* article and box score on the Yankees re-ascension to the top of the American League's Eastern Division at 9:40, and by 9:41 he had sprinted to the den to retrieve the periodical that he called his "baseball season bible." He thumbed through the pages of the book while simultaneously scouring the internet sites for some insight as to a new pitcher, one who was not already gobbled up by the other teams in the league.

The search for a replacement starting pitcher, however, yielded no viable alternatives. The best available man seemed to be Paul Connor of the Cleveland Indians. Connor was a journeyman whose season statistics included a 7-12 record, an E.R.A. of 4.27, and a ratio (hits plus walks divided by innings) of 1.403. These were not the statistics that could be counted on to resurrect a slumping staff, especially in light of the fact that Taylor's numbers were, despite his recent troubles, still more impressive than Connors' figures.

Jeff thought about what plan of action he should take. Maybe selecting a middle reliever, someone like Martin, would be a good idea; a reliever with a solid E.R.A. and ratio would certainly help in those two categories, but, on the other hand, would likely do little to aid Jeff's squad in the all-important wins category. Martin's numbers, his eleven wins the prior year and his five consecutive victories this year, were an anomaly among such relievers. While middle relievers are capable of picking up occasional wins, what Jeff's team really needed was a starter who could be counted on to win at least one game a week.

He decided to follow the Yankees' decision. If they kept Taylor in their starting rotation, he reasoned, then so would he. As he liked to say, "great managers think alike." Not that he was overly pleased with the Yankees' field general, despite the team's surge to first place, but at this point, he needed all the help he could get.

That evening, Jeff and Chris, having mended their short-lived rift, crossed Manhattan with another friend, to the East Side, and watched the Yankees-Red Sox game at a sports bar. The three men were met there by two other friends of theirs, and the five consumed four pitchers of beer and several appetizers before the game concluded at 11:00 P.M. They remained at the bar long enough to watch that evening's installment of *SportsCenter*, drinking two more pitchers during that half-hour span. After leaving the others behind, Jeff returned home, going immediately for his pillow. As he lay in the dark, he struggled to avoid thinking about Michelle.

Thoughts of her tormented him for some time as he tried to rest. They were thoughts that had been repressed while he was with his friends at the bar, but which were now enhanced by the liquor that he had consumed all night, until he was finally able to drift off to sleep.

CHAPTER 3

The cacophony of multiple taxi horns muddled the otherwise rhythmic sounds of vehicles passing the two women as they ate their brunch at the outdoor café on East 84th Street. Beads of sweat formed on their mimosa glasses from the morning sun's heat, and the plates sitting in the middle of the table contained remnants of bagels and vegetable omelets. As they sat, one of the women gasped in mock horror as her friend recounted the events of her previous night's date.

"Seriously, Michelle, I know it is a problem between you, but come on, really, it couldn't have been that bad," said Lisa Porter, lifting her glass to sip her mimosa while she awaited her friend's explanation.

Michelle Stein sighed. She brushed her long brown hair from her face, and Lisa, thinking that perhaps her comment came across as too insensitive, noted a tear slowly making its way down Michelle's left cheek. After an extended pause, Michelle sighed again and then replied, "Sorry, Lisa, but yes, it was. I don't want to be overly dramatic, but it was all of our problems manifesting themselves in one neat but horrible little package." Her tears began to flow freely. Lisa placed her glass back on the table and reached into her pocketbook for a tissue, but her efforts were waved off by her crying companion. "I have my own tissues," Michelle said, wiping the tears with her hands, "and I promised myself that I wouldn't cry."

Lisa stood and walked around the table, positioning herself behind a now-sobbing Michelle. She wrapped her arms around Michelle, who had buried her head in her hands, such that her arms formed a protective ring around

35

Michelle's. "It's OK to cry, honey," Lisa said, "we can sit here as long as you want. I'm not going anywhere." She slowly ran her hands up and down Michelle's arms to comfort her, and gently kissed her on the top of the head. One of the café's waiters stood impatiently next to Lisa, unable to squeeze between her and the table behind her. He cleared his throat in an attempt to convince her to move, but his efforts proved futile as Lisa lifted her head from atop Michelle's and glared at the waiter until he formulated an alternative path to his intended destination.

"It's not OK to cry," Michelle sniffled. "I knew who he was. I knew what he was like. I should not be surprised by anything he does anymore." She paused, and sat up straight, freeing herself from her friend's grasp and wrapping her arms around Lisa's waist. "Thank you for being here with me and listening to me complain. But we both know that he's never going to change, so I just need to accept that things are over."

Lisa looked down at Michelle's reddened face, again kissed her on the top of her head, and then returned back around the table and sat back down in her seat. "Nothing is final, you know," she replied. "Now what happened last night that was so terrible?"

Michelle looked to the sky, as if searching for the proper way to convey her thoughts so that she did not sound like she was over-reacting. In the sunlight, Lisa could see the bright purple pouches that ran along the bottom of Michelle's eyes, their vivid color testament to a lack of sleep and great deal of crying the night before. Michelle caught her friend staring at the bags under her eyes and reached down to the table to retrieve her sunglasses. "Oh my God, Lisa, I must look horrible," she exclaimed, placing the glasses over her eyes and pulling them slightly down on her nose to hide the discoloration. "I didn't have time to put make-up on this morning before I met you." She looked downward. "I am so sorry."

"Don't be ridiculous," Lisa answered, attempting to diffuse the tension in the air by making a joke at Michelle's expense. "To be honest, we should do it this way more often. I am enjoying being the better-looking one for once," she added, smiling. "When guys walk by now, they will look at me, rather than at the girl who looks like she has two black eyes. I could do this all day, you know."

Michelle chuckled at her friend's joke, the first time that she had allowed herself to laugh since she ran out of a bar the previous evening, leaving an incredulous Jeff Goldstein inexplicably wondering what he had done to cause her to leave in such a rage. "You're always the better looking one, Lisa," she said, "you know that."

Lisa puckered her lips in a mock pose and ran her hands through her curly blonde hair. "Thank you, darling," she said in an affected voice, "but we both know that you are lying." Her voice returned to normal. "You are stunning, Michelle. You know that. I would kill to look like you. Of course," she laughed, "I would have to lose about 15 pounds, grow bigger boobs, get a nose job, and bleach my teeth. But enough about my dreams. You still haven't told me what happened."

Michelle looked at Lisa. "Well, I can tell you one thing. My boobs aren't bigger than yours, Lisa," she said, looking downward at her friend's T-shirt and smiling. "In fact, I got rid of my biggest boob last night. You want to know why?" she asked.

Lisa leaned forward, pressing her breasts together in a mock competition. "Yes, I do. We all do," she said, looking downward into her cleavage. "The girls and I all want to know."

"Well what do the three of you think it was? The usual."

"Let me guess. Baseball, right?" Lisa said, leaning back into her chair and shaking her head. "Was there a game on that he insisted on watching?"

"Of course," replied Michelle, reaching for her own glass and sipping at her mimosa, the condensation from the glass falling onto her own T-shirt. "We went to that nice Italian place on West 76th. You know, the one where we went a couple of weeks ago with Diane. I figured it was a good time to discuss our relationship, where we were going, you know, the stuff we want to talk about and men never want to talk about. It's been a long time since we moved here after college, and I think it's time to determine where this relationship is really going."

"Makes sense to me," Lisa said. "So what happened?"

"You can probably imagine. There I am, trying to get him to actually have a real, adult conversation with me, and it occurred to me that he wasn't really paying attention to me. Instead of looking me in the eye, I realized that he was looking over my shoulder. I turned around, and for the first time, saw …"

"The little TV over the bar, right?" interjected Lisa.

"That's right!" exclaimed Michelle. "You knew about it?" she added as Lisa shook her head up and down. "I did not see the TV when we were there last week. To be honest with you, that was one of the reasons that I insisted we go there. It's bad enough with him looking down at his damned phone every five minutes for the baseball scores, I figured that if there was no TV there I had a chance of being able to talk to him. Well, clearly I was wrong."

"Did you confront him about watching the game?" asked Lisa.

"I tried to, but I could barely get out a sentence before I started to cry. I was so mad at him that I got hysterical. It was so embarrassing, to tell you the truth. I never thought that I would lose my composure like that, especially in a public place like a restaurant." She again lifted her glass and took another sip of her mimosa, the coolness of the drink serving as a calming force to prevent her from crying again while recounting the events from the prior evening. "And then, it was so bad ... so bad that I ran outside to the sidewalk because I couldn't even stand to look at him anymore. I was so frustrated, and then he came after me, which was clearly not what I wanted him to do at that point."

"Please tell me you didn't have another argument in the street," pleaded Lisa.

"I can't say that," Michelle said, shaking her head. "He came outside, and get this, he had the nerve to ask me what was wrong. I mean, seriously, even he can't be that stupid. So I told him that he wasn't paying enough attention to me, that he watched too much fucking baseball," she lowered her voice after dropping the f-bomb, and looked around her to make sure that she had not offended anyone. "I apologize for using that word, but he just gets me so angry."

"Really? You're apologizing to me? A little profanity never hurt anyone, so don't fucking worry about it," replied Lisa, again joking in an attempt to ease her friend's nerves. "Go on."

"So I told him that he watches too much baseball, which everyone knows, right? And guess what his answer was?" She paused, but decided not to wait for a response before continuing. "No, don't guess, I will tell you. Instead of recognizing what everyone else is telling him, he told me that I was crazy. I'm crazy! How is it possible that he doesn't see it?"

"Shut the fuck up!" Lisa replied, loudly, as the people from the next table turned in her direction. Luckily for the women, the people two tables over, the couple with the two small children, did not look up from their plates, apparently oblivious to her epithet.

"No, really," Michelle said, herself oblivious to the people who were now watching their conversation. "His response was that I am crazy. That was enough for me. I walked to Fifth Avenue, hailed a cab, and went home. He called me a couple of times after I got home, but I did not pick up the phone." She shook her head slowly. "I'm done. Crazy? Maybe I am crazy. You know, for staying with him that long."

"Well, I wouldn't say that it's over yet, Michelle, you know how things sometimes work themselves out," Lisa said, "but you know that whatever you decide, I am here for you."

Michelle looked around her, dabbed at her moistened eyes with a tissue that she retrieved from her pocket, and then lifted her glasses and looked straight at Lisa. "Of course you are, Lisa. But," she added, a faint smile creasing her lips, "now that I know how much you think about my body, I am having second doubts about your intentions. I don't have any more room for romance in my life, honey. Maybe if I keep these giant rings under my eyes you won't be so attracted to me."

She again laughed and reached for her mimosa, which was now comprised more of melted ice water than champagne and orange juice. Raising

40

the glass as if to make a toast, Michelle smiled at Lisa, who also laughed in response to Michelle's obvious attempt at humor. "Seriously, Lisa," Michelle added, "thanks for being here. It's good to know that I have friends I can count on, especially since my family is hours away."

CHAPTER 4

The next morning, the smell of freshly brewed Jamaican coffee, dashed with a hint of cinnamon, wafted through Jeff's apartment, combining with the smooth, almost imperceptible jazz sounds playing through his I-pod docking station to create what would appear to be a seemingly mellow, relaxed, care-free Sunday morning atmosphere. Sunlight poured in through the drawn shades, and several speckled goldfish swam gracefully and silently through the water of their twenty-gallon glassy home. The false serenity was broken, however, by the rustling of newspaper which betrayed the intensity with which Jeff pored over the Sunday sports section.

"Damn them," he bellowed, "why can't they just once have the scores of the late-night West coast games?" The clock on the wall, a paper maché depiction of the old Yankee Stadium purchased on a 2008 pilgrimage to the Baseball Hall of Fame in Cooperstown, read 9:05. "Gotta turn on the computer," he thought, as he strolled into the next room. Like a junkie looking for his next hit, he simply could not wait, even another minute, for information regarding the previous night's Angels-Mariners and Twins-A's games. Those were the two games from the previous evening that had been completed too late to be included on the late sports reports.

The entire coffee table, cleared of the prior day's bottles and snack foods, was now covered with papers of various sizes and consistencies. The Sunday sports section, the latest edition of *The Baseball News*, each major league team's preseason rosters, and the up-to-date fantasy league standings, printed off of the league website the previous evening, were strewn about the table as Jeff continued his agonizing, seemingly endless search for the perfect pitcher. Jeff glared down at the standings, and was overcome by feelings of disgust, which were not entire merited due to his current third-place standing. As of June 23, the standings were as follows:

1) The Emerson Boozers (Joe Emerson)	57
2) Bobby Fish and the Fins (Bob Fishman)	55
3) Golddiggers (Jeff Goldstein)	53
4) The Jew Crew (Keith Greenbaum)	50
T5) Frantastics (Pete Francis)	45
T5) Bergermeister-Meisterbergers (Mike Berger)	45
7) Bayonne Bombers (Joe Spadola)	41
8) Brians and Brawn (Brian Hunter)	38
9) Hang 'em Hy (Gene Hyland)	30
10) Martinizers (Barry Martin)	26

Four points from the top," he thought, "just four points from being in first place."

But Jeff was well aware of the fact that these numbers were deceiving and that the teams' relative positions could change wildly based on the statistics from just one game. A home run here or there, three more victories, and a handful of stolen bases could easily vault Jeff into the top spot that he so coveted. On the other hand, he knew, a few less runs batted in and another bad pitching week could potentially drop him all the way into sixth place, a fall from which his squad might be unable to recover, at least not for some time. With the way that Taylor had been performing over the past few weeks, and due to the unsavory dearth of quality starting pitchers still available, Jeff attempted to formulate an alternative battle plan.

His pitchers had been underperforming, but there was still the possibility that he could advance forward in the various hitting categories with a couple of strong weeks. "Maybe if I traded one of my better starters," he thought, looking at the latest stats for Chicago ace Pete Sammon, "I might be able to get a quality slugger to boost my homers and RBI's. Then I could pick up points with the hitters rather than the pitchers."

No, he quickly realized, he could not complete such a trade. At the very least, it would be extremely difficult to make such a trade with one of the top teams. The pitching staffs of his and the other teams closest to him - Francis', Spadola's, and Greenbaum's teams - were all within four victories of each other, and, in again reviewing the statistics he realized that his team was about a dozen homers behind his nearest competitor. Giving up a quality starting pitcher at this stage in the season could be even more dangerous than suffering through the remainder of Taylor's season should his horrendous outings continue. He searched through his papers again, trying to figure out what path to embark upon. His plans were further complicated by the fact that several members of his league were notorious for their inability or refusal to make trades, which cut down on his potential options.

The muffled, almost distant sound of a ringing telephone caught his attention. It was a fairly foreign sound to him, as so few people called him on his home phone, and he rarely answered it when it rang; the unsolicited callers could simply hear the answering machine message, hang up, and move on to their next victim. He briefly considered allowing the answering machine to pick up this time, but then decided to answer. Maybe it would be Michelle, calling to see if they could work things out. Or, better yet, maybe it could be one of the guys from his league, calling with a trade proposal that could prove to be the answers to all of his team's problems and questions. With his right hand, he fumbled clumsily underneath the mountain of newspapers and standings sheets, reaching the receiver just before the fourth ring. Much to his chagrin, however, the caller was not Michelle, nor was it one of his friends. Nor was it an

44

unsolicited caller. In fact, it was much worse; it was one of the last people with whom he was prepared to deal at this point in the morning.

"Jeffrey, when should we expect you today?" asked the instantly recognizable female voice on the other end of the line.

"Damn," Jeffrey thought, "forgot to look at the caller ID. Why do I even have it if I don't use it? Shit." He had to answer the question, but could not remember if he was to see his parents today. "Oh, hi, mom," he stammered, cradling the telephone under his right cheek as he continued to peruse his papers. "Expect me for what?" he asked, as his eyes scanned the minor league statistics from the past month.

"For the barbecue, of course," she answered. Jeff paused; he had completely forgotten that it was the last Sunday in June, the day of the annual family barbecue and get-together.

He put down the papers and grasped the telephone in his right hand, leaning over the table and placing his head in his left hand. He could feel the onset of a headache; the last thing that he wanted to do was go to his family barbecue, but there was no way of getting out of it now, at the proverbial eleventh hour. "When is everyone else coming?" he asked.

"We told people to show up at around 1:00, but that means that your aunts and uncles probably won't be here before two or three. Come as early as you want – I'm sure that there is some kind of ballgame that you and your father can watch."

"I'm sure you're right, but I'll probably be there when everyone else arrives. Let's say that I'll get in around two-thirty or three, O.K.?" Jeff stated hesitantly.

"What do you mean, you'll probably be here around two-thirty or three," his mother shot back angrily, "come down earlier than that. If you come around noon or one, that way we get to can spend some time with you. You know something, young man," she added, in a scolding tone, "just because you're 27 doesn't mean that you can't spend time with your parents anymore; you haven't been here in so long, it's hard to believe that you only live in New York as opposed to being across the country."

"Mom, don't give me that guilt. I've got some things to do," Jeff replied softly, referring to his weekly ritual of watching the morning' sports highlights and poring over the newspaper. Of course, he could not tell her that this was the reason, preferring instead to tell her that "I'll get there as soon as I can. Stuff to do here and then get the car and drive out. You know it's not the easiest thing of all time."

"Fine," she answered, her reply curt but her tone beginning to soften. He could hear his father speaking in the background, and then his mother as she responded, "he said that he'll be here around three." She paused, and his father's muffled voice could again be discerned. "I know that there is probably a ballgame on before then," she replied, speaking to his father but also directly into the mouthpiece of the telephone, "what do you want me to do? He told me that he would get here around 2:30 or three o'clock."

Having finished with his father, she turned her attention back to Jeff. "Are you bringing Michelle? We haven't seen her in the longest time."

46

"You and me both, mom. I don't know," he said hesitantly, not telling her about the fireworks that had erupted only two nights before, "I really couldn't tell you. Just tell dad to slip an extra burger on the grill. If she doesn't come with me, I'll eat it." He did not wait for her reply to the comment about Michelle. "Bye, see you later," he said, pressing the "off" button on the phone as he placed it back into its cradle.

He unplugged the phone and put his cell phone to silent mode; there could be no more disturbances. Actually, the mere thought of spending an afternoon with his entire family was more than distracting enough. He got along well enough with some of his relatives, but some were just pains in the ass. It wasn't a large family, but they had, as did so many families like them, this god-awful habit of all speaking at one time and so loudly that he would feel as if he was stuck on the floor of a political convention. He quaked with fear just thinking about it.

And they always peppered him with questions. Questions about his job, about why he lived in the city when his work often took him back to Jersey, about why wasn't married yet, and about Michelle. He had dated her for about six years, since they were both students at Franklin & Marshall College. She was a math major, he a business major. They had met early in their junior year in a statistics class, and had remained friendly and then began to date a year later. Both obtained jobs in New York following graduation from school, Jeff with one of the big accounting firms and Michelle as a math teacher at a private school in the city. He was from Northern New Jersey and wanted to return to living in the New York area. She was from Southeast Pennsylvania, a short distance from the Lancaster, Pennsylvania home of their college, but went to New York to be with Jeff and, he incorrectly thought, to escape her small-town roots.

47

For some time, the two of them were quite serious, and it appeared inevitable to all, including both Jeff and Michelle, that they would eventually end up getting married to each other. Lately, however, things between them were not the same, maybe, he thought, due to his hesitation on pulling the trigger on getting engaged or married. This had clearly been the case on Friday night. She was getting all worked up about a definite commitment and settling down, whereas he was not quite ready to get married and start a family. It was a debate that had been raging periodically for some time. Finally, when it became clear to Michelle that Jeff was not ready for the commitment that she desired, and with no hint that his mind would be changing in the foreseeable future, he thought, she was forcing herself to make a decision about their future, whether it would be together or separate. The answer that she had reached, based on her outburst at the restaurant and the fact that she had not been in contact since that time, seemed to be for them to split up. Moreover, as she made quite clear to him the other night, she would not play second fiddle to a baseball game.

Jeff was, of course, wrong about the real reason for Michelle's anger. While it was true that her rage had manifested itself in an argument which seemed founded on his lack of commitment to their relationship, the reality was that his making her take what she perceived to be a back seat to his desires to watch baseball was the main reason for their difficulties. She knew that the time he spent watching and reading about baseball and the players was excessive, to the point of being obsessive. She could not, however, make him see this, especially when her anger boiled into hysterics outside of the restaurant.

Compounding the problem was that his entire family had already taken her in, as if she were one of their own. She had been a constant part of their family gatherings for years now, and was always present when Jeff's parents came into the city to see him or when Jeff traveled to Jersey to visit their home.

48

They appreciated her deference to her elders, the product of her upbringing, and loved her wry sense of humor. It had gotten to the point where Michelle would go shopping with Jeff's mother when they would take the drive into New Jersey, and Jeff's parents sometimes referred to Michelle, seemingly with more frequency, as their "future daughter-in-law" when introducing her to others at family or other events. They just wouldn't understand that there were problems between the two of them; that he and Michelle had grown apart, and that deep down, they really had very little in common except for their attraction to each other.

It was not even just a matter of her refusing to take a back seat to baseball, Jeff reasoned, the reality was that she did not even like baseball. Also, her interests bored him. The idea of exploring Manhattan's museums and art galleries on summer weekends was completely foreign to Jeff, and he could not understand why Michelle would not be happy walking to a local bar and watching the Yankees play while drinking beer with friends. They were becoming bored with each other's stories of the workplace. They seemed to have fallen into a rut, more like an abyss, in their relationship. It was a chasm that had sparked Michelle's outburst, Jeff reasoned, again failing to realize the extent to which his baseball-watching was a contributing factor. And he did not know if he could build a bridge to span their differences, although he certainly desired to do so. There was no way, however, to properly describe the situation to his family, especially without making himself out to look like the root cause of the difficulties.

Besides, did it really matter what his family thought?

CHAPTER 5

There was one relative whom Jeff wanted to see at the family get-together, but whom he knew would not be there. His cousin, Greg Bloom, was an infielder's coach with the Milwaukee Brewers and was spending his weekend in Phoenix while the Brewers played a three-game series with the Arizona Diamondbacks. It was a sort of homecoming for Greg, who had been a star high school player and later excelled at shortstop for four years at Arizona State University, alma mater to no less than 100 major league players over the past 50 years. Considered small at 5' 7", Greg was a "throw-back" of sorts, having played following the emergence of Cal Ripken, Jr., Alex Rodriguez, and others, who served to lead the evolution of the shortstop into a large, powerful hitter.

Despite the criticisms of some that he was too small to play major league baseball, he was drafted in the third round of the 1992 amateur draft by the Boston Red Sox. He then bounced around in both the Red Sox and Brewers' minor league systems, displaying a fine glove but batting a paltry .223 for his six years of professional ball before a shoulder injury ended his career prematurely.

Only once did Greg make it to the majors, being promoted to Milwaukee for a two-week stint toward the end of 1998 and seeing action in eight games, most as a late-inning defensive replacement. He did, however, start two games. His offensive statistics for the eight games read as follows:

	G	AB	R	H	HR	RBI	SB	AVG
Bloom, Greg	8	11	2	2	0	0	1	.182

Greg's career highlight came on September 20, 1998, when he singled to start the ninth inning of a tie game against Texas, stole second, and came around to score the winning run on a double. Projected by some to make the major league roster in 1999 following his brief 1998 stint with the parent club, Greg injured his shoulder in the off-season, and then tore his rotator cuff in Spring Training before the 1999 season and never fully recovered from reconstructive surgery. Clearly, Greg did not amass Hall of Fame statistics, but did earn himself a spot in the Baseball Encyclopedia, sandwiched between Jimmy Bloodworth and Clyde Bloomfield. Coincidentally, Bloomfield was an infielder who also appeared in eight major league games, seeing action in 1963 with St. Louis and in 1964 with Minnesota. As he was quick to point out, in his own self-deprecating manner, Greg's career batting average was higher, at .182, than Bloomfield's career mark of .143.

Despite the relative brevity of Greg's major league career, however, his knowledge and understanding of the sport and its fundamentals did not go unnoticed by team executives. Also, despite his easy-going and affable demeanor off of the field, the intensity with which he played the game, as well as the determination with which he struggled to again play following surgery, further endeared himself to the Brewers' hierarchy. Once it was determined that he could no longer play due to his shoulder injury, therefore, he was immediately named a coach in the Brewers' minor league system. He honed his coaching skills at three levels of the minor league system over the next decade before earning a promotion to his position with the Brewers.

With the Brewers playing a weekend series in Arizona, there was no possibility of Greg being at the barbecue. In fact, since another relative's wedding approximately three years earlier, the two cousins had seen each other on only one occasion. The year before, Jeff and Michelle were vacationing in

51

Chicago, and had taken the hour-long drive north to meet up with Greg for a Brewers-Dodgers game in Milwaukee, complete with a visit to the Miller Park locker room after the game. They planned to get together whenever the Brewers traveled to New York to face the Mets, but the plans always seemed to fall through for one reason or another. They would speak to each other on the phone every month or so, though, and Greg would provide Jeff with inside information on some of the players in the league. While Greg was not flawless, he did possess a good eye for talent.

While still in high school, Jeff and his friends had become involved in their first fantasy baseball league. At first, they all stumbled through the machinations of the game together, but, after a couple of years, the league became competitive enough that each of the men was looking for an edge over the others. Throughout college, they continued the league, usually conducting their April draft during Spring Breaks from school. Jeff considered having someone connected with major league baseball to be an asset to be utilized, and he often called Greg, who by then was already well ensconced in his coaching career, for help. His cousin, with the insight of a former player and current coach, as well as with inside information that Jeff did not possess, was more than willing to provide him with the names of several players to draft for his team.

It was not as if all of the suggested players tore up the major leagues, and some of them did not even earn a promotion to the majors, but several of Greg's recommendations proved to be quite productive both for their real teams and for Greg's fantasy team. As a result, the late March, pre-draft telephone scouting reports became an annual ritual, as did the mid-season player updates. Greg could certainly provide insight as to some of the well-known players, such as whether or not certain players would be able to return to their past glory following injury, but he was especially helpful in steering Jeff towards young talent, those players whom the other fantasy owners would not have even heard of, much less have given a second thought to drafting.

Some of the other guys used to joke with Jeff that he had been given "inside information" from Greg before the draft. Jeff laughed off such comments, however, and was careful to avoid selecting more than one Brewer at any given draft lest his friends begin to think, or discover, that he was really trying to cheat.

Jeff, delaying his trip to his parents' house as much as he possibly could, first left the city that day at 2:30. He drove through the Lincoln Tunnel and onto the New Jersey Turnpike, cruising down his home state's most un-garden-like portion before turning onto the Garden State Parkway for the final leg of his journey. All the while, he was thinking alternately of Michelle and his baseball team. Exiting the Parkway, he fought his way through traffic down Route 9 until he eventually reached the jughandle turn which led to his parent's neighborhood. A couple of quick turns, and he reached the corner of the street where his parents' house was located. As he turned his car into his parent's street, Jeff glanced down at his dashboard clock, which now read 3:30. He had thought that it was even later in the afternoon -- the radio in his car was not working, and the resulting silence had made the long trip seem interminable. Still, he knew that he was late, and that was cause for concern.

He surveyed the situation as he approached his parent's house at the end of the cul-de-sac, just one in a seemingly endless row of two-story buildings. Each of these aluminum-sided giants shared the same white sides and dark slate roof. His brother's Honda Civic was parked in front of his parents' mailbox, and most of his cousins' cars, American cars all, were parked nearby.

A silver BMW revealed that even his aunt and uncle, they of perpetually late fame, had already arrived. Jeff was unquestionably the last to arrive; no doubt his parents would be greatly embarrassed by his tardiness and he would have to pile dealing with that issue on top of all of the other angst that he was already feeling.

Knowing that he would not be able to explain this one easily, he eased his car down the street and parked behind a dark blue Pontiac, a car which he recognized as belonging to his mother's brother, his Uncle Steve. His cousin Greg was Steve's eldest son. Despite the fact that Greg had earned significant amounts of money both playing and coaching in the majors, his father never wanted to accept any gifts from him. And while Uncle Steve also made a decent living, he was, as Jeff's father liked to say, extremely tight with a buck. In fact, the Pontiac was the same car that he had been driving for over a decade, and it still had an Arizona State University sticker in the back window from when Greg's younger brother had attended the school around the turn of the century.

Rather than go through the house, where he knew the women would be congregated, Jeff went around the structure, directly to the backyard. The distinctive smell of barbecued ashes, combined with the aroma of charring hamburgers, was already wafting through the still summer air. The 20-gallon garbage can at the side of the house, which he passed as he approached the site of the barbecue smell, was already littered with dozens of empty beer bottles, standing as testament to the alcohol consumption that was inevitable whenever the family got together. It also confirmed just how late Jeff was in his arrival, a fact that did not go unnoticed.

"Jeff, my boy," his father called out as Jeff rounded the corner of the house and strolled into the backyard. Standing next to his grill, he shifted a grease-covered spatula to his left hand so he could shake his son's hand with the right. "Look who finally made it here, fellas," he called out as he motioned to the others who were gathered in the backyard, "the prodigal son has returned."

He looked at Jeff disapprovingly and beckoned him to lean in closer so that he could speak to him privately. "You know that your mother is having a heart attack," Mr. Goldstein whispered, "she thought that you were going to try and make it here early." His voice became stern. "I don't ask for much from you, but you could try to make her happy once in a while." He motioned to his right, pointing to a man two years older than Jeff, and who bore many of the same facial features. "Your brother got here hours ago. Why couldn't you just get here on time for once?"

"Don't give me any shit, dad," Jeff answered, a scowl covering his face. He turned away, nodding in his cousins' direction as they sat at a table, stuffing their faces with snack foods. "I had some work to do."

"Work, my ass. Was there some important cable movie on this morning?"

"Give me a break, dad," Jeff responded with a grin, "I was working, and then there was traffic on the Parkway. You know how it is."

"My son," he murmured, not believing the excuse as he looked through the screen door where he could see the women in the kitchen. He reached down and thrust his hand into the red cooler situated next to the grill, which was filled with bottles of beer and jagged chunks of ice. Pulling his hand from the cooler with a beer bottle, he extended his now damp fingers in a rapid motion in an effort to dry them. Twisting off the bottle top, he downed a mouthful of beer, after which he pointed to the house with his spatula and said "work, traffic, whatever. I know one thing, boy, you'd better get yourself in the house and say hello to your mother before she comes outside and starts giving me hell."

Jeff reached into the cooler to grab a bottle for himself. The cold feeling of the ice raced up his arm. Jeff wasn't concerned with the cold or wetness of the ice, however, as a thought of a different kind raced into his head. He turned to his father, who had a radio sitting on the table alongside his grill which was tuned to the baseball game, and asked, "Who's winning the game?"

"You should get your radio fixed, you know. But don't worry about it now. And put that damned beer down," his father commanded.

"Give me a break, dad. I need a drink after that ride, especially before I go face mom and the others," pleaded Jeff, exaggerating slightly. "Plus, let's be realistic. I can just pull out my phone and find the score if I want to."

"No," his father said firmly. "Put the beer down and keep the phone in your pocket. Go in, say hello to the women and make your mother happy, and then you can come back out and drink and eat all that you want." He lowered his voice so that nobody else could hear. "It's bad enough that you are here alone," for the first time making note of the fact that Michelle had not accompanied Jeff, "and you know what your mother is going to say about that. You should have at least been here earlier."

"Don't listen to him," his Uncle Steve chimed in from behind the two men, "the score's tied. So far it's been a pretty boring game. You must be pretty excited, though, with the Yankees being in first place."

"You know it," Jeff replied, as he smiled and pointed to the blue Brewers' cap affixed to the top of his uncle's head, its brim hiding the wearer's receding, almost non-existent, hairline.

Now his uncle pointed to his own forehead. "But don't get too comfortable. The Brewers are only three games behind in the Central Division, you know. They're moving up smartly, and have a chance at making the playoffs also. We could be looking at an October meeting, you know."

Jeff laughed. "Oh, come on, Uncle Steve. You're among family here. Everyone knows that you grew up a Yankees fan, that you've always been a Yankees fan, and that you'll die a Yankees fan. You bleed Yankee pinstripes." Each time that he said the word "Yankees," Jeff extended one of the fingers of his right hand for emphasis, so that all four fingers of that hand were now pointing skyward. "Face it, it doesn't matter where your son plays, coaches, manages, whatever. You're still secretly rooting for the Yankees."

"That's not true," his uncle replied in protest, "and you know it."

"Oh, do I? Or have you forgotten how you couldn't root for the Red Sox when Greg, your own son, your own flesh and blood," he said, mockingly, placing added emphasis on the words "flesh" and "blood", "played for their farm team?" He smiled broadly, and then looked to the others for support. By this time, the others were laughing loudly while his uncle's demeanor began to change as rapidly as the reddening of his face.

"That was the fuckin' Sox," his uncle bellowed, as the others pleaded with him to keep his voice down so as not to incur the wrath of the women for using profanity with children nearby. "We're New Yorkers and a New Yorker can never, and I mean never, like the Red Sox." He pounded his fist down on the plexiglass table in front of him as he tried to explain. "It's as if we are born with some kind of chromosome that prevents us, even if we tried, from rooting for the bastards."

"So the Brewers are different?" Jeff asked, quietly.

"You're damn right they are," he sputtered, drops of beer exiting his lips and landing on Jeff's shirt. "There is no rivalry or hatred between them, so you can like both." He took another swig of beer. "The teams aren't even in the same league anymore. I can easily root for both. So how, pray tell, can you be forced to dislike them if they're not even in competition with each other?"

"Nice rationalization," Jeff laughed, and tossed his uncle a fresh bottle of beer as a peace offering. "Cool off for a bit while I go annoy the women." He pointed his bottle in the direction of his father. "Besides, it's OK to root for your son's team. We should support family." He smiled. "What we should be doing is ganging up on that brother-in-law of yours, the one that I'm ashamed to call dad during the summer when he's wearing that stupid Mets' hat."

"Don't bring me into this," his father cried from underneath his light blue Mets' cap as he again motioned to the house, "just get inside and say hello to your mother before I kick you there myself."

"All right," Jeff answered, "but don't dare start any more burgers until I get back outside. You know how much these scavengers can eat, so make sure there's enough for me."

He gestured to his cousin Doug, who had been busy the entire time attacking the dip and chips with a vengeance rarely seen in civilized people. He then looked back to his father, who nodded in agreement.

As Jeff stepped through the screen door and into the house, he was greeted by the shrill call of his aunt. "Jeff! Well, look who finally made it," she cried, looking down at her watch, "it's my long-lost nephew, the one who never arrives on time. Where do you live," she asked, mockingly, "in another time zone?"

"Hi, Aunt Susan. How are you?" Jeff, replied, kissing his aunt on the left cheek. He then turned to his right, where his mother stood over the counter, furiously slicing vegetables to re-fill the empty plastic tray conveniently located next to Doug. "Hi, mom. Sorry that I'm late."

"You could have at least called us," she answered, without looking up from her vegetables, "you know that your father worries about you. Would it have been so difficult for you to get here early once and give him a little bit of happiness?"

"I'll have a talk with dad," he replied, as his mother turned, wiped her hands with a towel, and grabbed him in a tight hug while kissing his cheek. He always found it amusing when his parents tried to pawn off their concerns on each other, to make it appear as if they were the cooler of the two heads.

"Did you bring Michelle?" his mother whispered before unlocking him from her embrace and peering behind him. "Everyone has been asking about her."

59

"No, mom," he immediately responded, under his breath, "she didn't come with me."

The brevity of his answer caught her off-guard. Her face quickly turned to a frown. "Is something wrong?" she asked, quickly leading him into the next room. "Do you want to talk about it?"

"No," he answered, as he looked over his mother's shoulder, through the window, to the men standing around the barbecue. "There's really little to talk about now. I'm not even sure of what's going on. Let's just say that we probably won't be seeing each other for a while. Maybe. I don't even know, to be honest with you." He paused. "Things are just a little weird between us. I'd rather not talk about it now."

"If that's the way that you want it, dear," she answered, sadly. "But don't forget, I'm here if you want to talk to me about it. You know how we worry about you, because we'll never stop being your parents. Maybe after everybody else is gone you will tell me what happened." She pulled him closer. "You know what," she said, her face breaking into a comforting smile, "I'm sure that everything will work out. It may just take some time."

"Thanks, mom," he said. He kissed her on the forehead, and in the next instant turned and walked toward the rear of the house. Mrs. Goldstein followed closely behind, but stopped when she reached the rest of the women. As she reached the kitchen, Jeff's sister and other relatives looked at her, puzzled, to which she responded with a shrug of her shoulders.

Jeff, trying desperately to ignore the motions and silent communications being exchanged between the women, exited the room and walked back onto the deck where his beer stood, waiting and sweating, on the fiberglass table. There the men stood, still as the beer bottle, listening to the baseball game on the radio.

Jeff reached down to the table and picked up his beer. As he strained to hear the radio, he turned to his father. "There, dad," he said, "I've gone and spoken to the women. I've done what you asked of me. What's the score of the game?" Mr. Goldstein, however, had his back turned and was in the process of turning over the seven burgers that were broiling on the grate of his barbecue. Puffs of white and grey smoke curled upward from the pieces of meat, and the moisture from the burgers fell to the coals below with a loud sizzle every time that the cook pressed his spatula to their round figures. Jeff waited for the response, but soon realized that none would be forthcoming. This prompted him to call out one more time, "Dad?"

"Yes, son," his father answered, his face still taking the full force of the smoke as he proceeded to move the burgers to one side of the grill and carefully placed five hot dogs side by side so that his guests would have a choice of what to eat with his wife's special potato salad. "Did you say something?"

"Yes, I did," Jeff said, moving closer to his father so that his face now felt the heat of the barbecue and the rich aroma of the cooking meat filled his nostrils. "I said, what's the score of the game?"

"Oh," his father answered, "to be honest with you, I wasn't paying attention. When last I heard, the Mets were down by one." He turned the hot dogs slightly, so that their initially-blistered sides were now facing up. "I'm sure that they've fallen behind more by now."

"Uncle Steve," Jeff said, turning to his right, "he's a lost cause. Some kind of fan he is. Help me out here. What's the score of the game?"

"Which game do you mean, Jeff?"

"The game you're listening to."

"You mean the Mets' game?" asked Jeff's cousin Mark, as he dug his hand into the plastic potato chip bowl. By Jeff's count, it was the fifth time that Mark had done so over the brief time that Jeff had been outside. "You want the score of the Mets' game?"

"Yes, you asshole" he replied to his cousin, "the Mets' game. Get your head out of your ass and your hands out of those chips."

The men laughed. "It's close, the Mets are down 4-3," Mark answered. Mark looked over at his father, still grinning broadly. Turning back to Jeff, he asked, "Why are you so concerned?"

"I just want to know, is that alright with you?"

Mark looked at him skeptically. "Does this have anything to do with that fantasy league? From what our dads tell me, it sounds like you're really into yours, I was going to get involved in one of those leagues but the purist in me wouldn't let me."

"Purist?" Jeff asked his cousin, "purist, my ass." He flicked his fingers together; the moisture that had collected on his fingers from the beer bottle's condensation flew in Mark's direction, spraying his face with the cold liquid.

"Besides, nobody in this game is of much use to me, since none are on my team, so my concern about the score is, how would you say, pure."

His father called from the barbecue. "Whoever wants a burger or a dog, come here now. The first batch is ready." The men all stood and walked to the grill. Mr. Goldstein took four of the burgers and a few hot dogs, placed them on a plastic tray, and brought them inside for the women. Uncle Steve went for a hot dog, leaving Jeff and his two cousins with three burgers and one hot dog. Citing the home field advantage, Jeff grabbed one of each, dousing the hot dog with mustard and sitting down at the table with his food and a fresh beer.

He was soon joined by his father. "I was just talking to your mother," he said as quietly as he could, which was still fairly audible to anyone within a ten-foot radius. "She told me something was wrong with you and Michelle. I know that you didn't talk to her about it, but she is very concerned. What happened?"

Jeff took a bite from his hot dog, and drops of mustard oozed from the sides of his mouth. He chewed the food deliberately, and then turned to his father. "It's nothing, really. I don't want to talk about it here, especially with everyone else around." He saw the worried look on his father's face, a look that he had not seen more than a couple of times before, and tried to reassure him. "Don't worry about me. And tell mom not to worry. Just like she said, it's probably something that will blow over soon." He wiped the mustard from his lips and smiled, using the same napkin to wipe away the sweat that had been collecting on his forehead due to the blazing afternoon sun. "I'll bet that Michelle comes with me the next time that I make it down here. Now let me go and get some of mom's potato salad. I forgot to get some before."

He stood and patted his concerned father on the back, thinking to himself that the situation with Michelle was anything but that easy, that it was possible that his family would never see her again. This was not the time, however, for him to discuss any of his problems with them. It was hard enough for them to understand some of the things that he did. If he told them that she had left him in a restaurant and broken up with him because he was making her feel secondary to baseball, they certainly would turn on him. He knew how they felt about her, how much they cared for her. And there was no reason to incur their wrath with the rest of the family there.

Besides, maybe things would work themselves out. If they did, then any conversations at this time would be useless. And why upset them for no reason? He loaded his plate with food and sat down next to the radio. Another run had just crossed the plate, and the Mets were now losing, 5-3, in the bottom of the seventh inning.

CHAPTER 6

"I'm half living my life between reality and fantasy at all times."

- Lady Gaga, Grammy-award winning singer

Jeff went to the gym directly from work. He had joined the club several years ago, and had recently made what amounted to his sixth or seventh commitment to getting into shape. For the first couple of months, he took the subway to the club, three times a week. He sometimes thought it odd, though, that he would ride a subway so that he could run around an indoor track, especially when the heat inside almost matched the blistering mid-July temperature.

It was also unmistakably humid in the gym, the natural result of dozens of people sweating off the burgers and pizza that they had consumed at lunch only hours earlier. There were some people in the gym who were truly dedicated to their bodies; most of the members, though, were just like Jeff, people who would eat what they wanted and then attempt to exercise to get into shape, if not only to break even after their fattening repast.

Jeff's routine consisted of a one-mile jog, eight times around the track that encircled the various weight lifting machines and equipment. This run, which often would amount to nothing more than a brisk walk, would be followed by a half-hour trek through the universal equipment and the occasional nautilus machine - alternately exercising the chest, arms, and shoulders. Only rarely would he use any of the leg machines, believing that running stretched out his lower extremities more than enough.

Even rarer were the days when he would venture into the room that contained the free weights. Jeff did not fit in with the Venice Beach wanna-bes that populated that room, nor did he try to act like them. Their goal was simple; to make Popeye resemble the stick figures that they considered true art. Jeff's goal was much different, and, at the same time, infinitely more difficult. In his mind it did not seem to be that tough -- he only wanted to work his chest up enough so that it stuck out further than his stomach. That, he believed, was more feasible than trying to flatten his stomach. He had already come to realize, however, that this goal, like so many in his life, was not nearly as attainable as he initially hoped or believed.

Lately, however, his rigorous work schedule had made it impossible for Jeff to get to the gym other than on the weekends. Friday afternoon, after work, he went home, grabbed his gym bag, and immediately went to the gym. He made sure that he finished his workout and left the gym by 8:00 so that he could get home and grab a quick shower before the Friday night baseball telecast began. Tonight it was the Boston Red Sox, that most reprehensible of ball clubs, visiting the granddaddy of all new-retro stadiums, Baltimore's Ballpark at Camden Yards, home of the Orioles. It was a surprisingly intriguing and important match up as the Orioles, riding a five-game winning streak, had climbed within two games of the second-place Sox and were safely entrenched only four wins behind the front-running Yankees. Moreover, although it was still too early to be thinking in such terms, under the league's mystical playoff system, the Orioles were only one game behind the Minnesota Twins for the league's fifth and last playoff spot.

As usual, though, the ballgame held Jeff's interest for other reasons. Tonight, there were three -- Boston third baseman Steve Conti, Orioles' left fielder Steve Wilson, and Baltimore left-handed starting pitcher Mike Linskey.

66

Wilson had been one of the biggest coups scored in the 2011 "Future GM League" draft. After two years of promise and well-publicized potential, he had still failed to crack the Orioles' 2011 opening day roster. Jeff, needing a stolen-base threat, drafted Wilson and placed him on his minor-league roster, obtaining him for the bargain basement price of one dollar. And he, along with the rest of the baseball world, waited.

In August that season, Wilson paid dividends for both the Orioles and the Golds by supplanting the trio who had shared Baltimore's lead-off spot for the previous three seasons. By the middle of September, he had amassed twenty-one stolen bases and was batting at a crisp .327 pace. This average dropped by the time October rolled around, but was still a respectable .293 by the end of the season. This was more than enough to earn him a starting spot in both the Orioles' and Golds' 2012 (and thereafter) lineups.

Jeff dashed from the shower, a dark blue Yankees' towel draped around his waist. Water dripped from his body, forming small puddles on the carpet beneath his feet, as he lunged for the remote control. Grabbing the remote in his left hand, he turned on the television just in time to hear the final words of the National Anthem. "The most beautiful song in the world," he used to tell friends, although he would not recognize it without the final two words - "Play ball!" He remembered back to his childhood, when he and his father would rise from the couch and sing along with Robert Merrill, his unmistakable tenor voice resonating throughout the cavernous stadium, as he belted out the anthem before Yankees' games.

Jeff thought about his father, who was, back then, the consummate Yankees' fan. On many a night he would keep Jeff entranced with his stories of the Bronx Bombers' glory years of the '50s and early '60s, when his own father rooted for the team, and of the "Bronx Zoo" Yankees of the '70s, tales of taking the subway to Yankee Stadium and sitting so high up in the stands that he could seemingly reach up and touch the celebrated facade that encircled the ballpark. Most of the tales focused on superstars that Jeff's grandfather watched, all-time greats like Mickey Mantle, Whitey Ford, and Yogi Berra. Even more interesting, however, were the times spent reminiscing about the lesser-heralded players. Steady performers like Johnny Blanchard, Jerry Coleman, and Gil McDougald, his father explained, formed the heart and soul of one of the most dominant teams ever to grace a baseball diamond, if not the greatest collection of athletes that professional sports has ever known. To hear his father tell the stories, one would think that he had been watching those men play with his own eyes, not those of Jeff's grandfather.

He remembered the sparkle in his father's eyes when discussing the 1976 playoffs against the Kansas City Royals, when Chris Chambliss' walk-off home run sent the Bronx Bombers to the World Series for the first time since 1964, and the joy that his father took in rushing home from school to watch that year's series against the Cincinnati Reds, when day games were still in vogue. The seventies brought a whole new crop of colorful heroes for Mr. Goldstein to watch and of which to regale his son with stories -- Jim "Catfish" Hunter, Thurman Munson, Graig Nettles, Reggie Jackson, and Mickey Rivers, among others. It also made one-time heroes out of unsung players who rose up during crucial times to leave their marks in baseball history and enjoy their fifteen minutes of fame - including of course, Bucky Dent.

October 2, 1978, was the day that, in baseball lore, David truly conquered Goliath. On that day, the Yankees completed an improbable comeback (they were more than a dozen games behind Boston late in the season) and won the American League's Eastern Division with a win over the

Red Sox in a one-game playoff at Boston's fabled Fenway Park. The final score of the game was 5-4 in favor of the Yankees, and the critical blow was a three-run homer by light-hitting Russell Earl "Bucky" Dent off of his former teammate, Red Sox hurler Mike Torrez. One swing of the bat, a lazy pop fly lofted by the five foot-something Dent into the screen over Fenway's twenty-three foot "Green Monster," had decided the fortunes not only of the players and coaches of the Yankees and Red Sox, but also the fates of two baseball-crazed cities. It was shocking in that Dent only struck 40 home runs in his entire 12-year career in the major leagues; and in his other 24 post-season (playoff and World Series) games, he did not hit even one home run. The blast even earned Dent a new nickname – "bleepin'," as in "Bucky Bleepin' Dent," as he is still known in Beantown and its surrounding areas.

For so long, his father would explain, the Yankees and Red Sox were, undisputedly, the greatest rivalry in professional sports. Not just baseball, he would explain, but all of professional sports. Dodgers and Giants? Lakers and Celtics? Canadiens and Bruins? All were mere child's play compared to the bad blood that had brewed and simmered between the Yankees and Red Sox for decades. Ever since Red Sox owner Harry Frazee had peddled arguably the greatest player in baseball history, Babe Ruth, to New York in 1919, hatred had festered between the two teams unmatched by any in professional, or amateur, sports. For decades, it was a lop-sided rivalry, to be sure. From 1919 through 2003, the Yankees captured 26 World Series titles while the Red Sox captured, in round numbers, zero.

That all changed in 2004, when the Red Sox finally exorcised their long-lingering suffering from the Ruth transaction, familiarly known as the "Curse of the Bambino," and won the World Series crown that had eluded them for 86 years. That was followed by another title in 2007, and for a few years the

69

dominating team in the rivalry was Boston, at least until the Yankees returned to the World Series and took home the title in 2009. Through it all, however, the animosity continued between the teams, unabated. Even defections to the Yankees by World Series-seeking hounds like Wade Boggs and Roger Clemens could not ease the tensions between the two squads. A Red Sox title in 2013 only added to the anguish between the two teams, which was heightened even further when the Yankees signed Red Sox starting center fielder Jacoby Ellsbury as a free agent following the 2013 season. The Ellsbury signing was seen by many as not just a manner by which to improve the Yankees' roster, but also as a way to stick it to the Red Sox by pilfering one of their best players.

When he thought of these times, of the hours that they spent watching the Yankees, it made his father's new-found allegiance to the Mets even more difficult to swallow.

The beginning of the seventh inning found a bleary-eyed Jeff struggling valiantly to stay awake. The Orioles led the Red Sox 5-4, with Conti having driven in a pair of runs for the Sox and Wilson's production limited to one single in four at-bats with a stolen base. Unfortunately for Jeff, Linskey had continued the futility shown by the pitchers on Jeff's fantasy team. He was long gone by the fifth inning, having surrendered nine hits and all four Boston runs in his four-inning stint.

Jeff could barely keep his eyes open, as the hazy glow of the television in the otherwise darkened room began to exercise its hypnotic powers. He vowed to stay alert, if only to see Conti's last at-bat. The aura cast by the television screen, however, had the opposite effect, bringing his game viewing to an abrupt halt.

As he drifted off to sleep, he began to have the dream.

Up until the previous year, Jeff would have the same dreams as every other heterosexual male. He dreamt of women of different shapes and sizes, whether they be blondes, brunettes, or redheads. A veritable smorgasbord of female beauties occupied his nights, and they served to fill the void in his life created by a lack of true romantic relationships, especially for those times when Michelle was not around. Other times he would have the dreams tied to stress, such as being late for school and not being able to get into his class, or arriving at school to find that there was a test for which he had not studied. Lately, however, the subject matter of his nocturnal cinemascope had changed dramatically.

This dream always began the same: a sweeping view of a sold-out stadium. It looked, for all intents and purposes, like Yankee Stadium; the old stadium, not the new one constructed as an homage to Yankee boss George Steinbrenner. Its cross-cut patterned green grass sparkled in the sunlight as the midday sun hung lazily over an urban jungle which seemed identical to the South Bronx beyond the center field stands. It was almost too perfect -- the grass was cut to the perfect length, the dirt of the base paths immaculately smooth. Circling the interior of the Stadium were the blue seats, which provided a sharp contrast to both the bright green grass and the glittering metal of which the stadium was constructed. The blue of the seats also provided a perfect contrast to the bright whiteness of the famous frieze which hung over the scoreboard in center field. More than 57,000 people filled the park's seats, their thunderous applause rising to the heavens where the ghosts of Yankees past resided.

Something in this scene, however, was different. The Yankees were not playing. Instead, the stadium, what seemed to be the Yankee Stadium, the "House that Ruth Built," had instead become the home of the Golds, Jeff's fantasy team come to life. The scoreboard showed one out in the bottom of the ninth, with the Golds trailing the Bayonne Bombers by a 4-2 score.

The stands were filled to capacity with screaming fans, and several people whom Jeff recognized, including Michelle, sat in box seats along the first base line. "Now coming to bat for the Golds, number 22, right fielder Stan Jefferson, number 22" intoned the unmistakably deep voice of the late Bob Sheppard, who had served as the stadium's public address announcer for over half a century prior to his death in 2010.

Jefferson, using patience at the plate, carefully eyed each pitch, running the count to three and one before stroking a single into shallow left field. Bombers' manager Joe Spadola, realizing that his starting pitcher's offerings were losing velocity, strolled slowly to the mound. He motioned to the bullpen, calling for his ace reliever, Joey Williams.

"Now batting for the Bombers," boomed Sheppard, "the designated hitter, number 34, Randy Garcia, **number 34.**" Williams was extremely careful in his pitches to Garcia, but the eagle-eyed slugger was patient enough to wait for his pitch. Five throws later, he reached first base on a walk. The next batter, catcher Brian Stevens, laid down a rare textbook bunt to sacrifice the runners to second and third. The slow-footed catcher was thrown out before reaching first base, the second out of the inning.

The Golds were now down to their last three strikes. Only one out separated the Bombers from the league championship, and the same result would relegate the Golds to playing the role of bridesmaid. The Golds' wily manager, though, had one last trick up his sleeve. "Now batting for Nicks," the voice of Bob Sheppard echoed through the stadium over the roar of the capacity crowd, "the player-manager of the Golds, number 48, Jeff Goldstein, number 48." Jeff selected a bat from the rack on the right side of the dugout, and strode to the batter's box with a swagger and cockiness usually reserved for only the most seasoned of veterans, the navy blue number "48" seemingly dancing across the back of his uniform as he walked.

The dreams' culmination was always the same. The first two pitches resulted in a one-and-one count, pending the third pitch. "Williams checks the runners, rocks, and delivers the ball plateward," exclaimed an excited Mel Allen for the nationwide television audience. Jeff's eyes widened as the spinning spheroid neared him, seeming to grow larger and larger as it approached the plate, eventually ballooning to the size of a watermelon. In one swing, Jeff brought home the championship for the Golds with a mammoth three-run home run. "How about that," Allen shouted, as the ball rocketed off of Jeff's bat and sailed well over the left-center field fence with plenty of room to spare, traveling at least 400 feet.

Up in the booth, Allen's broadcast partner, Russ Hodges, was re-creating, with a slight alteration, his famous call of 1951, when the Giants beat the Dodgers to advance to the World Series on Bobby Thomson's home run, still referred to as "the Shot Heard 'Round the World" -- as he yelled into the microphone that "the Golds won the pennant, the Golds won the pennant!" Jeff circled the bases triumphantly, his fist thrust skyward with his thumb extended, prancing like a Dali-esque hybrid of Chris Chambliss circa 1976, after his home run won the fifth and final game of the American League playoffs and propelled the Yankees past the Royals into the World Series, and Robert Redford's portrayal of Roy Hobbs in *"The Natural."* Just for good measure, two fans approached Jeff as he ran between second and third bases and patted him on the back, the same two interlopers who had done the same to former Home Run king Hank Aaron as he rounded the bases following his historic home run number 715.

When Jeff reached home plate with the winning run, all of his heroes, the superstars of his team, were there to greet and congratulate him. The celebrants were joined by a mob of joyous fans, including Michelle, who told Jeff again and again how she had faith in him and loved him. And then Jeff, the manager of this all-star collection, was hoisted skyward by several of the players and carried off the field on their hulking shoulders.

"World Champions," Jeff muttered softly to himself as he shifted in his chair, his consciousness and unconsciousness, his worlds of fantasy and reality, engaging in a nightly struggle to stay distinct from each other.

CHAPTER 7

The five men sat around the coffee table in the living room of Bob Fishman's apartment, their half-empty bottles and cans of beer leaving rings of moisture on the glass top as Mike Berger dealt the others a new hand of cards. In the background, the voice of Michael Kay was barely distinguishable as the television screen glowed with the images of the Yankees-Angels game. The brightened screen had an almost magically electronic aura to it; its luminescence penetrated through the haze of the cigar smoke which slowly curled upward from each of the three water-filled cups serving as ashtrays in the middle of the table, and it provided the room's only light aside from a bare, sixty watt bulb dangling precariously overhead.

"Hey, Jeff," asked Mike as he examined the cards in his hand, "how is Michelle doing? You haven't mentioned her much lately." When Mike said the name "Michelle," Bob Fishman quickly cleared his throat, hoping to gain Mike's attention, and ran his left hand across his neck, as if to signal Mike that Michelle was not a good topic for discussion. Mike did not realize what Bob was trying to do, though, and could only look at him, puzzled, and mouth the word "what?"

But it was already too late. The question had been posed, and a response was required.

Jeff looked intently at his cards for ten long seconds, his gaze strong enough to burn a hole through the three queens that were carefully positioned between the four of diamonds and six of clubs. Without looking up, he replied, softly, "not so good, man. I'd rather not talk about it." He took a deep breath, glanced at the silent faces surrounding him, and smiled, although it was clearly a forced smile. "Hey, how about those Yankees?" he asked, trying to break the uncomfortable silence while also sequeing into a new topic, and turned his neck

75

to see if he could make out the score of the game in the corner of the television screen. Lately, he found that he was having trouble reading the little numbers in the graphics posted during the games, and realized that it was probably time for a new glasses prescription.

"Does anybody know what the score of the game is?" He looked down at the few remaining chips stacked in two rows directly in front of him. "I can only hope that the Yankees are having a better night than me." He was hoping that nobody would realize that he was bluffing on this hand, as he expected his three queens to beat the others.

It became apparent that nobody knew the score, so all of the men placed their cards face down on the table and turned to the television in time to see a Yankee hitter strike out to end the fifth inning. As the game went to commercial, the Yankees led by a 3-1 count.

Pete Katz was a mountain of a man, with his six-foot, one-inch body burdened with the weight of over 280 pounds. It was not unusual for Pete to consume two six-packs of beer in slightly over three hours, and yet still be coherent enough to win the last hand of the evening. He was also the only member of the weekly poker game who was not involved in the fantasy baseball league. In reality, he was not even much of a baseball fan, especially compared to the others. Whenever the discussion would turn to the league, as a result, he would grimace and try to change the subject.

Tonight, however, Pete decided that it would be worth his while to play devil's advocate. "Guys, how's the fantasy league coming?" he asked. "Any of you boys winning? More importantly, are any of you going to make any money out of it?"

76

The others murmured in response as they examined the cards in their hands. "I thought that you hated to talk about the league," said Jeff, with more than a subtle hint of curiosity in his voice.

"Usually I guess that is true, but not tonight."

"I guess that it's going," said Mike Berger, as he laid his cards face down on the table. "The league, that is. This hand is a different story altogether. To put it simply," he added, "it sucks. I fold." He stood and stepped away from the table. "Does anyone want a beer?" All four men raised their hands, and Mike, ever the trusted servant, walked to the kitchen to assume his newly-appointed role of bartender.

"Well Jeff, tell me something about this league," Pete continued. "From what you guys have told me, a pitcher's earned run average and some form of hits to innings ratio are categories from which you can get points." He looked at the others, two of whom nodded. "If that's the case, then what happens when the Yankees are playing against one of the pitchers from your team? Do you root against them, hope that your man pitches a no-hitter?"

"Don't be stupid, man," Jeff answered while staring at his cards, hoping that none of the others would follow Mike's lead and would keep throwing chips onto the pile in the middle of the table. "You know I'm a Yankees fan. I don't care enough about the league to root against the Yankees. They're the key team in baseball, not the Golddiggers." His face remained expressionless as he spoke, and Jeff hoped that he would not smirk, for such a reaction would reveal that even he did not truly believe what he had just said.

"O.K.," Pete said in response while smirking. He glanced back at the kitchen, from which Mike was returning with the beers, and nodded in Mike's direction. "We'll see about that. I'm assuming that the 'Golddiggers,' as you referred to them, are your fantasy league team. Let's change the question a little. What if it is the last week of the season, the Yankees are two games out of first place, and you need an excellent pitching performance from one of your non-Yankee starters, who is facing the Yankees, to win the league championship. Then what?"

Jeff answered slowly, his hesitation serving to belie the inner conflict with which he was faced. "First off," he said, "please call them the 'Golds'. It's like the 'Mets' instead of their originally-given name of 'Metropolitans' in that we prefer the shortened version. Second of all, that's never going to happen, so why even think about it?" He paused. "But let's assume that it does happen," he continued, "if it were to take place, then, to be honest with you, that's an easy one," he added, "I root for the Yankees, but only that they should win by a 1-0 score, with the one run that is scored being unearned." He smiled and looked over in Mike Berger's direction, pleased with the diplomacy and neutrality of his answer. Mike, strolling in from the kitchen, handed Jeff a fresh bottle of beer as Jeff looked up.

"Oh yeah, smart guy," chimed in Bob, never one to back off from a good confrontational situation, "try this one. This is the ultimate situation, you know, between your real team and your fantasy team. What if," he began, "what it the Yankees are down 1-0 in the bottom of the ninth, two men are on base, and your pitcher is still in there. Then what?"

Jeff was growing weary of this game, as it was becoming apparent to him that the others were starting to align themselves against him. He still held the three queens in his hand, and wanted to confirm that he would be winning the pile of chips. "Fuck you, man," Jeff said in a clipped tone, "we are here to play cards, not hypothetical baseball exercises. I already told you what I'd do."

"No, you didn't," Bob replied. "Come on, it is the bottom of the ninth. Let's say that two men are on base, and the Yankees down by a run. Your pitcher is still in the game. Who do you root for in that situation?" He began to make noise like an imaginary clock: "tick, tock. Tick tock."

"I don't know, alright," Jeff stammered, his face growing red with anger. "There's always another game. Sometimes you have to go with your wallet, especially when the stakes are high; unlike this piece of shit card game." He looked at Pete's smiling, fat face. "Are you happy now? Can you stop browbeating me so that we can finish this fucking hand already?"

"Nice loyalty, Jeff," said Pete, "what happened to Mr. Yankee fan?" He laid his cards face down on the table, a jumble of different numbers and suits which, as Pete realized, was a definite loser. "I'm folding, guys, it does not seem like this is going to be my night. And by the way," he added with a devilish, knowing smile, turning to the others at the table as they stared intently at their hands, "I know you guys feel the same way. About this fantasy baseball league, that is. All of you bastards are the same -- none of you have any loyalty."

"Well, fatboy, what is loyalty? And when I say loyalty, I mean other than being loyal to food and beer." asked Jeff, taking his turn at being cruel to his overweight friend.

Pete's smile quickly turned to a reddened scowl. Always conscious of his weight problem since his younger years, the mere mention of any variation of the word "fat" would bring back a flood of bitter memories. All of the guys knew this, and would, if they really wanted to piss Pete off, make jokes about his excessive weight.

This time, though, Pete decided that he was not going to let Jeff get the best of him. His broad smile returned, with his cherubic face returning to its

79

normal flesh tone within seconds. "When you say 'loyalty,' Jeff, what are you talking about?"

"I mean, look at baseball. Who in baseball has any loyalty?" Jeff asked, with a puzzled look that exhibited his disbelief at the ineffectiveness of his carefully-placed insult. "Baseball today is so much different from how it was in the fifties and sixties, or even ten, twenty years ago. Free agency changed things, big money changed things, and the players themselves have no loyalty to their team."

Now it was Joe's turn to join the conversation. "He's right, you know. Think about it. How many players stay with the same team for their entire careers? It used to be common. Now, guys like the Yankees, you know, Derek Jeter and Mariano Rivera, are the exception. They are going to have to start making longer Hall of Fame plaques just so they can list all of the teams that these guys play for. That guy Octavio Dotel, in how many cities did he play? Twelve different teams? And Mike Stanton? Eleven?"

Jeff continued. "Because of the rapid movement of players," he tried to elaborate, "more often than not for the almighty dollar, and the way that the game is played today, on and off the field, it is getting easier for people to shift their allegiances. Look at how the players do it. Why can't we?"

Pete's smile grew broader, his happiness growing after seeing the look on Jeff's face. "Because you root for a team," he started to explain in a matter-of-fact tone, completely devoid of any discernible emotion, "and as a fan, you root for your favorite players." He was careful to stress the word "players," using a deep voice as if to add a Shakespearean-like dramatic flair to his diatribe. "You don't root for the Yankees because of Derek Jeter, because of Mariano Rivera, or because of any of the other current players. You root for the

Yankees, I believe, because that is how you were raised. You grew up a Yankee fan. You bitch about how your dad likes the Mets now. How do you justify that?"

The last question was met with a prolonged silence. Jeff's eyes began to narrow, and Pete sensed that the argument was his for the taking. It was time to go in for the kill. He stared directly at Jeff, invoking his most commanding voice, and said, in an almost scolding manner, "and you don't root for a player just because he is on your fantasy team. That's not how it works."

Now it was Jeff's turn to lay down his cards, exposing his royal trio to the others. He reached across the table and pulled all of the chips from the center to directly in front of his chair. "Think about how much better, how much purer, the game of baseball was in the past. When I say past, I mean before we were even alive. Back then there were allegiances, sure, but mainly because there were better players; players who fit the mold of superstar, of hero. That's a role that so few players fill today. The players of today, even those that we grew up with, couldn't hold a candle to the players of our fathers' generation. Or as Larry Holmes, that great historian, would say, the players of today couldn't carry the old-timers' jockstraps."

"That's not entirely true," said Bob, shuffling the cards as he prepared to deal the next hand, "there are plenty of excellent players today."

"And surely there are some with big dicks," Pete added.

"But you can count those guys on the fingers of one hand." He turned to Pete and shook his head. "Superstars, that is. I don't know about the sizes of their cocks, nor do I want to. I would guess, however, that those guys who are still doing steroids have little balls, from what I hear. You may know more about that than I." Jeff stood to stretch his legs, and continued his soap-box rhetoric.

"Just think about the past for a second. Look at the 1950's, at the quality ballplayers. One city," he stressed, holding up the index finger of his right hand for a dramatic flair of his own, "had three of the best center fielders ever to play, all at one time. Imagine growing up in New York back then. You had your choice of Mickey Mantle, Duke Snider, or Willie Mays. Actually, I'm wrong. You had your choice of the Yankees, Dodgers, or Giants. And once you picked the team, you rooted for the center fielder on that team. Those were just three of the players in town -- and let me remind you that both Mantle and Mays, and some might argue the Duke, were better than any guy who plays today."

"There are certainly some players today who can be considered all-time legends, though," interjected Bob Fishman, "don't you think? Surely you can think of a couple of dominating pitchers and some guys putting up tremendous home run numbers. Forget the steroids guys. There are still others, like ..."

Jeff began to respond before Bob finished his sentence. "Yes, there are some good players. But the old guys say that it's just not the same. Maybe it was because back then the guys played their entire careers for one team. When you think about Mickey, you think of the Yankees. Mays, the Giants. Snider, the Dodgers. And don't forget, The Yankees also had guys like Yogi Berra, Whitey Ford, and Joe DiMaggio. The Dodgers had Roy Campanella, Pee Wee Reese and Jackie Robinson."

Mike interrupted, joining in with a superstar list of his own. "The Cardinals had Stan Musial. Boston had Ted Williams. Cleveland, the freakin' Indians, had that awesome pitching staff -- Rapid Robert Feller, Early Wynn, and . . ."

He looked to Jeff for help. "How about Bob Lemon, who was just warming up for his stint as Yankee manager, and Mike Garcia?" offered Jeff, as he shuffled the deck of cards in preparing to deal a new hand. "Do you know that the four of them made up the Indians' starting staff from 1949 through 1955, and all of them, except for Feller, were still in the rotation together until 1958? That's a long string."

"Thanks. And Warren Spahn, he was a Brave."

Jeff began to circulate cards around the table, and then leapt in with more, albeit about a different decade. "The same is true with the sixties," he opined, adding that "Harmon Killebrew was a Minnesota Twin, even though he finished his career somewhere else. Willie McCovey and Juan Marichal, Giants. Bob Gibson, Cardinals. Sandy Koufax and Don Drysdale, Dodgers. Roberto Clemente, Pittsburgh. Ernie Banks, Mr. Cub. Al Kaline, Detroit. Brooks Robinson, always a Baltimore Oriole. All of them were awesome, and all, with the exception of maybe one or two years at the end of their careers, played with the same team. That's what it was like in the 50's and 60's. Not now."

Pete cleared his throat and glanced down at the five new cards in his hand, thinking for a moment before asking of Jeff, "Oh yeah, wise guy, I know that I don't know as much about baseball as you, but I do know a little bit about baseball history." He smiled. "So, then, what about Frank Robinson? How about Carlton Fisk? If memory serves correctly, each of them starred for two," he held up two fingers, "two teams. Not one. Two."

Jeff laughed. "There are always exceptions, you asshole. The point is, back then the players spent entire careers with one team, even if involuntarily and for less money than they thought they were worth. But that made it easier for their hometown fans to root for them and for the same team, throughout their playing time. I mean, I'm told that when the Dodgers left Brooklyn it was traumatic not because some of the players that were moving, but rather that the team, the mystique of the Brooklyn Dodgers, was leaving. According to some, the borough never recovered."

Bob jumped in, primed to offer his assistance to Pete, who up until this point had been waging his war alone. "But it was also true in the 70's, wasn't it? There were guys who you would call 'loyal.' Guys like Carl Yastrzemski, Johnny Bench, Lou Brock, George Brett, Mike Schmidt, and Jim Palmer, for example. All of those players are in the Hall of Fame, and all of them spent their entire careers, or at least the overwhelming portion of their careers, with the same team. And that was during the beginning of free agency."

"You're right," responded Jeff, "but Yaz, Brock, and Palmer were holdovers from the 60's so they may not even count. And look at the other stars of that era -- like Tom Seaver, Pete Rose, Nolan Ryan, Dave Winfield, and Reggie Jackson." As he stated each of these players' names, he repeated his earlier exercise of extending one finger as he said each name so that all five fingers of his left hand were out, and pointing in Bob's direction. "Each of them played with at least four different teams during their careers. And for all except Seaver, who, if you will recall, got the royal screw from Mets' management, their primary motivating factor in changing teams was to make more money in the free agent market."

"Think about this one, though," Bob interjected. He lowered his glasses to the tip of his nose to appear more intellectual, which drew slight laughter from the combatants. "You've obviously spent a tremendous amount of time, perhaps too much, thinking about this. But do you think that it's just a coincidence that Seaver, Rose, and Jackson, who were, I believe, three of your fingers, all returned to the Mets, Reds, and A's, their original teams, before retiring?" He paused, looking around at everyone else seated at the table. "Wrong -- they were attempts to go back to their original team, their original

84

fans, to re-kindle the memories of the past, to bring back some of the relationships that you're talking about. And that, my friends," he said, rising from his seat, "is what I consider loyalty."

"Don't get overly dramatic, Bob. Sit down," said Jeff as he again raised his right index finger; the others seated at the table were now bearing witness to a poorly emoted theatrical performance, not merely an argument about the merits of different eras of baseball players. "The point still is, back then there was more loyalty. Whatever you want to say about the past, the players and fans were loyal. Today, the game is ruled by money. Why do you think that the Hall of Fame people pick the hats that go on the players' plaques now? Because the Yankees tried to bring guys back into their fold, coaxing them with dollars and bogus jobs, just to increase the number of interlocking N-Y hats in Cooperstown."

Jeff rose from his chair, placing both hands on the table in front of him. "You can even throw the sacred names like Cal Ripken, Kirby Puckett, and Don Mattingly in my face as much as you want. The truth is, that if their home cities, be they Baltimore, Minneapolis, or New York, had not come up with the dinero, they would have moved on. Even Jeter toyed, at least publically, with leaving the Yankees a few years ago if they did not pay his asking price. And, more importantly, for every one of them there are dozens of whores who are openly available to the highest bidder. Loyalty is dead."

His voice lowered as he sank back into his chair and shook his head from side to side in exasperation. Each of the men picked up the cards which had been thrown in their direction and were now more focused on the next hand as opposed to Jeff's diatribe about the ills of baseball. Despite their indifference to continuing the conversation, Jeff added, "look, we can argue this forever. My point is really basic, so basic that even your pea brains should be able to understand. All that I'm saying is that the players of a couple of decades ago, who could pretty much whip the asses of the players of today with one bat tied behind their back, had more loyalty to their teams and fans."

"So?" murmured Bob, without looking up from his cards.

"So?" Jeff repeated incredulously. "Loyalty is a two-way street, don't you think? It made it easier for the fans to have the same fidelity to a team. That something is missing today, which makes it all the more logical that fantasy leagues are rising in popularity and guys are focused more on individual players and their statistics than they are on teams. Millions of people play it every year, you know. I don't remember exactly how many, but I'm pretty sure I heard somewhere that tens of millions play. Granted, the internet also makes it easy, but fantasy baseball is, to the guys who play it, a business. Being in a fantasy league lets them play general manager. It lets them imagine, lets them fantasize, about the job that they really want. Hence our league's name, stupid."

"Amen to that brother," added Joe, "and you're right, it lets us all do the job that we really want to have. Which one of us, except maybe Pete, wouldn't give up our day jobs to go and be the General Manager of a major league baseball team? I would do it in a heartbeat. You can't knock that, Pete. Or the 'Future GM League.'"

Pete looked at the others, all of whom now had smiles on their faces. "So I am surrounded by a bunch of frustrated baseball executive-wannabes? I guess I can live with that." He looked again at his cards, which were no better than his last hand, and sighed. "Again, my hand sucks. Somebody get me a beer."

CHAPTER 8

Greg Bloom was born October 17, 1971, in Stillhouse, Kansas, a town located forty miles northwest of Topeka and having a population of approximately 12,000 residents. He was the fourth child, and the first son, born to Steven and Linda Bloom. With one son being born after Greg, the seven Bloom family members constituted fully half of the Jewish population in Stillhouse. Despite their religious differences from the remainder of the overwhelmingly-Lutheran town, the Blooms were able to assimilate well and never experienced any form of the anti-Semitism that, sadly, continued to permeate so many other parts of the United States.

Steven and Linda had moved to Stillhouse in 1967, when Steve was transferred to be his company's sales representative for the rural Kansas area. He moved the family away from New Jersey, where he had been one of the best salesmen on the Eastern seaboard. He and his wife quickly warmed to the idea of moving, and, seeking the promise of a lucrative business in the Midwest, as well as an escape from the growing hustle and bustle of the East coast, opted for the clear skies and slower-paced days of Stillhouse. The location, aside from being peaceful and rustic, was also practical. Due to Stillhouse's proximity with Topeka, as well as other growing cities, Steve was able to earn a fine living in support of his wife and, eventually, five children. He missed being able to watch his beloved Yankees on television, but the lower cost of living, combined with his increased salary, more than made up for the sting of being forced to watch Cardinals' and Royals' (when they were founded two years later) games.

While Steve and Linda were originally blessed with three daughters, Judy, Monica, and Susan, many believed that Steve longed for a son. The three girls were born only four years apart, and friends and family often joked that Steve was determined to keep having children in rapid-fire succession until they had a son. This, however, was far from the truth, especially because Linda was determined to have a large family and wanted to have at least four or five children, while Steve would have been more than content to stop after Monica was born.

Still, when Greg was born two years after Susan, a baseball and football were placed in his crib, as if it were his destiny to become a ballplayer. Hours of daily practice time after school followed with father and son, and Greg became one of the stars of both the local pee-wee baseball and Pop Warner football teams. Greg was barely of average size, however, and by the time he was ten, it was clear that he was not going to be large enough to compete as a football player, nor would basketball be a possibility. Realizing that baseball would be his son's only possible career path if he was to be a professional athlete, all of Steve's energies were channeled into making Greg a complete baseball player.

The long hours of playing catch and hitting practice paid off, as Greg quickly developed into one of the greatest schoolboy athletes in Kansas history. He consistently led his junior league teams to their bracket titles, and developed a reputation that was well-known across the state and beyond. He furthered his legend during his four years of high school, leading his league in batting average three times, home runs twice, and runs batted in twice. Also, he served as the team's ace starting pitcher, compiling 27 wins in three years before being switched to shortstop to help his batting improve even further, a move that had paid off almost sixty years earlier for Babe Ruth. While he would never develop into a Ruthian-type slugger, he was still revered as one of the greatest baseball players, if not the greatest, to come out of the small Kansas town.

He was the darling of Stillhouse, a clean-cut all-American boy who was known to slug the game-winning home run and then celebrate at the local soda shop later that evening with an ice cream sundae shared with his girlfriend, Jane Moore. Jane stood five feet four inches tall, making her only about three inches shorter than Greg; when she wore her high-heeled rattlesnake cowboy boots and her strawberry blond hair was teased just right, she would actually appear taller than him. The fact that she wasn't Jewish was of no concern to the Blooms, and the fact that Greg was Jewish was of no concern to the Moores or, as everyone knew, to the rest of the town. Many spoke, sometimes in hushed tones and sometimes openly, about the future Mr. and Mrs. Greg Bloom and the possibilities of their lives together, whether in Stillhouse or elsewhere.

The night before the final regular-season game of Greg's junior year, Stillhouse was abuzz with the rumor that Jack Haines, a scout for the New York Yankees, would be coming to town to take a look at Greg. Only two boys from Stillhouse had ever been signed to baseball contracts before, and neither had ever played for a major league team. Greg was uneasy about all of the attention, and was especially nervous about performing in front of a professional scout. He slept no more than ten minutes that night, envisioning the possibility of stepping onto a major-league baseball diamond and thinking again and again about which number he would wear when he became a member of the Yankees.

In the end, this concern was of no consequence. Greg went three for four in the game, driving in three runs and scoring two others in Stillhouse's 10-3 romp over arch-rival Leesville. He also pitched the last two innings in relief, retiring six of the seven batters he faced, four via strikeouts. He walked off of the field after retiring the last out, surrounded by his teammates, and dreaming of his future with the Yankees.

Those dreams, however, were quickly dashed after Greg had dressed and walked out of the team's locker room. He was met by his father and Jack Haines; instead of offering him a chance to play for the Yankees, Haines told

Greg that he thought that Greg was too small to play major league baseball. He advised Greg to go away to college to play another level of organized ball, where he would have more time to add some size to his 5'7" frame and further hone his batting skills. Then, perhaps, the key word being "perhaps," the Yankees would consider drafting him.

When Jack Haines left Stillhouse that evening many, including Greg, were left with the unsettling belief that Greg's chances at playing professional baseball had gone back to New York with him. Haines, however, was impressed enough with Greg's raw skills to place a telephone call to his old friend Joe Deegan, who was the manager of the Arizona State University baseball team, and recommend that Deegan recruit Greg to play for the Sun Devils. Based on Haines' recommendation, Deegan flew Greg to the Arizona State campus for a look at the school and a tryout. Greg exhibited his skills for three hours with the Sun Devils' varsity team, and impressed Deegan enough to be granted an athletic scholarship to Arizona State following his graduation from high school. He saw sporadic playing time during the first two months of his freshman year, but began to see increased at-bats as the season went on. He platooned during his sophomore year and, by the beginning of his junior year, was the Sun Devils' starting shortstop.

When Greg was first told that he would be inserted into the starting lineup in the beginning of his sophomore season, even though he would be sharing the starting spot, he immediately phoned his father and then Jane. That night, too excited to sleep, he wrote a letter to Jane:

Dear Jane -- I can't fully express the feelings that I am going through today. It has been over three hours since I told you the news that I'll be starting the season as a regular player. For the first time, I feel like the winner that you and my dad have always told me that I was. I couldn't have done this without either of you. Please know that every time I get on base, or score a run, or make a play in the field that I will be doing it because of you.

I love you. I will always love you. One day I may be the starting shortstop, but you, my dear, will always be my first-stringer.

All my love,

Greg

Jane Moore was married to Jack Buckley, Stillhouse's dentist, on a sunny October day in 1994. She and John live in a four-bedroom house on the east side of Stillhouse, two miles from the old baseball field, with their three children, John, Jr., Patrick, and Marie. Greg's letter is neatly tucked away in the bottom drawer of her bedroom chest. Jack is unaware of the letter, and Jane is careful to hide it so that it will not be discovered. It was the last letter that she ever received from Greg. She had tried calling him once or twice after receiving it, but never received a return call. She never found out why.

*****

Candy Wilson was from Los Angeles, five foot two inches of bleached blonde, suntanned, California beach girl. Immediately upon her arrival at Arizona State, she became well-known around campus for her obvious lack of desire to restrain her well-developed body beneath too much clothing at a time, and, due to her tanning sessions in the smallest of bikinis, flashing the slightest of tan lines from underneath her short shorts. Her stated major was economics, but Candy truly only had three interests as the second semester of her freshman year began -- the sun, partying and having a good time, and the shortstop from Kansas who sat two rows beside her in her History 101 class.

She could tell that the handsome young baseball player was shy and would not approach her, so she did her best to try to gain his attention during class. One unseasonably warm day in February, she wore a cotton mini-dress which barely covered the tops of her thighs, and made sure to cross her legs just as Greg's glance was aimed in her direction. From the corner of her eye, she could see his gaze going up and down her tanned legs, and watched as his eyes grew wider and wider as they scanned the length of her well-toned lower body. She moved ever so slightly, allowing Greg to see the lower portion of her white lace underwear.

She then shot a glance in Greg's direction, in response to which he quickly turned away, knocking his pen and book off of the desk in the process. She giggled quietly, and then winked at the now red-faced Greg. He smiled faintly, and quickly turned his attention to the professor, who had also turned his way when the book snapped to the hard concrete floor of the classroom.

When the clock reached ten minutes to eleven, the professor dismissed the class with the admonition that they all were to be prepared for their mid-term examination, which was only four short weeks away. Greg gathered up his books and tried to hustle out of the classroom door. His path was blocked, however, by a tanned blonde in a cotton mini-dress. "Why don't we go out for a soda?" asked Candy Wilson, her tongue edging across her lower lip as she looked up at Greg. He nodded his head approvingly, and she placed her left hand in his right as they exited the classroom together.

CHAPTER 9

"I almost love the fantasy world of sports more than the real world."

- Norm MacDonald, Comedian/Actor

Jeff thought back to the day of that year's fantasy league draft. He arrived at the draft to find Keith Greenbaum, Barry Martin, Joe Spadola, and Bob Fishman already in their designated seats around the circular conference table. Two cartons of orange juice and three boxes of donuts, as well as two dozen bagels with cream cheese and butter, were heaped in the center of the table. As in the past three seasons, the draft was being held at the posh Manhattan law offices of Jacobs, Carlin, and Moskowitz, where young lawyers, including Bob Fishman, spent the majority of their waking hours, for most no less than 70 hours a week. There was an almost professional atmosphere to the draft, as printed name cards were placed on the table, designating where each team owner was to sit. The cards were arranged in order of the prior year's finish, with the reigning champion, Joe, seated across the room from the door, in front of the picture window which afforded a spectacular view of downtown Manhattan. Jeff walked to his right as he entered the room and settled into the seat in front of his name, directly to Bob's left, three seats from Joe.

Each of those already in attendance had staked out their territory, creating a semi-circle of materials in front of them for quick reference and consultation, when necessary. These materials consisted largely of pre-season rosters of each major league team, as well as various "baseball preview or "fantasy preview" magazines. Each of the men also brought I-pads or laptop computers, which were positioned directly in front of them, the laptops' power cords creating a maze of wires on the floor alongside the table.

Jeff placed his laptop on the table in front of his seat, typed in his password, 0722, which stood for Michelle's July 22nd birthday, and logged on to the ESPN fantasy site. He opened his zippered bag and unpacked its contents, neatly laying the materials, magazines and newspapers alike, in a similar semi-circle, knowing full well that the order of each person's materials would be replaced by chaos within the next hour. He had purchased no less than three preview magazines, highlighting and underlining those players and scouting reports which he would need to consult as the day dragged on. He also placed photocopies of each team's major league roster in two neat piles, one for each league, directly in front of him. Each page contained meticulous notes in the margins for most of the listed players, so that Jeff could refer to the notes at a glance.

On the underside of his Brewers' roster, in small, almost indecipherable letters, Jeff had scrawled three names: Steve Hilton, Mike Jones, and Larry Peters. In their pre-draft conversation a couple of nights before, Greg had given Jeff these names as players to draft with his later picks, assuming that they were still available.

By Jeff's estimation, the only one of those three players with any renown, such that the others might seek to acquire him, was Hilton. He was drafted by the Minnesota Twins out of the University of Southern California four years earlier, and had spent the second half of last season with the Brewers' AA Minor League affiliate in Huntsville, Alabama. Hilton was a left-handed pitcher with a 95 mile-per-hour fastball, a rare commodity in a league so devoid of young southpaw pitching strength. Jeff assumed that Hilton would be selected fairly early, perhaps as an eighth or ninth pitcher for someone to fill out his major league roster. Despite having spent the prior year in the Southern League, all pre-season magazines were predicting that he would leapfrog over AAA team Nashville and be included on the Brewers' opening day roster. Some of the pundits even went so far as to give Hilton a chance at cracking the Brewers' starting rotation.

Jones and Peters were different. Jeff expected that each would still be available for the minor league draft, that is, when each team selected five players for their reserve list, to be considered the property of the selecting team even though their statistics did not factor into the overall league standings. While the stated purpose of the reserve list was to have someone readily available to replace an injured player, two other reasons quickly emerged.

The first was to provide the team with a warm body to trade, because minor leaguers and real-life reserves were often included to sweeten deals that might not otherwise occur because it would be so grossly beneficial to one team at the expense of the other.

The other rationale was to obtain a player who would still be one or two years from the being promoted to the major leagues, but who could be protected for this period at a salary much lower than he would otherwise command once his ticket to the parent club was assured. As Jeff would explain it to those uninitiated into the world of fantasy baseball, a projected rookie superstar could, depending on the level of pre-season hype surrounding him, easily command a fantasy baseball salary of $20-$25 even if he had never stepped onto a major-league baseball diamond. As each owner began the draft with a limited bankroll of $260, a salary of this size was often tough to rationalize, especially for a rookie player who was essentially unproven. In contrast, a player selected for a fantasy reserve list had a fantasy salary of $0. Protecting him, or keeping on the fantasy roster, required only increased salary increments of $5 per year. In two years, therefore, this player's salary would only be $10, or half of what he could be expected to fetch should his name be thrown into the auction.

The only drawbacks to hoarding players in this fashion were that a limited number of players, generally five to seven, could be protected from the prior year's roster. As such, protecting such a player would preclude the roster from containing a different player who could start producing immediately, if one of the players on the starting roster was injured or simply was not helping the team.

Jeff knew that the others had scoured the minor league pre-season predictions almost as religiously as the major league scouting reports. He knew, therefore, that they would all know the name Steve Hilton. The other two, however, were a different story. Jones was an outfielder who had banged out 15 home runs while batting .285 at Class A Wisconsin, in the Midwest League, the previous year. His promotion to Huntsville was virtually assured, but no reports indicated that he would be promoted any further in the near future. In fact, the various experts had scarcely made mention of Jones, aside from listing him as one of the Brewers' outfielders still two or three years away from the major league level.

Jeff had contrary information. Greg had assured him that Jones would be promoted when the major league rosters expanded to 40 players in September, if not sooner. The Brewers' outfield was stocked with aging veterans, and injuries to any two of the over-30 crowd could lead to an early summons to Milwaukee for prospects like Jones. Because his name had not been mentioned by the media more than occasionally, however, Jeff was confident that he would still be available when the reserve draft was conducted.

If all went as expected, Peters would also be available by the end of the draft. A right-handed hurler with an adequate fastball who spent the last year in the Cardinal organization, Peters was still one or two pitches away from being promoted to AAA Nashville, much less Milwaukee. Greg had heard the name

Peters bantered about in trade rumors, and had given his name to Jeff almost as an afterthought. Jeff dutifully listed Peters below Hilton and Jones as players to watch, but had no intention of calling his name come draft day.

The first player auctioned off at the draft, as always, was a reserve outfielder. This year's honoree was Dave Alonzo of the Giants, a player who would be lucky to reach 200 at-bats by the end of the season. He eventually ended up on the Bayonne Bombers' roster, purchased for the princely sum of $5. The first dozen or so players of the draft were always reserves, a non-illustrious group who served to set the market value for the players, both stars and otherwise, who followed.

For the third consecutive year, Gene Hyland was committing what Jeff considered to be a cardinal sin; trying to base his team on pitching, spending over $20 apiece to acquire four starting pitchers and two relievers. In sharp contrast was Pete Francis, who devoted almost his entire budget to stocking his roster with productive hitters, leaving him with a pittance to select pitchers for $1 and $2 apiece when all of the other staffs were completed. Brian Hunter, meanwhile, stayed loyal to the hometown ball clubs, and was all but assuring himself of another ninth-place finish by drafting five players each from the Mets and Yankees.

In the middle of the 20th round of the draft, after 195 other players had been drafted, it was Jeff's turn to throw out a name. The piles of food were long gone from the middle of the table, and the remaining orange juice was beginning to sour. Two of the others stood to stretch their bones and looked out of the window, watching the traffic crawl along Lexington Avenue from their perch 30 floors up. Jeff shuffled his rosters with a puzzled look on his face, seemingly looking for a cheap player to complete his pitching staff, which was now comprised of an even mix of four starters, two middle relievers, and two closers.

Scratching his chin, which was now covered with a half-day's growth of dark beard, he shuffled the papers one more time, came to the Brewers' roster, and, looking at Pete Francis, said, almost sheepishly, said "How about Steve Hilton, pitcher, Brewers, for one dollar?"

"Who the hell is Steve Hilton?" mumbled Pete, as he clicked the mouse of his computer furiously to get to the ESPN review of the previously-unknown (to him, at least) Hilton.

Joe Emerson, scribbling furiously as he checked his remaining funds and roster spots, found Hilton's name on his list of players to draft and raised the stakes, yelling "three dollars."

Mike Berger then joined the bidding, and Mike and Joe went back and forth until the last bid reached $12. Jeff had long since dropped out, angered at himself for naming Hilton when both Mike and Joe had such funds to spare. Jeff, on the other hand, was down to his last few dollars. For him to compete with the bidding at this level would leave him with only five dollars for his remaining four roster places, ensuring that he would be scraping the bottom of the barrel to complete his squad. Instead of being a member of the Golds, Steve Hilton, pitcher, Brewers, soon became the property of the Emerson Boozers, when Mike leaned back in his chair and threw his pen in the air, exclaiming "too rich for my blood, Joe, you asshole, he's all yours."

Eventually all ten rosters were swelled to their 23 player limits, leaving only the minor league draft to be completed. The temperature in the conference room had reached an uncomfortable 80 degrees, and the men were edgy from sitting in the cramped quarters for over eight hours. Jeff would be selecting ninth in the opening round of the minor league draft, the order of which was determined by drawing numbers from a hat. Because the second round went in reverse order, he would also have the twelfth selection. Of the first seven names called out in the next five minutes, Jeff, for all of his preparation in the weeks leading up to the draft, could only recognize four. None of those names were Mike Jones or Larry Peters.

Keith Greenbaum, selecting eighth, chose Texas shortstop Jeff Gabrick, attempting a comeback after missing all of the previous two seasons with a severely torn left Achilles tendon. Jeff almost blurted out the name Mike Jones, but then checked the roster of Joe Spadola, who would be selecting tenth and eleventh. Spadola's pitching staff was thin, so Jeff assumed that he would be looking to select two pitching prospects, leaving Jones open for the twelfth pick. He studied at his list of minor league hopefuls, and called out the name of whom he believed to be the best remaining pitcher - "Steve Phoenix, pitcher, Oakland A's."

Spadola's expression turned pained, as he crossed out the name that he had scribbled on the top sheet of his notepad, the sheet that he had partially obscured by folding it over in half. Out of the corner of his eye, Jeff could see the names Phoenix and Howell written in black ink. "With my first pick," Joe mumbled, "I'll take John Howell, pitcher, Seattle Mariners." He paused for a moment, the others waiting patiently for his next selection. "Let me take a quick look for my second pick," he then whispered, casting a wicked glance in Jeff's direction.

"I need another pitcher, damnit," said Spadola, as he thumbed through his pre-season roster. "Too bad there's nobody good left." He eventually reached the Brewers' roster, and Jeff's eyes widened as he watched his friend's eyes seemingly scan to the bottom of the roster, toward the section reserved for outfielders.

Spadola appeared exasperated. He looked at his computer, his eyes darting right to left, and then ran his left hand through his thinning black hair as he said, "oh well, there are no goddamned pitchers left. I guess I'll just take this guy Jones."

"Who?" asked Pete.

Joe, filling in the name on his reserve roster, clarified his selection for those who had not understood him the first time that he said the player's name. "I said, I'll take Mike Jones. He's an outfielder with Milwaukee."

Eight of the faces seated around the round table showed surprise at the selection of Mike Jones, Brewers, an outfielder, who according to all published reports, was still two or three years from the major leagues. Jeff, meanwhile, buried his head in his hands, silently cursing himself for not selecting Jones earlier.

CHAPTER 10

"What consumes your mind, controls your life."

— *Author unknown*

The two cousins sat together in the bar of a Cincinnati hotel, reminiscing with each other and lamenting the fact that it was the first time that they had seen each other in almost two years. The hotel was located several miles from the Hyatt, across the river in Covington, Kentucky, where the rest of the Brewers' personnel were sequestered prior to the opening game of a three-game series with the third-place Reds. Jeff sat one stool to the right of Greg at the end of the bar, and the other patrons paid little attention to the two men reflecting on old times, none realizing that one of the men was the infielders' coach for the rival Brewers.

Both Jeff and Greg stared up, mesmerized, by the Kansas City-Oakland game being broadcast on the giant screen that loomed above. They sat, mouths agape, scarcely saying a word, like two children examining the piles of wrapped presents encircling the family tree on a crisp Christmas morning. Jeff had three fingers wrapped around the handle of a mug which held the remaining two ounces of a draft beer. At the same time, Greg was hungrily downing a wickedly-strong vodka and cranberry juice, the fourth such drink that he had consumed in a scant forty-five minute span.

Greg turned to Jeff, but his eyes never strayed from the magic screen hovering in their presence. "My life sucks, Jeff," he said, and waited for a response from his cousin which never came. After a prolonged pause, he asked, "Do you know why I never made it in the majors?" his raspy voice slightly slurred by the vodka coursing through his veins. "You know why I only played eight fuckin' games in the show?"

"In the show?" Jeff replied, in a mocking tone, "what are you, a movie? The show? Call it the majors."

Greg stared at Jeff, his eyes piercing through Jeff's forehead to such an extent that Jeff realized he had crossed a line. "Yes, the show," he replied, sternly. "That's what we, real fucking ballplayers, call it." He paused and waved his hand in Jeff's direction, adding "Fuck you." The long time between get-togethers had made Jeff forget that his older cousin was, for all intents and purposes, an angry drunk.

Trying to atone for his misstatement, Jeff replied, "Yes, I know why. Because you got hurt," his gaze focused on his beer to avoid further embarrassing eye contact with his cousin. "You had to retire," he said sadly, "But let's be realistic. You're not the first person to suffer a career-ending injury, you know."

Greg shook his head slowly, his left eye moistening with the hint of a tear. He reached out with his right hand, grabbing Jeff's arm. "No man, that's not it. My life is shit. I am at freaking rock bottom. You don't understand."

"Oh yeah, I know," Jeff chuckled, forgetting his misstatement from only seconds before and also his desire to be serious due to the dire tone of Greg's voice. He lowered his voice to a whisper and attempted to use a little levity to calm his agitated cousin. "It's a racial thing, isn't it?" he asked. "How could a small, white guy have competed? You were practically an endangered species out there, cuz."

His attempt at humor was not appreciated. "This is not the time to be funny, you bastard," Greg sneered, slamming his now empty glass to the counter with such force that it caused waves in Jeff's beer. He leaned forward. "You just don't understand," he cried.

The men and women at the other end of the bar, alerted to the possibility of trouble by the tone of Greg's voice and the thud of the glass hitting the bar, looked in Greg's direction. One, a burly trucker who looked to be six feet two, 250 pounds, and who had clearly not showered in at least the last two days, rose slowly and inched toward the cousins.

"It's O.K., dude, we're family. This is how we communicate with each other," Jeff said, waving off the intervener and then turning quickly back to his distraught cousin, who was now desperately trying to gain the bartender's attention for another vodka and cranberry juice. "What the hell are you talking about, Greg?" he whispered.

"Like everyone else, man," Greg barked, his voice remaining several decibels above Jeff's comfort zone. Jeff motioned with his arms for Greg to lower his voice, which he did. "Open your eyes and look around you." He pointed to his eyes, which were now opened to their widest. "Like everyone else. The only difference between the guys who got caught and the rest of them is that they got caught. Wake up, and see reality - this is life, buddy boy, not some fuckin' fantasy world." He turned to the man behind the bar, who was busy talking to another of the patrons, and called out, "hey bartender, can we get another round over here? Vodka and cranberry and a draft."

The bartender looked at Greg, shrugged his shoulders, and indicated that he would bring the drinks shortly.

103

"I'm not quite sure that I understand," Jeff said in response to his cousin's unintelligible comments, "you're kind of talking in circles, you know. Can you be just a little more specific with me? Everybody else what?"

"What?" Greg asked, incredulously. "You can't figure out what I am talking about?"

Jeff pondered for a minute. "What was everyone else doing?" he asked himself, and a possible answer popped into his head. Drugs! "You mean steroids?" he whispered.

"Steroids were child's play, you idiot," Greg answered. "If I had been doing steroids I would have hit 30 homers a year." He paused. "No, not steroids," he continued, "let me show you." Having already caught the bartender's attention, and with another two drinks on their way, Greg reached into his coat pocket and pulled out an amber-colored vial. He quickly placed it back into his pocket, but Jeff had enough time to see the white powder encased in the vial during that split second.

"Oh man, cocaine?" he blurted. He quickly caught his tongue, and lowered his voice so that the others in the bar would not be able to hear him. "Are you out of your mind? I can't believe that you're … still," he was speaking slowly, in disbelief, "… using cocaine. Are you out of your fucking mind?"

"Was, is, and will be," Greg replied. "This," he said, pointing to the vial in his pocket, "is what kept me from going all the way and having a great career. The little grains of white powder, that little demon inside, this is what kept me from being one of the best ever to play professional baseball." His voice trailed off, as his head slumped onto the elbow of his right arm, resting comfortably on the bar.

While Jeff knew that Greg would never have been one of baseball's elite and that his alcohol-fueled statement was more than just a little self-aggrandizing, his point was obvious. And while Jeff wanted to commiserate with his cousin, his mind was whirling at the revelation to such a degree that he could not think of anything intelligent or, at the very least, coherent to say. "When did you start using the stuff?" was the only question that he could muster.

The bartender walked over, armed with a fresh vodka and cranberry for Greg and beer for Jeff, and placed both glasses on the bar. "I assume we're adding these to your tab?" he asked. Both men nodded approvingly, and stopped talking until the bartender had returned to his post on the other end of the bar.

"Who can remember?" said Greg when the coast was clear. "Some girl, Candy something or other, turned me on to it in college, but it really got out of control when I was in the minors. Geez, everywhere you went, that is all that you saw. I tell you, it was unreal, wall-to-wall girls and drugs. All of these party girls wanted to fuck ballplayers. Some just for the fuck of it, and some were looking for rich husbands. It was almost comical," he chuckled, "you'd hear the same thing again and again – 'hey man, you want some, I can get you some good blow.' And at the risk of sounding crude, that sentence had two meanings attached to it."

He raised the index and middle fingers of his right hand. "If you were a ball player, in most places the women and drugs were both free. And there were all sorts of drugs, by the way. In a way, I am lucky that I only used coke. Some of the other shit is worse. Acid, heroin, shit like that will kill you much faster." He shook his head slowly, and Greg imagined that he was recalling fallen teammates, other players whose careers were derailed by drug use, or even players who ended up dead from drug use. "Anyhow, you think that the shit is free. At first, that is. I turned it down for a while, and tried to clean up my act, but I'm only human. And one time is all that it takes; don't let anyone tell you differently. But once you take for free a couple of times, they try to collect from you later. There are no free rides."

Jeff looked incredulously at his older cousin, the man who had been his role model for so long. Greg seemed to have it all. He was a professional baseball player and then coach, he always had an unbelievably gorgeous woman on his arm at family functions, and when he was promoted to the majors he was even named to Playboy's list of ten most eligible bachelors. And yet, here he was, baring his soul, a soul that was tormented to a greater extent than Jeff believed possible. He wanted to say something, but didn't know whether to console him or beat the shit out of him. His expression belied his inner conflict, and all that he could say was "cocaine?"

"Don't let them fool you, Jeff," Greg continued to preach. "One time. That is all it takes and you're hooked. It began with just a quick sniff, but by the time I reached the minors I was close to a gram a day habit. I stopped for a while, but then fell right back into it. Like I said, you could get it everywhere. I just kept going from there. Heck, I had to keep playing ball just so I could afford to use the stuff. Lots of salary monies up the nose, you know. Let me tell you, it was an obsession. I had to use it, and it controlled everything that I did."

"Controlled?"

"Yeah. I didn't use it, man, it used me." He stared directly into Jeff's eyes for the first time during the conversation. "That is what it is like when you are addicted or obsessed. You lose yourself and your identity. It, whatever it may be, drugs or anything else, takes over. And there is nothing that you can do about it. What was it that someone said, something like 'when you can stop you don't want to, and when you want to stop, you can't.' I read that somewhere. It's so true." He paused, deep in thought. "Holy shit!" he said, "I just remembered where I saw that quote – a guy named Luke Davies wrote a book called Candy. How fucking ironic is that? I just mentioned that girl Candy, remember? How fucking ironic." He chuckled, but in a sad tone.

Jeff listened to his cousin and looked at his trembling right hand, the hand attached to the golden arm that fired so many baseballs from deep in the hole between second and third bases, almost dart-like, into a waiting first baseman's glove. Now it was just the hand of a mere mortal, the hand which held Greg's fifth vodka and cranberry juice, and Jeff nodded his head in agreement with the observation espoused by his fallen idol. "Yes," he wanted to say, "I know all about being obsessed." And while Jeff's obsession was not with drugs, it was with something just as powerful – to him.

Jeff knew that he had an obsession of his own. Work to Jeff was just a method of making money, a necessary evil. Baseball was just a hobby, or so he thought. No, his true obsession, he believed, the one thing that occupied his mind more than any other, was a woman. But not just any woman. His obsession, he thought, was with Michelle.

He had not recovered from their break-up, and still believed they would be back together soon. He also had great difficulty in accepting the fact that he could have been to blame for their troubles, and could not comprehend that it was his overwhelming devotion to baseball that had led to them going their separate ways. He realized that he was often more than simply interested in baseball goings-on; what he still did not understand, though, is what Michelle already knew: that he was not merely a baseball fan, but that he was consumed by the game and its players. She knew that baseball was Jeff's real obsession, and in a perverse form of a power play, the stated obsession had recognized and attempted to eradicate her competition. Jeff simply did not see it clearly, or even at all.

She had tried to explain this to him, but somehow he was never fully able to grasp the message that she was trying so desperately to convey to him. Instead, he allowed her to slip away. When he thought about it now, he could realize the irony of the situation -- his life's true desire and obsession had removed herself from his life, because she felt that she was secondary to what she believed was his paramount obsession. Baseball initially had played the role of mistress in Michelle's eyes, and baseball was a mistress with which she could not share Jeff. In the end, however, Michelle came to believe that it was she who was the mistress, the "other woman," and that she was merely interfering with Jeff's unrequited love for a game, his love for baseball. His "understanding" of the situation, however, was still lacking in one fundamental respect – that he still did not recognize the depths of his obsession for baseball and how Michelle was correct in her feeling threatened by this obsession.

"Yes," Jeff said as he glanced up to see that the Royals were leading the A's by a 4-2 score, "I think I know what you mean when you talk about obsessions." Jeff paused, and then reached for his cousin's arm so that he could further the obsession that he denied. "By the way, I need your help with something," he whispered, and drew Greg's ear closer, so that the others in the bar could not hear the rest of their discussion.

There was a silence as Jeff looked about the bar. As his head moved from right to left, Greg grew impatient, asking "What is it, Jeff? Does it have to do with Michelle? I know that you guys are having problems but I mean, I hardly knew her. I doubt if I could do anything for you. I can talk to her, though. What's her last name again, and where does she live so I can send her something or find her in the phonebook."

"No," Jeff answered, as he continued to glance from right to left while shifting uneasily in his seat. "Her last name is Stein, and she lives a few blocks south of me on the Upper West Side."

"Stein, huh?" Greg replied. "Oh, that's right; I forgot that she was a nice Jewish girl. Never could seem to find me one of those."

"Forget about that," Jeff said, "This has nothing to do with her. That I'll work on myself." He paused and again furtively looked around before continuing. "I need some help with the fantasy baseball league. At the rate that I am going there is no way that I can win, and a lot of money is at stake, money that I can really use."

"I can give you some cash if you want, but, as I said before, money is tight." Greg replied, adding, "you want me to forget that her name is Stein? Too stereotypical, sorry. Would be hard to forget."

"Just drop it, OK? And as for money, no, thanks," Jeff said, "Money and family don't really mix, from what I've been told. I would never want to borrow money from you. I am talking about something else. A way that we can both make money."

"Shit, the baseball league again? What do you need, the names of some players that are going to be brought up? Need a jump start on the mid-season rookies? If you want, I can give you a short list right now. Even fucked up, I can tell you who some of the hot new players are. Have you got a pen?" he asked, fumbling through his pockets, clumsily searching for a writing implement.

"No, that's not it," Jeff replied, his tone more serious than before, "it's not about new guys. It's about the guys that are already there."

109

Greg looked up at his cousin, puzzled, not understanding that Jeff was going to ask him for much more than the names of young ballplayers. He continued to talk, oblivious to Jeff's growing irritation at his inability to listen to his request. "Because if you need to know stuff like that, you'll have to give me some time for guys on other teams, but I can let you know about our team now. There's this one guy, what's his name, that's been making alot of noise at double A. They're talking about him coming straight to the majors when the rosters expand, not even stopping off at triple A. He's a third baseman, but can play other positions too." He ran the fingers of his left hand through his hair. "I can't believe that I can't remember his name. I think that it was Bob something or other. I guess that I'll have to let you know his full name later. Same for guys on the other teams, once I can find out."

"No, Greg," Jeff interrupted, "you don't understand what I am asking you. Just listen to me for a second."

"When we're on the road," Greg tried to explain, "I'm a little out of the loop. When we get back to Milwaukee I can look into it and give you a call with some names." He could not find a pen, but did pull a yellow piece of paper from his back pocket. It contained the phone number of a woman whom he had met upon his arrival in Covington the previous evening. He smiled, remembering her sultry voice and taut body. "Jeff," he slurred, "you've got to hear about this babe that I picked up in the hotel last night."

"No, Greg," Jeff yelled, quickly looking down into his beer to avoid the stares of those seated at the other end of the bar and at nearby tables. His voice lowered. "Listen to me for a second."

"O.K., O.K., what is it?" Greg, falling into a moment of sobriety in response to his cousin's outburst, folded the piece of paper and placed it back

110

into his pocket. Glancing toward the bar, he called "hey, bartender, how about another round over here?"

The bartender looked over at Greg, clearly slurring his words, shook his head slightly, and sighed. He then surveyed the entirety of his establishment, which was only about ten percent occupied. He shrugged his shoulders again, in acknowledgment of his predicament. He was concerned about serving the two men, one of whom was already quite intoxicated, but selling drinks was his business, and tonight the business, other than the two cousins who alternated between whispering and yelling at each other, was sadly lacking. "Coming right up, fellows," he called to Greg, "vodka and cranberry and a draft, right?"

Greg thrust his thumb skyward in assertion to the bartender's inquiry, and then turned back to face his cousin. In a twist of the earlier events, he was now trying to be a calming influence on Jeff. "Alright Jeff, calm down and look at me for a second. What kind of favor do you need?"

"I need you to make a player change," Jeff whispered, in a voice barely audible above the clinking of the glasses being shuffled by the bar.

"That's what I just asked you, you asshole," Greg snapped in response. He could not help but notice the sweat that was beginning to form on Jeff's forehead, and the constant shifting of Jeff's eyes was beginning to make him nervous. "Give me a pen and I'll give you a couple of names, and I'll call you next week with a better list. Bob what? I'm telling you, his name is on the tip of my tongue. I can't believe this shit. I guess that my short-term memory sucks. They say drugs can do that to you. Hopefully I can locate some definites for you."

Jeff continued to shift his eyes from right to left. He leaned closer to Greg. "You don't understand," he said, pulling his head back, looking behind

111

him, and then leaning forward again to continue. "Stop your fuckin' rambling and listen to me for just a second. I don't mean help like you've been giving me in the past. This is a little more complicated."

"What?" asked Greg, his bloodshot eyes widening. "What do you mean by complicated?"

Jeff glared at his cousin. "That's what I've been trying to tell you for the last five minutes." He paused and again looked, furtively, in both directions before continuing. "I need to have somebody taken out of the lineup."

Greg's eyes grew even wider. "What do you mean out of the lineup? You mean taken out of the Brewers' lineup? You know I have no power over that." He shook his head slowly, sadly. "I'm just a coach, remember, I'm not the manager. Probably could have been a manager, you know," he mumbled, sadly, "if I had stayed straight." He swallowed the last of his drink, searching to his right to see if the bartender was making his way toward their table. "And besides, even if I did have that power, don't you think I would need some kind of a reason to make a change? I couldn't just pull a guy out without an explanation. The team would be all over me, not to mention the fucking media."

"There are ways of making a change without actually making the change yourself," Jeff whispered, lowering his head as he could see the bartender making his way toward the end of the bar. "There are other ways of making changes happen, if you get what I am saying."

Now it was Greg's turn to raise his voice, his words again growing more slurred by the vodka as the bartender arrived with the men's replacement drinks. He looked up at the bartender, nodded his head in appreciation, and then stared down at his fresh drink. A puzzled look came over his face as he tried to absorb Jeff's words. "What the hell are you talking about? What is your deal?

You sound like a fortune cookie." His voice grew even louder. "What the hell do you mean?" he bellowed, as Jeff tried in vain to silence his cousin.

Now it was Jeff's turn to look up at the bartender, as the man removed the empty glasses from the table. The bartender, catching Greg's roar flush in his right ear, stared down at the men with one eyebrow raised quizzically. Jeff reacted quickly to this look, so as to avoid any suspicion of problems. Pointing to his cousin and then to his own head, he motioned to the bartender. "He's a little out of sorts recently. Don't mind him. He's been having some woman trouble."

The bartender placed the empty glasses in his right hand and turned to walk back to his post at the bar, glancing back over his shoulder once to see the one man attempting to calm his emotional relative. When the bartender ducked back behind the bar, Jeff began to speak again.

"Listen to me. I need to win this fantasy league. My life is fucked. My job is fucked. I need this money. It's a hundred fifty grand at stake – one hundred and thirty five grand if I win. If I lose, I lose fifteen grand."

"Fifteen thousand dollars each?" Greg answered, incredulously. "A bunch of rich, young Jewish lawyers and accountants playing a game for fifteen thousand dollars." He raised his glass, took a sip of his drink, and slowly shook his head from side to side. "Now I guess I understand why you take the fucking game so seriously. Fifteen grand a person. How fucking cliché is that?"

Now it was Jeff's turn to glare at his cousin. "How dare you fucking judge me, you damned coke addict," he sneered. He grabbed his cousin's right arm, the wounded wing that had removed Greg from his hopes of starring in the major leagues. "Listen to me," he whispered, "if you help me win," he added, "there will be something in it for you."

"I don't like the sound of this," Greg cried, as a wave of his drink sloshed over the side of its glass, caused by the turbulence that resulted when Jeff grabbed his arm. "What is it that you want me to do, anyway?"

"Mike Jones," Jeff whispered cryptically.

Mike Jones had been elevated to the major league roster in mid-May, far earlier than anyone had expected or even anticipated when two of the Brewers' outfielders fell to injury. The same Mike Jones who Jeff had intended to select in his fantasy league draft. The same Mike Jones who was snapped up by Joe Spadola before Jeff could pick him. He had spent the last six weeks as the team's starting center fielder, and was already exhibiting the prowess at the plate and on the base paths that many, including Greg, had expected of him. His performance was not only benefitting the Brewers, but was also doing wonders for Spadola's team as well. Jeff feared that if he continued to play at that pace, Spadola would run away with the league title.

"Jones? That fuckin' cokehead?" Greg replied. "I gave you his name before the draft, remember? What do you want from him?"

"Yes, you gave me his name before the draft," Jeff said, sadly, shaking his head, "but I couldn't get him for my team. Look, I need him out of the lineup." He paused and leaned back in his seat, suddenly smiling and holding up his hand to prevent Greg from saying anything before he continued his train of thought. "Wait," he added, "did you say that Jones was a cokehead? That is interesting. I didn't know that he was into that stuff, but then again," he said, winking at Greg, "I didn't know that you were doing the shit either. That's very interesting. But cokehead or not, he's killing me out there with the goddamned numbers that he keeps putting up. I need him to be out for a couple of weeks. Maybe a muscle pull or something like that."

114

"How do you expect me to pull this off, asshole?" Greg growled at his cousin, struggling to keep his voice low enough not to cause any suspicion from the others in the bar. "Do you want me to just go up to him and pull his muscle?" His eyes were forming rivers of red that encircled his pupils, and the veins on his neck were becoming more pronounced. "In fact, maybe you want me to pull his groin muscle. What should I do, just go up to him and pull on his dick as hard as I can? As a matter of fact, I could ask him if it would be alright for me to give him a really hard hand job. That would really look good, wouldn't hurt my reputation at all. How am I supposed to do this?" he cried, "tell me."

Jeff again brought his voice to a whisper. "Surely you can think of something. And it certainly doesn't have to be his groin muscle. Do it in a way so that nobody knows what happened. It doesn't even have to be on the field. How about an out-of-control clubhouse prank? Or maybe an overzealous locker room wrestling match?" He paused and looked to the bartender, who was still standing on the other side of the bar. "We've all heard of players being involved in those types of scrapes in the past. Or maybe have him do some long tossing of the ball until he hurts an oblique muscle. I'm just asking you to be a little creative. It's not that difficult."

Now it was Greg who was looking furtively from side to side with his voice lowered. "No way, man, you've got to be out of your mind. I'm telling you now that I don't think I can, or will, do it, and I think you need professional help. It's pretty fucking funny, when you think about it. I'm the one who's sitting here bombed, which should tell you what kind of shape you must be in to ask me to do this shit." He shook his head slowly in disapproval, his vision blurred by the swaying motion. He paused, looked to the ceiling, and then asked, "by the way, when you say big money, how much are we talking?"

"I told you before, you stupid drunk. The pool is $150,000. Each of us put up $15,000, winner gets 135. And if you help me, I'll give you 20 grand of that."

"Only 20? Make it 35," Greg growled. "It is a lot of money, I guess. To tell you the truth, I could use it also." He paused and looked back up at the overhead television. "What the fuck are you guys doing putting up fifteen grand for a baseball league? Things must be good in the accounting game. Fucking yuppies." Greg said as he gulped down the last of his vodka and cranberry juice. "I would do Jones to get the thirty five thousand. But why do I feel that we will be having this conversation again? Is getting rid of Jones the only favor that you want?" He paused and again looked around the bar before adding in a whisper, "so many questions. Will there be others that need to be removed? Am I signing on to become a professional hit man?" He started to laugh as he reached down with his right hand to his belt, encircling his fingers as if they were gripping a pistol. "Should I carry a gun and holster in my uniform? How much will I have to do? Will I be chased by the baseball police?"

"Don't worry about that now, you paranoid bastard," Jeff said. "Just do this one thing."

"I don't know," said Greg, again shaking his head. "There's something that really smells about this. And we both know that there is never only one thing."

"Of course there is," Jeff replied. "Only one thing for now. I don't think there will be anything else, honest. And it does smell. But it doesn't mean that you shouldn't do it. Let me know. You know where to reach me." He stood, took four twenty-dollar bills from his wallet, and placed them on the table in front of Greg. "This should cover the drinks. I'll see you at the ballpark."

That night, Jeff sat in the second deck of the Great American Ballpark, watching the Brewers pound the home team by a 7-2 count. Mike Jones, that Mike Jones, had three hits in the game, knocked in two runs, and stole a base. He also made a spectacular diving catch to rob one of the Reds' hitters of a sure extra-base hit to end the fourth inning. The catch helped protect the lead for the Brewers, and also had the effect of controlling the ERA of Milwaukee starter Wily Peralta. Too bad, though, that Peralta was a member of the Frantastics.

Following Jones' third hit of the game, Jeff, peering through binoculars, searched for Greg in the dugout. Greg, somehow sensing that Jeff was looking in his direction, shook his head and extended his arms, palms facing skyward, in disbelief. He then reached down and touched his right hamstring, a faint smile creasing his lips. Jeff lowered his binoculars, and he also smiled. His hopes of a first-place finish were one step closer to becoming a reality. Greg was on board. All that was needed was a definitive plan.

The following day, the cousins met at the airport before the Brewers' plane was to take off. For the first time, Greg actually said that he would agree to help Jeff, but stated that he was still unsure as to how he would be able to cause injury to Jones. "You said he was a cokehead," Jeff opined, "surely his drug use can lead to something."

"Look, Jeff," Greg said, pulling Jeff to the wall, out of range so that nobody else could hear their conversation. "The organization doesn't know about my problem. Some people do, but they have been nice enough to look the other way. If I get into some trouble with Jones and the topic of drugs surfaces, I'm a dead man. So let me do it my way, O.K.? You'll have to trust me. I'll do what I can." He hugged his cousin, and then turned to walk back to the gate where the Brewers were boarding for their flight home. Pausing, he turned back to Jeff. "But don't expect any miracles. I can only do what I can do."

Jeff nodded in agreement, muttering to himself, "that's all I can ever ask, but I have confidence." He yelled to his cousin as he disappeared across the terminal. "Bye, Greg. I'll give your best to the family. Go Brewers." He felt the bile rising from his stomach as he finished the last two words, and immediately walked to the airport lounge. As the Brewers' team plane taxied down the runway en route to Milwaukee, Jeff raised a cold beer to his lips, as he awaited the boarding call for passengers traveling to New York.

CHAPTER 11

Jeff arrived home from the airport at eleven o'clock that evening. He checked his answering machine, but the only call that he had received over the weekend was from his mother, who was unaware of the fact that he had traveled to Cincinnati to meet Greg. After his conversation with Greg, Jeff had realized how much Michelle meant to him and was looking to partially re-arrange his priorities in an effort to regain her affections.

In fact, he was hoping that there was a message from her when he returned home, especially when he saw the red blinking light on his answering machine. When it was not Michelle, though, his heart sank deep into the pit of his stomach. He decided that he had to speak to her, and that he would have to make the initial contact.

It had been almost one month since the two of them had spoken. This was their longest span of time apart in over five years. When Michelle had to fly to Atlanta for a four-week training session for work a couple of years earlier, Jeff went down each weekend so that they could be together. He thought back to that time, and began to reminisce about when the two of them first began to date, when both were in their senior years at Franklin & Marshall College, a small, liberal arts college in Lancaster, PA better known to its students and alumni as F&M.

That year, the approaching Thanksgiving holiday had caused its usual rush of panic amongst the underclassmen at F&M, as the reality of a semester barely underway and yet almost at its completion smacked the students' faces with an urgent call for the completion of papers and studying for late midterms. There was no such panic felt by the seniors, however, many of whom were already decided as to their career path. They felt as if their senior year success, or lack thereof, would have little, if any, bearing, on their graduate school or job selection opportunities. This was true for Jeff, who had already accepted a position with a large New York accounting firm.

While the overwhelming majority of underclassmen flooded the library or locked themselves in their dorm rooms in an attempt to finish as much work as possible over the next two weeks, so that they would allow themselves the slightest peace of mind for their long weekend home for Thanksgiving, the senior class was otherwise occupied, many of its members busy meandering from bar to bar, drinking themselves into oblivion on a nightly basis. Jeff and his friends had four bars in Lancaster that they would frequent. While they certainly did not go to all of these watering holes each evening, the night always seemed to end at the same seedy hole in the wall located a scant few blocks from the college.

The group arrived at the tavern at approximately 10:00 on the evening of November 12. This was early by most standards, and, in fact, the four were pleased that the bar was not filled to capacity, as it most certainly would be within the next two hours. The bar appeared to be constructed to fit anywhere from 75 to 100 people comfortably. Usually, however, over 200 students and locals crowded within its walls, played its pinball machines, and threw down as little as three dollars for a pitcher of lukewarm beer. It was difficult to walk from one end of the bar to the other, and to sit down at one of the tables in the back meant that it could take, at peak time, up to thirty minutes just to walk back to the bar to obtain another pitcher.

After rattling the pinball machine for almost an hour, the men purchased three freshly-tepid pitchers of beer and made their way to a table, sitting down next to another group whose table was laden with enough beer to satisfy them for at least a couple of hours. The tables were also located in a convenient location, with a clear view of the side door, so that anybody entering the bar, until it became overly crowded, could be scanned in a matter of seconds. It was from here that the men viewed the women entering the bar, so that the rare move, if one was to be made, could be accomplished before the other testosterone carriers in the bar could interfere.

Michelle had attended Alfred College in upstate New York for two years before transferring to F&M. Her stunning looks, outgoing personality, and intelligence made adjusting to her new school a smooth process, and she made quick friends and joined a sorority during the second semester of junior year. She and her sorority sisters also frequented several of the local establishments, and the end of the evening would sometimes lead them to the same seedy bar as many of their classmates.

Jeff had seen Michelle often in the past, whether on school grounds or at these bars, as was inevitable considering the small size of the college. Through the grapevine he had heard some information about her, such as the fact that she had transferred from Alfred and that she had a steady boyfriend back home, a short twenty-minute ride from the college. Jeff knew that she had not dated anyone else during her time at F&M. He found himself deeply drawn to her 5'3" frame, with her dark, flowing hair and almond eyes. He and his friends, as men were prone to do, would often discuss the women at school who they would sleep with if they had the chance. It seemed that Michelle's name would always be mentioned; if not by Jeff, then by one of the others with whom he hung around. Of course, if any of his friends were to mention Michelle by name, Jeff would become irate and tell them to keep away from her. After a while, the others in his group began to call out her name just to invoke his temper.

121

Jeff had been at the bar for almost two hours that evening and had consumed five beers when Michelle and her friends stepped into the bar. She was dressed in a black denim miniskirt, with her nipples evident as they strained against her cream-colored sweater, the result of the unseasonably cold weather that had been gripping Southeastern Pennsylvania over the last few days. She and one of her sorority mates inched their way over to the bar, their hair tossing from side to side as they debated how many pitchers of beer they would purchase. Deciding that two would be sufficient for the six females, they paid the bartender and reached for the pitchers. As they did so, their chests brushed against the backs of the people who were huddled alongside the bar. A smile creased Jeff's face as he imagined those breasts being pressed against his.

The women sat down at a table on the opposite side of the room from Jeff and his friends, but Michelle sat against the wall, where it was possible for the two to make eye contact. Jeff looked over in Michelle's direction, but quickly turned away when she caught his gaze. Jeff later looked over at her table, and Michelle, who had been staring in his direction, quickly turned away in much the same manner.

The glances being exchanged between Jeff and Michelle did not go unnoticed by those sitting with either of them. Jeff's friends urged him to go over and speak to Michelle. Three of Michelle's friends were saying the same to her, but the other two seated with them tried to dissuade her from getting involved with Jeff, as they reminded her of the boyfriend back home. It was at that moment that Michelle revealed, for the first time, that she and her boyfriend had broken up at the end of the summer. She had not told anybody, she explained, because she did not know if she was sufficiently over the breakup and unsure as to whether she was ready to get involved in another relationship so quickly.

122

As she caught Jeff's eye for what appeared to be the tenth time that evening, though, Michelle realized that she was ready to be involved with another man. And Jeff was the one man with whom she was ready to be involved. Jeff, in the meantime, informed his friends that he intended to go over and speak to Michelle, boyfriend or no boyfriend. He was simply waiting until some of her friends left so they would not get in the way.

When the crowd at the bar began to dissipate, two of the women from Michelle's table, those who had tried to convince her not to become involved with Jeff, left to return to their sorority house. Another met up with a member of the football team and left to go back to his apartment. The three women who remained lived in the same dormitory, and all planned to walk back together within the next half hour. Together, that is, until Jeff walked over to the table and began to talk to Michelle.

Over one hour later, two of the sorority sisters put on their jackets and walked back through the cold night to their building. Only Jeff and Michelle remained at the table in the back of the bar. That night, Jeff walked Michelle back to her dorm. He asked her if she would like to see a movie that weekend, and she readily accepted, kissing him on the cheek as she walked into the warmth of her dormitory building and he turned to walk to his dormitory on the other side of the hill.

CHAPTER 12

The Brewers returned home from their series in Cincinnati riding the crest of a four-game winning streak, and those close to the team had renewed hope for the possibility of a pennant push. Advance ticket sales for that week's Tuesday through Thursday series with Pittsburgh were higher than any mid-week series in recent memory.

These aspirations, however, would come crashing downward when the early edition of Tuesday's newspapers hit the stands. Page one of the *Milwaukee Sentinel* contained an article which revealed the death of Mike Jones, rookie left fielder for the Brewers. Although details were sketchy, the article quoted unnamed local police as indicating that there was a possibility of foul play. At a hastily-called press conference, Brewers' management announced that evening's game would be canceled due to the tragedy.

Very few facts regarding Jones' death were revealed at this press conference. A team spokesman, adhering to the wishes of local police, refused to answer specific questions regarding the circumstances of the death, nor even speculate as to its cause. The only information confirmed was that Jones had been found dead in his Milwaukee apartment shortly after midnight by a friend who had come to call on him. Both the team and police refused to identify the friend who had discovered Jones' body, stating only that it was a person unconnected with the Brewers' organization. Speculation initially arose that this person was a female arriving for a pre-arranged encounter, but local authorities would neither confirm nor deny that possibility.

Manager Matt Garver spoke briefly at the press conference, but was overcome with emotion almost immediately and barely managed to blurt out two sentences before burying his head in his hands. He did manage to say that

Mike Jones had been a fine ballplayer and a good person, and that he could not understand why God had chosen to take him at this time, so soon after his ascension to the major league level.

Garver's speech was followed by comments from two members of the Brewers' coaching staff. While only hitting coach Steve Grimes and pitching coach Ben Guerrero actually spoke, all of the other coaches were in attendance. They were joined by ten members of the Brewers, three of whom also spoke and expressed both their sorrow and condolences to the Jones family. All of the players and coaches who spoke described Jones in glowing terms, and expressed disbelief at how quickly, and shockingly, he had been taken from their midst.

The 2014 season, the players announced, would be dedicated to Mike Jones. That night's game, however, was canceled.

After his late flight home Monday night, Jeff stayed home on Tuesday, preferring to stay home and rest rather than going to work and slaving away at his cluttered desk for the day. He did not set his alarm clock, and was able to sleep until 9:00 before being awakened by the beams of light filtering in from between the slats of his vertical blinds. He buried his head deep into his pillow to try to avoid acknowledging the new day, but decided to turn on the television to hear all of the late sports scores.

He reached up with his right hand, and, without looking up from the pillow, groped over the top of his nightstand until he found the remote control. He turned the remote toward the 32-inch flat screen television mounted to the wall across the room, and pushed the power button. As always, the set was tuned to ESPN, and the re-run of the previous hour's edition of *SportsCenter* was just beginning. The television clicked on just in time to catch the last strains of the show's opening music, and Jeff turned his left ear toward the set so that he could hear the opening story, which he expected would focus on one of the pennant races that were beginning to develop as baseball swung into the dog days of summer.

While the telecast's lead story dealt with baseball, however, it was not confined to the pennant race, nor was it even limited to on-field events.

"Good evening. This is Mark Wolfe, and alongside is Scott Parker. We begin this morning with the type of story that occasionally breaks into the world of sports, a story usually reserved for the 11 O'clock news, a story that, quite frankly, gives us a reality check and one that is without explanation."

Jeff, wondering what this horrible story could be, rubbed his eyes and sat up, turning to face the screen at the same time that the smiling visage of a young man wearing a Brewers' cap appeared behind Wolfe.

"Once again, tragedy has struck the world of sports," Wolfe began. "Once again, the young life of an emerging athlete has been erased by the use of a handgun. Mike Jones was in the middle of his rookie season, a season that enabled him to smell the cut grass of a major league ball field for all too short a period of time. Last night, Jones was cruelly murdered by an unknown gunman. Details are slow in being released, but we now go to Jack Smith for a live report from Milwaukee. Jack?"

"Thank you, Mark," said Jack Smith as the telecast cut to him in Milwaukee. "I'm here with Brewers' manager Matt Garver, who, only moments ago, stood at the lectern behind us and informed the world that one of his players had been shot and killed late last night, only hours after the Brewers arrived home from last weekend's series in Cincinnati. The series with Pittsburgh this week was going to be the biggest in several years for this team, but now the mere thought of participating in a pennant race has to pale by comparison to the impact of what occurred, the death of one of their own, late last evening." He turned to Garver and thrust the microphone in front of his face. "Matt, we know how difficult this is for you, but what do we know at this point?"

The Brewers' manager looked down at the microphone in Smith's hand, wiped tears from both of his eyes, and buried his head in his hands. Turning away from the camera, Garver walked slowly away from the reporter without uttering a word in response to Smith's question, managing an apologetic wave as the distance between the two men increased. The crowd to the rear shuffled nervously, and Jeff could see his cousin amidst the other Brewers' coaches as the camera surveyed the scene, while Smith provided details of what was revealed at the press conference. Jones had been shot and killed the previous night, reported Smith, and police were, as of yet, unsure as to either the identity of the gunman or his motive.

Jeff turned off the television, and slumped slightly forward as he rested his lower back against the pillows that were now propped up behind him. Mike Jones was dead. Just last night, he had spoken to Greg about causing some form of injury to Jones. And now he was dead. It all seemed so eerie.

Too eerie. Jeff's eyes opened wide, as the possibility that Greg could have had something to do with the murder of Mike Jones suddenly dawned upon him. No, that was ridiculous. There was no way that Greg had anything to do with the death. Jones was a coke user. He probably just got caught in a bad drug deal; he had gotten home from Ohio, wanted a hit, and ran into trouble. That is what must have happened, and the fact that the death was drug-related was being covered up by either the local authorities or by the team itself. He had heard about situations like this in the past. It would not look good for either the team or major league baseball if information about his drug use was revealed.

"Poor Mike Jones," Jeff thought, "he had it all and threw it away to drugs."

And yet, he was still not completely sure.

Later that afternoon, as Jeff sat looking over the fantasy baseball standings from the previous weeks, his concentration was broken by the ringing of his telephone. He reached over, pulled the phone from its cradle, and placed it to his ear, his eyes never straying from the paper in front of him.

Before he could even say hello, the unmistakably deep voice of Joe Spadola boomed from within the receiver. "Do you believe this shit? Do you fuckin' believe it? I finally get a guy who can play, and he's gone? Not injured, but fuckin' shot? What the fuck? Not that I care so much about the league, but what the fuck?"

"Oh, hi, Joe. I guess you heard the news," Jeff answered. "Too bad -- he was really producing for you. And fuck you with finally having a guy who could hit, you bastard. As I recall, you won the whole thing last year." He looked down at the rosters in front of him. "Looks like if you're going to win again you'll need an outfielder for your team."

"Very funny," Joe replied. "But seriously, Jeff, do you believe this? Stop thinking about the league for a second. The guy was only 22 years old. That's younger than we are, man. He was 22. Shit, we were in first grade when this kid was born. We were graduating from school about the time that he was first beginning high school. Yesterday he was a major league baseball player, and today he's dead. You figure it out."

"I never try to," Jeff replied. "Besides, not to minimize it, but people younger than us are dying every day. In the cities, they're dying of gunshot wounds. So many others are still dying overseas fighting for our country. This only seems different because he was a ballplayer. But in reality, it isn't much different than the statistics that we read about every day in the newspapers."

"I guess you're right, Jeff. I just get spooked when someone younger than us dies. It makes me feel really old. As if grey hair and receding hairlines weren't enough to remind us of our age and mortality." Joe laughed, but it was a nervous and hesitating laugh.

"Look Spadola," Jeff replied, "people die. It's a fact of life. Maybe it will turn out that this guy Jones was into something illegal, or that there was a reason that he is dead. Then again, maybe it won't. Maybe he was killed for no reason at all. I don't know. But we can't dwell on the fact that he was only 22. I'll bet if you look in the paper you'll see at least a couple of obituaries for people younger than that. The fact that he could hit a ball doesn't change that." He paused. "By the way, though, it really does look like someone needs an outfielder."

"Oh man, give me a break," sighed Joe, "How can you be thinking about that right now?"

"No better time than the present," Jeff said as he flipped the pages of his statistics, laying his team's roster next to that of Joe's Bayonne Bombers. "It's easy. I need a pitcher, and I can probably spare an outfielder for you. It looks like the perfect time to make a trade."

"I just got home," Joe growled. "I called to talk about a guy who's dead, and I don't feel like making a fuckin' fantasy move right now." He paused and took two deep breaths. "Tell you what - give me a call at work tomorrow afternoon. You have the number, right? We'll talk about it then."

"O.K., I'll talk to you tomorrow. And seriously, don't be too bent out of shape by this. It's not something that would happen to either of us." He clicked off the phone and placed it on the table beside him, and began to circle all of the pitchers on the Bombers' roster that he would want to take for his team. Then he did the same with the outfielders whom he considered to be expendable, so that he could formulate a trade by the next day. Maybe some benefit could come from Mike Jones' untimely death.

The next day not only brought a trade with the Bombers, but a six-player deal with the Frantastics as well. When the dust had cleared, Jeff had added two new starting pitchers, which enabled him to drop Kevin Taylor from his roster. He also replaced two of his outfielders, and added a new catcher, Pittsburgh's Larry Winthrop, who would hopefully provide help in the various hitting categories. Jeff had restructured his team to such an extent through these two trades, as well as two waiver pick-ups the week before, that his 23-man roster, at this point, only contained twelve people from his original opening day squad. Jeff felt that he had a team who could contend, but knew that he still would have to pick up at least one more hitter and one more pitcher to make a serious run for the league title.

But who would that pitcher and hitter be? From where would they come? And, most importantly, who would Jeff have to trade in order to get them? The Brewers had not yet announced who would be called up from the minors to replace Jones. Maybe if Jeff could get some information from Greg, he would be in a position to make a deal to get the new Milwaukee starting left fielder. Of course, he would have to get that information fast, to prevent anyone else from acting on the same impulse.

The clock in Jeff's kitchen read 5:45 PM. He reached for the phone and dialed Greg's cell phone number, forgetting that the time was one hour behind in

Milwaukee, and left a message on Greg's answering machine to get back to him, that he had something that he wanted to discuss. He went into the kitchen, fixed himself some boxed macaroni and cheese for dinner, sat back on his leather sofa, and settled in to watch that night's ESPN game of the week.

ESPN's Thursday night game of the week featured the San Diego Padres and the Montreal Expos, but much of the pre-game show, not surprisingly, was devoted to Mike Jones. After a retrospective on his brief major league career, as well as file footage showing his exploits while in the minors, brief interviews with various ballplayers were shown. These players, including several teammates and others who had played against Jones both at the major and minor league level, exhibited emotions which ranged from shock to anger.

This segment was followed by a segment on other major leaguers whose careers, and lives, had been cut short by tragedy, all of whom were familiar to Jeff and other students of the game: Ed Delahanty, Lou Gehrig, Ken Hubbs, Roberto Clemente, Thurman Munson, Lymon Bostock, and, most recently, Nick Adenhart. The portion focusing on Bostock was longer than the others'. While his career was not as distinguished as Gehrig's or Clemente's, the modern-day Hall of Famers in the group, he had died the same way as Jones -- cut down by a bullet. As Jeff watched this tribute, his thoughts again began to race back to Greg. What if Greg had something to do with Jones' death?

No, there was no way that Greg could have been involved. He would not have done something so cruel, so inhuman. It had been a struggle just to convince Greg to go along with the plan to injure Jones in the first place. He wouldn't have killed him. That was not Greg. Greg had told him about the drugs, not only about his use, but also that Jones was into using cocaine. Surely, the death had to have been drug-related.

131

But what if Greg were involved? What if Greg had hired someone to kill Jones, or, worse yet, if he had actually pulled the trigger himself? Now his mind was whirling, and it began to dredge up a number of worst possible scenarios.

If Greg was somehow caught and arrested by authorities and was charged with the murder, was there any way that Jeff could also be held responsible? After all, he had asked Greg to see to it that some form of misfortune befell Jones. The prosecutors could argue that Greg would not have done anything to Jones, much less kill him, if Jeff had never approached him and asked his favor. Could this be some form of entrapment? Could Jeff be considered part of a conspiracy, or be charged with aiding and abetting? Several of Jeff's friends had gone to law school, and he struggled to remember back to their first year, when they would discuss their criminal law classes. Could someone be held responsible for a crime if they did not actually participate? Or if someone took steps well beyond what the original person had requested?

He knew that there was a way that he could be responsible, but what was it? Was it solicitation? If you asked someone to do something that was illegal, could you be held responsible for them doing it? Was that a conspiracy? Could he, Jeff Goldstein, sitting at home watching a baseball game, have been an accessory to the murder of Mike Jones? Or worse yet, could he be arrested and charged as being the ringleader of the plot to kill Mike Jones? He was, after all, the one that started the entire episode.

Jeff stared at the phone situated on the table to his right and at his cell phone, imploring each of them to ring. He needed to talk to Greg. He wanted to hear Greg's assurances that he had not killed Jones, that he had not hired anyone to kill Jones, and that they were not going to be in any trouble, that no police officers were going to be knocking on his door in the near future. For what seemed like an eternity, however, no noise was heard from the telephones. Jeff even picked up each on several occasions to make sure that they were working. Each time, though, all that he heard were dial tones. The phones were working, but Greg was not calling. Nor, obviously, was Michelle. And for now, at least, he was not in the right frame of mind to call her.

Finally, in the bottom of the second inning, with the Expos already holding a three-run lead and the Padres' manager walking to the mound to summon help from the bullpen, the cell phone rang. Jeff nervously answered, and was pleased to hear the upbeat tone of his cousin's voice.

"Hiya cuz, how are you?" Jeff paused and listened intently to his cousin's voice. The tone of Greg's voice was not only upbeat, but seemed to possess a strange lilt, as if he were drunk.

"Greg, what the hell is going on there?"

"Oh nothing, just having a little party," said Greg. "As you may have heard, tonight's game was canceled, so I had a little free time and thought I would make the best of it." The distant voices of two women could be heard talking, and Jeff could barely make out what Greg was saying above the music, consisting largely of extended guitar licks, blaring in the background.

"Shit," Jeff muttered, realizing that Greg was probably high. The body of Mike Jones was not even cold, and he was already no doubt back on a cocaine binge, getting high with some bimbos, all three of them inhaling that white powder while Greg laughed about the fact that the game had been canceled.

"Listen to me," Jeff yelled into the telephone, "and turn down the fuckin' music. What the fuck happened?" He paused, and took a deep breath, preparing himself for the worst. His respect for his cousin was rapidly diminishing, such that he was now picturing the both of them spending the next 20 years behind bars, clad in matching prison stripes. When there was no immediate response, he rephrased his question in a more pointed manner. "What happened to Jones?"

"Jeffy, Jeffy. You worry too much," Greg answered in a condescending tone. "Things got a little out of hand. But don't worry about it," he whispered into the phone, "it's all taken care of."

"What do you mean, out of hand? All taken care of?" Jeff's voice was rising with each word, as he now began to believe that his worst thoughts were becoming reality, that Greg had been the mystery man who was the cause of Jones' death. "What the fuck are you talking about, all taken care of?"

There was a pause on the other end of the line. Then, for the first time, Greg's voice sounded serious, as he began to scold Jeff. "Don't you yell at me, you little fucker." Jeff could hear the sound of Greg's hand covering the phone's mouthpiece. He could also hear his cousin's muffled voice saying to the women in the room with him, "Girls, turn down the damned music and go into the bedroom. There's more in there. Now get the fuck out of here. I'll be in soon."

Beads of sweat were beginning to form on Jeff's forehead as his cousin removed his hand from over the mouthpiece and breathed deeply. The perspiration began to drip down his brow and down the bridge of his nose he heard Greg take another deep breath, followed by a third. Then it flowed more freely as Greg began to speak, as it became immediately apparent that Jeff's fears had turned into reality. "You wanted something done to him, right? Well, something did happen to him."

"But . . ." Jeff tried to protest in disbelief.

134

"Shut up, you little shit," Greg admonished before Jeff could utter another word. "As I recall, you asked me to take Jones out." His voice lowered, presumably so that the women in the next room could not hear his next sentence. "Well, I did exactly what you wanted, dear cousin, and went over to Jones' place the other night to see if I could help you out."

"But I didn't want him dead," Jeff interrupted.

"Let me finish," Greg bellowed. He took another deep breath and continued his explanation, his voice becoming slower and softer with each syllable. "I went over there with about an ounce of coke, figuring that we could do a few lines. I was going to try to piss him off and force him to come after me. If he was high enough, he would have probably tripped over something, and done some kind of damage. Like to his leg or something like that." He paused and exhaled deeply. "And you know that the team wouldn't publicize what had really happened, they would have made up some stupid story about him pulling a muscle somewhere. It happens all of the time, just like I told you before. Neither the team nor the league wants any type of negative publicity, especially when that negative publicity involves drugs. The league has enough shit going on with steroids that they try to keep every other drug-related incident under wraps."

"I understand that," Jeff replied. "But then what happened?"

""We each did a couple of lines," Greg responded, "and everything was going just the way that I expected. I made some kind of racist comment, since Jones was a really radical nigger bastard. I knew that he would be completely pissed off, and he was. I thought that he was going to jump up out of his chair and make a beeline for my head. No doubt he would have fallen over something and, you know, mission accomplished." He paused and took a deep breath. "But instead of coming after me, fuckin' kid pulled a pistol from underneath the couch where he was sitting and started to wave it in my direction. I almost shit my pants, and hit the floor right away. He started to walk toward me, waving the fuckin' gun, yelling that I was some sort of redneck bigot old man."

"Holy shit!" Jeff exclaimed.

"You ain't kidding," answered Greg, becoming more animated as he continued to tell his story. "He was coming at me, yelling that I was a redneck bigot, telling me that he was going to kick my old man ass, all the while waving that damned pistol at me. I didn't know if it had any bullets in it, but I couldn't take a chance. He cocked the hammer as if it was loaded, and all of a sudden I thought that it was all over for me. The last thing I wanted to do, though, especially in my own coke-induced state, was die lying on the ground. That would have been the sissy's way out. So I leapt to my feet and tried to lunge at him to knock the gun loose, but I accidentally hit the gun itself. Instead of falling to the ground, the damned thing went up in the air. I tripped and fell down, and Jones tried to catch the gun."

"And," Jeff said, hesitatingly, "and then what happened?"

"Let's just say he was better at catching a baseball than he was at snaring a weapon," Greg replied. "When he reached out the gun went off, and apparently it was loaded because the bullet went right into his fuckin' stomach."

"Holy shit! Then it was an accident, and you didn't really kill him," Jeff said, wishfully, as he wiped the drops of sweat from his face and gulped down a mouthful of beer.

"Not technically, but how would you have explained it to the cops?" answered Greg softly. "My fingerprints were on the gun, remember? What could

I have possibly said to the police so that they would have let me go? How about, 'Well officer, I know that my fingerprints were on the gun and that Mr. Jones was shot in the stomach, but it wasn't my fault.' For some reason, I just didn't think it would work."

Jeff tried to collect his thoughts. "Well then, what the hell did you do? How come they haven't caught you yet?"

"I'm not a complete idiot, Jeff," said Greg. "I was smart enough to keep my plans to myself, so nobody even knew that I was going there. After the shot went off and I saw that he was dead, I left him behind, already dead, and went home as fast as I fuckin' could. Before I left, I wiped my prints off of wherever I had touched, thank God for those cop shows on TV. I took the gun with me, and hid it and the clothes that got blood on them so that they would not be found."

"Are they in a safe place?" asked Jeff, nervously.

"Don't worry," said Greg confidently, "they won't be found. Look, like I told you, I took care of it. Nobody, except for you and me, will know what happened the other night. I just told you, nobody else even knows that I was there the other night. I sure as hell ain't talking, and I assume that you won't be telling anyone. So relax, have a drink, because nothing's going to happen to us."

"Oh, be cool like you, partying up with a couple of hookers even though you killed a guy the night before?" Jeff blurted. He glanced down at the beer in his hand, and, suddenly feeling queasy from the conversation, placed the bottle back down.

"Fuck you and your sarcasm, you little piece of shit. It was an accident, one that nobody is going to hear about. And instead of fucking with me, you

137

should chill out and relax, because you got exactly what you wanted. As I recall, you wanted him out of the lineup because of your fantasy baseball league." Now Greg's voice began to rise again. "Well, Chanukah came a little early this year. He's out of the lineup, just a little more permanently than you may have expected. So sit back, win the league, and then we'll have a nice little party at the end of the season with the money that we win. That way you can meet some of my, what did you call them, hookers?" He laughed. "Now I'm done talking to you. The hookers are waiting for me."

Jeff was speechless as Greg hung up the phone. Mike Jones was dead. Greg had, in one way or another, been responsible. Jeff was also partially responsible, since Greg had gone there to help him, And now, Greg was partying with women while Jeff sat, sweating profusely, in his suddenly lonely apartment. What was he going to do? He knew that he couldn't go to the police. If he did, both of them would go to prison.

Maybe Greg was right, he began to think. If they weren't going to get caught, he should forget that the whole thing ever happened. But his conscience would not allow him to completely forget. Mike Jones was gone, killed at the age of 22. The ramifications of his death would be far-reaching. "That's right," Jeff thought, as he began to think about the practical effect of Jones' death.

Moments later, his initial wave of nausea subsided and his face brightened, as he realized that his chances of the Golds capturing the fantasy league championship had increased dramatically due to Jones' death. His death was still mysterious and, based on what Greg said, would never be solved. A death committed by an unknown assailant for an unknown reason, and, most importantly, a death that the police could not link to either Jeff or Greg. Since Jones was killed, Jeff had already been able to re-work his roster, and his ability to do so was due entirely to Greg's efforts.

"Maybe things weren't so bad after all," thought Jeff. He turned up the sound of the television, opened a beer, and settled in to watch the last few innings of the Expos-Padres game. He realized, however, that he had not accomplished the purpose for which he had initially called Greg, because he never got to ask him who the Brewers would be calling up from the minors to replace Jones. Rather than try to speak to Greg again, though, he decided that it would not be a good time to interrupt him, based on Greg's state of mind, and decided that he could wait and find out with the rest of the world. He had already brought in enough new talent for his team to make a move for first place, he figured, so there was no need for him to find out about what young outfielder the Brewers would be breaking in over the coming weeks.

In the bottom of the eighth inning, with the Expos leading by a seemingly insurmountable 10-2 score, Padres manager Dave Charles sent rookie James Haworth up to pinch hit for the pitcher, who had been routed for four runs in just one inning of work. The ESPN announcer noted that this was to be Haworth's first at-bat, as the Padres had just called him up to the majors that afternoon.

Jeff had been watching the last few innings in the dark, with the only light in the room being provided by the television and the moon peeking around his window blinds. Upon hearing the name James Haworth for the first time, however, he immediately turned on the lamp sitting on the table to his right. He went to the other room, snatched his laptop computer, and carried it back into his bedroom so that he could search for any information on James Haworth.

Jeff kept a yellow legal pad and pen nearby while he was watching games so that he could write down the names of young ballplayers, names that somehow eluded him despite his intense preparation methods. It was rare that the pad would contain as many as two names on any given night, with the exception of when features were done on up-and-coming minor leaguers. These features provided Jeff with the chance to do some advance scouting for his team, whether it be for the current season or for the future.

James Haworth. Jeff thought back to his baseball guides, imagining himself thumbing through the sections on San Diego to try to remember any information on James Haworth. The name, however, did not trigger any memory. Jeff searched on the ESPN website and also picked up the last issue of *Baseball Weekly*. Sure enough, Haworth's statistics were included along with other members of the Padres' Wichita, Kansas AA minor league team. These statistics, while not spectacular, were enough to earn a promotion to the majors, and, given sufficient playing time, Jeff believed that he could be productive toward the end of the season.

Jeff thought of activating Haworth via a waiver wire pick-up. Surely there was an outfielder on his team that was expendable. The name of Dan Randolph immediately leapt to mind. In order to bring up Haworth and drop Randolph, though, he had to make sure that Haworth was nobody else's property. But who could have had Haworth on their roster? If he was on somebody's roster, wouldn't Jeff have remembered him being drafted?

Just to be sure, Jeff began to check the other rosters. Much to his dismay, he found that Haworth had in fact been drafted, by the last-place Martinizers. Perusing the ESPN site and league standings, he determined that Haworth had not been activated by the Martinizers, but was still sitting on the bench, where his statistics did not count. He thought of calling Barry Martin and making a trade for Haworth, but saw that his clock was showing 1:25 AM and decided to wait.

Wait, that is, for about five minutes. Haworth doubled off of the right field wall, and came around to score on a single by the next hitter. Now, Jeff had to have him for his team. He reached for the phone and dialed Martin's number. The phone rang six times before an obviously groggy Barry Martin answered. "Who the fuck is it?" he croaked, still very much asleep.

"Hey Barry, it's me, Jeff. Did I wake you?" Jeff grimaced at his own stupid question. Of course he had awakened him, but his feeble attempt at hiding this did not pass unnoticed.

"Of course I was sleeping, you piece of shit," cried an irate Martin. "It's the middle of the night! What time is it? 1:30? Are you out of your mind? Some of us have to go to work tomorrow."

"I know, so do I. Look, I just wanted to call and discuss a possible trade with you."

At the other end of the line, there was silence.

"Did you hear me, Barry, I was thinking of making a trade for a pitcher, which I know you need."

There was still silence at the other end of the line.

"Why don't you give me a scrub pitcher, and I'll take this kid Haworth from you. I heard that the Padres called him up this afternoon. He's not even on your major league roster, just wasting his time in your minors."

The silence came to a shattering end. "Are you crazy?" Martin bellowed, forcing Jeff to hold the phone at arm's length to avoid damaging his eardrum. "What the fuck are you thinking, calling me in the middle of the night to make some stupid fuckin' trade?" He paused. "You know," he said, his voice now at a more normal decibel level, "Joe was right. You are completely fucked in the head over this league. Now let me go back to sleep."

Jeff heard a click on the other end of the line, and then a fresh dial tone. He slowly hung up the phone, Barry's words still ringing through his ears.

Jeff left three messages on Barry Martin's cell answering machine and a message on his home phone over the next four days, but Barry never returned these calls. He also sent him two messages via Facebook, neither of which generated a response. With each passing day, Jeff grew more and more frustrated with his inability to trade for James Haworth, especially since Haworth had hit safely in each of his four games with the Padres. Jeff's frustrations, however, were slightly lessened each day as he watched the daily statistics and standings change following the death of Mike Jones.

Almost immediately, the loss of Jones' production was proving damaging to the Bayonne Bombers, whose batting average and home run positions each dropped by two places. In the meantime, the Golds, boosted by Jeff's most recent acquisitions, were beginning to close the gap in two pitching categories, earned run average and wins.

The Golds were still in fourth place, however, and the teams ahead were showing no signs of slowing down. Particularly troubling to Jeff was the fact that the Emerson Boozers were building a wide lead in the saves category, setting the stage for Joe Emerson to be in the position to trade one of his relievers for one or two power hitters. This, Jeff believed, would practically assure Emerson of victory.

Jeff tried to think about how this scenario be avoided. If only something were to happen to one of the Boozers' relief pitchers before such a trade could be consummated, he reasoned, he could stem the Boozers' ascension

142

to the top of the standings. Jeff knew that Joe had already spoken to at least two other teams about trading one of the two, but that the other teams had wanted to hold off for at least another couple of weeks. Jeff remembered, for example, that Emerson had spoken to Barry Martin about such a trade, and, considering the contempt that Martin was obviously feeling for Jeff, it was likely that Barry would do all that he could, via a trade, to help Emerson pull away from the pack.

Jeff consulted his schedule. The interleague portion of the schedule was beginning, and the Brewers were about to begin a home series against the Seattle Mariners. Following that three game set, though, they were traveling to Baltimore to take on the Orioles. Jeff checked the statistics one last time, picked up the telephone, and dialed Greg's number. He had not spoken to his cousin in over two weeks, since their conversation after the death of Mike Jones. Greg was not in, so Jeff left a message on Greg's answering machine, saying that he had a favor that he wanted Greg to do for him.

CHAPTER 13

The first two games of the Milwaukee-Baltimore series were fairly uneventful. In game one, Orioles' ace Justin Stevenson held the Brewers to six hits en route to a 3-1 victory, with first baseman Manny Gomez providing all of the offense that the O's required, driving in two runs with a fifth inning single off of Brewers' starter Giovanni Pacheco. Game two went to the Brewers by a 5-2 count, due largely to a three-run home run by second baseman Rob Patton.

Game three, however, produced fireworks. With the Orioles leading the Brewers in the seventh inning of a tight 3-2 game, Baltimore pitcher Mark Williamson plunked Milwaukee right fielder George Vaughn with a fastball to the small of the back. Despite the fact that both teams were clearly in a position to make a strong bid for the playoffs at this juncture of the season, both were obviously feeling the pressure of the mid-season's pennant races, and tempers quickly flared in the already tension-filled contest. Vaughn hurled his bat aside and charged to the mound in an attempt to take a swipe at Williamson, with the Baltimore catcher and home plate umpire in hot pursuit of the burly designated hitter. The benches and bullpens of both teams quickly emptied in response to the possibility of a melee, with more than fifty players and coaches galloped to the center of the diamond. As usual, there was some pushing and players jawing at each other, but very few punches were thrown.

There was only one casualty. Orioles closer Paul Frank, who had 28 saves up to that point in the season and was well on his way to shattering his own personal best for saves in one season, suffered a dislocated right shoulder during the melee. Frank, with the rest of his bullpen mates, had rushed to the center of the crowd that was milling about the infield once they saw Vaughn take his first steps towards the pitcher's mound. Due to the large number of people clad in only two different types of double-knit uniforms, however, individual players were obscured amid a sea of grey, blue, and orange such that television cameras could not detect how the injury to Frank had actually occurred, nor could a review of the brawl's videotapes reveal the person, or persons, who were responsible.

Local papers in the Baltimore area later reported that Frank claimed to have been grabbed by one of three people – Brewers' catcher Jose Dominguez, Orioles' pitcher Hank Millman, or Milwaukee coach Greg Bloom. Because of the large number of players and coaches who crammed onto the Camden Yards infield grass, though, Frank could not specifically identify which of the three had pulled his shoulder from its socket.

One of these men, though, had apparently grabbed Frank by the right arm, and the tug caused his pitching shoulder to dislocate. At the time, Frank was merely standing to the right side of the pitcher's mound, several feet away from Vaughn and Williamson, who had been separated but they were still jawing at each other. The news reports, noting that the loss of Frank dealt a severe blow to any Baltimore hopes of a respectable divisional finish, as well as one of the American league's playoff spots, speculated that one of the Brewers, either Dominguez or Bloom, had caused the hurler's injury. One pundit went so far as to opine that the tensions of a potential pennant race had overcome one of these participants, such that the injury was not caused accidentally, but that the action had been done intentionally.

What the media did not report was that Frank was not merely the Orioles' closer. Frank was also one of the two relievers who were racking up save after save for the Emerson Boozers.

Jeff had seen the highlights of the Baltimore-Milwaukee fight on that evening's *SportsCenter* broadcast. While three different camera angles of the

145

melee were shown, none offered a view as to what had happened to Frank. Jeff went to sleep that evening trying to visualize how the loss of Frank would affect the standings. The next day, he read about the incident in the newspaper, including the allegations surrounding Dominguez and Bloom. He smiled and chuckled lightly to himself. In contrast to his concerns and fears after hearing about the death of Mike Jones, as he read and heard about the injury to Frank, Jeff was content with the thought that Greg may have been the one who removed Frank's golden pitching arm from its socket.

Jeff received a call that afternoon from Joe Emerson. "What the hell did you do, Goldstein, have your cousin do something to Frank?" asked Emerson, quite seriously. "Did you have him go out there and pull as hard as he could on Frank? He was cruising in the saves category. Now what the hell am I going to do?"

It was the first direct allegation regarding his cousin's possible involvement in causing a player's downfall, and Jeff quickly brushed it aside. "I don't know what you're going to do, Joe," replied Jeff, who then dispelled any thoughts of Greg's involvement. "And think logically about this for a minute. How could I have spoken to Greg about this? Did I plan for Vaughn to charge the mound? Do I have some form of power over the Milwaukee lineup? Or better yet, what did I do, call Greg the night before and say, 'look, Greg, if there's a fight don't worry about anyone else out there, just go after Frank.' Come on, be serious." Jeff laughed aloud.

Joe thought that Jeff was laughing at the ridiculousness of the notion, but Jeff was secretly content with the knowledge that the last scenario was closer to the truth than Emerson could ever imagine. "Well, it looks awfully suspicious to me," Joe said, as he joined Jeff in laughter. He then added, "I know that I'm off base. There's no way that you could have planned this. But think about it, it does look really strange, especially since people are saying that Greg was the one who did the dirty deed."

"Sure, a major league coach is going to throw his career in the toilet by maliciously hurting a player from the other team," Jeff said, chuckling. "I don't think so." Although Joe did not know it, Jeff was speaking the truth with this last sentence. He didn't think that Greg had caused the injury, by this time he knew so. He could feel it, even though he had not yet spoken to Greg for verification. He broke out in laughter again, and then told Emerson that if he wanted to trade for a reliever, he should call back again later so that they could discuss something.

Returning home from a lackluster job interview that evening, Jeff ran into an old friend of his, Matt Stewart. Matt was from Maryland, and was obviously distraught over the Frank injury. "Can you believe it?" he asked Jeff, as the two descended the stairs to the subway station, "This one really hurts. I mean, this year the Birds really had a shot at it. Not only the division, but they could have gone to the World Series with their talent. I know that there's plenty of time left to go in the season, but it certainly doesn't look good at this point with their closer sitting on the sidelines." He looked up at Jeff, who was not even trying to hide his joy at the situation. "And your smirk doesn't help things any, asshole."

"Come on, Matt," Jeff responded. "What do you expect? I'm a Yankees fan." By now Jeff could not contain his laughter. In an awkward sense, it was becoming apparent to Jeff that Frank's untimely injury had provided him more with joy than he had experienced in some time. Instead of being remorseful or empathizing with his friend's plight, Jeff was growing more and more pleased with the positive effects that Frank's injury would have for both the Golds and the Yankees. "Who knows," he chuckled, "maybe the Orioles will do well

147

without Frank. I mean, closers are overrated, don't you think?" He pushed Matt from behind.

"Fuck you," Matt said, stumbling forward slightly.

Jeff placed his hand on his friend's shoulder, steadying him, and tried to look at him in a sympathetic manner. "All jokes aside, Matt," he said to his friend, "calm down." He could not contain his grin, however, as he added, "don't worry, at least you still have a shot at beating Boston this year. And even if you don't, I hear that the cellar isn't too cold these days."

Matt exited one stop before Jeff, promising that he would have his revenge. Jeff continued to laugh, and turned to one of the other subway passengers. Pointing to Matt as he walked away on the platform, Jeff informed his acquaintance that his poor friend was an Orioles' fan. This statement elicited laughter from all of those standing within earshot, which, thankfully for Jeff, was a carful of Yankees' fans. Jeff exited the train at its next stop and purchased a newspaper when he reached the street, wanting to read yet another account of the brawl and its potential effect on the pennant chase.

While walking in the hallway outside his apartment, Jeff heard his telephone begin to ring inside. Reaching for his keys, he put down his briefcase and unlocked the apartment door, leaving the door ajar with the keys still within its lock. He raced into the kitchen, and was able to pick up the phone at the same time that his answering machine clicked on. Over the noise of his own recorded voice, he shouted to whoever was on the other side of the line to hang on until the message finished.

After the beep, Jeff heard Greg's familiar voice, who again sounded like he was in the midst of a party. Much like their last call, two female voices were again discernible in the background, one of whom sounded familiar from the week before. "Hey Jeff, did you see the papers today? Looks like somebody did a bad thing to the Orioles, wouldn't you say?"

"You know it," Jeff replied, turning off the phone machine so that the conversation would not be recorded.

"Girls, just a second," Greg said with his hand over the phone, and then resumed talking to Jeff. "I told everyone, you have to look out for that Dominguez. He's a time bomb waiting to explode."

"You mean that Jose was the one who . . ." Jeff began to ask before he was interrupted by Greg.

"Well," Greg said, "let's just say that that is the version that I will be giving if anybody asks me." He laughed. "Have a good night, cuz. Let me know if you need anything else. We'll be home in about four days."

Over the next couple of days, Jeff reviewed the fantasy league standings even more than usual, hoping that Smith's death, combined with Frank's injury and his recent trading spree, had allowed his team to make a push upward. By the following Thursday, his hopes came to fruition.

The Golds had vaulted past Bobby Fish and the Fins, into third place. Moreover, they were only one point shy of the surging Frantastics. The Emerson Boozers were still sitting comfortably in the driver's seat, but their stranglehold on the saves category was beginning to erode due to the injury suffered by Baltimore's Paul Frank. The top five teams as the season reached the middle of August were as follows:

Future GM League (8/14)

1) The Emerson Boozers	57
2) Frantastics	53
3) Golddiggers	52
4) Bobby Fish and the Fins	50.5
5) The Jew Crew	49

Jeff picked up his cell phone and quickly dialed Brian Hunter's home phone number. Brian had not returned his past few phone calls, all to his cell phone, but Jeff was tiring of waiting for a response. He cradled the phone under his chin, as he held the statistic sheets in one hand and that day's *Daily News* in the other. After four rings, Brian's answering machine picked up: "Hi, you've reached Brian and Diane. We can't come to the phone now, because Diane's either out spending money or we're in bed. If this is about the baseball league, don't tell my wife, but my team is in last place and my players are ripe for the picking. Leave a message and we'll call you back."

Jeff waited for the tone, and then began to speak, in direct defiance of the message's instructions: "Hi Brian, this is Jeff. Hopefully you'll have some money left after your wife's shopping, because you're going to owe me some after I win this league." He paused momentarily. "Hey, do me a favor and call me back. I have a trade that I want to talk over. How does the name Johnny Boyce sound to you?"

Jeff clicked off the phone and threw it onto the bed. He thought of calling Joe Spadola to talk trade with him, but then realized that Joe would not be home until later that night, since he worked more hours in the summer when his father's business at the family-owned store picked up. He decided instead to peruse the classified pages, to make a more effective effort at locating a new job.

CHAPTER 14

"I think the more stressful our times get, the more we look for fantasy escapes."

- *Jeri Ryan, actress*

Thus far, the recruiters with whom Jeff had been speaking had been of little help. Daily scouring of sites like Monster.com and Craigslist also yielded little positive results. Over the past two weeks, he had gone on only two interviews. He had been clearly overqualified for both of the open positions, but knew that he had to find work somewhere and that accounting jobs were scarce in the summer months. He had not even told his parents that he had been fired, so he could not go to them for help with his rent and other expenses. Similarly, he had not told most of his friends about his firing, so he was not even relying on others to try to locate new employment for him. He decided to accept the first offer that he received and then move on later in the year if it wasn't working to his satisfaction. Heck, any paycheck was better than no paycheck.

Before his recent termination, Jeff had worked for Martin & Jerome, one of the world's largest and most prestigious public accounting firms. He had been at M&J for over four years, since his graduation from college. For the last six months of his tenure, he was involved in the audit of Benco, a manufacturing conglomerate with annual sales in excess of $10 billion. Unfortunately for Jeff, Benco did not work on a calendar fiscal year, but rather closed its books on April 30th. This meant that the audit of this company, which was considered one of the most rigorous (and, therefore, most prestigious) in the New York office of Martin & Jerome, led to long hours in the months of June and July, after the typical accounting busy season of January through April.

Jeff's desk at Benco was a veritable fallen avalanche of past financial statements, spread sheets, and audit books in need of corrections. The right side of the desk was dominated by a black telephone, which sat in front of the clock radio whose dial was permanently tuned to the local sports station. The radio was a constant source of distraction to Jeff's co-workers on the Benco audit, who were forced to listen to the talk radio and baseball games pumped out by the radio from early morning until they were finally released for the day, typically at somewhere between one and two A.M. "Jeff," they complained, "how often can you hear Joey from Brooklyn or Steve from Manhattan call from their stupid car phones and invent baseball trades that nobody in their right mind would actually consider?"

He knew that they were right. After all, some of the callers were ludicrous. Some idiot from Queens would call and say that team A should trade their starting first baseman, center fielder, and one of their starting pitchers to team B for a backup second baseman and minor leaguer. This trade, he would explain, would help both teams. In reality, of course, it would only be beneficial to team B, the one that was in the thick of the pennant race and, coincidentally, the team for which the caller was rooting. If the trade proposal was totally outlandish, it would make for great radio because more idiots would call in for the next two hours and try to fine-tune the trade so that it made sense, at least to them, each caller lambasting the previous one for adding a player that he felt should not be included.

Many of the callers proposed deals that made less sense than trades being considered in the fantasy league, and the fantasy league was devoid of considerations such as maintaining some form of team chemistry and the players' salaries. "Yes, they are ridiculous," Jeff would reply, "but they are still fun to listen to." To Jeff, that is. It was little more than annoying to those around him who did not yearn for the ever-present sports babble.

152

Things were even worse for John Robbins, the audit supervising senior who shared a room with Jeff at the local motel when the audit staff was kept late into the night, which had been more often as of late. Jeff insisted on watching the 2:30 A.M. edition of *SportsCenter*, even though he was aware of all of the day's sports news from his hours of radio listening. Many was the evening that Robbins would drive the two miles from the audit site to the motel with his eyes almost slammed shut due to fatigue and collapse in the foreign bed, only to be kept awake for thirty minutes by the highlights and commentary provided by the station's late night anchors.

It became apparent after several consecutive evenings of being kept awake against his will that Robbins would not stand for this routine much longer. As he was one year more experienced and one level above Jeff, though, he could exact his revenge in ways other than merely making Jeff turn the television off. The papers on Jeff's desk began to pile even higher, as Robbins, playing the role of work delegator, threw assignment after assignment to his overburdened underling.

Jeff was rapidly becoming more and more frustrated, in part due to the immense workload that he faced daily, and in part by his inability to pay what he considered to be an adequate amount of attention to baseball and his fantasy league team. His work began to suffer, something that did not go unnoticed by his superiors following a review of some of his work papers.

"Jeff, could you come into my office for a second?" asked Bob Linder, before he turned and strode down the hallway to the office at the far corner. Linder was the Martin & Jerome partner responsible for the Benco audit. A member of the firm for 22 years, Linder had acquired a reputation for working extremely long hours and expecting the same from those working under him. Linder also expected those working with him to dress appropriately while on the

153

job. To him, this meant that men were to wear dark blue or grey suits, solid color shirts and black wingtip shoes. The dress code extended to neckwear, as only repp and polka-dotted ties were permissible. Even the colors of the ties were monitored; any tie with dominant colors other than red, burgundy, or blue was frowned upon. This created wardrobe problems for the men, many of whom found that their olive or taupe suits, striped shirts, and patterned ties were left unworn for months at a time, relegating them to wearing the same two or three suits in rapid-fire rotation.

When Bob Linder asked Jeff to follow him to the corner office, thoughts began racing through his head. He had not said more than five words to Linder in the last six weeks. What could he possibly want to discuss? He wanted to run, but there was no escape. Jeff took a deep breath, tucked in his shirt, and straightened his blue and red striped tie. He then began to take the long walk down the hallway, shuffling his feet like a shackled prisoner being led down the corridor to his execution.

He knocked lightly on the door. Not even looking up from his desk, Linder waved Jeff into the office and pointed to the chair directly opposite his. "Take a seat, Jeff. Oh, and do close the door behind you."

Jeff's heart had been down in his stomach, but he now felt it coming up with that familiar bile taste as he closed the door and sat opposite Bob Linder. The partner gestured to a bowl of candy on his desk. The large desk that separated Jeff from Bob Linder was immaculately neat, with the exception of Jeff's latest audit binder pages strewn about. Linder asked Jeff if he wanted so try some candy, as he reached into the bowl and produced a red, plastic-wrapped oval.

Jeff declined, and waited for the partner to tear into him for whatever it was that he had done wrong. A verbal lashing, though, was not forthcoming. Instead, Linder leaned forward, folded his hands on the desk, and asked, innocently, "is anything wrong? Your work appears to be suffering a little, and we both know that you're capable of doing better." Jeff was taken aback by the sincerity in Linder's voice, and at the same time was slightly amused by the similarity that all of his conversations were taking on.

Several things immediately leapt to his mind. As always, however, he decided that these were best kept to himself. What could he say? "Well Bob, where do I even start? You no doubt know that I'm having a problem with that asshole Robbins who is always kissing your behind, but who is not too busy to pile enough work on my desk to keep half of freakin' Minnesota employed. There's also the fact that I have 135 grand at stake in a baseball league that I can't focus on because I'm stuck in this hellhole doing a fuckin' audit for 14 hours a day during the summer. And did I mention my girlfriend? Or should I refer to her as my ex-girlfriend, who hasn't spoken to me in weeks and who before that had been giving me shit about my priorities and fun stuff like that." No, clearly he could not say any of that.

He managed a slight smile, looked at the photograph of Linder and his family that sat on his desk, and said "I'm probably just a little tired, Mr. Linder. But don't worry, because it's nothing that I can't handle. I'll catch up, and I'll fix whatever papers were wrong." Jeff hated himself for demeaning himself in this way, but knew that his job depended on such promises. He felt weak due to his inability to confront Linder, especially as the smiling faces of Linder's wife and two young daughters peered at him from the photograph, their smiles mocking him.

"Alright, Jeff," Linder said, leaning back in his chair, "but if you have any problems you know that my door is always open. And please call me Bob." The red light on Linder's phone began to blink. "We'll talk more later on," he said, as he reached for his telephone receiver. Jeff stood, nodded at the partner, and exited the room, closing the door behind him as he left.

That evening, the blue light of the television screen filled the motel room, providing a small space of artificial light piercing the darkness for those who would be passing by the room's window on the way to their own cubicle for the night. Inside the room, Jeff lay in his bed, watching the baseball game, and silently voiced his support for the visiting team. Or, rather, silently rooted for a player on the visiting team.

The breathing in the next bed became slower and deeper, as its occupant slipped into a deeper sleep. Jeff, however, could not close his eyes, despite the fact that he had worked for almost 15 hours the previous day. He glanced at the standard-issue motel clock: 3:35. He then directed his gaze back at the 19-inch color television on the bleached oak dresser opposite his bed. The screen was displaying a look at the waning Safeco Field crowd, as well as graphics indicating that the game between the Texas Rangers and Seattle Mariners was tied 2-2, with the game mired in the bottom of the 16th inning. No sound emanated from the television, so as not to awaken Jeff's sleeping roommate.

The Texas pitcher, obviously tired in his third inning of work, walked the first two batters whom he faced, throwing only one strike out of nine pitches. The next batter, the Seattle left fielder, strode to the batter's box as the Texas manager hurried to the pitcher's mound to calm his fatigued hurler.

The manager removed his blue and red cap, scratched the graying tuft of hair that lay matted atop his head, and looked anxiously to his team's bullpen. The bullpen, however, was occupied by only one person – a catcher. He scratched his head once more and barked a few words of encouragement before returning to the dugout, as the pitcher was permitted, by necessity, to continue.

In the motel room, the fantasy manager scratched his own head and began nervously biting his lower lip. The fatigued hurler who was playing the role of sacrificial lamb to the still active Seattle bats was not only a member of the Texas Rangers, but also of the Golds.

The outfielders moved in several steps apiece, hoping to cut down the runner at second base should he attempt to score on a base hit. The strategy was foiled, however, when the batter swung at the first pitch and sent the ball rocketing into the deepest part of right-center field. The outfielders could only watch helplessly as the ball caromed off of the outfield wall, the runner at second crossing home plate with the winning run seconds before the ball came to a rolling stop on the outfield grass, a scant few feet from where the center fielder stood only seconds before..

In his motel room, Jeff muttered "shit," barely audibly, but he carelessly slammed his hand down upon the edge of the bed with a resounding "whack." The breathing in the other bed halted momentarily, and the blankets rustled as the body underneath slowly moved.

Jeff lay still in his bed, but did not turn off the television as the cameras continued to roll, capturing the obviously-tired Mariners celebrating their hard-fought victory. As the celebration continued, John Robbins slowly lifted his head from the pillow and attempted to open his eyes, squinting hard in Jeff's direction. "Turn the fuckin' television off, Goldstein," he growled, reaching for his watch. "What time is it, anyway?"

"Just one more minute, John," answered Jeff, "I want to see the scores before I turn it off."

Robbins bolted upright and reached out for the remote control. "The scores will be the same in the morning, which, if you look at the clock, you will know is only four hours away. Certainly you can wait that long, can't you?" His voice reached a fevered pitch as he searched in vain for the remote, which was hidden underneath Jeff's blanket. "Where the fuck is the remote?"

"Just one second, alright?" Jeff pleaded.

Now Robbins leaped from the bed and went to the television to turn it off manually. He turned back to Jeff. "No, asshole. Not one minute. Not one second. Not one fuckin' baseball score. I need to sleep. You should be getting some sleep. I have a job to do. You have a job to do. Or have you forgotten about your little meeting with Bob?"

Jeff looked at him, mouth agape, with more than a hint of disbelief.

Robbins continued his tirade. "What do you think, that I didn't know about it? Surely you must know that your job performance, or lack thereof, has been quite the topic of conversation. And this is not a good time for that, my friend. As you are no doubt aware," he snickered, "there will be layoffs soon. Most people are working twice as hard as usual to protect their jobs. You're doing the opposite."

Jeff swallowed hard. "What are you talking about?," he croaked, as he turned the lamp off next to his bed, leaving only the small white circle remaining in the center of the television screen to illuminate the room.

158

John's voice was muffled now, and Jeff realized that he had buried his face into his pillow. "Get a fuckin' grip, Jeff. Let me just say this. If you don't improve, and I mean really improve, now, you're gonna be out on your ass. The economy sucks. People have to want to work, or they are gone. You will be one of them."

Jeff started to speak, but could only eke out the word "what?" a second time.

"What? Is that all you can say?" John's voice grew stronger as he continued to rip into Jeff. "Try this on for size. Linder has been asking me for weeks why your work has been so lousy. Benco is his biggest client and is very, very important to him. Believe it or not, I've been covering for you, buddy boy. But guess what, I'm not going to do it for you anymore. I'm sick and tired of making excuses for you when you can't give me even the slightest courtesy." He laughed. "So sleep well, because this may be the last time that you'll stay in this room, and the last time that you will keep me up to watch a meaningless baseball game."

Jeff turned away from John Robbins and pulled the blanket up to his neck, trying to fall asleep while he wondered whether his superior, the man attempting to sleep only six feet away, was bluffing or if he would be out of a job by the next morning.

It did not take long for Jeff to find out. At 10:00 the next morning, his phone rang. On the other extension was Bob Linder. "Jeff, could you come here for a minute?"

This time Jeff could feel the bile rising in his throat as soon as Linder said his name. "O.K. Mr. Linder, I mean, Bob," he gasped, "I'll be there in a minute." He again walked the long hallway to Linder's office, in the same

159

shuffling motion, passing by several of his co-workers busily working on their own facets of the audit. "What the hell did I do wrong?" he wondered to himself, as the corner office, and his inevitable professional execution, both grew nearer and nearer.

When he reached the office, he could see John Robbins standing off to the right, approximately two steps behind the chair that sat directly across the large desk from Bob Linder. The partner, from his own chair, motioned with his right hand for Jeff to sit down. This time, however, no candy was being offered. For ten seconds, what seemed to Jeff like an eternity, no words were spoken by any of the three men. Finally, Bob Linder cleared his throat and began to speak.

"Jeff, I don't know quite what to say. When you started here, we thought that you were going to be a valuable member of our Benco team. I know that this is one of the toughest assignments in our office, but, based on your abilities and past experience, it was felt – I felt - that you could handle the workload." Jeff leaned forward and opened his mouth to respond, but Bob waved him off. "Jeff, let's be straight about this. I think that you can be a good auditor. Right now, though, you're not. I don't know if your mind is on something else, but we just don't have room for you here now. My confidence in you is not strong right now, Jeff, and without that confidence I cannot have you here on my team."

The words "mind is on something else" echoed through Jeff's ears, so much so that he missed the next sentence that Linder spoke. "We feel that it would be best for both you and the firm to let you go. Once you've worked out whatever is wrong, then you can feel free to apply for a job with the firm again. In the meantime, we will give you eight weeks' pay to carry you through until things get straightened out."

160

Tears welled up in Jeff's eyes, and he looked sheepishly in John Robbins' direction. Robbins, though, did not make eye contact with Jeff, instead looking out of the large office window with a small, almost imperceptible grin creasing his face. Without saying a word, Jeff stood and turned to leave the room. As he reached the doorway, he heard Bob Linder's voice for what would be the last time. "I really am sorry, Jeff," Linder said, "I wish you the best, and I do hope that we will have the opportunity to work together again in the future. Please close the door on your way out."

Jeff packed up his desk, carefully placing his few belongings in a cardboard box that once held reams of copy paper. Before walking to his car, he took out his Yankees' schedule, and realized that the team was playing a matinee that day, a 1:05 businessman's special. He decided that he had nothing better to do, so that he would try to make the game. To do so, though, he would have to hurry to the Bronx. Surely, Yankee Stadium would be the perfect place for him to escape, for him to forget what had just transpired. He fled the office, never bothering to pause and say goodbye to his co-workers.

Jeff almost bowled over a co-worker in the hallway as he rushed past her, and only waved his hand in her direction as his final form of farewell. He loped to his car, tossed the cardboard box in the trunk, and drove to the motel and did the same with the remainder of his belongings, twisting and gnarling his suits and shirts in the process.

Traffic on the George Washington Bridge was unusually light for mid-afternoon, and Jeff reached Yankee Stadium by 12:30. He presented his Martin & Jerome business card at the ticket gate, and paid half-price for his Grandstand ticket. He thought himself to be quite intelligent for using the card in this manner, especially since he no longer worked for the firm. But what could possibly happen? What was the ticket salesman going to do, call to verify his

161

continued employment? When he thought about it afterward, he realized that the half-priced admission was the best thing that the job had done for him, instead of vice-versa, in as long as he could remember.

He climbed the stairs to the Grandstand, taking off his jacket as he ascended the stadium steps. By the time he settled into seat number 3, row 15, section 418 of the Grandstand level, located slightly to the right of home plate, his sleeves were rolled up to his elbows and his tie loosened, the top button of his starched shirt undone. He leaned back in the metallic blue seat, and watched the center field scoreboard intently as it showed highlights from the previous week's major league action. He scanned the outfield stands, and lamented the loss of the old Stadium, the one in which he had seen so many games as a child.

When the highlights finished, he walked to the concession stand and bought himself an overpriced beer and pretzel, then returned to his seat just in time for the playing of the Star Spangled Banner. As the crowd's cheering intensified over its final strains, Jeff looked up, squinting, at the bright blue sky and thought of John Robbins, Bob Linder, and the other members of the Benco audit. Those people were still entombed in that office that they called home, working around the clock like slaves to complete an audit of an unfeeling client. The poor slobs.

"Yeah," he thought to himself, "this is the life. No more of Bob Linder's shit for me. 'I really am sorry, Jeff,' he says, like he meant that. No fuckin' way." He gazed up at the intensely bright sun that loomed over the outfield frieze. "Fuck John Robbins. Fuck Bob Linder." The first batter, Angels' center fielder Dan Carlin, stroked a single to left field. "Fuck all of them." His face broke out into a smile. "As a matter of fact, fuck Dan Carlin."

Five innings and several beers later, though, Jeff began to reflect on what had transpired that morning. For the first time, he realized that he had been fired, that he would not be able to go to work the following day. Worst of all, he would not be getting his paycheck after his severance period expired, the end for which work was his means. "Now I've done it," he thought, "what am I going to do? What am I going to tell everyone?"

"Oh shit," he realized, bolting upright as those in the Grandstand seats rose and craned their necks to see an outstanding catch in the right field corner, "what am I going to tell my parents?"

Going into the bottom of the seventh inning, the Yankees were on the short side of a slim 3-2 margin. The Los Angeles starting pitcher, however, was beginning to show signs of fatigue, which was not surprising in light of the 100 degree temperatures that turned the Yankee Stadium field into a giant oven. The leadoff batter in the seventh lined out to the shortstop, but the pitcher's tired arm was evident as the next two batters reached first base through walks.

With one out and runners on first and second, first baseman Todd Ride strode to the plate. The crowd initially hushed in anticipation, and then began to roar as the pitcher began his windup. The pitch sailed almost two feet above the catcher's head, and the catcher almost separated his arm from the rest of his body straining to haul in the rising projectile. The pitch also brought the Los Angeles pitching coach scurrying to the mound. The coach reached the pitcher's mound and grabbed at his left sleeve, indicating to the bullpen that he wanted the lefty to pitch to the Yankee first baseman. Moments later, the weary starting pitcher trudged off the field, quickly doffing his cap, to a smattering of polite applause from the capacity crowd.

As the reliever took the first of his warm-up tosses, Jeff looked up at the scoreboard, which until the sixth inning had been devoid of any out-of-town scores. Now, however, a score of 4-1 was flashed for the Minnesota-Boston game, with the visiting Twins holding the edge. Several people seated behind Jeff had also seen the score, and cheered loudly at the hated Red Sox' fate. Jeff, however, quickly frowned when he saw the score flashed, as he realized that Boston's starting pitcher had been Joe Markham, who was also a member of the Golds.

Jeff glanced alternately at the scoreboard and the playing field, hoping for run-scoring rallies by both the Yankees and Red Sox. Only one was to be, however. As Jeff glanced up to see the Boston score, the reliever delivered his first offering to the Yankee hitter, who sent the ball sailing far into the right field seats, giving the Yankees a 5-3 lead. The crowd erupted as the ball was caught by a fan, the base paths suddenly becoming full of pinstriped joggers.

At the same time as the ball landed in the fan's glove, the scoreboard operator increased the Twins' lead to 8-1, with the game still in the second inning. "Shit," Jeff cried as the change was flashed, burying his head in his hands while everyone around him was rejoicing and calling for Ride to emerge from the dugout and tip his cap.

"Hey buddy, what's your problem?" boomed a voice from behind. Jeff turned, and saw a six foot tall, round man wearing a faded Yankees t-shirt that was two sizes too small and adorned with the number 23 staring in his face. The man's chest strained against the fabric, separating the '2' from the '3' by a wide margin, and his flabby stomach obscured the top three inches of his elephant-sized blue jeans.

"What?" Jeff asked, and turned back to face the action as the next hitter had settled into the batter's box.

"You heard me, what the fuck is your problem? You're in New York, asshole, up here we root for this team." The fat man was slurring his words, and had obviously consumed far in excess of the three beers that Jeff had downed.

"Yeah, asshole," chimed in his equally rotund friend. "Who the hell are you rooting for, pretty boy, in your white shirt and tie?" He punctuated this statement with a belch so loud that people in the next section turned to see from where the rumbling had emanated.

"I'm rooting for the Yanks, guys, I'm one of you."

"Not when you're complaining when Ride hits a home run, you're not," yelled the fat man, as he moved slowly toward Jeff, tripping and falling into a seat two rows behind. Jeff looked to see if his path was clear to the aisle, but then decided to stay when he saw two security guards approaching.

He turned to the fat man, who was still struggling to regain his balance. "Sorry, man, but believe me, I'm a Yankees fan. I've had a really fucking bad day, OK? I got fired today, and I am a little distracted." He paused. "Tell you what," he said, looking at the two mounds of girth facing him, "I'll buy you both a beer."

A look of reason suddenly enveloped both the fat man and his friend, and they both licked their chops in anticipation of what was a clearly unnecessary drink. "No, dude," the second one said, also slurring his words, "you lost your job today, so we are buying for you." Jeff hailed the next beer vendor, the other guys paid for three beers, and they all raised their cups in

165

appreciation to the Yankees as two more runs crossed the plate, giving the home team a 7-3 advantage that they would never relinquish.

Jeff also smiled with the satisfaction that he had dodged a potentially harmful situation. He imagined how he would explain getting beaten up at the game, especially to Paul and the others who had questioned his fidelity to the Yankees. He did not want to give them any further ammunition to use against him, especially when he felt that they were wrong.

CHAPTER 15

"One essential to success is that your desire be an all-obsessing one, your thoughts and aim be coordinated, and your energy be concentrated and applied without let up."

- *Claude M. Bristol, The Magic of Believing*

Jeff drove home after the game, and emptied the contents of his car's trunk, representing his time spent at Martin & Jerome, into the lobby of his apartment building. He then parked his car in the underground garage, and, returning to the street, stopped at a corner newsstand to purchase the latest edition of *Baseball Weekly*. He entered his apartment and went to his answering machine to see if anyone, including Bob Linder or John Robbins, had called. The light on the machine, however, was unblinking. He slumped into the leather chair that sat opposite his television, and exhaled deeply. "Shit," he thought, "I've really lost my job. What am I going to do now?"

His concern over his job situation was short-lived, however, because in the same instant, he realized that Brian Hunter had not called him, either. About four days had passed since Jeff had left the last of his messages on Brian's answering machine. Jeff wondered whether Brian was still upset about their disagreement, but that had taken place a month ago. Besides, Jeff needed to work out a quick deal with Hunter, and could not sit around for him to call back.

Jeff checked on Facebook. Spadola had set up a group on the site for the league several years ago, but most of the men never thought to even check the page. Earlier that week, Jeff posted a comment that he was looking to make a trade, a general inquiry that he hoped would lead to at least one offer being made. Up to that point, however, nobody had commented or called him.

167

It was 6:30. Brian could never talk on the phone while on the train from work, so calling him on the cell phone would prove futile. He usually arrived home from work at about 6:15, so he had probably just walked through the door -- it was the perfect time to catch him. Jeff picked up his cell phone and, luckily, it contained Brian's number with his contact information. He pressed the home number, possibly for the first time ever, and hoped that Brian would be there. After the second ring, the unmistakably sweet voice of Diane Hunter, a southern belle transplanted by her husband, as she told her friends, into the wilds of the big city, answered. The simple "hello" which she drawled into the phone had an almost musical quality.

"Hi Diane, this is Jeff. How are you?"

She paused. "Jeff?"

"Yes, Jeff Goldstein. It's been a while since we've seen each other. How are things going over there?"

"Oh, Jeff," she said, the lilt gone from her voice. "I suppose you want to talk to Brian about that stupid baseball league."

"Stupid league?" Jeff responded in an offended tone. "How can you say that?"

"I can say it because all of you are acting like little children. When Brian started it was supposed to be a game. Now, it's like a competition between you and Joe Emerson to make stupid trades with Brian, and he's lost already. It's just like last year, only he's out of the running earlier now. And don't think that we didn't need the money that he'll be losing to one of you. Maybe you can spare fifteen thousand dollars, but here in the Hunter household, that much money can go a long way."

Diane was beginning to sound upset, so Jeff decided to lighten things up a little. He forced a slight lilt in his voice, as if to sound apologetic for bothering her. "I'm really sorry for bothering you, Diane. Can you do me a favor and have him give me a call back?" he said in his best sing-song voice. "I'll be at home all night, so he can call me either on the cell or on the phone here. He knows both numbers."

"O.K., Jeff, I'll tell him you called," she said, sighing audibly. "But just so you know, he has to call his mother and Joe before he gets back to you, so it probably won't be for a while." She then added, in a lighter tone, "Oh, by the way, how is Michelle? We haven't gone out as a group in so long. I called her a couple of weeks ago, but she hasn't gotten back to me."

"Oh, she's alright, I guess," he replied, knowing that she had not returned any of his calls, either. "One of these days we'll all go out. Maybe I'll take you guys out for dinner when I win the, as you called it, 'stupid' baseball league. Just have Brian give me a call when he gets the chance. Thanks, Diane," he said as he hung up the phone, his mind consumed with the dueling troubles of Michelle and the fact that she still was not calling him, as well as thoughts of the conversation that Joe and Brian would have, and the possible trades that they could make, before Jeff had a chance to speak to Brian.

The Emerson Boozers were still in first place. If Joe Emerson could steal a player from the lowly Brians and Brawn, and make a new late-season surge, or even just maintain his current position, then that trade could be the death knell for any hopes of Jeff's reaching the top before season's end.

Jeff waited for Brian's return phone call, pacing nervously in front of his television as the sports highlights of the previous day flashed across the screen. Finally, his cell phone rang. "Hey, Jeff, it's Brian. I'm sorry that I didn't get back to you earlier in the week. Work's been a bitch. This is the first night that I've been home before 11."

"No problem, Brian, I know the feeling all too well," Jeff answered, although he realized that he would not likely know it for some time, or at least until he found another job.

"What's up? But make it quick, I've got to go and spend some quality time with the wife, if you know what I mean." Brian paused and lowered his voice so that nobody else would hear him. "Plus, she's a little ticked off at you. I don't know what you said to her before, but I wouldn't do it again if I were you."

"Honestly, I don't know," Jeff answered. "I think it's the league in general that's pissing her off. If I had a wife like yours, dude, I don't know if I'd be on the phone with a schlep like me now. But since I do have you, I've got that familiar trading bug." He turned down the sound of the Yankees' game, which he was watching on the television to his right. "Want to move any players?"

"Well, what have you got in mind?" Brian answered, obviously between bites of his dinner.

"I was thinking about one of your pitchers," Jeff offered. "How about Charlie Van Horn? I see that your pitching has been slipping lately, but I can give you a hitter to strengthen the power categories."

Jeff heard a loud gulping sound on the other end of the line as Brian swallowed hard. "No can do, amigo. I traded Van Horn to Emerson a couple of minutes ago. Can you think of anyone else that you may want?"

As Brian finished his sentence, Jeff's heart sank deep into his stomach. A wave of nausea came over him, as he realized that Joe had gotten to Brian first. Just like that, Jeff felt as if the season was slipping away, that any chance that he had of catching Emerson had disappeared in that instant. Despite his overly-melodramatic reaction, he tried desperately to organize his thoughts. "Let me think for a minute, Brian. Who else do you have?" he asked, searching furiously for the Boozers' roster.

"You know, Jeff, I don't even know who I have anymore. I think that I have about three guys left from my original team. I've been doing so much wheeling and dealing with you guys lately that it's impossible for me to keep track."

"What do you mean, you guys?" Jeff asked, breathlessly. He felt like he was having heart palpitations as he awaited Brian's response.

"Oh, I thought that you knew. I thought that you kept on top of everything that went on in this league. Me and Greenbaum pulled off a major deal yesterday. I guess it didn't hit the site yet. He caught me at work about five minutes before a big meeting. We traded six guys, I think. To tell you the truth, I don't even remember who was involved. But I do recall that I got rid of John Spahr. I mean, come on. The guy hit twenty homers in the first half of the season. That's more than he hit in the last three years combined. He's got to tail off at some point, right?"

Maybe, Jeff thought to himself, but Spahr hadn't shown any signs of slowing down in the last few weeks. He was second in the league in home runs, and fourth in RBI's. Jeff wasn't even going to ask for him; he thought that someone with such power, who had come so cheaply in the beginning of the season, would have been an untouchable. Brian had spent only six dollars for him in the April draft. Surely he was one that Brian would have wanted to hold onto for another couple of seasons.

But now, Spahr was banging out homers and driving in runs for the Jew Crew, one of the teams hot on the Golds' tail. Jeff felt less air entering his lungs with each breath, as he struggled to cope with the information that Brian was so bluntly hurling in his direction. "You're kidding me, right?" he gasped, as he clicked on the internet to determine the remaining members of Brian's team.

"No, man, I'm dead serious. I got a couple of good young kids for next year." Brian explained. "One of them is that third baseman from Chicago. He is going to be one of the greats, or so they say. I heard his name mentioned as a hot young prospect on ESPN last week. Face it, this season's over for me." He paused. "Look, not to be rude, but I've got to run, Diane's calling me. Think about what you want to do and give me a call at the office. You might want to wait until next week, though, because I'm really not too sure of which guys are on my team anymore and who I can spare."

"Uh, O.K.," Jeff said hesitatingly, "I'll give you a call next week. You guys have a good night."

"Get some rest, man, you sound tired," Brian said, adding, "and in the future, just call me at the office. Diane really is sick of the league."

"So you did know why she was mad at me."

"Yep. She had steam coming out of her ears when she told me that you had called the apartment. Be careful in the future. I could barely convince her to let me call you back. And speaking of that, have you spoken to Michelle lately? How are things between you guys going? Has there been reconciliation yet?"

"I wish that I could say yes, believe me," Jeff responded. "Unfortunately, we haven't spoken in weeks and I really doubt that she wants to hear from me. I'm just going to ride it out for a little while longer. If I don't hear from her by the end of August, I'll call her. Hopefully we'll be able to work something out." He sighed deeply. "You really are lucky to have a wife like Diane, you know."

"Yeah, I know. But I can't let her hear me saying that. She's been on my case for us to buy a house, that she's sick of renting an apartment. What a pain in the ass that would be. The prices of homes are fuckin' outrageous. And me losing again this year hasn't helped -- her view is that if I can blow fifteen grand each year for a stupid baseball game, then I have no right telling her that we cannot afford to move to a house in the suburbs."

"The grass is always greener, my friend, especially when there is grass," Jeff replied. "But trust me, you've got it really good. Whatever she wants, give to her. Take it from one who knows. When she's gone, you'll wish that you had. I will give you a call next week."

CHAPTER 16

Jeff hung up the phone, and glanced nervously at the flickering computer screen that showed the most updated fantasy league standings. Brian told him to wait until next week to call him, but next week could be too late. The season was rapidly approaching its end, and player moves had to be made as soon as possible to maximize their statistics before October rolled around.

Next week was definitely too late. Jeff had to make a trade tonight. As he scrolled down his cell phone looking for Mike Berger's telephone number, he felt a slight itch in the crook of his right elbow. He paused, and began to scratch the itch with his left hand. Soon he was scratching furiously, until the inside of his arm was a vivid shade of pink.

Suddenly he stopped, and laughed out loud. Not a deep laugh, but more of a knowing chuckle. The reason for this laugh was that he realized the almost ironic nature of the situation. The itch was probably caused by a mosquito bite. And yet, here he sat, nervously scratching at the inside of his arm like a drug addict who was searching for a quick fix, shuddering at the thought of coming down from his high.

He realized that making a trade was his quick fix. For the first time, he realized that if he had an addiction, it was the baseball league. It was almost like Greg had described it in the Detroit hotel -- the addiction could take a person over. For Greg, it was his cocaine habit. Jeff had thought at the time that Michelle was the only thing that he was addicted to, but was now beginning to think that baseball, the fantasy league, was his addiction. He lost his job because of his desire to watch baseball. He had also lost the girl who could have been his wife, who he wanted to spend his life with, due to his preoccupation for baseball, or at least that was the explanation that she had given him when she

174

walked out of the restaurant that night. And tonight he would be satisfied, with his world being complete, if he could only make a trade. Maybe she did know something. But he could control it … or so he thought.

He sat back in his chair, stretched out his legs, and stared down at the mark on the inside of his elbow. His eyes drifted upward, his weary pupils focusing on the ceiling. Scrolling aimlessly up and down the contacts list on his phone, he felt the printed pages of his weekly standings between the toes of his right foot. He felt a sharp twinge in his middle toe as the paper sliced into it, and bent over to see if any blood had been drawn. A mere drop of blood had come to the surface where the skin was split, but no other blood was visible. The stinging feeling, though, lingered as a reminder. It was just an additional pain caused by the fantasy league.

Jeff picked up the sheet and looked at the list. There, in black and white, stood the story of the baseball season, indicating the Golds' third-place status. He had to be able to reach someone. His failure to do so exasperated him. He again logged onto his Facebook page, scanning the right side to see if any of the other league members were also on the site – which would give him a rapt audience with which to correspond. To his chagrin, none of the other league members were listed.

Jeff again picked up his phone, and this time, with deliberation, scrolled upward to the "B" section to find Mike Berger's contact information. He reached for the cordless phone and slowly punched out the numbers, but the phone went right to voice mail. It seemed odd to Jeff, but perhaps the phone was off or he was already talking to someone else. Heck, maybe Mike was otherwise engaged and had unplugged the phone, because his girlfriend hadn't walked out on him.

Jeff picked up the television's remote control, and turned to the movie station to see what they were showing that night. As usual, it was a film that had been shown more times that month than while it was in theaters, so he quickly turned it off and ran the scale of channels, stopping when he arrived at the Playboy Channel. He sat in the darkened room, watching video playmates romping in the surf, all the time thinking of Michelle.

He closed his eyes, thinking back to how soft Michelle's body had felt to his touch, the smell of her hair, and how her panting voice would beg him for more. He could almost feel and smell her in the room with him, and remembered the last time that they had made love.

It was in his apartment, and he could recall the exact date -- June 21. It was raining, and they stood, naked, watching the rain pelt the windows of his apartment while he rubbed her body from behind. She turned to him, her nipples hard as rocks as her firm breasts pressed against his. As he was seven inches taller than her, he had to lean over slightly to kiss her, which he did for some time. He then picked her up and carried her to the bed. They began to have sex, and, several minutes into the lovemaking session, the phone rang.

"Leave it," she whispered, as the phone rang for the second time. "They will call back later if it's important," she added, as she leaned up to kiss his chest.

He glanced down at her as the phone rang again, and sighed. "I have to get it. It might be important," he said, as he moved from on top of her and reached for the phone as it rang for the fourth time. As he began to answer, he could hear Michelle talking behind him, asking what could be so important that their lovemaking had to be interrupted. "He...Hello," he stammered, still breathing heavily.

176

"Hey amigo, what the hell are you doing on a rainy night like this?" It was Bob Fishman.

"Oh nothing," Jeff answered, moving slowly to his left until he was sitting on the edge of the bed. He looked back at Michelle, but she was wrapped in a sheet, walking toward the bathroom. "What is going on there?"

"Baseball, my friend. The baseball season's almost at the halfway point. We're getting to the homestretch, and you know what that means. It's time for us to make our annual blockbuster trade. I've got a ton of possibilities drawn up. Go get your rosters."

"Are you off the phone yet?" Michelle poked her head out from the bathroom and yelled in Jeff's direction. "If not," she added, seductively sticking her right leg outside of the door, "you'd better get off right now if you know what is good for you."

He cupped his hand over the receiver as he turned on the lamp next to the phone. "Just a couple of minutes," he called to her, "Why don't you climb back into bed?"

Now she strode back into the brightened room, the curves of her body evident under the white sheet as she passed from darkness into the light. "Why? What the hell are you doing on the phone? Don't you have any respect for me?" Her last sentence was significantly louder than the previous one, leading Jeff to believe that Bob had to have heard her yell.

If Bob had heard her voice, though, he certainly wasn't giving any indication to that effect. Jeff could still hear his voice calling through the phone as he tried to calm Michelle. "Hey dude, are you there? I've got players to move."

Jeff looked at the phone, and then over at Michelle, whose body was red from head to toe, at least the exposed portions seemed to be red. He held up his right index finger, and mouthed the words "one minute" to her, indicating for her to climb into bed and rest her head on his lap. He looked away from her, into the pieces of paper that sat on his right thigh, and began to speak into the phone. "O.K., Bob, who are you thinking about dealing?"

"Baseball! Is that what this is about? You can't be serious! You're talking about baseball!" Michelle exploded, running back to the bathroom, clothes in hand, and slamming the door shut behind her. Jeff quickly and quietly explained to Bob that he would have to call him back the next day, and then walked over to the bathroom door.

He knocked on the door several times, but there was no response from within the bathroom. "I'm sorry, honey. Please come out. I'm off the phone. How about we go back to bed?"

"Are you crazy?" she yelled, locking the door so that Jeff could not enter. From his side of the door he could hear her crying, her whimpers followed by the sound of her blowing her nose and running water.

"No, I really am sorry," he tried to explain. "It won't happen again. I turned the phone to vibrate. Besides, I didn't ask him to call me, he just did. It's not like I wanted to be interrupted."

The door opened, and Michelle stepped out, fully dressed and rubbing her already reddened eyes. "I don't care if you asked him to call or not, you swine. I also don't care if you wanted to be interrupted. The simple fact is that we were having sex and you stopped to talk about baseball. He did call. We were interrupted. And you did not seem to mind." She paused, and then continued in an even louder voice as she shook her finger in his direction for

178

added emphasis. "Do you hear me? We were having sex," she repeated, placing extra emphasis on the word "sex," "and you stopped to talk to one of your friends about baseball, about that league. You really don't see anything wrong with that?"

Jeff paused and reached out to caress her arm. He really did not think that he had done anything improper, but knew that he had to admit to some wrongdoing in order to placate his hysterical girlfriend. "You're right. I guess so, but there's nothing that I can do about it now," he mumbled. She broke free from his grasp, rushed out of the bedroom and toward the front door. Wrapping a Yankees' towel around his waist, he followed her, this time grabbing her by the arm as she unlatched the front door. "Don't go, please don't go," he pleaded, but to no avail.

"I have to go," she sniffled, and turned away, tears running down her cheeks. She walked out into the hallway, and disappeared into the elevator.

Jeff closed the door at the same time that the elevator doors came together and walked to the kitchen, pulling a cold bottle of beer from his refrigerator. He slumped in the chair that sat across from the television, the chair from which he had watched so many baseball games, and closed his eyes. He began to think of the other times that his love for baseball, his desire to watch every game possible, had led to friction between he and Michelle.

There was her cousin's wedding, which was held on a Sunday afternoon in late September two years ago, as the Yankees were in the middle of a tight pennant race with the Toronto Blue Jays. Michelle was a bridesmaid, and as her cousin Allison strode down to the aisle to the light serenade of a harp and organ, Jeff sat in the fourth row of the wedding hall's chairs, off to the right. A thin, almost imperceptible, white wire ran from his ear, where it was connected to an

179

earpiece, down to his chest, where his I-phone lay, neatly concealed within the breast pocket of his suit jacket. He dared not tell Michelle that he was going to listen to the game during the service, but she and those around her became aware of his deception as he pumped his fist in jubilation when the Yankees jumped out to a quick 3-0 lead in their game against the Jays.

Michelle avoided him for the entire wedding reception, leaving him perched at the bar, forced to drown his boredom in an endless stream of vodka tonics. Very few of the family even dared speak to him during the four-hour affair. Michelle's silent treatment lasted for the next five days, and his rudeness continually stared him in the face at later Stein family functions in the form of icy stares from Allison, her parents, and her new husband, none of whom had ever forgiven his ill-timed celebration.

One other incident that had led to Jeff incurring the full force of Michelle's wrath was her sorority semi-formal during their senior year at college. A seemingly meaningless game that May evening between the Yankees and A's was being televised and the bar situated in the reception hall was tuned to the game. The game began at 7:05, and at a few minutes past nine Jeff had wandered into the bar area to see if he could find out the score. At that point, the teams were knotted at three, with two men on base for the Yankees in the top of the sixth inning. There were two outs, and Jeff sat and watched the Bombers push across two more runs before the inning ended.

Unfortunately for Jeff, a few minutes after nine was also the time for he and Michelle's table picture to be taken. The rest of the table members and the photographer waited for ten minutes, and, when Jeff did not show, took the picture in his absence. Michelle was humiliated, especially when he told her the reason for his disappearance. She refused to talk to him until he showed up at her dorm room three days later with a dozen red roses and a promise that he would never ignore her for a baseball game again. Her anger returned, however, when the photographs from the semi-formal came. This time, Michelle's forgiveness was bought with another dozen roses, dinner, and a renewed promise.

A renewed promise, but, like the previous one, a promise that would be broken. The latest incident had only been the last straw in Michelle's eyes. The weekend after Bob Fishman interrupted their lovemaking led to the restaurant incident where she ended their relationship.

He had called her several times following that night, but she had not returned these calls. Even calls to her friends proved futile, so there had been no communication between the two in over a month. His last visions of her, those that were most firmly emblazoned in his memory, were her reddened face, tears running down both cheeks, as she stood in the corner of an elevator, and the back of her head, hair flowing wildly, as she fled the restaurant, hailing a cab, and disappearing off into the night.

CHAPTER 17

Diane Hunter felt her cell phone buzzing. Taking the phone from her purse, she glanced down and saw the smiling Facebook profile picture of Michelle Stein staring up at her from her phone's screen. Pressing the "answer" button, she raised the phone to her face. "Michelle, is that you?" she asked.

"Yes," the voice on the other end of the phone croaked between sobs, "it's me, Diane, I apologize for not calling you back sooner, and I apologize for bothering you now, but I thought that you would understand."

"Understand what?" Diane asked. "What's wrong?"

Michelle sighed deeply. She cleared her throat, and then replied, "It's not even what's wrong anymore. Everything is wrong."

"If you mean with Jeff, honestly, I am not surprised."

"It's the fucking baseball league," Michelle cried. "The league. Oh, wait, I'm sorry for cursing. I am just so frustrated with him. I know he calls Bob, right?"

Diane paused, intending to choose her words carefully. "Yes, he calls the apartment once in a while. For all I know, those two talk every day on the cells or at the office, but Brian knows better than to tell me because he knows how mad I will be." She again paused and sighed. "You know the fifteen thousand dollars that Bob already lost in the league this year could have been put to much better use, like toward a down payment on a house or a school fund for our children."

Michelle gasped. "Did you say *fifteen thousand dollars*? I had no idea they were each contributing that much ... that much money," she stammered, "there is no way I would have let Jeff give that much. Not that it matters now, of course."

"Dare I even ask what happened this time?" asked Diane.

"I don't even know how to explain this," Michelle replied, her voice growing stronger. "Let's just say we were … we were in bed, and the phone rang." She paused and took a deep breath before continuing. "Oh, jeez, I'm just going to tell you. We were having sex, he was on top of me, and in the middle he took a call from one of the baseball idiots."

"Please tell me that you're kidding me," Diane pleaded.

"Wish that I were," Michelle said. "Anyway, he picked up his phone and answered it, so I figured it was important – like work or something like that. I got up and went into the bathroom to clean myself up a little so that we could, you know, resume when he got off of the phone. When I walked back out of the bathroom, I realized that he was talking about baseball. I am standing there naked in his bedroom, and he is talking about baseball!" Now Michelle was shouting, so much so that Diane had to hold the phone away from her ear. "I couldn't get dressed fast enough and get out of there. I am done, Diane. I am done. I simply cannot do this anymore. I thought that I loved him, but he loves baseball. I can't compete."

"Calm down a little, Michelle," Diane replied in a calm voice. "You love him, and we both know that Jeff loves you."

"He says so, but he does so much to prove otherwise. He may love me, but he loves baseball more. There have been too many instances like this. How much can I possibly be forced to take? Tell me, how many times had Brian interrupted sex with you to take a stupid baseball call?"

Diane knew that there was only one correct answer. "No," she said, "I can't say that he ever has."

"Of course not!" she yelled. "What idiot stops fucking his girlfriend to take a call about a stupid baseball game? It's not even real baseball. And quite frankly, I don't care how much money those idiots are blowing, he never should have taken the call!" She began to cry again. "He never should have taken the call."

"You're right, Michelle," Diane interrupted. "Do you want to get together for lunch? It sounds like you could use some time out today."

"No, not today, Diane. I need to be alone. I need to think. Sorry for bothering you." She sniffled deeply. "I will call you in a couple of days."

CHAPTER 18

Following the death of their young centerfielder, the Brewers began a slide that left them in fourth place, a full twelve games off the pace being set by the front-running Cincinnati Reds. The mysterious circumstances surrounding Mike Jones' death, as well as the hole left in the outfield due to his untimely departure, had left the team in a funk from which they did not appear likely to emerge. With each game, the Brewers would appear more and more listless, their will to play seemingly drained.

Manager Matt Garver, watching his team slide closer to the cellar, assembled his coaching staff for an emergency meeting, not for the purpose of creating a game plan, but rather to discuss how to best deal with the situation. Following Jones' death the team had tried to go about things in a business-like manner, barely acknowledging their loss except in the form of black armbands worn on their right uniform sleeves. That obviously was not working, so it was time to take a different approach.

The coaches huddled together in Garver's office on an off-day, while the players were given the day to rest, both their bodies and their minds. Several of the players did still come to the ballpark to utilize the weight room and get in some extra batting practice, but they were expressly told that they were not to interrupt the coaches' meeting. Those players who gathered in the locker room, however, could hear occasional outbursts coming from behind the closed door.

"What are we going to do?" bellowed Garver, as he held up the most recent National League standings. These standings showed that the Brewers were a scant two games ahead of the last place Chicago Cubs, with the Cubbies riding a three-game winning streak and closing the gap nightly. "We certainly can't go on like this."

"What do you expect from these kids, Matt?" asked first base coach Johnny Spartan, "I mean, these players are not mature adults like us. Most of them are in their early 20's and probably don't know how to deal with this type of thing, especially the guys that played with Mike in the minors. You barely knew the kid. Some of these guys played with him for extended periods of time. He was like family to them."

"The way that he died didn't help matters any, either," added third base coach Pete Sanders, "and the rumors that are beginning to surface about it being drug-related are only adding fuel to the fire. More than a handful of the players have told me that they've been approached by reporters asking questions about whether or not Jones was a drug abuser. Some of the guys say that they never saw him using any kind of drugs, and others are talking about the fact that he smoked pot and used cocaine while he was in the minors. The conflicting stories and rumors about such drug use, if nothing else, have got to be a tremendous distraction to these kids, and they can only avoid the questions for so long before something breaks. And none of them want anything bad said about him in the media, so they're internalizing everything."

Garver looked at the 2014 team photograph hanging on his wall, taken during Spring Training, his gaze fixed on Jones. Without turning back to those sitting behind him, he began to speak softly. "Look, forget what the players know or don't know. All of us in this room, we all know that Jones was involved with the drugs. We hoped that it wouldn't affect his play, and it didn't seem to for the time that he was here with us. But that was not public knowledge. Nor should it become public knowledge, especially from anyone associated with the team. I don't know who started these rumors," he said, his voice gaining volume as he turned to Sanders, "but they can't be based on fact. I think that whenever a young man is killed in this country, especially a young black man, the presumption is that drugs played some role."

186

The two black coaches nodded in agreement. Sanders stood and walked toward Garver. "I certainly did not mean to say that drugs were involved, Matt, I just wanted to point out that the rumors that I heard invoked some form of drug involvement, and I know that some, and I have to assume all, of the players have been hearing the same shit."

"So what do we do, call a team meeting and try to dispel those rumors?" asked the exasperated manager. "Some of the players knew what he was into, as you've already said. I'm sure that some of them knew about it before we did, and they also are aware of whether or not the rumors could be true." He paused, and placed his right hand underneath his chin. "No, I don't think we should do that. That would probably just make a bad situation worse." He paused. "Greg," he said to one of the men sitting in the rear of the room, "you've been quiet for a while. What do you think?"

In unison, all of the coaches turned to Greg Bloom, who had been uncharacteristically quiet for the duration of the meeting. When they turned to face him, the reason for his silence became quite evident as he was fast asleep in his chair, his head resting on the rear office wall.

"Greg?" called Garver, but there was no response. Garver picked up an eraser from his desk and threw it in Bloom's direction, striking him in the nose, startling and awakening him.

"What?" Greg mumbled, as he rubbed his nose and tried to adjust his eyes to the bright florescent lights dangling overhead. "What the fuck is going on?"

"Gentlemen," Garver said as he turned back to the others, "I think that it would be a good idea for you to leave me alone with Sleeping Beauty here for a few minutes. There's something that we have to discuss now." He turned back to his desk and sat down, his eyes fixed on the blotter atop his desk until the door closed behind the exiting coaches, at which time he looked up at Greg. "Bloom," he bellowed, "sleeping during our meeting? What the fuck is going on with you?"

"What are you talking about, skip?" asked Greg, innocently. "I'm just a little tired, that's all."

"Don't fool with me, Bloom. I have known you for way too long. Never, in all of your days as a player or coach, have you fallen asleep in a meeting." He leaned in closer to Greg. "Even when you were using. Here we are talking about drug rumors and Mike Jones, and you're sleeping in the back of the room, looking like a poster boy for drug use. Look at you. You look like shit." His voice grew louder. "You look like a fuckin' bum. And I've noticed how red your eyes are all of the time."

"What can I tell you?" Greg answered, his eyes looking away from Garver and his voice becoming defensive, "I guess that I'm just not getting enough sleep."

"Not enough sleep, my ass," Garver shouted, as he jumped from his chair and came around his desk, grabbing Greg by the collar. "I know what you're up to, you stupid, stupid ass. I've been around too many drug users in this game to not recognize the signs. I don't know when you started or how much you're using, but I know that you're doing something." His eyes were becoming as red as Greg's as he continued to berate his cowering coach. "And I'm telling you right now, so you'd better listen carefully, straighten up or get the hell off of my staff. There's no room for that kind of shit on my team. Especially after what happened to Jones," he growled, "that's the kind of shit that can destroy you, and you'll just be taking all of us down with you. It's bad enough that people are saying that Jones was killed over drugs. How would it then look if one of our coaches was caught using the stuff? I can't let that happen."

Greg lifted his right arm, and in one swift motion separated Garver's grip from his shirt. He stood up, and looked his manager in the eye. "You're wrong," he barked, "I'm not doing any drugs. And fuck you for your bullshit." He turned and walked out of the office, slamming the door behind him as he yelled, indignantly and with more than a decent amount of misplaced self-righteousness, "this has got to be the only fucking job where you're not allowed to sleep." He stomped through the locker room without stopping, past the stares of his fellow coaches, and strolled all the way up the tunnel into the dugout, where he sat and stared out at the field.

Two of the Brewers' players were running in the outfield, and several others were playing catch around the infield. Greg watched the Brewers' young middle infielders, shortstop Juan Sanchez and second baseman Rob Patton, practice turning double plays. They went through their motions in an almost poetically fluid motion, and Greg realized that both of the youngsters, playing in the middle of the infield, the area that he had hoped to rule in the past, moved far more gracefully than he ever had. "Maybe," he thought to himself as he sat, "I wasn't as good as these guys are. Maybe I've been deluding myself all of these years. Maybe."

When he arrived home to his apartment that night, Greg went straight to a bottle of vodka sitting on top of the refrigerator and poured himself the remaining fluid, adding three ice cubes to ease the sting of the hot liquor as it slid down his throat. He quickly gulped down the vodka, three shots worth, and searched in vain for another bottle in the wooden cabinet located in the next room. He did find, however, some bourbon, which he opened and drank directly from the bottle.

As he wiped the remains of the last gulp from his lips, he walked into the second bedroom of his two-bedroom apartment, the room which held all of his playing mementos. He turned on the light and looked quickly around the room, briefly staring at each of the team pictures and plaques that adorned the walls, as well as the pictures showing him standing with some of the best players of his time. On the far wall, behind the desk that sat in the room, hung his Brewers' jersey, the shirt that he was wearing when he stroked the first of his two major league hits.

The jersey had been cleaned before he had it mounted inside of its current frame, but a small spot of dirt directly below the number 12 emblazoned across its back remained. To Greg, that small patch of dirt reflected his career as a player, as it indicated the work ethic and drive with which he had approached every game as a player, or the ethic and drive that he believed that he had brought each game. That "win at all costs," always giving 100 percent attitude, had catapulted him into the major leagues, albeit for a brief time, but that had been derailed by the combination of an injured arm and his cocaine use. That spot of dirt, no doubt imperceptible to most but which stood out like a beacon for Greg, reminded him of where he had come from, where he had been, and, sadly, indicated to him where he was going.

Now he stood in front of the jersey, before the shrine that represented his playing days, and began to think of Sanchez and Patton, the duo that currently comprised the middle of the Brewers' infield. He thought of the ease with which they moved, and tried to remember himself at his best. The memory burned away at his mind, as he again realized that he was never that fluid in his movements, that he was never as good as the kids that he had been watching, nor could he even hit as well as they could. He had watched some old videos of himself playing on the internet. He cringed when he compared his performance to these young kids. Sure, it was a different game back then, but they were much better than him. He began to think that he had deluded himself into thinking that he could have ever competed on the major-league level. He looked down into the half-empty bottle of bourbon nestled in his right hand, and sank to his knees, with tears welling up his eyes.

Sitting on the floor, directly to Greg's right, was a framed picture of the 1998 Brewers that he had, for one reason or another, never hung on the wall. He glanced over at the team photo, which was autographed by all of the team members and coaches, and then gazed up again at the jersey which loomed over him, rapidly becoming a cruel reminder of his past. He reached over to the photo on the ground, picked it up, and stood, walking back toward the other side of the room. Suddenly wheeling around, he flung the picture at his framed jersey, shattering the glass of both frames with a deafening crash.

Two weeks later, the Milwaukee team plane landed in the rain at Newark Airport, and the players and coaches quickly boarded buses for the drive to their midtown Manhattan hotel. Many of the players looked forward to traveling to New York; some had family in the area and others enjoyed taking in the nightlife. This was especially so when they were in town for a weekend series, so that games were played in the afternoon. The Saturday games, concluded by late afternoon, left the evening open for the players to enjoy healthy bites of the city known as the "Big Apple."

Jeff was waiting in the hotel lobby when the first group of the Milwaukee players and coaches arrived. He stood with the young children who watched their heroes whisk by them on their way to the elevators, each of the youngsters, as well as several adults, clamoring for autographs from their favorite stars. Jeff was there for an entirely different reason; he searched in vain for his cousin, and, when he did not see Greg, he then sat in the back of the lobby, content to wait until the next bus arrived.

191

The next group arrived approximately ten minutes later, and was led by members of the coaching staff and the team doctor. Greg walked in with the rear of the group, chatting with two of the Brewers' players who had accompanied the coaches on their bus. As he entered the lobby, Jeff called out to him above the cries of the assemblage cluttering the hotel's first floor. Greg saw him and lifted his right hand, holding up fingers alternately in an attempt to gesture for Jeff to go up to room 815, where he would be staying.

Jeff waited until the crowd in the lobby thinned out, with the exception of a few stragglers, and then rode the elevator to the eighth floor. There was only one other person in the elevator, and Jeff immediately recognized him as Howard "Lefty" Grant, one of the aces of Milwaukee's pitching staff. He turned to the pitcher, who stood eight inches taller than his five-foot-eleven frame, and introduced himself as Greg Bloom's cousin. Grant extended his right hand, and the size of his fingers enveloped Jeff's as the two shook hands vigorously.

"Will you be coming out to see us play this weekend?" the twenty-five year old fireballer asked in a friendly southern drawl, as he fidgeted with the large gold chain that hung from his neck.

"Of course," replied Jeff, "but it's only fair to warn you that I'm a Yankees fan, so you know that I'm going to have to root against you guys. With the interleague schedule it's not like you play them that often, anyway."

Grant gasped and clasped his hands over his mouth in mock horror, and stepped out of the elevator as its doors opened for the sixth floor. "Whatever you say, Jeff, wasn't it?"

Jeff smiled broadly with approval. "Yes. And no offense but you better get the shit kicked out of you on Saturday. You're pitching way too good this year, Grant, and you're killing me in my fantasy baseball league."

192

"Oh man," Grant said, instinctively reaching out with his left arm, the arm that earned him a five million dollars per year salary, to prevent the elevator doors from closing. "I am so sick of these fantasy leagues," he said, the friendliness quickly evaporating from his voice. "Do you know what it's like to be on the mound and have some jerk in the stands rooting for a walk, or for some idiot to get a hit so that some other guy can score a run?" He looked to Jeff for some type of response, but none was forthcoming. "You guys may not think that we hear you in the stands when you say crap like that, but we sometimes do. And the same people are ruining the game for us, you know. Some of us like to think that we have an actual fan base for the team, and that the fans are at least a little loyal. Even in a place like New York."

"You shouldn't pick on New York while you're here, you know. The big city isn't so scary, Grant," answered Jeff, "we may not know all of our neighbors like the little town you come from, but eventually you learn your way around. And we certainly have our loyalties. Three million fans per year in attendance for the Yankees certainly show some loyalty, wouldn't you say?"

Lefty Grant was born and raised in a small town in Arkansas. Like Greg Bloom, he was arguably the best schoolboy athlete ever to come from his high school, a school which housed only two hundred students per class. Even in the new millennium, Grant's hometown of Waldron, Arkansas, located in the westernmost county of the State, still seemed, to many, to be locked into the mid 1900's, a modern day Mayberry. For an athlete like Grant who moved beyond the town's boundaries, the big cities could be intimidating. He had attended the University of Arkansas on a baseball scholarship and had used his time in Fayetteville to acclimate himself to a more populous environment, but was still, admittedly, much more comfortable pitching in a mid-sized city like Milwaukee as opposed to the bustling metropolis of New York.

"It isn't a matter of being scary, my friend," Grant said, his tone growing more serious, "it is a matter of loyalty. Back home, or back in the country, as you would call it, we are loyal to each other. Everyone takes care of everyone else. But it doesn't matter whether there are thousands of people in a town or millions of people in the city. It doesn't matter whether you have two doctors around or two thousand doctors. There is no reason why everyone can't be nice and loyal to each other. There's no reason why it shouldn't be like that even here, and you fantasy guys are the worst example of people who have none. You have no loyalty at all. You go to Yankees' games, part of the three million, but you will root against them for the right pitcher from my team or any other team. That's what I am talking about."

The irony of Grant's comments was not lost on Jeff, whose smile shortened to a slight smirk as he silently mouthed the word "loyalty." How could a baseball player complain about the loyalty of the fans, especially when the players were the ones who exhibited no such loyalty in chasing the highest bidder from city to city whenever their contracts expired? Grant was puzzled by the expression on Jeff's face. "You heard me, Yankee lover," said Grant, "I'm talking about loyalty." His eyes narrowed. "So you can root for the Yankees. And root against me when I pitch against them. I appreciate that. But don't root against me because of your stupid league. That's bush. Can you remember that?"

"You're damn right I will, Lefty," Jeff responded, feeling more and more confident in the presence of the giant hurler. "But do you actually think that you can stand there and preach to me about loyalty?" Now it was his turn to preach. "I mean think about it. Surely you don't believe that the players are loyal. How about you? What's going to happen come contract time if you win 20 this year?"

"Don't be too sure about what you believe, buddy boy," growled Grant, as he dropped his bag to the floor and moved closer to Jeff. "Plenty of us have more loyalty than the fans could ever feel for the team." He paused and looked around, even though they were the only two in the elevator. "And I'll deny saying this if any reporters ask me about it, but when my contract is up I'll take less money from the Brewers than from other teams, say the Yankees, for example, to stay in Milwaukee when my contract is up. I've been with the team for so long now that it's like my second family, and that includes the fans."

Stepping back out of the elevator, Grant picked up his bag and turned to walk away. As he strode into the hallway, he added, "don't be naïve, Jeff. And never make generalizations without first knowing the facts. Just because some of the players follow their wallets doesn't mean that we all do."

"Some?" asked Jeff, holding the elevator door open with his arm. "I would venture a guess to say that it is much more than some."

"You know what I mean, you fucking cynic. Even if it is half, or more, that still doesn't mean that it's everyone," admonished Grant, turning back and again stepping into the elevator. "Look, I'm done with this conversation now. Get your ass upstairs to see Greg. And you better come to the locker room after one of the games so that I can whip your butt in front of him." He flexed the bicep on his pitching arm and smiled. "And just so you know, if you don't come down to the locker room, I'll have to waste your cousin instead." He looked intently into Jeff's eyes for a few seconds and then laughed. He extended his right arm to shake Jeff's hand and then turned, walking out of the elevator. Once in the hallway he turned to his right and continued walking down the hallway to his room as he continued to flex his bicep in mock aggression.

Jeff remained in the elevator alone for the thirty seconds between the sixth and eighth floors, laughing to himself about the conversation that he had just had with one of the National League's best pitchers. He wondered if Grant was being honest about taking less money to stay in Milwaukee. And if he was telling the truth, was he the exception or the rule?

CHAPTER 19

"In the depths of a mind insane ... Fantasy and reality are the same"

- *Tomas Enrique Araya and Jeffery John Hanneman, Slayer (lyrics from the song "Dead Skin Mask" © 1990)*

The elevator doors opened again when the car reached the eighth floor, and Jeff stepped outside and glanced at the gold-plated plaque that hung on the wall across the narrow hallway. The arrow for rooms 812 through 820 pointed to the right, so Jeff turned to his right and began to walk, passing three doors before coming to room 815. He was surprised to find the door ajar, with a stream of faint light reaching out into the hallway. He slowly pushed the door open so that he could enter the room, the door's hinges creaking slightly as its full weight came into contact with the wall behind it.

Inside the room, a lone figure sat on the bed, bathed in the light of the television which was playing a *"Seinfeld"* rerun. The person on the bed held a glass in his right hand, and the ice cubes within the glass clinked together as the glass was being moved about in a deliberate, clockwise motion. Jeff struggled in the darkness of the room to see if Greg was the man on the bed, and, as he neared the figure, could make out the familiar features of his cousin's face.

"Greg? What's up, cousin?" he asked, stopping and standing to Greg's left. "I didn't know that you Midwestern boys watched *'Seinfeld'*. Is this a good episode?"

Greg's eyes did not move from the television, although Jeff could see his face reflecting in the mirror situated across the room from the bed. His eyes appeared to be staring at nothing, almost trance-like, as if the television did not even exist. He lifted his left arm, the one that was not holding a drink, and motioned to the bar near the front of the room. Without even looking in Jeff's direction, he mumbled, "of course it is a good episode. They all are good." He paused, continuing to rotate his glass as the ice clinked rhythmically together. "Fix yourself a drink, Jeff. Then come over here and sit down in this chair." He motioned to his right, near the window that overlooked the busy Manhattan streets below.

Jeff placed several ice cubes in a glass, and poured himself a vodka and cranberry juice. Looking at the large bottle of vodka in his hand, he noted that it was already half-empty. He estimated that Greg must have consumed at least three strong drinks in the past half-hour. Picking up a handful of pretzels from a plastic bowl that sat near the liquor, he moved across the room, through Greg's field of vision, past the television, and sat down in the chair as instructed.

For two minutes there was silence, as Jeff waited for Greg to speak to him. Perhaps appropriately, the *"Seinfeld"* episode was one in which George was working with the Yankees, and he was talking with then-manager Buck Showalter about different uniforms for the players. Jeff laughed to himself as the scene developed, but Greg's stoic face never strayed from its trance-like position. In order to break the silence between the men, Jeff cleared his throat and asked his cousin what he wanted to discuss. Greg looked down at his glass, and began to swirl the melting ice cubes around with his left index finger. He looked back at the television, and then to Jeff. He opened his mouth as if to speak, but instead took another large gulp of the vodka from his glass. Swallowing hard, he closed his eyes and said "Sanchez."

"Sanchez?" Jeff asked, as if he had missed some of what Greg was trying to say to him. "You're going to have to be a bit more specific."

"Sanchez," Greg repeated, softly, forcing Jeff to quickly interpret his cousin's cryptic message.

"Juan Sanchez, the shortstop?" Jeff asked, "Is that who you mean? What are you talking about?"

"Whose team is he on?"

Jeff was beginning to think that his cousin had inhaled a lot more than just vodka fumes before he arrived at the room. He decided to take an easy tone with Greg, however, so as not to instigate any outbursts. "Juan Sanchez is on your team," he said slowly, in an overly condescending tone, "the Brewers, remember?"

Greg's head pivoted sharply in Jeff's direction, his bulging eyes riddled with rivers of red. The veins in his neck were becoming more visibly tensed, and drops of vodka were coming over the sides of the glass as his hands began to shake with anger. "No, you asshole," he barked. "I know he's on the Brewers, you stupid fuck!" he yelled, saliva spurting from his mouth. "Don't treat me like an idiot." He pointed his index finger in Jeff's face. "How fucking stupid do you think I am?" He paused, composed himself, and then said, quietly, "what I meant is, what team is he on in your little fantasy league?"

Jeff brushed his right hand across his cheek to remove the saliva that had spewed from Greg's mouth when he called Jeff a "stupid fuck," and moved his head backward to avoid any contact with Greg's finger. He thought for a second, but could not remember the team that included the Brewers' shortstop. "I don't know, dude. I am sure that one of the guys has him because middle infielders who start are all taken, but I don't remember who. I could get on-line now and check it out if you want me to. Why do you ask?"

"Is he on your team?"

"Don't you think that if he was on my team that I would know it?" Jeff asked, this time returning some of his cousin's anger.

"I don't know," Greg answered in a mocking tone, "would you? You seem to be a little slow on the answers today."

"Give me a little credit," Jeff pleaded, feeling the tension in the room rising with each word. "I'm not a kid anymore, and you're way too drunk for this time of day. Perhaps it is time for you to slow down a bit." He reached out for the glass in Greg's hand, but Greg pulled it away and took another large amount of vodka in his mouth before placing the glass on the edge of the bed.

"No reason for me to slow down," Greg replied. "I don't need to be anywhere for a little while. This is my rest time. This is how I rest." He looked at his cousin, completely disregarding Jeff's concerned look. "Now, if he's not on your team," Greg continued, "then it couldn't possibly hurt you or your team's chances if something were to happen to him, right?"

Jeff looked at his cousin, trying hard to determine if he was joking or serious. The question, however, could not be properly addressed with a simple yes or no answer. "Well, that really depends on which team he is on," he began in response, "and how that team is doing relative to my team and the others." He was not being difficult – whether or not he could be hurt by something happening to Sanchez really was based on how that team was performing relative to the others in the various statistical categories, unless he was on one of the two teams above the Golds.

He saw that Greg was growing impatient, though, and knew that he did not have sufficient time to properly explain this position to his drunk and surly cousin. He decided that it would be best to simply give Greg the answer that he knew was desired, so after a slight pause he said, simply, "no, I guess it couldn't hurt my team. Why do you ask?"

"Look, you wanted me to help you win this thing, right?" Greg asked, his voice an alcohol-induced growl. "Well, this is another way that I'm going to help you." He paused, and lowered his voice to a whisper. "Come to the game on Saturday afternoon. I'll leave a ticket for you at the gate. I do believe that you will like what you see, but come to the Stadium very early or you'll miss the excitement." For the first time in the conversation, Greg lifted his head and looked at Jeff. "Now get out of here. I have a friend coming up to visit, and she should be here any minute."

"Somebody that I know?" asked Jeff.

"Don't worry about who it is or whether you know her," replied Greg, "I can tell you that she's never been to one of our family reunions, if you get my drift. Just make yourself scarce. I will see you on Saturday."

Jeff stood up from the chair, and walked back to the other side of the room. He carefully placed his glass next to the half-empty vodka bottle, and then turned back to Greg. "Oh, I almost forgot. There is one other thing that I have to ask you." Greg lifted his head as if he were listening, so Jeff continued. "My parents were hoping to see you before you left town. You think that will be possible?"

Greg waved him away with his left hand. "I don't think so. I'm not really in the mood to see anyone else this time around. Do me a favor and make up some bullshit excuse. They'll believe you." He turned back toward the television. "Don't forget. All that you need to do is come to the game on Saturday, and get there early. I'll leave a ticket for you at the window. Actually,

I will leave two. See if you can get that girlfriend of yours to come to the game so I can see her. Michelle Stein is her name, right? If she's with you I will come out of the dugout and have you two waved down to field level so we can chat. Maybe she'll be a little impressed and it will help you out."

The first contest of the three-game series was captured by the Brewers, who prevailed by a slim 4-3 score. The winning run crossed the plate in the top of the eighth inning, when New York reliever John Morse issued a bases-loaded walk to the Brewers' center fielder, Lou Goren. The Yankees staged a rally in the last half of the ninth inning, but their hopes of victory were crushed when Milwaukee second baseman Rob Patton speared a line drive with one out and two men on and then tagged the lead runner off of second base, completing an unassisted double play, to end both the inning and the game.

The Milwaukee infield turned two other double plays in the ballgame, but wasted a chance for a third in the seventh inning when shortstop Sanchez caught a toss from Patton but then could not properly remove the ball from his glove and threw too late to first base to catch the speedy Yankee base runner. That mistake led to the Yankees scoring the then-tying run, a tie that was erased a half-inning later with the walk to Goren. After the game, Bloom made it a point to speak to Sanchez and Patton. He informed them that they were to take extra fielding practice before the Saturday afternoon game, that he would instruct them in the proper way to complete a double play.

The next day's game was scheduled for a 1:05 p.m. start. As the clock struck noon, most of the Brewers were gathered around the batting cage, flexing their muscles as they belted pitch after pitch into the center field bleachers. Batting practice pitcher Jake Morrison, who also doubled as the team's reserve catcher, was only too happy to serve up slow offerings for his teammates to crush into the stands.

While the hitting display was enthralling the few fans who had settled into their seats for the pre-game festivities, Bloom gathered Sanchez, Patton, and backup first baseman John Darren around the second base bag and began to instruct them in the fine art of making the pivot at second base and successfully completing a double play. Jeff, who had arrived at the park only ten minutes earlier, shielded his eyes from the midday sun as he strode down the aisle to his box seat along the first base side, courtesy of his cousin Greg. He slowly ate the bagel with cream cheese that he had purchased before leaving for the ballpark and casually sat, alternately watching the gathering in the middle of the infield and the batting practice power display. He was alone, his call to Michelle the previous night having gone unanswered. He did not feel that it would be proper to bring anyone other than her to the game so he sat on the aisle, with the seat next to him to remain unoccupied for the game.

"The problem is that you're not transferring the ball from your glove to your bare hand, or releasing the ball at the right time, which was why you had the problem last night," Greg told Sanchez. The young shortstop shuffled his feet slightly in the infield dirt, listening intently to the tutorial being offered up by his coach. "Let me show you how it's done." Greg jogged to his left, positioning himself approximately ten feet from second base. He crouched down as if playing the field, made a noise to simulate the crack of a bat connecting with a ball, and jumped toward the base. Acting as if a baseball was being tossed to him from an imaginary second baseman nearby, in one motion, he stepped on the bag, whirled in the air, and threw the imaginary pill to first base. "Now you do it," he said, motioning to Sanchez, as he jangled his arm slightly, the throwing motion having caused a current of pain which ran from his shoulder to his hand. The young players eyed their coach and his wounded arm warily, but then assumed their positions when Greg caught their stares and motioned to them that he was fine.

203

The shortstop went through the same drill as his coach, and then Greg stood by the pitcher's mound, tossing a ball to Patton so that the three infielders could practice their technique together. Greg clapped his hands together as the threesome slowly executed a fictional double play, and then turned to Sanchez and informed him that he was still having trouble with throwing to first base when the runner approached second standing up. "Don't forget, Juan," he instructed, "you can't leap, pivot, or throw over a man who is not sliding in front of you. If he comes in standing up, you should plant yourself near the bag, not jump, and fire the ball to his left side … your right side, since you're right-handed, over to John." He took the ball in his hand and motioned for Patton to stand between first and second bases. "Here, let's try it."

"Wait a second, coach," Sanchez asked in his heavy accent, "which side was I supposed to throw it?"

"To his left," Greg answered. "You're right-handed, aren't you? So throw the ball with your right hand, around him." Greg moved his right arm in a sideways throwing motion. "He's coming at you, so his left is your right. Understand?" The players looked at each other as if they were trying to digest this piece of information regarding how to tell their left from their right, and, seemingly at the identical moment, understood the concept and nodded. "O.K., then," Greg instructed, "let's give it a whirl. And don't forget, there are people in the stands. Don't embarrass any of us."

Sanchez took the toss from Patton, dragged his left foot across the second base bag, planted his right foot in the infield dirt, and hurled the ball sidearm to Darren. The throw was several feet wide to Darren's left, however, and he had to leave the base in order to catch the ball. Had there been an actual runner barreling down the base line in an attempt to cross the first-base bag, he and Darren would have unquestionably collided as Darren lunged for the errant throw. Greg, watching the entire scene from the rear of the pitcher's mound, crossed his arms and shook his head, telling the players that they would have to do it again. This time, he would act as a base runner and run from first base to second as if he was trying to prevent a double play.

"Sanchez," Greg said, loudly enough so that all three players heard, "you need to be able to gauge how far to my left the throw has to be so that it doesn't hit me and still be close enough to first base so that Darren can catch it without his foot leaving the bag, got it? We don't want him getting creamed by the guy running to first, and there's not a great deal of room for error so you need to know how much to his side you need to make the throw." Greg walked slowly to first base, stretched his aging legs out, and took his stance next to the base.

"Do it now," Greg yelled, as he took off from first base and ran toward second. Patton scooped up the ball, which was now being fed to him by the team's batboy, and tossed it to Sanchez. The shortstop dragged his foot along the right side of the second base bag, dug his right heel into the Yankee Stadium dirt, and threw the ball just inches from Greg's left side, where it landed in Darren's glove with a resounding pop. The first baseman did not have to move from his perch, right foot planted on the side of first base, in order to haul in Sanchez's perfect throw. "Looked good that time, boys," Greg panted, as he bent over and placed his hands on his knees, gasping for air due to his 90-foot sprint. "Let's do it one more time," he said, extending his index finger skyward. "Make sure that you throw as close to me as possible. That way Darren will have the best chance of catching it."

Greg again walked slowly to first base, and slapped Darren on the back in an encouraging manner before motioning to the batboy to throw the ball to Patton again. Once the ball left the youth's hand, Greg began to sprint to second base as he had before. Patton caught the ball on a short hop and took a step towards second before flipping the ball to Sanchez, who was covering the bag. Sanchez dragged his left foot along the right side of the base, as he had before, and planted his right leg to position himself to complete the relay throw around the charging runner. He eyed the runner, trying to determine the best way to throw the ball to his side as he came into second, still standing.

This time, however, the runner did not come into the base standing up. Rather, as Greg was approximately five steps from the shortstop he ducked and began to roll forward, his momentum carrying him directly into the shortstop's right leg. Sanchez's leg, with its cleats deeply imbedded in the infield dirt and facing Greg, was unable to bear the brunt of Greg's slide and buckled, the ligaments in the right knee being torn to shreds as Greg's shoulder struck his knee and leg. Following the contact, the two men rolled in opposite directions, with Sanchez coming to rest on the infield grass directly in front of second base. Greg stopped rolling several feet past second base, in the middle of the base path between second and third. Greg climbed to his feet almost immediately, and began to wipe the dirt off of his uniform.

As Greg stood and dusted himself off, Sanchez continued to roll in the infield grass in agony, clutching his injured right leg. Tears welled up in his eyes as he tried desperately to straighten his leg, but the excruciating pain that emanated from his right knee would not permit any such movement. Others realized immediately that something was wrong with Sanchez, and several players and coaches rushed to his side. Those in the crowd gasped as the players huddled around the injured shortstop, and, minutes later, gave him a polite round of applause as he limped off the field, his arms wrapped over the shoulders of two of his teammates, unable to place any weight on his right leg and shredded knee.

When Sanchez cried out in pain and began to writhe on the grass, Greg joined the other team members in rushing to his side. He repeatedly apologized for what had happened, and tried to cradle Sanchez's head in his lap while they waited for the team's doctor to come to the scene. When the team doctor arrived, Greg stood back, burying his head in his hands and muttering to himself that the whole thing was his fault. Several of the players came over to console Greg, putting their arms around him, and attempted to lessen his concern by telling him that it was just an accident and that it could have happened to anyone. Greg thanked them and turned away, slowly making his way back to the dugout. When he reached the sanctity of the dugout, he sat on the right end of the bench, again hiding his head in his hands. He did not want anyone to see the faint smile creasing his lips.

"What the hell happened out there?" barked Matt Garver, who had emerged from the dugout tunnel when one of the players had rushed to his office to tell him about Sanchez's injury. He saw the assemblage gathered on the field around their fallen teammate, then looked to his left and saw Greg with his head in his hands. Moving to his left, he went to speak to Greg. "Tell me, Greg," he asked, placing his hand on Greg's shoulder, "what the fuck happened?"

A tear glistened in Greg's reddened left eye as he looked up at the concerned manager. "It was an accident, Matt. I was trying to show the guys how to turn the two." He shook his head slowly. "You saw how they flubbed that one in the game last night. I just wanted to show them the proper mechanics. You know, I'm trying to do what you told me to do in the meeting."

Garver, who had been munching on sunflower seeds, spit out the shells of the seeds and sat down next to Greg, again gently placing his right hand on his left shoulder. "You were showing them how to turn a double play. They practice that all the time. So what happened?"

207

Greg turned away and bit down hard on his upper lip, as if he was attempting to compose himself before answering the question. The reason for his bite, however, was to cause him pain and force his tears to flow anew, an old actor's trick that he had heard about years before. He hesitated, looking out onto the field as the first tear rolled down his cheek from the pain, directly at the location where he and Sanchez had collided. "There must have been some miscommunication between us. I told them that we were going to try different ways that a runner will use to break up the play. The time before I came in standing up, and wanted Juan to throw the ball around me to first base, which he did. I guess he thought that I was going to come in the same way again, but I did a hard slide and roll instead. He should have just jumped over me," he said, his voice cracking as he paused to collect himself, "but by the time I was into the roll it was too late for either of us to do anything. His leg was set down, and I couldn't stop my forward momentum. I tried to shift my weight at the last minute, but it wasn't enough, I guess, to lessen the force on his knee."

He looked at Garver, this time making full eye contact with his boss. "I'm really sorry, skip, especially after the discussion we had last week. I'm really trying to make a positive effort. That's why I wanted to practice with them, to show you how serious I am about the job," he explained, essentially pleading for his manager's absolution as his eyes glistened with moisture. "You have got to believe me. I certainly didn't want this to happen." He stood, and slowly walked down to the other end of the dugout. He laid his head on top of the water cooler and leaned, his head and shoulders slumped forward, against the visiting team's bat rack.

Garver followed, and again placed his hand on Greg's shoulder. "That's alright, Greg, of course I believe you," he replied. "Now let me go see how Sanchez is doing. Maybe it isn't all bad. You've been around long enough to know that injuries usually aren't as bad as they look at first." Moving his hand

208

to the back of Greg's neck, he squeezed it lightly. "You take care of yourself. Try not to worry too much. Don't forget, the rest of the team has a game to play today." He turned, and walked down the tunnel to the trainer's room, where Sanchez was being prepared to be taken to the hospital for x-rays and, if needed, an MRI on his swollen right knee.

While Bloom and Garver were discussing the incident in the dugout, Rob Patton stood, several feet away, chatting with some of the other players. He was able to hear much of the conversation between his manager and coach, including Greg's explanation of how he was trying to teach the players different methods of handling base runners when they were going from first to second. His recollection, however, differed from Greg's. He did not remember Greg telling anybody that he would be running in different ways, only that they were to work on handling the runner who charged into second standing up.

Patton walked away from the others and thought about whether he should bring this difference to Garver's attention. He knew that the manager would have a great deal on his mind before and during the game, but wanted to clear his mind as soon as possible so that he could concentrate on playing nine innings without thinking about how to broach the topic. The start of the game, though, was only an hour away. He decided that the best course of action would be to go to the manager before the game started and inform him of this discrepancy.

He got his chance five minutes later, when Garver emerged from the dugout, holding a lineup card with Sanchez's name crossed out of the leadoff spot. The manager informed the few players who were sitting in the dugout that their starting shortstop had probably suffered some form of ligament damage, most likely a meniscus tear, based on the team physician's initial examination. While he was taken to the hospital for definitive tests, it appeared that he would be lost to the team for a minimum of four to six weeks. That figure would increase dramatically, Garver warned, if the damage to the knee was worse than expected. They would have to wait to find out for sure because the test results would not be available until later that night.

While most of the assemblage went out on to the field to tell their teammates of this update, Rob Patton stayed behind and walked up to Garver. "Uh, Mr. Garver," he asked quietly, "can I speak to you in the clubhouse for a minute?"

"How many times do I have to tell you to stop calling me Mr. Garver? I'm not that much older than you, you little shit." He shook his head and grimaced before asking Patton, "Rob, what do you want to talk to me about? Can it wait a little while? As you can see, I'm kind of busy."

"Well, uh," Patton stammered, "it's kind of important, Mr. Garver, I mean, skip. It has to do with what happened with Juan and Mr. Bloom."

Garver looked at Patton with a puzzled look on his face. The second baseman looked him in the eye and moved his head slightly in the direction of the dugout. Garver paused, and then turned to walk toward the tunnel which led inside, from the dugout to the clubhouse. He waved Patton along. "Come on, Rob," he said, looking around to see if anyone else had been paying attention to their exchange, "let's go inside and talk for a couple of minutes."

Greg was standing behind the batting cage a few minutes later and chatting with some of the Yankees' coaches when one of the batboys ran to his side and told him, hesitatingly, that his presence was requested in the manager's office. He turned to the batboy, who was no more than 14 years old, and told him not to bother him while he was with the other coaches, that he was busy talking. The batboy, however, was persistent. "But Mr. Bloom," he implored,

"I'm pretty sure that Mr. Garver really wants to talk to you now." He motioned toward the dugout, as if to stress his point even more.

Greg excused himself and walked, with the boy, away from the batting cage. When the two were a sufficient distance from the others, he bent over to whisper in the boy's ear. "He really wants to talk to me right now? Is it something important?" he asked.

"I think so," the youth in the miniature uniform replied. "Mr. Garver doesn't look very happy." He sighed when he saw Greg begin to fidget nervously. "But he didn't tell me why he wants to see you, so I really do not know."

Greg turned back to the other coaches and made some joke about the need to take care of some important team business. He walked toward the dugout and made his way to the manager's office. The Yankee Stadium clock read 12:20, so it was only about forty-five minutes before the game was to begin. He could hear muffled voices inside of the office. He knocked on the visiting manager's office door, which was closed, and waited for Garver's acknowledgement before entering. The voices stopped, and he could then hear Garver beckoning him to enter the office.

Greg opened the door and, when he stepped inside the doorway, he could see Garver standing behind the worn desk that occupied much of the room. Off to his right stood Rob Patton. The young second baseman appeared uncomfortable, as he fidgeted with the strings of his glove and shuffled his feet nervously, never making eye contact with his infielders' coach. Greg wondered what the two had been discussing prior to his arrival.

"You wanted to see me, Matt?" asked Greg as he entered the room.

"Yes, Greg, please come in," answered Garver. "And please close the door behind you."

Greg entered the room and shut the door, walking to the chair across the desk from where Garver was standing. The manager held out his arm and motioned for Greg to sit. Preferring to stand rather than sit, Greg politely declined the offer. "What's this all about, Matt?" He looked again at Patton, who was looking directly at Garver. "Why is Rob here?" he asked, "If it's important, shouldn't we just discuss it between you and me, coach to manager?" He laughed nervously.

"Well, Greg," Matt replied, looking alternately between Greg and Rob Patton, "Rob has been taking care of some stuff for me, and now he tells me that your version of what went on between you and Sanchez may not be exactly as you told me. I thought that it would be best to have both of you in the room with me so that we could take care of this quietly. I don't want to make a scene, or have this in front of the media. This team certainly does not need extra publicity, especially if it's going to be negative."

The manager walked over to the second baseman, and, in order to reassure him, placed his hand on Patton's right shoulder. It was the same hand that had been on Greg's shoulder only minutes earlier, a tacit, if not intentional, move that Greg took to mean that Garver was already accepting Patton's version of the events over his. "Rob, tell me what you were saying before Mr. Bloom got here."

Rob Patton continued to shuffle his feet over the worn carpet, and cleared his throat before beginning to recount his version of the events. "As I was saying," he stated, "Mr. Bloom, uh, told us last night that we had to take some extra practice today, that we had to work on our double plays."

212

"I'm sorry, Matt," Greg interjected, "but I already told you that. The game's starting in less than an hour, and I don't see any reason for us to be here now." He turned and walked toward the door, reaching out with his left hand for the doorknob before being stopped by Garver.

"Don't leave this room," commanded Garver. "You're going to stay here and listen to what this young man has to say. And might I recommend that you take a seat. You may be here for a few minutes more than you expected." Greg, now realizing that his honesty was being questioned, removed his hand from the doorknob and returned to the chair in front of the desk, this time sitting down as instructed. As he sat, he sighed audibly, looking over at Patton, who continued to look in the other direction so as to avoid direct eye contact. Garver waited, and then turned to Patton. "Go ahead, Rob, please continue."

"Well," said Patton, hesitatingly, "we were going through the double play motions out there. It was Coach Bloom, Juan, me, and Darren was playing first base. Coach was trying to show us how to do the pivot when the runner comes into second without sliding."

"You mean standing up?" asked Garner.

"Yes, sir. Coach Bloom was going to play the runner coming to second base, and I was supposed to flip the ball to Juan. He was to try to throw the ball around Coach, and the first time that we did it his relay throw pulled Darren off of the bag so Coach made us do it again. The next time we all did it pretty good, but Coach said that we should do it one more time just to make sure I expected, I mean, we all expected that it would be the same as the time before." He paused and sighed audibly. "That was the time that Juan got hurt."

There was a prolonged pause. Garver, who was by now as uncomfortable as the other two men in the room, realized that Rob needed some

213

coaxing before he would tell the rest of his account. "What happened, Rob? How did Juan get hurt?"

For the first time, Patton looked over at his coach, but now it was Greg who was avoiding eye contact, as he squirmed in his chair from side to side, obviously uncomfortable. This movement did not go unnoticed by the manager, who asked, "is there a problem, Greg? Is there anything that you'd like to tell me?"

"No, skip," Greg answered, although beads of sweat began to form on his forehead as he shifted positions in his chair. "There's no problem, and I don't have anything to tell you just now. That may change, but for now I just want to hear the rest of what Robby has to say." He gestured for Patton to continue.

"Well, we ran the drill again," Patton began to explain, "and Juan did the same thing that he did before. He was probably expecting Coach to keep coming in standing, because Coach never said anything about sliding. I know that I was expecting him to come in standing up, because that was the drill we were doing. I was off to the side, and all of a sudden Coach hits the dirt in a hard slide, and rolls right into Juan's leg. I'm not saying that he did anything on purpose," he added, as for the first time he and Greg made eye contact, "just that Coach never told us about practicing different kinds of situations. We were only working on the runner who comes in standing. That's why Juan's leg was planted and why he couldn't jump. And that's how he got hurt." He again turned to Greg, his eyes looking down at the floor. "I'm sorry, Coach, I just had to tell Mr. Garver what I saw. I owe it to Juan."

"I understand that, Rob. And don't worry about me," Greg answered, wiping the sweat from his brow. He shifted his eyes and looked at Garner, pointing his right index finger in the air and mouthing the words "just one second." He then returned his gaze to Patton. "Rob, look up at me. Did Juan and I have any discussion without you being right there?"

"I don't understand what you're saying," answered Patton, who was now looking Greg in the eye.

"Were you there for every conversation between Juan and me?" Greg continued. "Is it possible that we discussed what we were going to do and you just didn't hear it?" He waited, but no answer was forthcoming. "Don't forget, you were just giving him the ball. You didn't have to know how I was coming into the base, did you? It really didn't matter for your job, did it?"

This time Patton was bold enough to respond forcefully, his fears about angering his coach having dissipated due to what he perceived to be an improper line of questioning. "Well, I guess not," he replied, "but I'm pretty sure that you didn't give Juan any instructions without me or Darren hearing you."

"Darren was over at first base. I'm sure that he didn't hear half of what I told you guys." He looked at Garver, and shrugged his shoulders, extending his outstretched palms skyward. "Now pay attention, Rob, and please just answer the question I am asking. Were you there every time that I said something to Juan? While you may not think so, it's very important to me and Mr. Garver."

Patton shook his head vigorously. "This is not about what I think is important, coach. Even if I wasn't right there," he answered, looking at his manager instead of Greg, "I'm sure that I would have heard everything that you said to him. We were right there by the second base bag. And as for my hearing, I heard you guys talking in the dugout from a few yards away, didn't I?"

"I guess so, but that doesn't mean anything with respect to a conversation between me and Juan." He turned to the manager, who was standing behind the desk. "Matt, I certainly understand why you wanted to clear this up, and I appreciate it and appreciate you giving me the chance to hear it directly and respond." Turning again, he walked over to Patton, and extended his right hand. "Rob, no hard feelings. You did what you had to do. I probably would have done the same thing if I were in your shoes. You've got a lot of guts, kid. And Juan is a lucky man to have a teammate as devoted as you."

"And Rob, you'll have no problem standing in there and taking those guys sliding hard into second, even when they come in standing up," he added, chuckling lightly.

Neither of the other men laughed. A visibly exhausted Matt Garver slumped down in the chair behind the desk, thanking Patton for his time and telling him to warm up for the game. Both Greg and Patton turned to leave the office, but Garver added "you stay behind for a second, Greg. I just want to tell you something before you leave."

He waited until Rob Patton left and closed the door behind him before beginning to speak. "I don't know what actually happened out there, Greg, and I'm sure that Juan won't be of much help. I'm really trying to believe you." He paused and shook his head. "But it looks like the players don't have a lot of confidence in you, which is a problem. We talked about this the other day. You're their coach. They have to be able to put their faith in you and respect what you try to teach them. You know that I don't want you to be let go, but you're putting me in a very tough situation. If this continues I don't know if I'll have much choice. It's just too much shit, all at the same time. I can't afford it now. We, as a team, can't afford that now."

He stood, walked around the desk, and sat on its edge so that he was sitting only inches from Greg. "Look, Greg, this is the perfect opportunity for you. The team's going to have to bring up some kid to replace Juan. Odds are that this kid will be raw and desperately in need of major league coaching. Work your magic with him. Show him how to be a big-league shortstop. Work with him, alone, on the pivot. On throwing. Even on hitting. If he responds favorably, I will see and management will see. If so, your job will obviously be secure." He stood. "Your best talent is your mind for the game. All the owners want is for you to share some knowledge with the players, especially with the younger ones. Be a coach. Think about it."

Greg stood and motioned toward the door, silently requesting permission to be excused from the meeting. "Not yet," Garver said, "the team owner is on his way down to talk to you. I'll tell him what we just discussed, but the final decision on what's going to happen from here is his, not mine. So sit tight for a minute; we need to get this done before we go back out there for the game."

From his vantage point in the box seats along the first base line, Jeff had spent the past few minutes intently watching batting practice as the players took their final swings, each trying to outmuscle the others and place the ball further over the outfield wall. Several young women had gathered at the edge of the Yankees' dugout, and were screaming their approval with each long shot. The players took note of the impressionable beauties gathered nearby, and did their best to please their audience, taking mightier cuts with each swing.

For Jeff, though, watching batting practice was not merely an appreciation of the players' power. It was another version of his scouting. Maybe if he saw a player belt the ball well in practice, he would be worth a chance on a fantasy team. Jeff knew, though, that performance in batting

217

practice had little, if any, bearing, on how a player would perform in a game against actual full-speed pitching. He thought back to Leon Wood, possibly the greatest pre-game shooter in NBA history. Unfortunately for Leon Wood, his practice prowess was rarely, if ever, matched during an actual game, so his career was not only mediocre, but lasted only six years, with stops in six different cities.

As the last three sluggers were taunting each other at the cage, each daring the others to try to hit the ball to dead center or to the opposite field and see if they could reach the seats, Jeff saw a commotion erupting near second base. From the corner of his eye he could see his cousin wiping dirt off of his backside and knees while other players rushed to a fallen player on the left side of second base. He could not make out the identity of the injured Brewer because so many were crowded around him, but thought that it had to be either Rob Patton or Juan Sanchez because those were the players with whom Greg had been working a few minutes before. When he saw Patton's number 21 hovering over the crowd, however, he realized that it was Sanchez who was down.

He immediately thought back to his conversation with Greg of two nights earlier, and began to wonder if Greg had intentionally caused injury to Sanchez. Turning to the two teenagers seated behind him, he asked if they had seen what happened. One of the two told him that he had seen Sanchez get hurt, that he was injured when one of the coaches slid into him. According to the youth, it looked like they were practicing infield play when it happened. In response to Jeff's next inquiry, the youth stated that it looked like a freak accident; no fight had broken out and no punches had been thrown by anyone. In fact, Jeff saw many of the players going over to console Greg, such that he questioned whether the injury had been deliberate or, possibly, accidental.

The Brewers captured the second game of the series, romping by a 7-1 margin, marking the first time in four years that they had won back-to-back games in Yankee Stadium. Filling in admirably for Sanchez at shortstop was rookie Jose Benitez, normally a second baseman, who went two-for-five and scored a run. It was Benitez's third game at the major league level, and his single in the third inning was the first hit of his major league career. He also played a flawless defensive game, even ranging far to his left on one play to rob the New York hitter of a sure base hit.

Not wishing to disappoint Lefty Grant, Jeff made his way to the visiting locker room following the game. He was prevented from entering the locker room area by stadium security personnel at first, but was able to contact Greg, who sent out an emissary to bring him past the guards and into the Brewers' quarters. A group of reporters were clustered around Grant's locker, peppering him with questions about his complete-game victory. During the game, he had yielded but four hits and one unearned run. Because of his height, Grant was able to see over the media throng surrounding him and spotted Jeff making his way across the room.

"Hey, Yankee boy," he yelled in Jeff's direction, "what do you think? I hope that I didn't mess up your little fantasy league. You know that I was thinking of throwing a few juicy ones to those Yankees," he added, sarcastically, "just so your little team would do better."

Jeff grimaced and nodded in Grant's direction. "Damn," he thought, "I can't believe that Lefty Grant remembered what I said about the league, and even that he remembered who I was." He stopped, and walked closer to Grant's locker. He could see Grant pointing in his direction, and explaining to the media about how his coach's cousin was rooting against him not just because he was a Yankees fan, but also because he was involved in one of those "infernal fantasy leagues." A few of the scribes dutifully took notes on this explanation, but Jeff, starting to walk away, did not believe that any of it would make it into print the next day, especially in light of the pre-game injury suffered by Juan Sanchez.

Jeff asked one of the other reporters about where he could find Greg. He was told that Bloom was not available to the media, and that Matt Garver would be answering any questions regarding the Sanchez incident. Jeff explained that he was Greg's cousin and searched in vain for someone who could tell him where Greg was, but nobody would provide him with that information. He walked over to the manager's office, where Garver sat with his feet on the desk, speaking to approximately ten media members. The bright lights of the television cameras shone throughout the room, raising the temperature well above the comfort zone for those writers and broadcasters dressed in shirts and jackets. The heat did not seem to bother Garver, however, as he sat there in his undershirt and uniform pants and calmly answered questions about his starting shortstop and the unfortunate incident that had felled him only hours before.

"I told you boys, it was all just an accident. They were out there practicing the double play and there was a miscommunication between the coach and the players. It happens all of the time, but this time someone got hurt. It's really not much different than a player being struck by a ball in the field during batting practice. It shouldn't happen, but if somebody isn't careful or misses a sign, there's the possibility of injury." He fidgeted with some of the items on the desk. "As far as the extent of the injury, we have no comment at this time. Once the results come back tonight, you'll know as much as we do."

He leaned back further in his chair, the back of his seat touching the wall behind him. "How about we talk about what a bang-up job Benitez did for us out there today. The kid was thrown into the fire, into an impossible situation, and he responded brilliantly. I'm fortunate as a manager to have players not only in the starting lineup, but also on the bench, who can produce when necessary. Now if you boys will excuse me, I have some other things to take care of. Go talk to Grant or Benitez -- they were the stars of this show."

As the reporters filed past Jeff toward the players' lockers, he could hear two of them talking about the incident. One of the writers was explaining that he had seen what had happened from the press box and that he was convinced that it was not an accident. He was going to ask Rob Patton, who was the closest player to the scene, about his reactions and thoughts. The other writer agreed to accompany him, and the twosome made their way to Patton, trailed by Jeff. One of the men, the beat writer for the largest daily newspaper in Milwaukee, asked Patton what had happened on the field between Bloom and Sanchez.

Patton looked at the writers quizzically, stating that he was under the impression that, having already spoken to his manager, they should already know what happened. "Weren't you gentlemen just in skip's office asking him about what went on?"

"Yes, Rob," the beat writer answered, "but he told us that it was an accident. From where I was sitting, it did not look like an accident, and we know that you were right there. We also know that you spent a great deal of time in Garver's office today, and, from what I've been told, you have been spending time there quite often over the past few weeks. That makes you the best source for information. So tell us, what really happened out there?" The other writer thrust a mini-cassette recorder under Patton's nose to preserve his account.

Rob Patton took a deep breath, and slowly began to button his shirt. He leaned over to slip on his shoes, striking his nose against the writer's tape

221

recorder in the process. He then stood, and finally began to speak to the writers. "It's just like skip told you. It was an accident. Juan must have misunderstood something that Coach said. In fact, I think that you guys are just wasting your time looking for anything else." He turned and reached for his paisley tie, which was still dangling from a hanger in his locker, and added, "don't worry about where I spend my time. I'm just trying to do right by the team."

"Let us be the judge of that, Rob. You know it's our job to find out the truth, and how interesting these stories can be." The writer tapped Patton on the shoulder, and the player whirled around, the long end of his tie whacking the writer across the bridge of his nose. "Look, Rob," the writer said, his nose only inches from Patton's, "we're going to get to the bottom of this one way or another. Either you help us out or we get the information from someone else. And if we get it elsewhere, you're going to look like an asshole for covering it up and not helping out." He paused. "Again, what happened before the game between Greg Bloom and Juan Sanchez?"

Patton's face reddened, and his usually polite demeanor began to erode as the writer's threat sank deeply into his mind. He took the recorder from the reporter's hand, pushed the "record" button, and began to speak slowly, deliberately, into its microphone. "The incident on the field today before the game was an accident. The same thing has probably happened somewhere in the past, and it will probably happen again sometime in the future. No matter how hard you assholes look, you're not going to find any evidence to the contrary. So give it up." He turned off the recorder and hurled it in the reporter's direction. The machine hit the scribe in the chest before falling to the ground, the tape popping outside of it when it hit the carpet.

CHAPTER 20

Jeff left the ballpark and, intending to speak to Greg, went directly to the Brewers' hotel. Unfortunately, many of the local media, as well as the Brewers' beat writers, all appeared to have had the same idea. The members of the media were crowded into the hotel's lobby, where the Brewers' press secretary was busy handling their questions. A sign posted near the hotel's doors indicated that Greg would not be available to the media for the remainder of the weekend.

As Jeff would later find out, Greg was whisked from the stadium almost immediately following the game, and had arrived at the hotel almost an hour earlier. He had told the clubhouse workers to allow Jeff into the locker room, but by the time Jeff entered, Greg had already left in a New York City police officer's squad car. The story about his being unavailable for comment was created to divert the media's attention from his escape. Nobody was at liberty to tell Jeff about Greg's departure for fear of spoiling the plan.

"The team has no comment on today's events aside from what Mr. Garver told you following the game, other than what I am going to read now," the press secretary added. He removed a prepared statement from his pocket and began to read from the piece of paper, waving off any further questions. "Today an unfortunate incident occurred; as you are all aware, one of the bright young stars of the Brewers' family was injured during pre-game practice. The club is satisfied that there was no wrongdoing involved, and that Juan Sanchez's injury was caused by a simple but unfortunate miscommunication between he and one of the team's coaches." He held his hand over his face to shield his eyes from various camera flashes. "No further investigation into this matter is being pursued at this time. The sole focus of the team at this time is to help Juan on his road to recovery, so that he may prove to be a valuable asset to the Brewers both this season and in the years to come. We ask that all of you include Juan in your prayers so that he is able to return to the playing field as soon as possible."

He answered no other questions regarding Greg, Sanchez, or the leg injury, except to re-iterate Garver's prior comment regarding the possible severity of the injury. "At this time, we do not know how severe the damage to his leg is, or even if there is any tangible evidence of damage. He is currently undergoing preliminary tests, and will be flown back to Milwaukee tomorrow for further evaluation. We will notify you as soon as we are told about the test results."

As he finished his statement, a team bus carrying many of the Milwaukee players pulled up to the front of the hotel, and the players strode directly into the hot lights which filled the lobby. Most of the players declined any comment regarding the accident, choosing instead to focus on the stellar pitching performance of Lefty Grant and the possibility of their climbing back into playoff contention. Some spoke of dedicating the remainder of the season, and their push for a playoff spot, to both Mike Jones and Juan Sanchez. Rob Patton, tired of speaking to reporters from his earlier encounter, simply walked through the throng, and did not stop to answer any questions before boarding the elevator which would take him to his room.

Jeff stood in the far corner of the lobby, away from the sportswriters and players, and plotted how he was going to reach Greg's room. When the hotel posted security guards at the ground floor elevator doors and all stairwells, however, it became clear that doing so would be difficult. He went to the front desk to try to call Greg, but was told by the hotel personnel that Mr. Bloom was not to be disturbed and that he could merely add his name to the list of 20 others who had already left messages for Greg. He tried to explain that he was Greg's cousin, but was informed that two of the others before him had also claimed, clearly improperly, to be family members, and that they had to put their names on the list as well.

Jeff was about to give up hope when he spotted Lefty Grant, on the other side of the lobby, signing autographs for two young fans. Making his way across the crowd, he walked up to Lefty and asked him for his assistance in getting upstairs. Grant nodded, grabbed his bag and walked toward the elevator, informing the security guard that Jeff was with him. The guard stepped aside, and both men climbed onto the elevator.

When the door closed, Jeff began to thank Grant for his help. He was interrupted, however, before he could finish his sentence. "Since we're alone, tell me something," the tall southpaw said to Jeff, "what the hell was he thinking?"

"What are you talking about?" asked Jeff.

"You know what I mean," answered Lefty. "I didn't see what happened, but it all seems pretty suspicious to me. What the hell was Greg thinking? I find it difficult to believe that Juan would have messed up simple instructions. Everyone out there was a professional. Something went wrong there."

The look on his face belied Jeff's surprise at Grant's line of inquiry. "Are you saying that Greg intentionally...?"

Grant shook his head. "I don't know what I'm thinking, Jeff. All I know is that the team just lost its best shortstop to a freak play, but the play occurred in practice, not during a game. And it wasn't another player that caused the problem, but one of our own coaches." He shrugged his shoulders. "I haven't seen these guys practice double plays before a game with Greg for months now,

225

probably even since spring training ended. Why were they out there doing it today? And how did the impact happen?"

Jeff tried to interject, but was unsuccessful.

Grant continued. "These are the questions that I'm asking myself; I would never do it out loud because it would only hurt the team. But this shit should not have happened to Juan. He's such a nice guy. If you want to think that I'm blaming Greg, then I guess you can think that." He paused, and looked at ceiling as if searching for the proper words to express his feelings before continuing. "But to be honest, I don't even know if I'm blaming him. I'm just trying to figure out what happened. And part of that is figuring out what those guys were thinking."

Jeff looked up at the man two years his junior, the pitcher whose face wore a pained expression as he tried to comprehend the events that had transpired. He thought back to his conversation in this very elevator of two days earlier with Grant. The left-hander had spoken at that time of loyalty, about how some of the players were loyal to their fans and teams. And now, here he was, refusing to gloat about his own victory of only two hours ago and instead choosing to wonder why one of his teammates had suffered an injury which would interfere with that person's season.

Not only that, but Grant seemed to be genuinely concerned for the team's fate. "It's like I told you the other day, Jeff," he explained, "it all comes down to loyalty, being true to the team. No matter what you may think, we don't go out there for ourselves, but we go out there for the good of the team. Look at it this way. If I win 20 games this year but the team doesn't make the playoffs, then the season will be a disappointment to me. It's not just a game of personal accomplishments. For some it is, but not for most of us. It certainly isn't for me.

Losing Juan may be the end of any chance of the team doing something great together."

Grant shook his head in dismay. He could stride out to the mound every fifth day and do his best to pitch the team to victory, he reasoned, but what about the other games? The team was comprised of a blend of players young and old. For the older, more established players, some of their careers were nearing the end and this could have been their last realistic chance at a World Series appearance or victory. For the younger players, the excitement and drama of a pennant race was being put on hold. Some of the players would not be with the team next year, and the loss of their starting shortstop may have been the death knell for their chances of raising a championship banner above Milwaukee's Miller Park.

As Lefty Grant exited the elevator on the sixth floor, Jeff could not help but notice that his step had slowed from their previous encounter. His six-foot-seven frame somehow seemed shorter, as his shoulders slumped as he walked, weighed down not only by the bag in his hand but also his concern for his fallen teammate and his team's misfortunes. Jeff's compassion for Grove's feelings of loyalty to the team made him realize the irony that was, as yet, unknown to the players and media. Lefty Grant had just pitched the game of his career in front of a national television audience, and was now forgetting about his triumph to focus on the team's good. On the other side of the fence stood Greg, who had just damaged his team's chances of success due to what Jeff perceived to be his petty jealousy of the younger, faster, and more talented Juan Sanchez.

The elevator came to a halt on the eighth floor, and Jeff went to walk to the hotel room where he and Greg had discussed Juan Sanchez only nights before. As he approached room 815, he could see that the room's door was being guarded by a member of the hotel's security force. The security guard was

227

seated in a chair directly to the right of the door, the glow of a lit cigarette dangling from his mouth, and a pair of steely handcuffs and a thick black nightstick hanging from his belt. Jeff approached the room, stopped several paces from the guard, and asked if it would be possible for him to see Greg.

"I'm sorry, son," the guard replied, "but I'm under strict orders from management that nobody gets in to see Mr. Bloom. If I let you in I wouldn't be doing my job." He took a long drag from his cigarette, his free hand lightly tapping the nightstick which dangled from his belt in a tacit show of potential domination. "Why don't you go downstairs with the rest of them? There's nothing up here for you to see."

Jeff stopped and addressed the security guard. "I'm not one of them, sir. I'm Mr. Bloom's cousin. If you'll just ask him, he'll tell you that it's alright to let me in." He motioned toward the door. "My name is Jeff Goldstein. You've got to believe me. Please ask him."

"I was told not to disturb him," the guard replied, coldly, "so I can't." It was obvious to Jeff that the guard was not the least bit concerned about whom he might be, or whose relative he was. The guard's left hand inched its way downward, and its fingers were now wrapping tightly around the handle of the nightstick. He lifted his free hand and pointed his index finger in Jeff's direction, and then pointed to the elevator located at the other side of the hall. "Now please leave, sir, before I have you ushered out on your behind."

"You don't understand," Jeff said, inching closer to the door, as he quickly decided to take a different approach. "I'm his cousin. I think that he needs to see me now. Just let me knock on the door. If he wants to see me, fine. And if he asks me to leave, I will gladly leave."

The guard, becoming angry, refused to grant this request. "You're not touching the door, and I won't knock on the door for you," he growled, "now get the hell away from me before I call the police and have them kick your ass out of here!"

Jeff stood, motionless, and watched as the guard stood and began to walk toward him, his left hand still firmly clasping the nightstick. "O.K., pops, you win," he said. "I'll leave. But first, there's something that I have to do," he added, and rushed toward the door and pounded it with his fist, yelling to his cousin inside. "Greg, it's me, Jeff. Open the door!"

The guard whirled and drew his stick, flailing into the air as Jeff ducked out of his range. As the stick was raised for the second time, the door to room 815 opened, and its occupant inquired, "What the hell is going on out here? Jeff, is that you?"

"Yeah, it's me," Jeff called out. "The Gestapo here is giving me a hard time about seeing you." Jeff walked toward the open door, with the guard grabbing at his shirt from behind. He pushed the door open with his right hand, and shook the guard's grasp from the back of his blue polo shirt. "If you don't mind, I'm going to go into the room and speak to my cousin," he said to the guard, as he stepped into the hotel room and slammed the door behind him. The security guard, breathing heavily from the exertion, slumped back into his chair and resumed his watch on the room. He radioed his superiors downstairs, who advised him that he should not allow anyone else to pass, even if that person's presence was requested by Mr. Bloom, other than as otherwise directed by team management.

The scene in the room was very much the way it had been two nights earlier. The curtains were drawn, and the room's darkness was pierced only by the light of the television; there was no sound, however, as the television appeared to be muted. Empty glasses littered the bar, and another opened bottle of vodka, a different brand from the previous conversation, stood, half-empty, next to a bucket of ice. Three lemon wedges lay on the counter, along with an unopened plastic bottle of tonic water. Greg sat on the bed, facing the television. Much like Jeff's previous visit, Greg did not acknowledge his presence except to wave him over to fix himself a drink at the bar.

Jeff twisted off the cap to the tonic bottle, the hissing of the escaping air providing the only sound in the room. He took three ice cubes and placed them in the glass, and then added vodka, tonic water, and one of the lemon wedges. The silence was again broken as he gently stirred the concoction, the ice cubes striking the inner walls of the glass as they swirled around. Jeff walked over to Greg, and, without instruction, sat down in the chair next to the window, his body facing the television.

Neither man spoke for several minutes, as they watched a tape of 1975 World Series highlights. The only sound that was apparent, aside from the movement of vodka and ice cubes in the men's glasses, was when Jeff rustled lightly in his chair, the leather creaking underneath his body. The two sat, silently, watching the film of Carlton Fisk's famous Game six home run. When the first commercial flashed on the television screen, Jeff turned to his cousin, who was still sitting silently on the edge of the bed. "Hey Greg, can I ask you something?"

There was no response.

"Greg?" he said again, this time a little louder, "Can I ask you something?"

Greg turned away from the television and walked toward the bottle of vodka. Reaching down with his left hand, he picked up the bottle and raised it to his lips, slowly drinking as he placed more ice into his empty glass. He poured more of the clear liquid into the glass, and turned back to the bed. Returning to his prior seat on its edge, he responded, "That depends. What do you want to ask me about?"

"I want to know about what happened today."

Greg rolled his eyes, and opened his mouth as if he was going to provide information regarding that day's events. Instead of discussing the incident, however, he turned to a different topic. "Jeff," Greg asked, "I can't remember. Did I ever mention the name Candy Wilson to you?"

Jeff was caught off guard by his cousin's non-sequitor. "No, I don't think so. Why are you mentioning her now? What the hell does she have to do with what went on between you and Sanchez on the field before?"

Greg reached down and picked up a crumpled piece of paper from the bed. It looked to Jeff like a page from a magazine. Greg smoothed the paper, looked at it for several seconds, and then thrust the page toward Jeff. "Take this," he said, "and read the part that I have circled."

The top of the page read "In Memoriam" and the bottom of the page, in the lower-right hand corner, read "Sun Devils Magazine" – the monthly magazine for Arizona State Alumni. It was dated six months earlier, before the season had begun. "Which part should I read?" asked Jeff, as he scanned down the page.

"The part that's circled!" exploded Greg, the loudness of his voice startling Jeff. "What are you, an idiot? Read the circled part!"

Jeff looked down and did not see any circle on the page. He turned it over to its back side, and there saw, amidst the obituaries of past Arizona State students, an entry with a familiar name – Candy Wilson. "Former Sun Devils cheerleader Candy Wilson, class of 1991, died in December of heart failure at the age of 46," the obituary began. Without continuing to read the remainder of the page, Jeff turned to this cousin, who was looking in the other direction. "I'm so sorry, Greg," Jeff said, "I didn't realize that your friend had died. And yes, you had mentioned the name 'Candy' to me before, but I can't remember why." That was a lie; he remembered the name 'Candy' being mentioned in connection with beginning Greg's ordeal with cocaine, but sought no need to pick a fight with his already overwrought cousin.

"Man, she was beautiful," Greg said, as if he had not heard a word that Jeff had said. "Just thinking about her makes me hard. She was a girl that I dated in college. What an amazing body she had on her. You should have seen her, cousin, she was about five three, long blonde hair, and awesome tits," he said, holding his hands out in front of his own chest. "She was from California, had a perpetual tan, and was much more forward, if you know what I mean, than anyone that I knew back in Stillhouse. God, she was the sexiest thing that I ever saw." He paused. "In fact," he added, "she was probably the sexiest woman I have ever been with, even counting all of the groupies and women since I started playing professional ball. And that's saying something."

"You did mention someone named Candy before, but are you getting somewhere with this?" Jeff asked.

Greg continued his reminiscing as if he had not even heard Jeff's interruption. "If you remember, well, I am sure you've heard, I was dating Jane, my high school girlfriend, when I first went to Arizona State. I thought, like so many kids, I guess, that we would keep going and eventually get married." He looked up at the ceiling. "It was a different time, though. No cell phones. No texting. No e-mails. There was little way to keep in touch with her, other than through the phone in my dorm. "And then, one day, there was Candy. She was in one of my classes. She always wore shorts or short skirts, and with an ass like hers, all of the guys appreciated it. Anyway, one day she comes in wearing this blue sundress, and starts flashing me in class."

"Flashing you?" Jeff asked.

"You know, pulling up the dress and showing me her ass and her pussy under beautiful white lace," Greg answered as he sipped his drink. "I'm sitting in the class, and getting this massive stiffy while the professor is trying to tell us about some ancient history that nobody gives a fuck about. It was like a fuckin' movie. So I'm trying to play it cool, as if she wouldn't know that I was staring at her, but she knew."

"So?"

"She looks at me, sees that I'm looking right at her legs, and she starts to lick her lips. Then, she's got her right leg crossed over her left. She picks her right leg up and starts to scratch her thigh, moving slowly up until she's at the bottom of her ass." He feigned scratching his thigh for added effect. "And she's pulled up her dress so that she could scratch there, so I'm looking at half of her butt right there in the classroom. I'm telling you, I was in heaven. I almost shot my load right there. After class, she comes up to me, and I start to sweat, thinking that she's going to yell at me or something. But instead, she asks me out, and we started dating that day."

Jeff, growing increasingly impatient, pleaded with Greg to get to the point of his story, that there were more important things for the two of them to discuss.

"Man, was she good in the sack." He lowered his eyes. "Me and Jane never fucked. She didn't think that we should do it before we got married. I respected that, and didn't push it. Small-town values, I guess." He sat back in his chair. "But Candy was the exact opposite. She was a wild woman. To this day, man, even after all of the groupies and girls that just want to sleep with ballplayers, I've still never met anyone like her, or with her talents. And I doubt that I ever will."

"You already told me that," Jeff said, exasperated, "but you didn't answer the question that I asked you before. What happened today?"

Greg continued to ignore his cousin's questions, seemingly remaining oblivious to his voice. "But there was a bad side to Candy. She was beautiful, was a great lay, but she was also deeply into drugs. Shit, it was college, it was a time of experimentation for everyone, especially for her. You know what? I don't think that there was a drug at school that she didn't try at least once." He turned to Jeff, and tapped his left index finger against the side of his nose. "She's the one that got me started on coke, you know." Jeff nodded, because he already did know, and Greg nodded in response and continued his sermon. "She tried to get me to try heroin and stuff like that, but I didn't want to get into any of that shit." He shook his head. "I should have said no, refused the coke, but thought that I could handle it well enough. And at first I could, or so I thought. That shit takes over faster than you can imagine. One day you're normal, and the next you're out of your goddamned mind searching for one more line. You give it all up, man."

Jeff decided that it would be best to patronize his cousin's discussion and then to bring him back to the topic that he wanted to discuss. Leaning back in his chair, he asked, "Alright, I am sorry. Let's talk about her, if you want to. We can talk about the other thing later. What happened to Candy, Greg?" He paused, realizing that he knew the eventual end to his question. "I mean, other than her dying."

This time, Greg responded to a question. "You know, I'm not even sure. You should have seen her; she was like a poster child for abuse. Her face was destroyed by all of the use by the time she left school, and she became emaciated from all of the coke." He puckered his cheeks tightly. "It was terrible, man. I don't remember, but I think that she dropped out and went home to California. Either way, I haven't seen her since my junior year of college. But I guess that her spirit stays with me every time that I do a line or smoke a joint."

Jeff nodded in understanding. "But what about today, Greg?" he asked, "Let's talk about that."

"Do you see the obituary?" Greg asked. "She died of heart failure, it says. Heart failure my ass!" he yelled, "heart failure my ass!" He buried his head in his hands, sobbing. Still crying, he mumbled, "Heart failure my ass. She died of a drug overdose. I know it. I can feel it."

Jeff walked over and placed his hand on Greg's shoulder. "I'm really sorry, Greg. Really," he said, "but why is this hitting you so hard today? She died months ago."

Greg reached up and swatted Jeff's hand from his shoulder. "You insensitive putz," he bellowed. "It doesn't matter when she died." He paused, and then looked up, staring at Jeff with wide, crazy eyes. "Don't you get it?" His reddened eyes narrowed. "Don't you fucking get it?"

Jeff hesitated, again treading lightly for fear of not wanting to give the wrong answer to his highly agitated cousin.

"You don't fucking understand, Jeff," Greg sputtered. "She died of an overdose. I'm going to fucking die of an overdose also." His tears began to fall anew. "I'm going to fucking die of an overdose, and I can't stop it. That's what has been bothering me for so long. You think that I would have just gone out and killed f'ing Jones for you if everything had been fine, you asshole? I'm gonna fucking die soon. I have known since I saw this obituary. Why else would I risk my job? Would I do it for 35 thousand dollars? Seriously? Even I'm not that stupid." He opened his eyes wide again and stared at Jeff, a maniacal stare that sent shivers up Jeff's spine. "It's all about me dying. I can't quit the stuff, and it's going to kill me. Just like it killed Candy."

Jeff took a long sip from his glass, trying to allow his cousin to compose himself. "No you're not," he said after a long silence. "You can control yourself, and admission is the first step. Don't let it get you, just because it got Candy. We can get you help to make sure that you don't end up like her." He paused again. "But for now, let's focus on what happened today, please. Let's talk about what happened with Sanchez."

"I don't think so," Greg replied. The sports show had ended several minutes before. Greg picked up the remote control and pressed its buttons furiously as images of the multiple channels appeared on the screen for moments at a time. Greg continued to change the channels in this manner until the weather channel's maps appeared on the screen, at which time he placed the remote down on the table next to his chair and reached for his glass of vodka. "We don't have to talk about Candy anymore, but I also don't want to talk about Sanchez. Let's talk about something else. I don't want to talk about that."

"No," Jeff said, as he reached for the glass in his cousin's hand, wrapping his hand around the top of the glass. "I really think that we should talk about what happened on the field today."

"Fuck you, man, what are you getting at?" asked Greg, as he reached out with his free hand and tried to pull the glass from Jeff's outstretched arm. Half of the liquid from the glass poured to the carpet as Greg tipped the glass to its side in order to prevent Jeff from taking it in his hand. "What exactly is it that you want to talk about?" he asked, angrily.

"Calm down, Greg," Jeff tried to explain, "I only want to know what happened with Sanchez today. Is that so much to ask?"

Greg stood, and walked behind the chair where Jeff sat. "Why don't you tell me?"

"What?" Jeff asked, incredulously.

"Well, what did you hear at the ballpark after I left?"

Jeff tried to explain what he had heard. "Just that there was some type of incident and that it was an accident. The press secretary downstairs said that there would be no further investigations done."

Greg looked at him disapprovingly. "Oh, but you feel compelled to do some investigating of your own, is that it?"

"No," Jeff answered, "I just want to know what went on. It all seemed kind of strange. I mean, I didn't see what actually happened between the two of you, but after our conversation the other night, I couldn't help but wonder . . ."

Jeff's sentence was interrupted by the shattering of glass as Greg hurled his glass of vodka over Jeff's shoulder and through the television screen. Sparks flew from the shattered screen as shards of glass fell to the ground in front of Jeff, some striking him on his legs like tiny flies. Suddenly he felt two hands on the back of his neck, squeezing to the point where his shoulder began to ache.

237

"Wonder what, my friend?" Greg whispered in Jeff's left ear as his grip on Jeff's neck tightened.

Jeff was overcome by a choking sensation, and tried to stand up from the leather chair and escape his cousin's grip. As he tried to stand, though, Greg pushed down on his neck with increased pressure, preventing him from moving away. "What was it that you wanted to know? Go on, ask me! Ask the fucking addict what self-destructive shit he pulled today! Go ahead, ask me!" bellowed Greg.

Tears welled up in Jeff's eyes, both from the pain in his neck and the emotional strain that his cousin was inflicting upon him. He could barely choke out his thoughts, and could not lift his head to see his cousin, but croaked that, "all that I wanted to ask you … all I wanted to ask, was if you hurt Sanchez on purpose."

Greg released his grip on Jeff's neck. He stepped back and looked at his hands, almost as if shocked at what he had just done, and Jeff quickly jumped from his seat to avoid a possible repeat of the act of aggression, alternately rubbing his eyes and his sore neck with his hands as he glared at Greg. The elder cousin retreated to the far corner of the room, and began to fidget silently with the curtain rod. His voice barely distinguishable as he peered out from behind the curtain, as he calmly asked, "Is that all that you wanted to know?"

"Yes," cried Jeff, "that is all that I wanted to know. Well, now I also want to know why you are so afraid to tell me. I just want to know the truth. I didn't come here to get abused, either verbally or physically."

"I know that, Jeff, and I am sorry," Greg answered, his voice barely above a whisper and sounding, at least to Jeff, apologetic. "I don't know what came over me. I think it was just all of the emotions coming out at once. But what does it matter, anyway?" Greg moved to his right and sat on the bed, burying his head in his hands as he continued to talk, his voice now taking on a decidedly sadder tone. "They're flying me back to Milwaukee tomorrow. The press is going to be told that it is for my protection, that I need some rest after the unfortunate incident."

"But they said that it was an accident," Jeff said, a slightly lilt in his voice making his statement sound more like a question, "and that they would not be doing any more investigating."

"That's just what they said," Greg answered, lifting his head to reveal reddened eyes and a single tear floating downward from his left eye. "But it may be over for me. We had a little meeting with the owner today, and he told me that they're sending me home. They know about my drug problem. It's been a terrible fucking year, and now they know. Garver's known for a while, but this was just the final straw for management. They told me a while ago that I was one mistake from the end. And this may be the mistake."

"What about Garver? What did he say?"

"Garver tried to talk him into letting me stick around, but he said that management had already made its decision. They don't even know if I did it intentionally, but that doesn't even matter. Between the allegations over that fucking pitcher in Baltimore and this, they said that there's too much circumstantial shit to keep me here. The mere fact that I was involved in some more shit may be enough for them to bounce me." He looked up at Jeff. "What if they do? What am I going to do then? My whole life is baseball." He looked away, and then began to sob.

Jeff moved toward his cousin, the pain in his neck beginning to vanish. "Look, Greg," he said, placing his right arm around his older cousin as he sat down on the bed, "it will all work out. They won't fire you for this. It won't look good for them. And if you go back to Milwaukee and take it like a man, I'd be willing to bet they won't let you go. You're still too popular with the fans."

"Even with this shit?" Greg asked, wistfully.

"You know it. Drug user or not, you're still a hero for the little guy, the person who's had to work hard for everything in his life, a blue-collar guy. You're like a folk hero there, a rock star. You know that." He placed his hand on his cousin's shoulder for reassurance. "And don't worry, Greg, this conversation doesn't leave the room, so you're safe with me."

For once, Greg was looking to Jeff for comfort, and Jeff was delivering as best as he could. Greg wiped the tears from his face and stood, walking to the bathroom. He rinsed his face with cold water and returned to where Jeff was sitting, careful to avoid the tiny pieces of glass that still littered the carpet in front of the bed. "There's just one thing, Jeff, I won't be able to do any more stuff for you about your league. I've got to straighten myself out, and I can't take any more stupid chances. If you need a tip, that's alright. But that's it, nothing more."

Now it was Jeff's turn to be alarmed, and his concerned tone quickly turned to controlled anger, betraying a selfish turn of events in the cousins' conversation. "But I'm so close, man," he protested. "Let's see how things develop. Maybe I won't need any help, but maybe I will," he said, forcefully. "And if you want your money, don't forget, I have to win to get my money first."

The shift in Jeff's demeanor, and especially in his voice, did not go unnoticed. "You've got to be fuckin' kidding me," said Greg. "You just sat here and told me that everything would be fine, and now you're telling me that you may want me to put my ass on the line again so that you'll win the league. The fantasy league! Let me make this clear so that maybe you even understand it – you want me to risk my life in the *real* league so that you can win the *fantasy* league!" He raised his voice again, this time shaking his head while pointing at the side of his head with his right index finger. "You must be out of your fuckin' mind."

Jeff slammed his hand on the edge of the bed. "Hey, cousin, you better get your facts straight," he said, pointing his own right index finger at Greg, "you didn't do shit to Sanchez for me. Whatever you did out there today was for you and you alone. You went out there and hurt your own player due to your own petty jealousy, not to help me. And if you don't play ball with me, people may hear about some stuff."

"Hey, keep your voice down, man," Greg said quietly as he reached out for his cousin's arm, suddenly realizing that there was someone perched directly outside of the room, "the guard outside may hear what you're saying if you keep yelling." He paused, as Jeff's words sank deeper into his brain. "Wait a minute. Did you just threaten me? Who the fuck did you think you are, and who the fuck do you think you're dealing with? Don't fucking threaten me, Jeffy!"

Jeff looked up at his cousin, realizing the harshness of his comments and less-than-veiled threat, and apologized. He lowered his voice so that what he said would not be overheard. "You're right, I shouldn't have threatened you. And the fact that I may have benefitted is a justification. Maybe it's just an excuse. But either way, the fact is that you did it for you. The player got hurt because you can't deal with the fact that he's better than you, and that you can't play the game anymore. Sound right to you? Does that sound like an accurate description of the events?" Greg stood silently. "I thought as much," added Jeff, as he turned and walked to the door. "I'll be in touch. And do yourself a favor. Lay off of the coke, man, you're beginning to have some wild delusions. You'd think that you would quit the stuff after the shit that it's gotten you into lately." He paused, and then added, coldly, "If you don't want to fucking die, then stop doing the shit. Seems pretty easy to me." As he closed the door behind him, he could hear the sound of vodka being poured into a glass on the bar.

He also heard his cousin's pitiful voice, repeating the same words again and again. "What did I do? I just promised that I was going to get better. I totally fucked up again."

CHAPTER 21

The Brewers lost their last game to the Yankees, and then dropped three of four to Toronto. They were outscored over the five-game stretch by a 44-13 margin. Their performance had been lackluster since Lefty Grant's brilliant pitching performance over the Yankees, and even Grant was lit up for seven runs in only three innings against the Blue Jays. The team returned home to Milwaukee following the disastrous interleague road trip mired in fourth place, only one game out of the cellar. If was the furthest that they had been from first place all season.

Greg had flown to Milwaukee on Sunday morning, his plane touching down moments prior to the start of the Brewers-Yankees game. Several members of the media were gathered at the airport in an attempt to speak to him, but team officials had him deplane on the runway to avoid him having to answer any questions. A car was waiting next to the plane, and he was immediately driven, unbeknownst to writers and reporters, to Miller Park for a meeting with team officials.

Mike Tanney, speaking on behalf of the Brewers' owners, reiterated what had been said to Greg by another of the team owners during his meeting with Matt Garver, informing Greg that the team's administration was greatly concerned about the negative publicity that was being generated by the prior day's incident. The team, he said, had already been through a tremendous amount of pressure during the year, due in large part to injuries to some key players and then, more importantly, Mike Jones' death.

In order to ease this pressure and in an attempt to keep the incident from remaining in the news, however, no official sanctions would be levied against Greg for his role in Sanchez's injury. In what amounted to music to his ears, Greg was informed that he would rejoin the team when it returned home from Toronto, and resume his regular duties as infielders' coach.

After the meeting, Tanney pulled Greg aside to speak to him. "Greg, I've known you for several years," he began. "And, the other guys told me what happened before I was even here, when the team first acquired you from the Red Sox. You may not have ever heard about this, but Boston didn't want to part with you in the deal. They offered some other people, but the brass had heard good things about you and thought that you had both the work ethic and potential to be a fine major leaguer, so they insisted on you being included in the deal." He paused, and looked over Greg's shoulder. "In the spirit of complete disclosure, they also heard the rumors about your substance use, but had confidence that you had enough drive and common sense to put your best effort forward."

Greg cleared his throat and started to say thank you, but was quickly quieted.

"And you did. You busted your tail, and did make it to the big club, until you got hurt. That effort is also what earned you your coaching job with this team, and has kept it until now." He pointed to Greg's head, and then to his chest. "Now is the perfect time for you to use that common sense and internal drive again to overcome. As an organization, we want to put this incident, actually this entire season, behind us. I would suggest that you try to do the same. Make us proud. No more coke. That's the main thing. Stop doing the drugs, and buckle down on being a model citizen and coach. The fans love you; and we love having you here as long as you're not a threat to yourself or others. Simply put, we're behind you as long as you don't do anything to embarrass us or cause us any reason to doubt that you are putting forth your best effort."

He patted Greg on the shoulder and then shook his hand. Greg thanked the team owner for his support, and then slowly walked to the locker room. He walked over to the middle of the lockers on the east wall of the room, and sat down at the locker belonging to the team's starting shortstop. He remained, seated on the stool in front of Juan Sanchez's locker, and wept.

When the Brewers opened their home stand that Friday night against the Colorado Rockies, Greg was in the dugout with the rest of the coaches. That day was the first time that he had spoken to any of the others since he had left Yankee Stadium the previous Saturday, and each of the coaches told him that they were glad to have him back on the bench. Manager Matt Garver did the same, as did some of the players, some of whom had spent time with Greg either with the Brewers or in the minor leagues.

The members of the Milwaukee media were likewise gracious to Greg, allowing him to mentally prepare for the game without the hassle of having to answer questions about the incident and about his meeting with team management, a few details of which had been leaked to the press after it occurred. The official statement issued by the team was that Greg had been flown back to Wisconsin immediately following the incident so that he could meet with team officials and provide his account of what had transpired, rather than wait until the entire team returned from its road trip. In this way, the incident and any inquiry into same were resolved before the team returned, and with little, if any, distraction to the team. The team also announced that a similar meeting was conducted with Juan Sanchez, and that his account also cleared Greg of any wrongdoing. Greg did not know if Sanchez had even met with the team ownership, but was so thankful for the chance to rejoin the team that he never even sought to determine whether or not such a meeting had actually taken place.

The only group that had an adverse reaction to Greg was a small cluster of fans. When he first emerged from the dugout during pre-game warm-ups, many of the fans already in attendance cheered lustily. Embarrassed, he tipped his cap and strode back into the dugout. As he stepped on the top dugout step, a small contingent of fans seated behind the Brewers' bench began to jeer, with some holding up photographs of Juan Sanchez.

One fan even held a hand-made sign that read "Bloom is out for Blood -- fire the coach." Members of the stadium security force quickly confiscated the sign, however, and Greg was not even aware of its presence until he was told about it later.

The previous day, doctors had performed the last of a battery of tests on Juan Sanchez's leg. Their findings had confirmed the team's worst hopes -- he had suffered a torn right medial meniscus as well as a torn right anterior cruciate ligament. He would have to undergo reconstructive knee surgery, and would not be available until at least the beginning of the next season. It was possible that he would be shelved even longer, but doctors did not want to speculate at this early juncture as to when Sanchez could return to playing full-time.

The players were all notified of the severity of Sanchez's injuries prior to the Colorado game, but their spirits were lifted when he appeared in the clubhouse only minutes before his teammates were to take the field. He sat on the bench for seven innings, and received a standing ovation from the home crowd when his presence was acknowledged by the public address announcer after the playing of the Star Spangled Banner. As the crowd cheered, he walked, with crutches, over to the other side of the dugout. There, he and Greg shook hands to the obvious approval of the roaring crowd.

That evening's sports report noted the truce between Sanchez and Bloom along with their coverage of the game that followed; a 4-2 Milwaukee victory. As if spurred on by the dugout handshake, the Brewers jumped out to an early 3-0 lead, adding an insurance run in the seventh before the Blue Jays cut the lead in half on a ninth-inning home run by Ramon Munoz. One out later, however, victory belonged to the Brewers, and they entered the clubhouse after the game to find a message on the blackboard in their dressing room – *"Knock 'em dead, guys. I'm with you."* In the lower corner of the board, Sanchez had scrawled his signature, along with the words *"onward and upward -- 1st place."*

CHAPTER 22

Jeff watched the highlights of the game that evening, along with the film of his cousin shaking hands with the man whom he had intentionally injured only days earlier. He had read the prognosis for Sanchez's knee on the internet that afternoon, and had been surprised to see Sanchez speaking to Greg, much less sitting on the bench after receiving such dismal news. Perhaps, Jeff thought, Sanchez was as much of a "team player" as Lefty Grove, and that he was simply putting the interests of the team ahead of his own.

As the clock on Jeff's nightstand changed to 11:30, his phone rang. He answered, and was surprised to hear Greg's voice on the other end of the line. "Jeff, did you see the sports news tonight? It looks like things are going to work out alright."

Jeff turned off the television, and dropped the remote control on the bed in front of him. "I'm glad. Especially after the shit you told me you were afraid of last week. Did they do anything to you?"

"When I got to Milwaukee, I went right to the stadium. I met with some people, including Tanney."

"You mean the team's owner?" Jeff asked, excitedly.

"The one and only," Greg answered, in as excited a voice as Jeff's. "It was the first time he ever spoke to me."

"And you met with him on Sunday?"

"Yeah," said Greg. "Now this part is between me and you, right?"

"Of course."

"Well," explained Greg, "they told me that they were worried about publicity and all of that, so that they weren't going to take any action against me. As you could see, I was back with the team already. As far as they are concerned, I think the whole thing is past history. If I keep myself clean, that is. He actually mentioned the coke thing and told me that I had to stop using if I wanted to stay with the team. So I have to quit. This time I have to quit for real." He paused. Jeff could hear Greg's voice breaking on the other end of the line. "I'll tell you, I really lucked out."

"That's great, Greg," answered Jeff. "I mean, you're really lucky. That was a potentially dangerous situation that you put yourself in. You've got to be careful -- to do stuff on an open field when people are around is just asking for trouble."

"I know, and believe me, it won't happen again," Greg promised. "Besides, I've decided that I'm going to kick the coke thing on my own. I haven't had any since last Friday night, the night before the incident. To be honest with you, I was scared shit to do anything after what happened, but then a couple of days passed and I realized that, maybe, I can do this. That means it's been a week. I think that's the longest that I've gone without the stuff in about five years." He paused and coughed a hacking cough which resembled that of a long-time smoker. "Yes, it may be the longest in years. And it's not easy. I don't care how people will tell you that kicking an addiction is simple. It's been hell these last few days, but it's a hell that I am more than willing to endure."

"A whole week?" Jeff asked. "That is great news. What brought this on? Is it really the fear of losing your job? Or was it something else?"

"Actually, this may seem surprising to you, but it was support from the owners. Originally, it was fear. But then Tanney pulled me aside after our

249

meeting and gave me a little pep talk, about how I had been such a hard worker when I was a player and that is how I got places. He showed confidence in me, Jeff; he told me that the team will stand behind me as long as I don't fuck up."

"That was nice of him," Jeff replied. "He didn't have to do that."

"You're telling me. And I've got to prove to them that it's not a mistake. I'm laying off of the coke, and trying to reduce the alcohol also." Greg paused, allowing the words to sink into his own mind for a couple of seconds. "That one will be a little tougher, but I'm going to stick to a drink or two at a time instead of getting drunk every night. Maybe someday I'll be able to cut it out altogether." His voice rose. "It's a new day, cuz. I'm trying to make the most of it."

"I'm really glad to hear you sounding so upbeat," Jeff replied. "It's quite a refreshing change from the way that you've been lately Just don't become a total recovering alcoholic guy and start telling me to stop drinking, because then I'd have to kick your ass."

"I have no need to preach to you, but I will tell you that you can't live in the past, sport." Despite what he had just said, Greg was clearly preaching to, or at, Jeff. Both of them knew it. "You can't sit around and think about what was. That's what I was doing. I was feeling sorry for myself because of the shoulder problem and the fact that I was never as good as the guys that play today. And it wasn't healthy for me, especially when I began to drop deeper and deeper into the coke and drink."

"It's like when I think about the way that I fucked things up with Michelle," added Jeff. "I'll tell you man, it drives me crazy."

"Then you've got to do something about it," urged Greg.

250

"And what do you expect me to do, Mr. Evangelist?"

"Pick up the phone and call her. You guys had way too much invested in each other to give it up so easily. Anything that is bothering her can be fixed, and vice versa. A little give and take is what you need," explained Greg. "I could never do it, and that's why I'm still a bachelor at my age. But you're different. So is she. I only met her a couple of times, but she definitely seemed like she was something special, at least that's what I heard from everyone else. See what you can do about getting her back. I noticed she wasn't at the game with you."

Jeff's tone hardened. "You're right. She wouldn't return my call to say if she would meet me at the game. But I'll call her tomorrow, if I can get the nerve up. It's been a couple of months now, and that's so long that I don't even know what to say to her."

Now it was Greg's turn to support and cheer on his cousin's efforts. "You'll think of something, and I am certain that you will be somewhat intelligent and keep the baseball talk with her to a minimum," Greg insisted. "Hey, before I forget," he added, "speaking of baseball, how's the fantasy baseball league going now that you're doing it without my own special brand of help?"

"Pretty good, I guess. I'm on the verge of second place, but there isn't much time left in the season. It's almost the end of August, and the trading deadline is September 1." He paused. "I know what you've been saying, and I do respect your concerns, but I think that I may need your help once or twice more before all is said and done." He paused and tried to ease any fears that might develop. "Nothing too rough, though, don't worry about that. I'm not going to get you into trouble."

"We'll talk about it later, then," answered Greg, in a calm voice. "Now, the answer is no. I'm trying to straighten things out, and don't want to do anything to put it into jeopardy. The team is really looking over my shoulder now. I can't get my name even suggested as being involved in something right now." He paused, and then hedged on his comments a bit. "But give me a call in a couple of weeks. I'm not saying that my answer won't change, but I can't make any promises."

Jeff's mind was awhirl with fears of moving forward without Greg's help, and his subsequent tone turned to one of scolding, as he feared that his chances of winning the league were slipping away with Greg's words. He hoped that his words, contrived to cut at Greg's psyche, would sink in deeper. "I certainly hope that it would. If you're suddenly feeling some crazy sort of loyalty to the team, don't bother. The only one that you need to be loyal to is yourself. And if you're going to be loyal to anyone, then you should be loyal to me. And you know why? I'm family. The team can fire you in an instant, even without a reason. Family is always there."

"I don't know, cousin," replied Greg. "I admit that there's not a lot of real loyalty in sports, and I've heard your speeches about the players having none so don't give it to me now. But what Mr. Tanney said to me last week was something out of the ordinary," Greg explained. "He certainly did not have to speak to me, much less give me the shot in the arm that he did. Especially after he told me that he knew that I was using cocaine. So if I feel loyal to him, you'll have to forgive me." Greg heard Jeff clear his throat in an attempt to cut him off, but kept on talking so that he could finish his point. "Listen, for the first time in a very long time, somebody showed concern for me that made me want to do something for myself. You don't hear that very often, and I at least owe the man something for that."

"I don't want to belabor this point," Jeff answered, thinking quickly about how to diffuse Tanney's comments, and quickly, in his mind, thinking angrily back to how Bob Linder, when confronted with a similar situation, fired him rather than give him a similar second chance. "But do remember one more thing. At least part of what he did, quite possibly the largest part, was aimed at the good of his team. You told me that he told you of his concern for the team and any possible negative publicity that could come out of any disciplinary action being taken against you."

"So?" asked Greg.

"Well, it's obvious that the reason that nothing was done to you was because of the press, and not due to his concern or loyalty to you. That's the first thing." He stopped to catch his breath, believing that Greg was buying into his own self-serving comments and wondering why he did not feel any guilt feeding his cousin information that could undercut his efforts at healing and self-improvement. "And second, his little pep talk was also along the same lines -- if you do your job well, the team doesn't suffer. If the team doesn't suffer, then he doesn't because his investment is being protected. You have to remember to look at the big picture."

"Look at the big picture?" Greg responded, condescendingly, even as he wondered to himself whether Jeff was correct and if the owner was only looking out for the team, rather than for him. "What a cliché."

"I know it is," Jeff admitted. "But for all of the thoughts that the owners have about you, I would bet that their concern for the Brewers and for their monetary investment is hundreds of times greater. And that is the big picture. Sure he cares a little about you, and he should." Now Jeff's tone turned condescending. "But here's the reality, Greg, and you already know this so it's nothing new to you. You're really nothing more than a piece of property to him. If he saw you on the street, he probably wouldn't even recognize you."

"That's not true," Greg protested.

"Maybe after your meeting it isn't. But walk past him in the street three months or a year from now, and he won't give you the time of day. I don't want to hurt your feelings," he added, even though that was his direct intention at that time in order to get Greg to agree to help him again in the future. "I know that your chat with him meant a great deal to you. But I just hate to see you get disillusioned about his priorities, especially when it may unduly influence yours. His concerns are aimed at his well-being. Yours should be at your well being."

Greg's voice began to break. "But my interests are for my well-being, as a member of the team's coaching staff. It's all I know how to do, Jeff. And he told me that the team was behind me on this one."

"I understand that he told you that," Jeff answered, his tone growing more condescending with each sentence. "But how supportive do you think that he would be if he found out about that you were the person who killed Mike Jones; that you were the person who hurt his team by taking away its new prized rookie, something that he undoubtedly felt directly in his wallet? Didn't he tell you that one of the biggest problems for the team this year was, not surprisingly, Jones' death? If you told him that you had killed him, or contributed to his death, do you think that your friendly owner would pat you on the back and tell you that it was alright, that he understood what had happened, and that the team was 100% behind you? Let's be a little realistic. I certainly don't think that would be the case."

"But he won't find out about it," croaked Greg.

"This is true. Neither of us intends to tell him about it and, if you are correct, then nobody else even knows about what happened in Jones' apartment that night, so there is no way that it will come to that. But it serves to prove my point. His concerns are for his personal benefit. He's the owner of a corporation. As always, the big guy is going to take advantage of the little guy, Greg. And here, you're the little guy. He states that his concern is for the team because when the team profits and makes money, then he profits and makes money. Not that I'm condemning him, to be honest with you, but if he profits, he's concerned about it. If the team is going to suffer, he wants to bury it under the carpet. That's what he's done here."

"You're oversimplifying," Greg interjected. "They could have simply fired me or suspended me and not said why. Clearly they care about me. You're oversimplifying the entire situation."

"Am I?" replied Jeff. "I don't think so. And since his concerns are geared toward his well-being, then your concerns should be aimed at your well-being. The owners, including him, want to suppress the players and the coaches, make them do what they want done. They cry poverty all of the time and how big salaries are ruining them, but they continue to raise prices and live high off the hog."

"So what you're saying is that not only are players disloyal, but the owners are too?" questioned Greg, "but what about the fans? What about you, Mr. Fantasy League?"

"Well, how do you expect fans to react to this shit? Of course I am, I mean, of course they're cynical about the whole thing. Can you blame them, or blame me? And as far as the fantasy league, it's just an outgrowth of that discontent." His voice reached a fevered pitch as the words came faster and faster. "You can call it selfish if you want, but that's the way everybody connected with the game behaves. Call it a justification, but it's true." He paused, took a deep breath, and then continued as his voice lowered to a more reasonable level. "That's why family and friends are so important, so that the cynics among us have someone, something, that they can depend on. That's why we have to stick together."

"And, pray tell," Greg pondered, "how does your baseball league come into that equation?"

Jeff thought for a few seconds, and then slowly began to give his reason. "The league is important, first of all, because it means money. If my team wins the league, I win 150 thousand dollars. 150 thousand dollars! Of that total, you will get 35 thousand, like we agreed. That amount of money should be enough. But on top of that, your concern should be with your family and their well-being. Family is always there, like I said before. And you know that I lost my job. My severance is running out. I need the money. So for my benefit, not just for yours, you should help me win. That's how the league is involved."

"I hear you, cousin," replied Greg excitedly. "But if you stop your little diatribe for a second, you should think about this basic point. I worked all my life toward a goal. That goal was to play baseball. And I can't do it now. But what I can do is be a coach, and maybe become a manager in the future. That is my job. And it's a job that I'd like to keep." He paused, and then began to speak in a calmer voice. "I'm not going to sacrifice my life so that we can both gain a little profit. Perhaps your energies should be devoted to finding a job of your own, one that you can work at not only to earn money, but also to gain some form of satisfaction. That's the part of my life that I'm trying to regain, and I would suggest that you do the same. I'll talk to you next week."

Jeff started to respond, but it was too late. Before he could answer, he heard a click on the other end, followed several seconds later by a dial tone. He thought briefly about what Greg had said about loyalty to oneself and about achieving personal satisfaction. He understood. In fact, he understood clearly, or so he thought. That was what he was trying to do with the league -- he was seeking to obtain the personal satisfaction of winning. He was consumed, obsessed, with winning the league. The money that he would win, he reasoned, wasn't really the primary motivation. Instead, once the satisfaction was gained, the money would inevitably follow.

His other motivation was to get back together with Michelle. He thought of heeding his cousin's advice and picking up the phone to call her, but he could not bring himself to do it. His fear of rejection, that she would dismiss him again, possibly for the last time, haunted his conscience. "I figured that time would make it easier to call her," he thought to himself, "but instead it makes me grow more and more afraid of the possibility that I'll screw things up again and that there won't be a next time." He would be better off waiting until after the baseball season, he reasoned, to reach out and try to patch things up. The baseball league was a prime factor in their split. Surely he could not seek to reconcile with her until the distraction of baseball had been removed, as if it could ever be totally removed. He wanted to commit to her, but knew that he would be unable to commit to her one hundred percent while there were still games to watch and players to root for and against.

Also, such reconciliation was not that far in the future, as the baseball season was winding down. There were only five weeks left, and the Emerson Boozers were still in first place. Jeff reached for the standings sheet, which showed the Golds in a tie for second.

257

The printout from August 20 read as follows:

1) The Emerson Boozers	58
T2) The Jew Crew	53
T2) Golddiggers	53
4) Frantastics	50
5) Bobby Fish and the Fins	49
T6) Bayonne Bombers	43
T6) Hang 'em Hy	43
8) Bergermeister-Meisterbergers	36
9) Martinizers	32
10) Brians and Brawn	23

He reached for the newspaper, and scanned the television section to see if any games were being broadcast late that evening. He was pleased to discover that the sports station was broadcasting that night's Braves-Dodgers game, which had begun 20 minutes earlier. Turning the television back on, he walked into the kitchen and took a beer from the refrigerator. Returning to his bedroom, he sat on the edge of his bed and stacked three pillows against the headboard. He leaned back against the pillows, and began to drink as the bottom of the second inning commenced. The Braves were leading the visiting Dodgers by one run. The last inning that Jeff could recall watching when he awoke the next morning was the sixth, but he could not remember the score or which team was ahead at the time.

CHAPTER 23

"Real is not Dreams, Dreams are not Real, unless you find the fine line ... and erase it."

- C. Elizabeth, <u>Absolute Obsession</u>

The shining sun glinted off of the stadium seats, and bathed the decaying buildings beyond the outfield in an angelic light. The stark white frieze hung over the center field seats, its brightness seemingly powered by electricity. The white horsehide glowed as it was tossed around in the afternoon sky, and the outfielders were forced to shield their eyes in order to see any balls hit their way. It was the bottom of the ninth inning, there were two outs showing on the massive center field scoreboard. The home team was on the short end of a 4-2 score. The Emerson Boozers, having jumped out to an early 3-1 lead, were now one out away from defeating the home Golds and taking home the league championship. There were two men on base, and the manager of the hitting team was facing a crucial decision regarding who would be the next person, and possibly the last person, to step into the batter's box.

In the home team's dugout, manager Jeff Goldstein nervously paced. At the same time, the runners at second and third bases each paced in their own little circles, anxiously awaiting their opportunity to score what would be the tying runs. The player whose turn it was to bat, Pete Nicks, was slowly making his way to the plate, reluctantly marching to what would either turn out to be his chance at being a hero, or failure which would haunt him for the foreseeable future. To his relief, however, he only reached half-way to the batter's box before he was waved back to the dugout by Goldstein.

The manager decided that the team's fortunes would rise or fall on his shoulders, not on the back of a second-year, inexperienced kid, and he would be the one chosen to play the role of either hero or goat. He grabbed a bat from the dugout rack and bounded onto the field, taking several practice cuts as he walked to the batter's box. "Now batting for Nicks," boomed the field announcer, "the player-manager of the Golds, number 48, Jeff Goldstein, number 48." The wide number 48 sparkled on the back of the pinch-hitter's pinstriped uniform as he strode to the plate.

As he looked to the crowd jamming the seats on the first base side, he could see a familiar face, his beloved girlfriend, Michelle, standing in the aisle, her long brown hair gently blowing in the breeze as she mouthed the words "I love you." Dressed in a white sweater and navy blue shorts, both of which served to accent her body's curves, she puckered her full, red lips and blew Jeff a series of kisses as he took his swings, measuring, in his head, the timing of how he would need to strike in order to make the game-winning hit. Laughing, Michelle ran her left hand through her flowing tresses, and Jeff was blinded by a flash of light -- the sparkle of the sun reflecting in the two-carat diamond engagement ring that encircled her finger created two light beams, rays of light which represented an omen of the at-bat to come, one that flowed to the batter's box and one that pointed directly to the left field stands.

The pitcher threw two pitches to Goldstein, a ball and a strike, neither of which was good enough to cause the batter to take the bat off of his shoulder. The crowd noise reached a fevered pitch as the hurler prepared for his third offering. Mel Allen described the action for his enrapt television audience. "Williams checks the runners, rocks, and delivers the ball plateward." The hitter's eyes, focused intently on the approaching spheroid, widened as the white ball with the red laces grew larger and larger as it approached. The batter grabbed the 33 ounce stick tightly, and whipped it around in a fluid semi-circle as the ball entered his reach. The sound of the projectile colliding with the polished ash reverberated high into the stands, and the ball rocketed skyward, eventually ending its flight in the outstretched arms of a young boy seated in the left field bleachers, inches to the right of where the light from Michelle's ring had reached only seconds before.

In the broadcast booth, a speechless Allen leapt from his seat. His partner, Russ Hodges, thrust off his headset, yelling again and again that the Golds had won the championship. While bedlam erupted in the stands, the manager circled the bases triumphantly and deliberately, his arm thrust triumphantly skyward, and stomped his right foot solidly on each of the three bases as he passed over them. As he touched home plate, an adoring crowd of players and fans alike was there to greet him. Before he touched home plate, however, he paused and looked back over his right shoulder at the center field scoreboard. The lights now, presumptuously but correctly, reflected the Golds having won the game by a 5-4 score.

He touched home plate amidst the gathering of players and fans, and ran directly to the left side of the first base dugout, reaching up with his right hand and squeezing Michelle's left hand. Two members of the stadium's security force lifted Michelle by her waist and lowered her into Jeff's arms, her arms and legs wrapping tightly around his uniform. As he gazed into her eyes, she lowered her mouth to his right ear and whispered that she loved him, and that she never wanted the two of them to be apart.

They were briefly torn apart when two of the players lifted Jeff on their shoulders in celebration, but Michelle soon joined him as two of the other uniformed figures grabbed her by her shapely legs and sat her atop their shoulders. The four support men moved closer so that Jeff and Michelle could grab each other's hands, and the two leaned over and kissed as fireworks exploded in the distance beyond the center field scoreboard.

CHAPTER 24

Jeff thought back to when he and Michelle first moved to New York following graduation. She had previously visited the city with him, but she had never lived in any city, much less a city with eight million inhabitants. She had grown up in a suburb of Lancaster, Pennsylvania, nestled in the heart of Pennsylvania Amish country, and had spent two years attending school in upstate New York before returning to Lancaster to attend Franklin and Marshall College. And although Lancaster, adjoining the school, was a city, she had spent her two years at F&M living in the cloistered environment of a dormitory. Moving to an apartment on the West Side of Manhattan (the biggest city she had ever seen) was therefore a tremendous step for her, but the allure of living with Jeff was strong enough for her to take her chances there.

Finding a job was easier than expected. One of her math professors at F&M was friendly with a major donor to a Upper West Side private elementary school, and one phone call, coupled with Michelle dazzling the administration at her one and only interview, proved to be a potent combination as she was offered a position on the spot. The school was a scant ten blocks from their apartment, and the Upper West Side was packed with exciting restaurants and places for two young college graduates to visit. Midtown was a subway ride away, and they were walking distance from the Museum of Natural History. The more cultural museums were a brisk walk or cab ride to the other side of Manhattan, and she spent her initial days in New York plotting how to take in all of the culture as quickly as possible.

Jeff, however, was not what she would consider to be a willing participant. He would accompany her on occasion to a museum or Broadway show, but more often than not he wanted to either stay in the apartment and watch some sporting event or just go to one of the local bars with friends and watch games there. Several of his friends from high school had relocated to the city from his hometown in New Jersey, and another group of friends from F&M also resided in or around the city. Jeff's support system of local friends, it seemed to her, was endless. On the other hand, she had few close friends nearby, and her efforts at making friends with her co-workers were often stymied by Jeff's refusal to go out and see these people in social situations.

The obvious differences in their interests began to wear on Michelle as she approached her three-year anniversary at work, and the benchmark only intensified her desire to enjoy what she considered to be the New York "experience". All of her friends from other places would tell her how jealous they were of her for living in Manhattan, and asked about what it was like to enjoy its amenities. She would often lie to them because she was ashamed of the fact that she and Jeff took advantage of so few of the city's cultural offerings. She wanted an experience that went beyond merely watching baseball games. What started as little fights between her and Jeff as to their activities and interests began to escalate as a result, and soon she was sleeping on the apartment's couch.

When the animosity became too difficult for her to bear, she moved from the apartment to her own place, located ten blocks south.

After she moved out the tensions eased, and they began to attempt to re-kindle their romance. Now, Jeff was more receptive to attending plays and going to museums, but Michelle could not help but notice how often he would check his cell phone for scores of whatever games were taking place while they were walking the halls of the Guggenheim or other museums. Usually these times would just be met with a disapproving stare, but at times her temper would flare and an argument would result. Jeff would always apologize and say that he would not check the scores again, but then his bathroom breaks became more frequent or his need to go back and again look at an exhibit, while he urged Michelle to move forward to the next room, would also increase. She was also hurt that he thought so little of her - he clearly believed that she would not be able to figure out his score-checking ruses, which was also another reason for her growing discontent in their relationship.

Eventually days would pass without them seeing each other, or even speaking. She thought of dating others, but could not bring herself to spend time with any other man while Jeff was still in her life. Even after their last fight, in the restaurant, she still did not date. She would go out with her friends, especially her co-workers, but she had no need for male companionship at this time.

CHAPTER 25

"To me, baseball was a passion to the point of obsession."

- Brooks Robinson, Baltimore Orioles' Third Baseman, major league baseball Hall of Famer and 18-time All-Star selection

The fantasy league's trading deadline was September 1. When the league first began, the deadline was the all-star game. After that game the only teams that an owner could trade with were those teams directly above or below him in the standings. That rule prevented the weaker teams from having "fire sales" at the end of the season, or so the men thought. Instead, it had the effect of chilling most trade activity, because there was little, if any, impetus for the second-place team to make a trade with the team in front of him during the last two months of the season.

As a result, the trading deadline was extended between all teams. Now, any team could trade with any other until the first of September. While there were some instances of curious deals, those that caused other owners to questions the motivations of the weaker teams involved in those trades, it was a better system with respect to player movement. Besides, a blatantly one-sided trade could result in a reactionary and similar trade between two other teams, as owners chose sides to determine the eventual winner.

It was now August 27, and the trading deadline was less than a week away. If Jeff was going to make a trade before that date, he had to formulate a definitive plan not only of which players to acquire, but also those that were expendable and the best teams to involve in a deal. It was important that he not help his closest competition while bolstering his squad, so the obvious teams with whom to deal were at the bottom of the standings. Unfortunately, his last dealings with Brian Hunter had left him with a bad taste in his mouth, so it was unlikely that he would be cooperative. Better options lay with Gene Hyland,

Mike Berger, and Barry Martin. A glance of those three rosters did not reveal a tremendous amount of talent, however, which Jeff reasoned could help to explain why those teams were at the lower end of the point spectrum.

Several players caught Jeff's eye, though, and he set out in a quest to formulate deals with Gene and Mike for some of their players that would be acceptable on all sides. It was almost noon, so Jeff decided to wait before calling either person, because they would likely be on their lunch hours. While they were at work, Jeff was still home, dressed in shorts and a Yankees t-shirt. He had watched the entire Rangers-A's ballgame from Oakland the night before, and had not gone to sleep until 2:30 AM. One of the advantages to his unemployment was that he was better able to stay awake and watch the late-night West coast games due to his ability to sleep late the next morning. Today, he had rolled out of bed at almost 10:30, quite a far cry from the days when he would wake up, shower, and be out the door before seven to arrive at the Benco office.

As his joblessness dragged on, moreover, his desire to obtain gainful employment waned. Whereas he had been in constant contact with recruiters immediately following his dismissal from Martin & Jerome, now he would call each of the four recruiters once or twice per week at most. He had also become more selective in the positions for which he allowed his name to be submitted. At first he would give authority for his name to be forwarded to any company with an opening, realizing that he would require a paycheck to pay his bills and live like a human being. Once his unemployment checks began, however, he was provided with a steady income, albeit at a level significantly lower than with which he was familiar. And this income would continue for six months.

What the unemployment checks could buy, he reasoned, was time. He felt that he had the time to find the perfect job, even if it took weeks or months for him to find such a place and position. Already he had been out of work for over a month, and the opportunities were decreasing rather than multiplying. He also still had his severance checks coming for another couple of weeks, which meant that he was, for now, bringing home more money than he was while slaving away for an ungrateful employer.

Instead of worrying about the prospect of not working for an extended period of time, therefore, Jeff chose to focus his energies on the baseball league. He was well aware of the fact that the season would be over in little more than a month, and that a $150,000 brass ring lay at the end of the tunnel if he could overtake the Emerson Boozers. Even after giving Greg his $35,000 cut, he would still have a windfall of $100,000 filling his bank account, in addition to not having to pay someone else $15,000 of his own money.

It made perfect sense to him. After all, where could he find a job that would pay him a $100,000 starting bonus? Such a job was clearly beyond the realm of possibility. Winning the league, on the other hand, was well within his grasp. But it would take a little more planning and execution, and the time to undertake such actions was expiring in the next four days. It was a small window of opportunity, one that he would have to exploit as best as possible.

On a yellow pad, he had made two lists of players. The player list to the left was headed "*Ones to Spare*," meaning players that he would be willing to part with in trades with Gene and Mike. The other side of the page was headed "*Ones to Get*," those players whom Jeff sought to acquire from his two friends. The list to the left contained five players whom he would be willing to trade; the one on the right showed twelve, seven from Hyland's team and five from Berger's. Four of the five players from his team were not seeing any playing time with their major league clubs, but were minor-leaguers or reserves, prospects that could pay dividends the following season. In contrast, each of the dozen players sought were starters, whether position players or pitchers. Each was contributing to their respective teams, and Jeff believed that each, or any combination thereof, would have the effect of dramatically improving his team for the stretch run.

The three glasses of orange soda that Jeff had consumed while formulating these trades were beginning to take their toll on his bladder. He walked to the bathroom, newspaper in hand, and sat on the toilet. He closed the door behind him, a habit which he had never broken despite the fact that he lived alone in his apartment. As he settled in and turned to the sports section, he heard the sound of his telephone ringing from the next room. Not wanting to be interrupted, he allowed his answering machine to respond to the call. "What perfect timing," he said aloud, "Who the hell is calling me?"

Five minutes later, he emerged from the bathroom and, walking to the bedroom, pressed the "play" button located on the lower right corner of the answering machine. As the familiar female voice began to speak from the machine, Jeff was unnerved to discover that it was his mother who had called him, especially because she had knowledge of some information that he had been keeping from her. "Hi, Jeffrey, it's your mother. Why didn't you tell us? I just called you at work to invite you down this weekend because your relatives are coming in from California and I thought that you might want to see them. They told me that you didn't work there anymore, and that you haven't been there for over a month. What have you been doing with yourself?" She began to cry. "I can't believe that you lost your job and didn't even have the consideration to tell us. I don't even know what to tell your father. Anyway, I don't know where you are now, but I'm guessing that you're not at a new job or you would have told us what happened. When you get in, give me a call."

Jeff had wondered if he would be able to find a new job before he had to tell his parents about what had occurred at Martin & Jerome. As the weeks dragged on, his concerns waned but he decided not to tell his parents what had happened in a mistaken belief that he could keep the information from them without ramifications. Now he realized that his concerns were moot. He had to make a phone call and confront his mother's wrath. Taking a deep breath, he slowly dialed his parents' phone number. On the third ring, his mother answered.

He decided that he would try to diffuse the situation with humor. "Hi mom, it's me. I guess that my little secret is out, don't you think?"

"That's very funny, Jeffrey," she said, without even the slightest hint of laughter. "Why didn't you tell us? Why did I have to find out from a total stranger that you were fired from one of the best accounting firms in the country?"

"I was going to tell you, honest," Jeff replied. "I was just waiting for the right time."

"And when would that have happened, when you had already found a new job? Or when you ran out of money and had to come to me and your father to support you?"

"Probably the first," Jeff said, chuckling, "that way there would have been no reason for you to be upset."

"Be upset?" she cried, "of course I'm upset. Who wouldn't be if their son was fired? It's not every day that someone loses their job, you know, especially someone as smart as you."

"I know, mom, I'm sorry," replied Jeff, sadly.

"No you're not," his mother shot back. "I was going to ask if you had found another job yet, but I guess not since you called me back so fast."

"No, mom, I haven't yet, and there's no need for you to be so sarcastic," Jeff said, his demeanor turning serious. "It's not like I'm enjoying this."

"Well then why don't you just find another job? Maybe you are enjoying sitting home and doing nothing all day."

"No mom," he answered, "I'm not. It's just that jobs are very tough to find these days. They have been for some time. Do you not read the newspapers or watch the news? It isn't as easy as when dad was working."

"How can you afford to live in Manhattan?" she asked. "Maybe you should think about leaving that apartment and moving back home with us."

"That was just the type of response that I was worried about. I appreciate the offer, but no thanks. There is no way that I'll be moving back in with you guys. I need to be out on my own. And hopefully something will turn up soon. Until then, I got some severance, I'm collecting unemployment and I've saved some money so I'm making do."

"So what happened there?"

He thought about the question for a minute. He couldn't tell her the real reason - he was paying too much attention to baseball. "Well, mom, it's really not that important. I'd rather not talk about it right now, if you don't mind."

"You're damned right I mind," she shot back. "Your father and I didn't put you through four years of college so that you could fritter away a job for no reason. Now tell me, what happened?"

He thought the question to be overly intrusive, but realized that he would have to supply some form of answer to placate his angered mother. "It was just a personality conflict between me and one of the guys above me. I'm sure that it happens all of the time. We just weren't getting along. I was miserable, and I think that I'm better off this way."

"They couldn't transfer you to another audit?"

"No, mom, they didn't. Now let's drop it, alright."

"I said couldn't," said his mother, "not didn't."

"I heard you the first time. Now drop it."

"What am I going to tell your father?"

Becoming more exasperated with each annoying question, Jeff reached his boiling point at his mother's concern for his father's reaction. "Quite frankly, mom, I don't give a shit what you say to him," he barked into the phone. "And I don't care if he's disappointed, if he thinks that I'm a piece of shit for losing my job, or if he's worried that I'll never work again. Do you hear me? I just don't care. Tell you what, I'll save you the trouble and call him myself right now. Is that good enough for you?"

"Don't be upset with me, young man," his mother scolded. "We are entitled to be concerned about you. We're your parents, for God's sake. So curb that fresh mouth. First you break up with Michelle, you spend all of your time with that stupid baseball thing, and now I find out that you lost your job a month ago. And to top it all off, you give me attitude. You seem to be forgetting one very important thing."

"And what is that?"

"You're forgetting about your family."

"What?"

"I said, you're forgetting about your family. That when all else fails, when everyone deserts you, your family is still going to be there. Your friends can leave you, you can change jobs, but you've only got one family. And they'll stick behind you. Now, I expect you to treat me with some respect. I think that I've earned it over these 28 years, and I think that I deserve better."

"Oh, do you?" replied Jeff, ignoring the fact that her mother's speech about the importance of family essentially mirrored the one that he had given to Greg when seeking his help. "Well," he continued, "how about some respect for me. I'll make my own choices and my own mistakes. I don't need for you to point them all out to me. The thing with Michelle had nothing to do with this, and it had nothing at all to do with you. And, tell me, what could you possibly think that the baseball league had to do with all of this?"

"I don't know," she said quietly, "I guess nothing."

"You're damn right," he fired back, although he knew that the reality was that the baseball league had been a key factor, if not the overwhelming reason, for his dismissal. "Look, I'm really sorry for all of this," he said, in a lower and calmer tone of voice. "Let's both of us cool down, and I'll call the house later and tell dad what happened."

"If that's what you want, sweetheart," she said. "It's just that we worry about you. We hate to see bad things happen to you. You can't criticize us for that."

"I guess not, mom. I'll talk to you later."

CHAPTER 26

"We want to follow a dream, yet it's true, but it's one thing to follow a dream and another to follow an obsession ... A dream is more pure than obsession."

- Jose Mourinho, winner, FIFA (international soccer) Best Coach Award

By that evening, Jeff had formulated several potential trades that he could make between his team and either Hang 'em Hy or the Bergermeister-Meisterbergers. He called both Gene Hyland and Mike Berger on their cell phones that evening, but was forced to leave messages for them when neither answered. He also sent text messages to each, but, these were similarly futile as he did not receive a response from either. He dutifully logged on to Facebook to see if there was any activity on the league page, but that page was devoid of any new entries except for a premature "Happy Birthday" post from Joe Spadola to Brian Martin He was, therefore, forced to wait. As the night dragged on, however, he grew impatient and decided to call both Gene and Mike at home. As was the case with their cell phones, however, neither answered and he was forced to leave messages on their answering machines.

Neither Gene nor Mike returned Jeff's calls that evening. As he continued to watch that evening's highlights on the Baseball Network, Jeff realized that several of the key members of his team had fallen into minor slumps as the season dragged to a close. Moreover, one of his best hitters, Seattle's Jeff Matthews, was seeing decreased playing time as the Mariners' manager, with his team far out of the playoff chase, was providing increased on-the-job training for his younger players.

273

Now a trade seemed infinitely more necessary. When the show went to commercial, Jeff reached for the phone and dialed Mike Berger's cell number for the third time that day. Along with the sound of the ring, he heard a beeping sound, which indicated to him that Mike was already speaking with someone else and was ignoring his call – but at least Mike had his phone and, hopefully, could talk when he was done with that call. He decided not to leave a message, knowing that Mike would see the "missed call" indication on the phone, and instead attempted to call again five minutes later. As had happened earlier, however, the phone rang twice before the call went to Mike's voice mail. Puzzled by the fact that the line had been busy only five minutes earlier, Jeff decided that he would reach out to Mike at his office the next day.

Efforts at reaching Mike the next day were just as futile. He did not answer his cell phone or a text message sent that morning. Then, Jeff called Mike's office, and spoke at length with his secretary but was unable to speak with him directly. According to the secretary, Mike was in a conference all morning and then was out of the office for another conference during the afternoon. While Jeff politely left four messages with the secretary that afternoon, he began to wonder if she was telling him the truth, or if Mike was avoiding him for some unexplained reason.

Jeff could not locate Gene Hyland's telephone number at work, so he was forced to wait until that evening to try and work out the details of what he believed would be an almost certain trade between the two. He also did not want to bother Gene at work, lest he have similar problems to his efforts at speaking with Mike Berger. At 7:00, he dialed Gene's cell phone but there was no answer. He then dialed Gene's home number and spoke to his wife, Ashley. She informed Jeff that Gene would not be home for the entire evening and that she would tell Gene to return his call the following day. Before Jeff could thank her, she added that she would appreciate him not calling again, that three phone calls over the past two evenings were more than sufficient. He apologized profusely, and attempted to explain the urgency of why he needed to speak to Gene.

"It's important that I speak to him before the end of this month," he told Ashley Hyland, "because we need to make a trade in our baseball league and the deadline for making trades is September first." There was a clicking noise on the other end of the phone, signaling Mrs. Hyland's call waiting. She told Jeff that she had to answer the other call and that while she couldn't care less about whether Jeff and Gene made a baseball trade, that she would relay the message to her husband. She then hung up on Jeff before he could respond.

Two more messages left on Mike Berger's cell phone that evening went unanswered. Jeff furiously searched his standings and the team rosters to devise trades with other league members. Despite the fact that he had not spoken to Brian Hunter in some time, he decided that he would try to speak to Brian about trading for one of his pitchers. He also had another excuse for calling, he realized, as Brian's birthday was the following day and he could say that he wanted to be one of the first to wish him a happy one; second, at least, to Spadola after his Facebook post. He decided that the best way to reach Brian would be on his home telephone. After the third ring, he heard a click on the other end of the line, followed by the unmistakable southern drawl of Diane Hunter. "Hi, Diane, it's Jeff Goldstein. Is Brian around?"

"He's here, Jeff, but I think that he's in the bathroom. Hang on for a second." Jeff could hear muffled sounds from the other end of the telephone line, and assumed that Diane had covered the mouthpiece of the phone with her hand. Jeff thought that he heard Diane and Brian talking in the background. While the voices were almost imperceptible, Jeff believed that Diane's last words were that she didn't want to talk to him, and that Brian would have to handle the situation himself. Jeff was unaware of the situation that Diane was talking about, unless she was referring to what had occurred weeks ago or something with Michelle.

Finally, Brian took the phone from his wife's hand. "Jeff, long time no speak," he said to Jeff, "what do you want?"

"Well, it's almost trading deadline time, and have I got a trade for you. How about . . ."

Brian interrupted Jeff in mid-sentence. "I don't think that I want to make a trade right now."

"Well, shouldn't you wait until I tell you who?" Jeff pleaded.

"No," Brian answered quickly, "Listen to me carefully so I don't have to repeat myself. I don't want to trade."

The brevity of Brian's answers was beginning to bother Jeff. "Come on, Brian, at least let me tell you who I'm thinking about," he stammered, "let me tell you before you say no."

"No, I'm sure that you've cooked up a nice one-sided deal that will greatly benefit your team." He paused. "Listen to me for a second. I'm just not in the mood. Really, I'm not."

The tone of Jeff's voice changed from anger to surprise. "I don't get it. What do you mean 'one-sided?' You know that all of the trades that we've discussed in the past have been fair. How could you say that they were one-sided?"

Brian sighed. "Well, you can look at them any way that you want. Here's the skinny. I'm sick and tired of the constant phone calls and the stupid talk over this league. I've got other things to do, you know. I've got work. I've got my wife."

"What is this," Jeff blustered, "Is the wife getting mad at you?" His voice grew louder and filled with more sarcasm with each word. "Did she tell you that you can't play with the boys anymore? Could you sound any more pathetic?"

Even though Jeff's voice was raised, Brian remained calm in his response. "If that's what you want to think, then that's fine. But you're the one who's pathetic, my friend. Don't bother calling me again for this league. I won't make a trade with you, so it's not worth your time."

""Well, fuck you man," Jeff yelled in return. "I don't need your shitty players anyway. There are other teams, you know."

Brian chuckled lightly. "Sure there are. Just remember, the constant phone calls have probably pissed off some of the others also. Good luck trading with them." He paused. "Oh, and, one other thing, you piece of shit, make sure that you say hi to Michelle for me." He hung up the phone, laughing.

"Fuck you!" Jeff screamed into the receiver, although all that he heard in response was a fresh dial tone. He was annoyed at what Brian had said about his trades being unfair, but the comment about Michelle was what hurt most. "That malicious asshole," he said to himself, "what the fuck does he know about things? Obviously his wife wears the pants in that family. Who wants that? I'm better off not dealing with him."

He walked over to the refrigerator, pulled out two bottles of beer, and placed them on the table next to his leather chair. He then went back into the kitchen, and produced a bag of corn chips and a bottle of salsa from one of its cabinets. He sat down in the leather chair, turned on the television, and consumed the entire bag of chips and two beers while watching a movie. By the time he fell asleep in the chair that evening, he had emptied three more beer bottles. The bottles lay at his feet next to the empty chip bag, and the light of the television engulfed the room as he slept, his head resting on the side of the chair.

CHAPTER 27

"Passion is a positive obsession. Obsession is a negative passion."

- *Paul Carvel, Belgian writer*

Early the next morning, Jeff was awakened by the opening strains of the Star Spangled Banner being played on the television while the United States flag filled the screen. Still not fully conscious, Jeff thought that a baseball game was about to begin, and strained to open his eyes so that he could see which teams would be playing. When he was able to open them, however, he could see that his apartment was dark with the exception of the television.

The Yankee Stadium clock that hung on the wall had both of its hands pointing downward and to the right, closer to the five than to the six. When he looked at the clock, Greg realized that it was almost 5:30, but it took him several moments to realize that it was 5:30 AM and that he had fallen asleep in front of the television again. "Shit," he thought to himself, "those shitheads didn't call me back." He began to panic, realizing that the trading deadline was approaching with the speed of a runaway freight train. "What am I going to do?" he said aloud, as he laid his head back on the side of the chair.

Almost immediately, he jerked his head from its resting position and bolted to his feet. "The interview," he cried, as he remembered that he had a job interview at 9:30 that morning. He had completely forgotten about the interview, and had done nothing to prepare himself for the three individuals with whom he would be meeting. He knew nothing about the company, or even the position that he would be seeking. All that he knew was that his father had called a friend and somehow was able to arrange the interview in one day's time; more importantly, his father told Jeff that some type of job at the company was almost assured as long as he arrived and presented himself adequately. It was to be the easiest interview he would ever have.

He realized that he could not even do that right. He had intended to spend time scouring the internet the previous afternoon to retrieve information about the company, such as the products that it manufactured. Or was it the products that it sold? He was not even sure about the company's business, which made it difficult for him to determine which facets of his accounting background would be best off highlighted at the interview.

His appointment was four hours away. He still had plenty of time to prepare. He could eat and take a shower early, and then get online and perform his research. It would provide him with sufficient time to complete research on the company, its business, and partners, even if only to provide himself with a thumb-nail's sketch of its product and main personnel, if there even was a product to describe. He would only need a half hour or so for travel to the office, so as long as he was done by a little before 9:00 he would still be able to make the appointment on time.

Walking to the bathroom, he turned on the fluorescent light that hung over the sink and peered into the mirror situated beneath the bulb. The lower portion of his face was dotted with small whiskers, testament to the fact that he had not shaven for several days. Rivers of red ran from the pupils of his eyes outward, no doubt manifestations of the five beers consumed only hours ago. Jeff, wanting to make a good impression and thinking that he would be better off with eyes which weren't streaked with red, decided that some more sleep would be beneficial to his appearance. He turned off the bathroom light and walked to his bed, taking care to set the alarm clock to 7:15 so that he would have sufficient time to prepare before going to the interview.

He quickly drifted off to sleep, which was surprising in light of the nervousness that he was feeling about the interview. After an hour and a half of deep sleep, he was once again awakened, this time by the music coming from his clock radio. He rolled over and glanced at the clock, which read 7:15. He turned the alarm to "off," and went into the bathroom to shave and shower. He moved an electric razor back and forth across his cheeks and chin several times, taking more care when gliding the steel over his neck. Once his face was smooth, he proceeded to take a hot shower, making sure that he was done by 7:30.

After completing his shower, he wrapped a large towel across his stomach and walked out into the bedroom. Reaching out with his right hand, he picked up the television remote, he pushed the power button and turned the station to the 24-hour sports station. The clock on his nightstand now read 7:32, so he had missed only the first two minutes of *SportsCenter*. He wiped himself off with the towel while standing in front of the television, and sat on the edge of the bed while pulling on his clothes while the prior night's baseball highlights were broadcast.

Only two of baseball's 30 teams had rested that night, so the show was full of baseball as highlights and scores from 14 games were squeezed into 20 minutes of the half-hour show. Jeff was sure to watch all of the scores, hoping that some information would be included that could prove beneficial for his league. He then returned to the bathroom and dried his hair, adding a small amount of hair spray to ensure that his curls did not run amok later that day.

Believing that he had more than enough time before he had to leave for the interview, Jeff opened the front door to his apartment, removed the day's newspaper from atop his welcome mat, and sat down with the newspaper and a box of cereal. He read the sports section of the newspaper and studied the box scores while he ate, placing the cereal bowl into the kitchen sink as the clock read 8:22. He brushed his teeth and finished dressing, and went to leave for the subway as the clock reached 8:33. As he retrieved his keys from their position on the kitchen counter, he remembered that he had intended to do his online research that morning. Glancing at his wristwatch, he realized that he only had about a half an hour within which to do any such research.

To complete any research on the company, however, Jeff would have to possess the name of the company. He quickly realized that he was not in possession of this critical piece of information, nor did he even know the full name of the person whom he was scheduled to meet. The first person that he was slated to see was his father's friend, and he was then scheduled, he had been told, to meet with two other employees of the company, both of whom were accountants. Nervous because he had never met his father's friend, however, he had forgotten the man's last name. His father had always referred to him as "Charlie," so Jeff had written Charlie's full name on a piece of paper with the company's name and address. Realizing that he had forgotten to telephone the office the previous day to confirm the interview, Jeff was not aware of where he had placed the paper. 15 minutes later, a search of his apartment failed to reveal the paper, and Jeff was growing more and more nervous with each passing tick of the Yankee Stadium clock.

His only hope was to telephone his father. It was almost 9:00 and Jeff would have to leave within the next ten minutes in order to arrive on time for the interview, less if he wanted to make a good show by being early, even if only by a few minutes. He knew that his father would read him the riot act for having lost the information, but also recognized that his father was the only person who could give him the company's name and address. He dialed his parents' telephone number, but his distress reached new heights when their answering machine clicked on after the fourth ring. Leaving a frantic message for his father to return his call when he received the message, he slammed the phone down and walked to the bedroom. Sitting on the bed, he took two pillows and placed them behind his back. He again turned the television on, and sat, on the bed, watching the prior evening's highlights the second time that morning.

Two hours later, Jeff's father had not called. By this time, Jeff had given up all hope of appearing for the interview, and had taken off his suit and placed it back into the bedroom closet. He sat, still on the bed, dressed in his Yankee sweatpants and a blue shirt, cursing himself for being unable to remember the name of the man or his company and, moreover, for losing the piece of paper. As he watched three women on a talk show explain why they stayed with their husbands even after the men had pointed loaded pistols at each of their heads, he suddenly remembered Charlie's last name. Because he was still unable to recall the company for which Charlie Freeman worked, however, his recollection of the man's name was of little consequence at that time. Even a quick internet search for the name "Charlie Freeman" proved futile, providing Jeff with no results in the New York area.

His father called him at ten minutes past noon. He would not tell Jeff the name of Charlie Freeman's place of business, choosing instead to berate his son for the careless manner in which he had handled the situation, as well as the shoddy way that he had gone about trying to find a job. Reiterating his prior threat that he would not support Jeff financially, and noting that his wife was in full agreement with this position, Mr. Goldstein told his son that he did not want to speak to him again until after he had found some form of gainful employment, or at least taken proper steps toward acquiring such employment. Within seconds after he hung up the phone, Jeff went to the refrigerator and pulled a beer from its second shelf, downing its contents and reaching for another before closing the refrigerator door.

Later that afternoon, Jeff again decided that he would be better off trying to focus on his fantasy baseball league in light of the rapidly impending trade deadline. He still had not spoken to either Mike Berger or Gene Hyland, and the deadline was less than 48 hours away. He went to the table where his baseball materials lay, and picked up the prior week's standings. Turning to Hang 'em Hy's team statistics on the last page of the standings, he saw indentations where someone had written on the back of the paper. Turning to the other side of the page, he was horrified to see the words "Charles Freeman -- Lansing and Co -- 45 E. 51 St., 212-555-2020" written in black ink.

He telephoned Charlie Freeman to see if it would be possible to schedule another interview. Despite the fact that Mr. Freeman's secretary assured Jeff that he would receive a return phone call, he did not receive one that day, or even the next. Jeff assumed that his father had already spoken to Charlie Freeman, and that the two had agreed that the job that had been promised to Jeff would be withdrawn due to his dilatory conduct. Jeff was upset by that possibility, but did understand the reasons for such action.

Jeff's telephone was similarly silent with respect to calls regarding the baseball league. For the third day in a row, no phone calls, or any texts, were received from either Mike or Gene.

The Yankees-Red Sox game was being televised that evening, and Jeff knew that Gene, a devout Boston fan, would be fastened to his couch watching the game at home, as he was whenever the two bitter rivals met. Jeff had once invited Gene over to watch a battle between the teams, but Gene had explained that it was of paramount importance that he be seated on the right side of his couch for the game, as he had sat in the same position for the previous 15 years of New York-Boston tilts. Even when he moved out of his parent's house for a brief period of time, he still returned to the couch in their family room whenever the two teams squared off. When the game reached the bottom of the second inning, Jeff dialed Gene's number. The telephone was answered by Gene's brother, and Jeff could hear Gene's voice in the background yelling as the first of what promised to be many Yankee runs crossed the plate.

Within seconds, Gene was on the phone. "What's up, man?" he asked, breathlessly, "make it quick. You know that I've got to be on the couch for this. You should have called me on the cell."

"So take the phone into the other room, you idiot," he said, as he heard Gene sigh in admission that he could merely walk into the other room with the phone. Jeff paused, turning his statistic sheet to Gene's team and the possible trades that he had written in the margins of its page. "Let's talk trade, amigo. The deadline is just about upon us."

"I don't know, man, I'm not really in the mood to make any trades this year." His voice trailed off as his head turned from the telephone's mouthpiece and back over his shoulder at the television, and he called out to his brother to find out if any more runs had scored while he was away from the couch and television. Jeff could barely make out Gene's brother's voice in the background, as he replied that the score was now 2-0.

"Gene, I have the ballgame on. I can tell you that it's 2-0," Jeff interjected. "Now what do you mean you're not in the mood to make any deals? You and I both know that you're always ready to pull something off."

"Not this time, dude," replied Gene. "Look, I've got to go. I'll talk to you in a couple of weeks."

Fearful that Gene would disconnect him, Jeff yelled out for him to stay on the line. "We don't have time, Gene, that's why I'm calling you now. In case you've forgotten, tomorrow night is the trading deadline. If we're going to trade, it's got to be now. Not in two weeks."

"I don't think so," said Gene, clearly indicating, again, that he would not make any trades with Jeff.

"You're kidding me," said Jeff, confused. "Look, just hear me out. I've got some great deals worked out. I guarantee you that in five minutes we'll have completed something. What do you say?"

"Still no. I just don't feel like it."

Jeff, concerned that he would be unable to convince Gene to make any deals, remembered the conversation that he had with Brian Hunter only days before. "O.K., Gene. But before you go, let me ask you one question."

"Sure, man, shoot. But make it fast." He paused, and then began to yell, presumably at the television screen. "Come on, ump, are you blind? That pitch was nowhere near the strike zone! Can you believe this shit?"

Jeff ignored his friend's tirade, not even looking at the television to attempt to confirm or deny his perception, and focused on the topic that he wanted to discuss. "Brian told me that he wouldn't trade with me because I called him too often. He said that the trades that I wanted to make were unfair."

"Uh huh," grunted Gene.

"And he also said that some of the other guys felt that way. Is that why you're blowing me off now?"

There was a prolonged pause before Gene replied. "What are you talking about? I'm not blowing you off."

"Well," Jeff explained, "you didn't call me back for a couple of days and now you're not even going to talk about a trade with me. What would you think?"

"Well, I guess that if I was a woman, and an overly sensitive one at that, I would be thinking the same thing that you are thinking," Gene replied. "But you're not a woman, and you shouldn't be thinking that way. Besides, I haven't been ignoring you any more than I've been avoiding anybody else. I've been extremely busy with work. You know how that can be."

"No, not lately," Jeff answered, grimacing, "that's a cheap shot."

"Sorry, I forgot, man," said an apologetic Gene. "As I said, I've been busy, and I just don't feel like making any last-minute trades that could ruin the team for next year. Don't read anything else into it, alright? Now let me go and enjoy the game. And look out, Yankee lover. The Sox are primed for a comeback."

"Alright, Gene," said Jeff. "I'll talk to you in a couple of weeks. We'll go out and grab a burger and some beers."

"Sounds good. Later. Go Sox."

Jeff hung up the phone and stared at the pad in front of him. He was caught off-guard by Gene's refusal to make a trade, and was less than convinced with his friend's explanation. Maybe Brian was right about what the others were thinking. But he'd have to wait to hear from Mike Berger, if that call ever came, before he knew for sure.

Mike Berger never called. Jeff decided that he didn't want to chase after Mike anymore, so he refused to call him on the evening of August 31. The trading deadline passed when the clock struck midnight, and Jeff had nothing to show for it with the exception of his discussions with Brian and Gene. He was still confused about the accusations that Brian had thrown in his direction. He looked back over some of the trades that he had made during the season, including the one deal that had been consummated with Brian. All of the trades had all benefitted his team at the expense of the others, but that came as no surprise to him. The whole purpose of the trade, he reasoned, was to improve your team. If it had to be done with the other team's quality being diminished somewhat, that was a natural result.

But the majority of the trades did not appear to be one-sided at all. In several, players of equal ability, but who could provide help in different categories, were exchanged. And in others, what looked one way on paper to Jeff could look another way to the other team making the trade. He remembered when he traded one of his starting pitchers for two reserve outfielders. One of the players was being primed to step into a starting position, so it made sense for Jeff to acquire him. The fact that the player never cracked the starting lineup was of no consequence. Any trade was a risk, especially in baseball where injuries were so prevalent and today's productive player could all too easily become a member of the next day's disabled list. So to say that all of his trades were unfair was, ironically, an unfair statement.

Jeff searched for the perfect word to describe the way that he approached dealing players. "Shrewd," he said aloud, "I'm a shrewd trader. If that's what he thinks is one-sided, then he's certainly got a lot to learn." He was no different from major league general managers, he reasoned, some of whom he idolized, who were skilled at recognizing raw talent and acquiring those players before their market value soared.

The history of major league baseball, as well as all major sports, was replete with trades that eventually turned out to be grossly one-sided. If Jeff could be involved in a trade that would prove to be overwhelmingly beneficial to his interests, then he had done his job correctly. The job that he always wanted, and, at this moment, the only job that he had.

With the passing of the trading deadline, however, Jeff was suddenly constrained in his ability to improve his team to make a run at the league championship. He had been slowly closing in on the first-place Boozers, but his approach had been stunted by the slumps of several of his players. In contrast, the members of the Boozers appeared to be hitting their stride, as if on cue, for the late-season playoff push. It was almost as if they were a real team, with all of them peaking at the same time and working together like a well-oiled machine. Something would need to be done, and Jeff knew just the person whom he could call to ensure that such an event would come to pass.

Checking his season's schedule, Jeff saw that the Chicago Cubs would be visiting the Brewers for a three-game series the next week. One of the Cubs' outfielders, Barry Allen, had slugged seven home runs and swiped five bases in the previous three weeks. His power had allowed the Boozers to pad their lead in the home runs category over the second-place Golds, and he was showing no signs of slowing down. The only way that his production would decrease, it appeared, would be involuntarily. Surely there would be some way for Greg to cause Allen some misfortune when the Cubs visited the Brewers.

Greg did not answer his cell phone, so Jeff's call resulted in a simple message for him to call back. The cousins had not spoken to each other since the heated discussion that followed the Sanchez incident. Although Greg had appeared hesitant at that time to provide any further help with the baseball league, Jeff hoped that his emotions had calmed to the extent that he would be able to perform one more act before the season ended. If Allen could be removed from the Cubs' lineup, and, therefore, from the Boozers' roster, then no more assistance would be required and Jeff would have a strong chance of winning the league title.

Adding to the plan was the fact that Allen's current backup in the Cubs' outfield was Joe Koordin, who was also a member of the Golds' minor league roster. If he was to gain increased playing time and produce reasonable statistics, the Golds would be doubly benefitted from an injury to Allen. Koordin had faced only twelve pitches in his major league career, but his success at all levels of the minor leagues had earned him a promotion to the parent club when rosters expanded on September 1.

Greg returned Jeff's call the following afternoon. "I figured that I would find you at home, you lazy shit," he said, laughing, when Jeff answered the call. "Don't you think that it's time for you to get a new job? How long do you expect to sit around and do nothing with yourself?"

"Very funny, Greg. I will have you know that I'm looking for a job," Jeff answered, although he neglected to mention his failure to capitalize on the job lead that his father had provided.

"Aren't you bored?" Greg asked. "I couldn't sit around the house all day. Just doing that is enough to drive a person to drink. Too much idle time, you know." He chuckled lightly.

"I don't know what you're talking about," Jeff said, not even cracking a smile at his cousin's obvious attempt at self-deprecating humor as he glanced down at the opened beer bottle that sat precariously on the edge of the coffee table.

"What I mean," Greg explained, "is that I couldn't sit around and do nothing day after day. When I first got hurt, I was laid up and couldn't practice.

I'll tell you, I was climbing the walls trying to find something to do. Maybe I'm just a hyper person, but I can't sit still for more than ten minutes at a time. That's why the off-seasons are also tough on me and many of the other guys. Once we're out of our routine, that's when most problems start. What's that phrase? Idle hands? It's true."

"I thought that it was the drugs that made you like that."

"No, smartass," replied Greg, "'the drugs,' as you so delicately said, did not cause me to be jumpy. They're more the result of the large chunks of idle time. The jumpiness was just my normal disposition, although I guess that it may have been exaggerated somewhat by the cocaine. I'm told that that could happen. I was just never one to sit on my ass and do nothing."

"Speaking of the white powder, Greg," Jeff asked, in a voice which betrayed his concern, "are you still off of the stuff? How is the recovery going?"

"Well, there's a slip-up here and there," allowed Greg. "It's a tough road, let me tell you that. But I'm going to beat it. I've cut it down dramatically. Cold turkey is tough, but I'll have wiped it out soon." He sighed. "Hopefully soon. And then, eventually, I may even be able to give up drinking. That's one of the ways that this shit starts, you know."

"Sure, but like I told you before, don't even think about preaching to me about the ills of drinking, alright?" Jeff asked. "I don't care if you stop drinking one night and never so much as taste a beer again, but don't even think about condemning me for my drinking."

"No problem," Greg answered, chuckling. "Why'd you call? It's been a while. I figured that I wouldn't hear from you again until after the baseball season ended."

"Well," Jeff said, "I need one more favor."

"One more favor? I told you the last time that we spoke that I wasn't going to do anything like that anymore," Greg replied.

"I know, but it's just a little favor."

"No, man," Greg said. "I'm not gonna do it. I put my career in jeopardy a couple of times in the past, but I'm not going to do anything to wreck it now. It's too important to me. We've already been through this."

"And the money that we can win should be important to both of us," urged Jeff. "Come on, it's almost over. Just one more."

"I thought that it would be over after Mike Jones," said Greg with a sigh. "You know, I still have nightmares about that." His voice became a whisper, as if he was hiding something from others in the room. "I killed a man, goddamnit. And I know that I killed him, and you did not ask me to kill anyone. But no matter what you say to explain or justify it, the simple fact is that I wouldn't have been in that position if you hadn't asked me to help you with the league."

"But you did the shit, man, I didn't ask you to. And don't forget, the Sanchez thing was all yours. I had nothing to do with that."

"You're right about that, but it doesn't change my answer. I won't do it," said Greg sternly. "You can keep all of your money; I don't even want it anymore. You do your thing, and I'll do mine. My thing now is to preserve my career. I would hope that you would appreciate that and support me, even though it's apparent that you've done nothing short of torpedoing your own livelihood."

"A small setback for me. It's nothing that I can't fix," yelled Jeff, as he grew increasingly frustrated at his inability to gain assistance from Greg. Coupled with his inability to trade any players before the deadline, Jeff was worried that he was losing his ability to effectively play the fantasy game. Worse still, he feared that all hopes of winning the league, of reaching the elusive cash payout, were disappearing. His emotions were running amok, and culminated in an act of pure, and unwarranted, outrage. "I can't believe that you won't help me," he yelled at his cousin. "Well, don't come crawling back to me when you need some drug money, you backstabbing asshole." Jeff slammed the phone into its cradle with such force that it cracked in three places.

Jeff gulped down the remainder of his beer, and hurled the bottle against the wall above his leather couch. It landed against the wall with a thud, breaking into hundreds of pieces. Rather than cleaning up the mess that he had just created, he went back into the kitchen and pulled a fresh bottle from inside of the refrigerator. Twisting off the bottle cap, he downed the cold beer in a matter of seconds, throwing the almost-empty bottle against the wall a scant two inches to the left of where the previous bottle had impacted.

"I'm going to have to do it myself," Jeff thought.

He ran back to the table and picked up the most recent batch of fantasy league standings, tearing the pieces of paper into shreds and hurling them upward. As a sea of white confetti rained down on his head, he pulled a Yankees' schedule out from a yellow manila folder resting on the table. He unfolded the schedule so that the months of August and September were shown.

"If you want something done, you've got to do it yourself," he said aloud, although he was alone in the room. He peered at the wall to his right, where thin rivers of beer had left stains which extended from the floor to the points where the thrown bottles had exploded minutes before. "If Greg won't help me," he murmured, "it's up to me to make sure that I can win this league. Let's see, now," he said, as he scanned the schedule for the next series of games to take place at Yankee Stadium, "who's coming to town next?" Much to his dismay, the Yankees were on the road for the next two series, concluding an extended trip that would take them through Detroit and Baltimore.

They would be back in the Stadium the next Thursday, though, opening a ten-game homestand against the Texas Rangers. "Shit, I'm lucky," Jeff thought, because one of the other main hitters posting phenomenal numbers for the Boozers was Texas center fielder Diego Gomez. "Who needs help from Greg?" he asked himself, "because if I can just get to Gomez and take him out, I'd be sitting pretty." Actually, getting into close proximity of Gomez was the easy part. Buying a ticket for the bleacher seats would put him close to the action in the outfield. As the Yankees had already clinched a playoff spot, the game was not likely to be a sellout, so that getting seats near the field was a virtual certainty.

The difficult facet of the plan, of course, was deciding how to cause the injury to Gomez. Stadium security had been extremely loose as of late, even in spite of calls for heightened security after a series of events at sporting events over the past couple of years, so smuggling in some form of weapon was not out of the question. But what should be done to harm Gomez? The injury had to be severe enough to cause Gomez to miss the remainder of the season, so he had to be put out of action for three weeks at the very least. It also had to be something that could be accomplished from some distance. If Jeff was to stand within ten feet of Gomez and something was to occur, he would automatically be considered a suspect. No, he had to be some distance away, perhaps within the crowd, when the incident was to take place.

Jeff's mind had become more than slightly askew by his overwhelming desire to win his league. Whereas he was thinking completely clearly, such as in planning for Gomez's demise, his thoughts were irrational in one important way – that part of his mind that controlled his understanding of the ramifications of his actions. The most logical choice, he reasoned, was to shoot Gomez. He gave deep thought to how he could actually carry out his plan, but never once stopped to think of the fact that he was planning on shooting someone, of causing them great bodily harm. He figured that he could do it from a distance, such as from the stands when Gomez was roaming in the outfield. It was possible to carry a small gun, one that could be easily concealed in his coat pocket, and one which would be disposed of easily. If a proper silencing attachment was affixed to the barrel of the gun, even those seated around him would not be capable of identifying him as the perpetrator.

Searching the internet, Jeff located several websites advertising the sale of guns. He perused several of the sites that dealt in handguns, but was unable to locate a pistol that was small enough or quiet enough to enable him to complete the plan as he had imagined. He finally located a snub-nosed pistol that was equipped with a silencer, but became discouraged when he was advised of the five-day waiting period that was required before he would be able to purchase the weapon.

He knew that he could buy a gun on the street, but was afraid of the characters with whom he would have to contact in order to arrange such a purchase. After he returned to his apartment, he became despondent that he would be unable to affect the outcome of the league due to his inability to remove Gomez from competition. Never in his thoughts did he breathe a sigh of relief that he was essentially precluded from engaging in such criminal activity. Rather, in what was becoming a recurring scene in his life, he reached into the refrigerator and withdrew one of his three remaining beers. He had intended to stop at the liquor store earlier that day, but had forgotten to do so because his mind was so preoccupied with other concerns, like baseball and guns.

Taking a mouthful of beer, he walked into the next room and sat down in front of the table. Shreds of paper still littered the carpet, and bits of glass rested near the wall, forming two semi-circles on the carpet below where he had flung the two bottles that afternoon. Staring at the many shards of glass and then up the wall, which was still stained from the streams of brew that had inched their paths to the ground earlier, Jeff suddenly had an idea of how he could injure Diego Gomez, an idea that would not require a waiting period or licensing of a weapon.

CHAPTER 28

A beer bottle, he thought. He could carry a beer bottle into the stadium in his jacket pocket, since no glass bottles were given at the concession stands, and hurl the bottle onto the field in Gomez's direction. He remembered hearing about a football playoff game in the mid-1970's when a fan threw an empty bottle that struck a referee, knocking the official to the ground. He could not recall if the referee had lost consciousness after being struck, but believed that a solid enough blow to the back of the head could cause a concussion and knock Gomez out of the lineup for at least a week. While baseball did not have a formal concussion protocol similar to the National Football League, Jeff knew enough about concussions and their effects to know that a properly-thrown bottle could be debilitating to Gomez. Even days later, he could be suffering from headaches and possible double vision that would prevent him from seeing the ball properly, thereby inhibiting his ability to hit.

Jeff stood, with his hands on his hips, and stared at the marks on the wall. A bottle. In his delusional mind, a well-thrown beer bottle was all that was separating him from the championship. And if he could throw two bottles at a wall from across the room without even aiming, and have them land only inches from each other, he thought, then hitting a player in the outfield from a bleacher seat would be simple. It was perfect. And finding a bottle would be no trouble, as there were no less than twelve empty bottles on his living room carpet alone. They would still likely all be there by the time that the Yankees retuned to town, as Jeff had no real intention of cleaning his apartment before then.

That week's fantasy league standings were static as to the top three positions, as the Boozers continued to hold their lead over the Golds and Fish. The lead over the second-place Golds, however, had decreased by one-half point, such that the two were now separated by only two points, the closest that the Golds had been to the top spot all year. Not only had the team climbed to within this narrow margin, moreover, but it had also cut into the Boozers' leads in the home runs and runs batted in categories and was perfectly primed for an eleventh-hour run to the top. This run would be much easier, of course, if Gomez was removed from the Boozers' lineup, which made Jeff's plan all the more imperative.

On the night before they were to travel to New York, the Texas ballclub was playing a nationally-televised game against the Red Sox. Jeff watched the game at a local sports bar, and was careful to watch Gomez' movements in center field every time the camera focused in his direction. Jeff was able to ascertain that Gomez played a deep center field, and often was forced to run a long distance in order to reach an otherwise routine pop-up. Even bearing in mind that the outfield configurations of Boston's Fenway Park and Yankee Stadium differed greatly, Jeff still believed that Gomez would play a similar depth, in the shadows of the outfield fence, when the Rangers came to the Bronx.

This would make his mission even easier. If Gomez assumed a position several yards from the center field fence, a thrown bottle would not have to be completely accurate for it to reach its intended mark. And the closer that Gomez stood to the wall, the less chance there was of missing him completely. If he stood close enough to the fence, Jeff thought, it might even be possible to toss the bottle from a sitting position. That would decrease the chances of anyone identifying the person who threw the bottle, so that Jeff would have a greater chance of going undetected.

The television announcing crew also noted one peculiar habit that Gomez possessed. After each catch, he would turn to the crowd and walk closer to the fence, arms outstretched, as if he were begging for their applause. This was a curious move, especially when his team was on the road, and the response from the Boston crowd, as expected, was less than scintillating. The TV announcers, however, opined that Gomez was feeding off of the crowd's disdain. This habit could also prove beneficial to Jeff. Should Gomez make a play in the outfield and then walk back toward the crowd, he would be walking directly into Jeff's path and, quite possibly, into the path of an oncoming bottle.

Thursday afternoon, Jeff pulled a bottle of beer from the six-pack that he had placed into his refrigerator the night before. He drank the beer slowly, pausing after each gulp to stuff a handful of tortilla chips into his mouth. When he finished, he ran hot water over the empty bottle and carefully removed its labels. The temperature in the city was a seasonable 65 degrees, but the forecast called for the mercury to drop by as much as seven degrees by the beginning of that evening's game. Jeff pulled his faded denim jacket from the front closet, and checked to see if a bottle could be concealed within its left inside pocket.

The pocket was perfectly sized for a bottle. The depth of the pocket was such that the top of the bottle would come up to a level approximately one-half an inch below the pocket break. That way, the bottle would not fall out inadvertently, and, at the same time, Jeff would be able to reach in and pull out the glass in one fluid motion. He stood in front of a full-length mirror, like Robert DeNiro in *"Taxi Driver,"* and practiced pulling the bottle from his jacket and throwing it downward. He went through this motion several times, but on the last run-through he lost his grip on the bottle. It fell against the bottom of the mirror, and both the bottle and a small portion of the mirror shattered. Several of the shards flew up in his direction, and he ducked, shielding his eyes, and backed away from the wall.

His hands were shaking. For the first time, he began to doubt if he would be able to execute his plan. He clasped his hands together in an attempt to

299

stop their movement, and stared hard at the mirror. "I can do it," he said, as he pulled his hands apart. He held his right hand out in front of him, and then extended his left arm as well. Unlike the trembling that he had seen moments before, his arms and hands were effortlessly extended in mid-air, solidly, without movement.

He walked over to the table behind him and bent down, feeling with his left hand for one of the bottles that had remained on the carpeting since the previous week. He located one and lifted it onto the table, standing up straight before picking up the bottle again and bringing it into the kitchen. As he had with the other bottle, he ran the amber piece of glass under a stream of hot water and slowly peeled off its identifying labels. He dried the bottle carefully with a paper towel, and thrust it into the inside pocket of his jacket. Pulling the jacket's zipper up to a point slightly above the top of the pocket, he walked back in front of the mirror and eyed his reflection suspiciously.

To his relief, he was unable to detect a noticeable bulge where the bottle rested. He turned to his right and then to the left, each time examining his profile in the mirror to see if a security guard would be able to spot the hidden weapon. He was unable to see the bottle's outline from any of these angles, and was satisfied that there would be no reason for any of the security guards to see any differently. Just to be sure, he took a half-used roll of toilet paper and shoved it into the right outside pocket of the jacket. This was placed as a decoy; if he was to be checked over, or even frisked slightly, before entering the stadium, the guard was certain to find and confiscate the toilet paper. Jeff thought that the guard would then be satisfied and not desire to check him any further.

On the subway ride to the stadium, Jeff plotted out what would be the best time to throw the bottle. He couldn't do it in the first two innings, because everybody would be paying close attention to the game at that point and there was a better chance of his getting noticed. It would also be wrong to wait until after the seventh inning, because there was no guarantee that Gomez would still be in the game. There was always the possibility that the Texas manager could pinch-hit for Gomez should circumstances warrant, or he could even send in a late-inning defensive replacement.

The third and fourth innings were similarly discounted. Those innings would be too early for Gomez to showboat in the field. If Jeff was going to wait until Gomez played to the crowd and walked perilously close to the stands, the best time to throw the bottle would likely be somewhere during the bottom of the fifth or sixth innings. There was no real difference between these two innings as far as Jeff was concerned, and he decided that either one would be an effective time.

Jeff arrived at the stadium approximately an hour and a half before game time, and stepped into the short line that was waiting to buy bleacher seat tickets. Stepping up to the ticket window after a wait of approximately ten minutes, he asked for one ticket, and, having paid the person behind the ticket window and received it, walked toward the entrance gate. As he approached, he grew anxious; he could feel his palms begin to sweat and his heart begin to race faster. The reason for this burst of anxiety was that he could see two members of the stadium security force eyeing those people who walked through the gates, and suddenly felt as if the bottle in his jacket weighed one hundred pounds and protruded several feet from his body.

He paused, and started to turn around. Looking down at his chest, and, seeing no actual evidence of the bottle's existence, he reassured himself that neither of the guards would be capable of seeing the bottle which was tucked inside of his jacket. He turned back toward the gate, and slowly walked toward the guard, his hands thrust deeply into his coat pockets. As he stepped to within three steps of one of the uniformed men, he withdrew his right hand from the coat pocket and showed the man the ticket that was wrapped in his clenched fingers. The man motioned for him to stop, and he did, turning slightly to the right as the guard slowly felt the outside of his jacket. He looked up into the guard's face, and saw a wave of disapproval staring back at him. "What were you going to do with this, sonny?" the guard asked, as he pulled the roll of toilet paper from Jeff's pocket. "I hope that you weren't planning on throwing this onto the field. You know that you're not supposed to do that kind of thing here."

"Actually, officer," Jeff replied in a whisper as he pulled the guard off to the side, "I know that you can't throw it on the field. That's not what I was planning to do."

"Oh, no?" asked the officer skeptically.

"No," explained Jeff. "You see, I hate using the cardboard that they pass off for toilet paper in the bathrooms here. I just bring that along in case I have to use the facilities, if you know what I mean. I've had some, shall I say, issues lately."

The guard laughed. "Well, son, I can't disagree with you on that. But rules are rules, so I've got to take this away from you. Just stay away from the bad food if you don't want to be running to the bathroom."

"Thanks, officer," replied Jeff, "I'll take your advice." Jeff winked at the guard, who waved him on to the turnstile without any further search or inquiry. He handed his ticket to the elderly woman who stood to the left of the turnstile, and casually strolled to his seat, the empty beer bottle bouncing slightly within his pocket as he walked. Holding his ticket stub between his left

302

thumb and index finger, he proceeded to the sixth row of seats from the fence and sat down in the third seat from the aisle. People were beginning to filter in and sit all around him, and some of the players from each team were playing catch on the sidelines. Two Texas pitchers, most likely late-season call-ups to the team's roster since neither of the names on the backs of their jerseys looked familiar to Jeff, jogged by on the dirt that separated the outfield grass from the base of the outfield wall. When they passed by Jeff's section, they appeared so close that he felt as if he could reach out and touch them.

From his sitting position, he moved his left arm in a throwing motion, as if to practice hurling the bottle in Gomez's direction. To those around him, he hoped, it would just look like he was moving his arm as if loosening up a cramp or pain. The seats directly to his left and behind him were empty, so he determined, happily, that there was no chance of his striking anyone with his arm during such a throw. For the remainder of time prior to the game, he eyed all oncoming people warily, hoping that they would not be sitting in either of the two seats. Unfortunately, two young boys arrived with their father approximately ten minutes before the game was to begin. The family sat in the seats directly behind Jeff, which caused him to panic at first. This quickly subsided, however, when Jeff realized that the seven-year old sitting behind him could not possibly interfere with his throwing motion, unless the youth was to stand up and lean over the seat.

Feeling strangely relaxed, Jeff hailed the next beer vendor that walked by his aisle and purchased a cold beer. The outrageous price that the concessionaires charged for a simple beer always perturbed Jeff, but he decided that he would be better off drinking at least two beers before he attempted to carry out his plan and injure Gomez. More than two would possibly be a problem if his ability to properly aim became impaired, but since he had fallen into the habit of drinking several beers each night, then certainly two would have no discernible effect on him or his efforts. The beginning of the game grew closer, and Jeff gently caressed the bottle through his jacket when the crowd rose for the national anthem. To everyone seated in his section, it appeared that he was patriotically covering his heart with his hand during the playing of the anthem, but he was in reality adjusting the bottle into several different locations to see which way would be the easiest for him to grab.

New York starting pitcher Chet Johnson set the Rangers down in order in the first inning, and the teams exchanged sides as Jeff ordered his second beer. As the Rangers trotted out into the field, Diego Gomez tipped his hat to the crowd. Many of those seated in the bleachers, anticipating that this gesture was merely the first of many that would follow that evening, jeered Gomez loudly. Ever the showman, the young outfielder turned to the derisive crowd and tipped his hat once more, bowing slightly as he did so.

As Gomez bowed, Jeff estimated that the two men were less than ten yards apart. Jeff thought that the distance from one side of his living room to the other was only slightly less, and he chuckled lightly to himself, comfortable with the knowledge that striking Gomez square on the forehead would be a relatively simple task from that short a distance. He realized that he probably would not be offered as perfect a chance to throw the bottle as when Gomez had his head down, but was determined to wait until at least the fifth inning. Besides, the two beers were starting to work in tandem with the two that he had consumed immediately before he left for the game, giving his head a nice light feeling. He had forgotten that he had consumed the beers while still in his apartment when he began to drink during the early part of the game, and realized that would need to sober up a bit before trying what would be his one and only chance at striking Gomez.

At the end of four innings, the game was scoreless. Jeff was beginning to grow nervous, his palms drenched with sweat. He vigorously rubbed his left hand against the top of his pants, trying desperately to keep his hand dry to avoid the possibility of the bottle slipping out of his hand and falling harmlessly to the ground, or, worse yet, flying out of control and striking one of the other fans. The Rangers failed to put a single runner on base in the top of the fifth, and most of the fans sat calmly in their seats, waiting for the home team to come for their fifth time at bat.

In sharp contrast, however, Jeff was anything but calm at this time, and was nervously fidgeting with the bottle that rested in his pocket. He looked all around him, and could see people in almost all of the bleacher seats. Suddenly paranoid, he thought that the other members of the crowd were all looking in his direction, and, needing to escape from their collective stare, he jumped up and ran to the men's room. Turning one of the faucets on full blast, he cupped his hands under the cold water and flipped them upwards, splashing the water against his face. He rubbed his wet hands through his curly hair, breathing deeply as he tried to gather up enough nerve to carry out his mission.

From the crowds' reaction, he could tell that things were not going well for the Yankees in their half of the inning. He realized that the teams were changing sides once again when the public address announcer told the crowd of the Texas hitters scheduled to bat in the sixth, and knew that his time for striking Gomez was dwindling. Rubbing his hands over his face once more, he decided that the next inning would be it. There would be no more backing down.

"Well, I guess you didn't listen to me," thundered a voice from behind Jeff as he reached for a paper towel to dry his hands. The towel dispenser was empty, and in its steel exterior Jeff could see the reflection of the guard who had taken his roll of toilet paper prior to the game.

Turning around slowly, with rivulets of water dripping from the bottom of his chin, Jeff spoke to the guard. "What can I tell you, officer? I knew that I'd end up here at some point. But it was just to take a leak, so I'm good without the paper."

"Some game out there, wouldn't you say? I tend to like games that are low scoring. I appreciate the pitching." The guard's last sentence was slower and more deliberate than the rest of their conversation, and Jeff realized that the guard was staring at his chest.

"Any fan of the game appreciates good pitching, officer," Jeff replied. He eyed the guard warily, waiting for the moment when the security officer would reach out and feel the bulge that protruded from underneath his jacket. Moments passed, however, without any such movement, and the guard did not even say anything further to Jeff. "Well, I guess I'll get back to my seat," Jeff said, still paranoid, fearful that the guard was then going to ask him to open his jacket. "I'd hate to miss the rest of a close game."

The guard looked at Jeff's face, and his eyes slowly made their way down Jeff's body as Jeff's eyes widened in fear. "Have a good time, son," the officer said, obviously unaware of the concealed weapon, as he unzipped his fly and moved toward one of the porcelain urinals.

Jeff turned and briskly made his way out of the bathroom as new rivers of sweat formed on his brow, testament to his sudden realization of the madness of his intentions. Actually, he did not suddenly have an epiphany as to the impropriety of his intended actions regarding Gomez, but he did realize that he could get caught, and that he would then suffer the consequences. While he did not see a problem with striking the ballplayer with a bottle and knocking him out of commission, he did have a problem with being punished for such an action.

"That was too close of a call," he thought to himself, and, forsaking the remaining four innings of the game, he did not return to his seat. His heart pounding ferociously, his gait became a sprint as he exited the stadium and ran all the way to the subway station, pausing only to toss the bottle from his jacket into a mesh garbage can that stood on the corner of 161st Street. He never looked behind him, not even as the subway pulled out of the station and made its way back to Manhattan.

CHAPTER 29

Jeff fled the subway when it reached his stop, and sprinted the entire distance to his apartment, narrowly avoiding being struck by two speeding taxis as he crossed one block under color of a red light. Rather than waiting for the elevator, he bolted to the stairwell and rapidly climbed the steps to his apartment, although his rate diminished gradually as he ascended flight after flight. When he reached his apartment door, he was wheezing loudly and sank to his knees to catch his breath.

A neighbor was in the hallway, and walked over to him to see if any assistance was required. Without even looking up, Jeff waved the concerned neighbor off, saying only that he had just finished with jogging and merely needed to catch his breath. The neighbor again offered his assistance if any was needed, and, seeing Jeff shaking his head in a negative fashion, continued on his way. Jeff was relieved that no more questions had been asked, particularly any questions with respect to why he would have been jogging in jeans and a denim jacket.

Climbing to his feet, Jeff reached inside his pants pocket and withdrew his keys. His hand was shaking as he pushed the key into the door's lock, but he was able to turn the key and open the door, remembering to remove the key only after he had closed the door behind him. He opened the door once more and, without looking into the hallway to see if any other neighbors were present, reached around the frame and grabbed the keys, bringing his arm back into the confines of the apartment and closing it for a second time.

Almost instinctively, he walked over to the couch, reached for the remote control which was sitting on the table in front of the couch, and turned on the broadcast of the game from which he had fled. It was now the bottom of the eighth inning, and the teams were knotted at one. When the Yankees' Ken Dowd came to bat, the television cameras focused on the stadium scoreboard. The scoreboard showed a replay of the home run that Dowd had stroked in the sixth inning, up until that point accounting for the Yankees' only run. The ball had come to rest a mere three rows from where Jeff's seat had been located. As the crowd rose to attempt catching the ball, Jeff recognized the faces of those who had been seated around him earlier that evening, and lamented that his panic-induced run to the men's room had possibly caused him to miss an opportunity at catching the home run ball. The game also had later excitement, as Dowd provided the crowd with an encore of his earlier shot, blasting a home run almost 15 rows deeper than the first shot in the bottom of the eighth inning to give the Yankees what would prove to be their only offense in a 2-1 victory.

Diego Gomez was hitless in four times at bat during the game, and had also made a seventh-inning error in center field. Jeff was disappointed, however, by the fact that Gomez was still in the lineup at the end of the game and had, in fact, made the second out of the ninth inning on a weak groundout. He stared at the screen as the post-game show ran, cursing himself for not having the stomach to carry out his plan, especially since he had come so close to doing so.. He cursed himself again for his fear, especially since that moment of fear had quite possibly cost him any chance of overtaking the Boozers. He never once compared himself to Greg; not once did he consider the fact that his own internal struggles with his conscience, his reluctance to carry out his intentions against Gomez, in a way, mirrored Greg's latest refusal to undertake any further actions which could cause a player harm or injury.

The telecast brought even more bad news for Jeff, and provided what would prove to be the final nail in his team's coffin. After the recap of the Yankees-Rangers battle, highlights and reports from that evening's other games were shown. For what seemed to be the first time in months, Jeff was not

309

intently staring at the screen when these highlights were provided. Instead, he sat with his head in his hands, lamenting his lost hope of victory. When he heard the name Andy Carpanda, however, his head snapped to attention. Carpanda, who had emerged as one of the finest members of an improving Minnesota rotation, had won ten straight outings after the all-star game and had lifted the Golds a place or two in all pitching categories except saves. The report out of Minnesota was that Carpanda had strained his elbow during that evening's game with Oakland and that he would be lost to the Twins for the remainder of the season.

Jeff looked skyward, as if to ask why his chances of winning were disappearing before his eyes. He silently mouthed the words "shit, I can't fucking believe this," to himself, and then walked to the refrigerator to retrieve yet another beer.

*****

Whether or not Jeff's belief that he had cost his team any hopes of winning the league due to his inability to sideline Diego Gomes were of little consequence over the next month. In reality, the Golds could not recover from the loss of Carpanda, as the pitcher whom Jeff called up to replace him had two horrific starts before the season ended, costing the team two places in each of the ERA and ratio categories. The loss of those four points proved to be the final nail in the Golds' coffin, although the team's inability to catch the leaders in any of the hitting categories also proved to be a detriment to any potential advancement in the overall standings. Jeff spent the month trying desperately to will his players to perform better, but his efforts proved futile.

When the season concluded in the last week of September, the Emerson Boozers were still atop the standings, with the Fish having climbed over the

310

Golds to finish in second place. The Golds finished in third, four points behind the Boozers and only one point ahead of the fourth place Jew Crew.

Jeff's only consolation was that the Yankees had captured the American League East Division crown and cruised through the playoffs, reaching the World Series before falling to the Los Angeles Dodgers in six games. With the pressure of the fantasy league removed from his mind as September drew to a close, Jeff was able to enjoy the post-season, watching all of the World Series games with friends, including recently-reconciled Brian Hunter and Mike Berger, either at one of their apartments or at sports bars.

After the Series concluded, and without the constant distraction of baseball and the fantasy league, Jeff set about restoring some level of normalcy to his life. He borrowed money from his mother, over his father's objection, so that he could pay Joe Emerson his portion of the winner's share, and agreed as a condition of the $15,000 loan that he would consider moving back to New Jersey to live with his mother and father when his lease expired in January should such a move be required due to lack of finances. He hoped that such a move would not be necessary; during the final week of the Series, he had accepted a temporary job as an accounts receivable clerk with a sportswear company. While the job description was certainly beneath him, the salary was acceptable and he was hired with the promise that he would be working on a two-month probationary period; his performance would be evaluated at the end of the year, at which point he would either be released or promoted to a full-time accounting position.

During this entire period of time, however, he made no attempts to speak to Greg. His cousin had earned an early vacation, along with the rest of the Brewers' personnel, when the team had failed to make the playoffs. From the information that Jeff received, it appeared that the newly-found idle time had awakened Greg's demons, just as he had discussed with his cousin in the past. Jeff's father had spoken to his Uncle Steve; he was been told that Greg was taking the lack of postseason play badly, and that he had begun to drink even more than he had in the past. His uncle had implored Mr. Goldstein to talk to Jeff about intervening and trying to talk some sense into Greg, since he knew how close the cousins were to each other. Jeff was extremely hesitant to do so, however, in light of their recent past dealings with each other, dealings of which his father and uncle were, and would continue to be, unaware. Jeff also took the reports of alcoholism to mean that Greg had also returned to his drug habit, and was uncomfortable about calling his cousin to see if that was true.

The one other attempt that Jeff did make at reconciliation was with Michelle. He sent a dozen long-stemmed roses to her apartment the first week of November, after the season ended and when he could devote time to her without her ever-present fear of being forsaken for baseball, but this gesture, as well as several telephone calls, went unanswered. After two more weeks of trying to reach her both at work and at home, Jeff reached the unhappy conclusion that their relationship had ended. Brian Hunter informed him that Diane could set him up with a friend of hers, but he declined, explaining that he needed some time to recover from the break-up before he would be able to consider dating other women. Even though he and Michelle had split months prior, it was only after the baseball season ended and his nights became emptier that Jeff realized the true extent of how much he missed her, and that he truly did love her. As Greg had told him, the thoughts increased with idle time.

Only now, there was nothing that he thought he could do to win back her favor. Diane Hunter had taken pity on Jeff and offered to speak to Michelle for him, but her only report was that Michelle did not want to discuss him or speak to him. She did not tell Jeff, at Michelle's request, about the lonely nights that she had spent wondering if there could be reconciliation between the two, especially as Thanksgiving and the holiday season approached; she was planning on traveling back to Pennsylvania for Thanksgiving that year, her first such trip for the holiday since her move to New York and her first to be spent without Jeff. Nor did Diane relate Michelle's realization to her that as time passed she came to realize that the two were fundamentally incompatible and that, despite their past history, that they could never again become lovers. Michelle did not want to hurt Jeff, at least any more than their breakup already had, and wished aloud to Diane that she could help him straighten out his life. But to do so, she added, would be too difficult a job for her to undertake emotionally.

Even without hearing this, though, Jeff slowly came to the same conclusion, that they would never reconcile and that he needed to straighten out his life and priorities. And from his perspective, this belief was even more troubling because he had brought on the breakup himself, and many of the rifts that had developed between the two were due to his lack of consideration for her, as well as what she believed to be his overwhelming fascination with baseball. He still wondered if the last part were true, even in the face of others telling him the same.

CHAPTER 30

The four men gathered in the Miller Park weight room, alternately hefting the twenty-five pound bar loaded with steel discs as a radio blared rap music in the background. A television monitor hung to the right of the room, and the set was tuned to the local Fox affiliate and its broadcast of that day's Green Bay Packers-Detroit Lions game. The four men were of various sizes and ethnic backgrounds, but all were clad in grey and blue sweats, each of which bore the Brewers' team logo. One of the men, surveying the fashion scene of the room, pointed out that they were wearing Detroit Lions' colors, but all were quick to distance their allegiance from the Motor City gridders and proclaim their support for the hometown, or, more appropriately, home-state Packers.

Outside the steel gates of Miller Park, it was a typically cold Wisconsin fall day. The mercury of the thermometer was beginning a merciful climb, inching slowly upward above the freezing mark, and the two inches of snow that had fallen the night before were beginning to melt. Those brave souls who walked the streets were bundled up to protect their flesh from the winds whipping around the stadium, their hands thrust deeply into pockets and their hair matted and tangled under their woolen hats. A woman walked cautiously with her two young children. The children, each dressed in multiple layers of clothing and their little bodies topped with down jackets, resembled the astronauts of Apollo 13. Their mother held tightly onto each by their hand, fearful that their slight frames could be uprooted by the periodic gusts of wind that caused them to lose their balance and reddened their cherubic and laughing faces.

The weight room in the stadium provided a sharp contrast to the scene on the other side of its walls. The extreme heat in the room was beginning to take its toll on the current and former athletes, causing them to peel off their

314

sweatshirts and continue their weightlifting regimen clad only in their t-shirts and shorts. Their body heat only added to the tropical climate, and the mirrors lining two of the room's walls were clouded with mist.

"Hey coach," yelled second baseman Rob Patton to his coach over the din of the music, "what is this shit that these assholes are making us listen to? Is it music, or a jailbreak? I can't believe that anybody would listen to this garbage." The white middle infielder looked over to his equally pale coach, and both broke out in laughter.

The hulking figure lying prone on the bench exhaled deeply, a fine mist of saliva spouting upward as he pushed the steel bar skyward, the veins in his arms protruding well above the level of his skin. Placing the bar on the holders behind him, he sat up and slumped forward, grasping the sides of the bench with his dark arms. The four 25-pound discs on either end of the bar quivered slightly as the bench moved under his mass. "What the fuck are you whiteys complaining about? This is the music of today, man, you'd better get used to it."

He wiped the sweat from his brow and turned in Greg Bloom's direction. "Even you, old fuckin' country man. This shit is the most popular music in the United States today. We ain't in no fuckin' hoedown." He shook his head. "Ain't no Hee Haw being played this day and age." He stood, steadied himself through a quick head rush, and walked over to a towel that hung from a nearby chair.

"Hee Haw?" asked Greg, his left eyebrow arching slightly as he glanced over at Rob Patton. "Hee Haw? You have got to be kidding me, Johnson. That lacks any sense of creativity, my man. Surely even you can think of something better than that." He walked over to the Brewers' designated hitter, Jerome Johnson, and pushed his 170-pound frame up against Johnson's sweaty

315

255-pound mass. "What kind of a redneck do you think I am?" he asked, poking his right index finger into Johnson's chest, "just because I ain't a brother doesn't mean that I'm a piece of white bread. Besides, one does not need to be black to appreciate good music." He took one of the steel discs from each end of the bar, and then sat down on the bench, reaching back to grab the bar with his left hand. "And when you play some good music instead of this ghetto crap, you will see what I mean. Right, Robby?"

"You got it, coach. Give me some Springsteen over this hip hop shit any day. The Boss puts these guys to shame. Instead of making music, if you can call it that, these guys should go back to killing and stealing." Johnson moved closer, and Patton sensed that his words had struck a raw nerve in his immense teammate. Instinctively, he took a couple of steps backward, well out of Johnson's long reach.

Greg picked up Patton's thought in mid-stream, as the two men continued to taunt Jerome Johnson with stereotypes about his race. "You know, guys, this rap music business is getting to be like boxing," Greg laughed, "if you haven't served jail time, you're doing something wrong."

"And the names," said Patton, "if you can even call them names." Johnson had taken a step toward Bloom, but turned back to Patton when Rob elaborated on his latest point. "Look at the discs that these idiots are churning out. And the kids just eat it up. Master this, MC that, L'il this, Young that. You have got to be kidding me with the stupid ass names that some of these guys call themselves."

Greg laughed. "No, Robby, maybe they have something there. As a matter of fact, I'm thinking of changing my name for professional purposes. The name Greg Bloom is just too boring. I think that I'll call myself 'Homey

Glove.' What do you guys think? Do you think that the brothers will start to dig me? I think that it has quite a homeboy ring to it."

"You mean that you should start calling yourself 'Homo Glove," answered Johnson. "You guys just don't get it. There's a statement behind the music. And as far as the trouble with the law, lots of you white boys have the same problems. You just want to have this stereotype of the young black criminals."

"If the stereotype fits ..."

"Hey, fuck you, Bloom. I'll kick your ass across this room. Coach or no coach, you listen to me," any sense of humor had disappeared from his voice, "the fact that these guys are usually just kids, like ballplayers, is forgotten. They're fresh from the streets. How do you expect them to act? One minute they've got pocket change and the next they're millionaires. People suddenly love them and chicks are throwing themselves at them. Does that remind you of anybody?" he asked, pointing to the photos of ballplayers that adorned the room's walls. "And let me tell you, enough shit goes on with guys in this league that they are not much different from the rappers."

"What kind of shit are you talking about?" quizzed Bloom.

"You know what I mean, Bloom," Johnson answered, "all the drugs and stuff. And how about guns? I'll bet that over half of the guys on this team carry guns. And I don't mean rifles like you country shits keep on the wall at home in a wooden rack. These aren't guns that red-fucking-necks use to shoot the heads off of little bambis out in the woods. I'm talking about pistols that these dudes carry everywhere, whether in the glove compartment of the car or brought into the clubhouse. They carry guns because it's a different kind of jungle out there. Shit happens everywhere, man. You think that shit in

Washington a couple of years ago was an isolated incident? When that basketball player pulled a gun on his teammate in the locker room? Don't be fucking stupid."

He turned to Greg and burned a hole through his forehead with a stare, adding that, "you better not make any little jungle jokes, whitey, or I'll come over there now and kick the shit out of you." Greg stayed on the bench, and pulled his right hand across his closed mouth as if to simulate zippering his lips shut. "You got anything to add, Patterson?" he asked, looking in the direction of the up-until-that point silent fourth member of the workout crew.

"Patterson? Please, call me by my rap name, F.U. Whitey," right fielder Jim Patterson said to roars of laugher from Bloom and Patton. And what players use drugs?" he asked, innocently as he reached his left hand into his pocket, "do we know any?"

Bloom and Johnson looked at each other for a second, and then all of the men burst into laughter as Patterson pulled a rolled joint from the pocket of his sweatpants. "None that we know of," they said in unison. Johnson reached for the illegal cigarette, but Patterson quickly pulled his hand away. "Hey man," said Johnson, "is there any more where that came from?"

"No," replied Patterson, "this is the end of my stash. But I have an idea. Do any of you guys have any shit? We can have a little party later. It's been a long time, and I think that we've earned it. We've been working pretty hard here lately."

"I've got a little in my apartment," chimed in Bloom, "but it won't be enough for all of us, much less special guests. We've got to score some. Who has a connection so that we can get some quickly? My guy got busted last month and I haven't found anyone new, that's why I'm a little low at the moment."

318

"I thought that you were quitting, coach," asked Patterson.

Greg glared in the player's direction. "I am quitting," he explained. "I am quitting using the shit often. Once in a while won't hurt anyone, Patterson."

"From what I've heard, that's not what they tell people when they go into rehab. And from what you're saying, it sounds like much more. But who am I to judge?" replied Patterson.

"Well, it's O.K. in my personal rehab, and until you have a medical or other license that says to the contrary, then, no, you are not one to judge me," explained Bloom. "Now, more importantly, which one of you guys has a connection?"

There was a brief silence, until a voice from the corner of the room called out, "I do."

Three faces turned to the doorway, where Rob Patton stood, his towel draped over his shoulders. Jim Patterson spoke first. "You, Robby? We didn't think that you were into this shit. What with that choirboy face, I can't believe that you would be one to smoke the devil's poison."

"Life is full of surprises, Patterson," Patton said sternly. "Besides, there's a lot about me that you guys don't know. We used to have some wild parties back home. As a matter of fact," he added, turning to face Johnson, "we used to grow the stuff in our backyard. And there's nothing better than homegrown, let me tell you that."

All three of the others gasped in mock horror. "Do you have any of that homegrown shit now?" asked Johnson.

"No, but I can make a quick phone call and have it delivered right outside of the clubhouse door," said Patton. "Just let me know how much and for when, and I'll come up with the shit. But you guys have to buy the food. I don't want to be buying food for you monsters when you start to get hungry. That goes especially for you, Johnson. The team doesn't pay me enough to keep you in food."

Johnson simply smiled at Patton's comment, content not to respond verbally. He did, however, rub his stomach for effect as he broke out into laughter.

"You got it," replied Patterson, smiling. "Just call your guy and get a couple of eighths. That should keep us and a couple of women happy for the night. We can go back to my place, if you want. I have food there."

"No way, Patterson, I've seen your place," interrupted Bloom. "We'll go back to my place. It's even a little clean. I think that the cleaning woman was in yesterday. We can listen to some of that ghetto music and have a little party with some of my favorite women." He motioned to Johnson. "You know how white women go for big black men."

Johnson nodded approvingly, still laughing, as did Patterson. "You're on, guys," said Patterson, "go make your call, Robby. It's time for a little fun tonight."

Patton reached for his cell phone, walked away until he was out of earshot from the others, to a quiet spot on the other side of the locker room, and made a quick phone call. He then called out, "done," to the other three men, and walked into the locker room to shower. The others then joined him in the shower, and when they all dressed and exited the locker room, they were met by a man approximately Johnson's size who handed Johnson a small brown bag in exchange for four crisp twenty-dollar bills. The players and Bloom then walked to Bloom's car, and drove off to his apartment.

None of the men noticed the white car that was parked five spaces from Bloom's. As they pulled away, the Toyota slowly followed, keeping a city block's distance from the rear of Bloom's Mercedes. Three men sat in the Toyota, one of whom held the four 20 dollar bills that he had just gotten from Johnson.

CHAPTER 31

Brewers' Coach Indicted For Player's Murder; Also Arrested With Two of Team's Players For Drug Possession

November 14, 2014 (AP)(Milwaukee) -- The professional sports world was rocked yesterday when Milwaukee Brewers' infielders' coach Greg Bloom was charged by a Grand Jury with committing the shocking murder of Brewers' left fielder Mike Jones four months ago. The former ballplayer was arrested late Sunday evening along with two current Milwaukee players after the threesome, along with another Brewers' player, purchased small quantities of marijuana from an undercover federal narcotics agent under the left field entrance gate of Miller Park, where the Brewers play their home games. A trio of Drug Enforcement Agency agents then followed the players and coach for several miles, to Bloom's apartment, where three of the four men were arrested.

The other member of the group, Brewers' infielder Rob Patton, was released soon after being taken into custody. Sources close to authorities have identified Patton as one of several players currently cooperating with the DEA in its attempt to further squelch steroid and other performance-enhancing drug use in baseball and other professional sports, which has continued to climb, according to sources, to epidemic proportions despite the drug tests currently in place and the number of suspensions handed down by baseball during the 2013 season. Patton could not be reached for comment following the arrests of his teammates and coach, and a Brewers' representative declined to be interviewed, citing the ongoing investigation. The DEA refused to confirm or deny the existence of such a program, but a ranking official stated that there have been discussions regarding gaining assistance from professional athletes in the past.

Various items of drug paraphernalia were discovered in Bloom's apartment when it was searched after his arrest. Federal officials exhibited the various items for the press, which included several glass freebasing pipes, a small quantity of cocaine, and more than two ounces of marijuana.

322

A subsequent search of Bloom's bedroom closet revealed, according to arresting officer Patrick Murphy, a handgun identical to that used in the Jones murder. The gun, according to state records, was registered to Jones. Fingerprints matching Jones' were reportedly lifted from a blood-stained sweatshirt found buried in another closet. Other blood-splattered items of clothing were discovered at that time.

The Grand Jury, which was convened almost immediately pursuant to the Prosecutor's power in high-profile cases, took only five hours to indict the once-popular coach for the murder once the prosecution's evidence against him was presented. Other counts were handed down against him for lesser charges, including possession of firearms and narcotics. If Bloom is convicted of all counts facing him, he could spend the remainder of his life in jail.

This week's events were only the latest in a turbulent season for both the Brewers and their scrappy infielder-turned-coach. Jones' brutal murder and the inability of the police to identify any suspects shocked and befuddled the city's residents early in the summer and it was thought by many that the police would never break the case. As for Bloom, he was already considered in less than glowing terms by many Brewers' fans due to the freak accident in which he collided with starting shortstop Juan Sanchez during a pre-game practice in New York before a game against the Yankees, shredding the ligaments in Sanchez's knee and sidelining him for the remainder of the season; it was said at the time that this injury cost the Brewers any hope that they may have had of contending for the National League Central Division title, as well as one of the League's playoff spots. Various reports also alleged that it was not an accident; no proof, however, was ever uncovered which would verify these allegations, and no formal investigation was ever undertaken by either the Brewers or Major League Baseball.

Bloom was also identified, along with several players and coaches, as playing a key role in the mid-season brawl between the Brewers and the Baltimore Orioles which left star Orioles' closer Paul Frank sidelined for two months of the season. Frank later accused Bloom of being the person who *separated his shoulder, and that he had done so intentionally and maliciously. Again, no evidence was ever proffered that could substantiate Frank's account of the events.*

Jones began the 2014 season with one of the Brewers' lower minor league teams, but quickly earned a promotion to the major leagues with his quick bat and speed on the base paths. When Brewers' center fielder Matt Distern fell to injury in early May, Jones was summoned and immediately stepped into the Milwaukee lineup, earning the leadoff spot within two week's time. Jones' season ended in an untimely fashion due to his murder, which had baffled investigators for months, but his eleven home runs, 20 stolen bases and .298 batting average during his time with the Brewers were enough to earn him a posthumous second-place finish in the balloting for the 2014 National League Rookie of the Year.

A long-time coach with the Brewers, Bloom's major league playing career was even briefer than Jones', as it was limited to eight games with the Brewers late in the 1998 season before he suffered a career-ending shoulder injury. Immediately after his career ended, he began his coaching career. Prior to his time with the parent club, he had spent several seasons in the Brewers' and Red Sox' minor league systems, and gained popularity with fans and players alike for his head-first style of play.

Jury selection for Bloom's trial could start as early as next March. Until then, he is being held on $1M bail in a Wisconsin state prison. Each of the players charged with drug possession, identified by authorities as Designated Hitter Jerome Johnson and outfielder Jim Patterson, were released on $150,000 bonds and will most likely plead guilty to lesser charges within the next month. All three individuals have been suspended from the team pending the outcome of the cases against them. It is anticipated that the players will be reinstated prior to the beginning of next season, but that the indictment against Bloom will signal the end of his association with organized baseball. The Commissioner is scheduled to meet with Bloom's attorneys next month, and sources close to major league baseball say that he will receive a lifetime suspension, with the ability to appeal after five years.

CHAPTER 32

Michelle left work at 6:30. The bitter November wind, cutting through her overcoat like a knife, sent a chill up and down her spine, so much so that she decided to take the subway home rather than walk the almost 20-block distance to her apartment. She bowed her head, and, facing the wind like a bull squaring off against a matador, hurried to Times Square to take the A subway train uptown to her West 61st Street apartment.

Once inside the subway terminal, she purchased a copy of *New York Newsday*, and began to thumb through the comics as she waited, still shivering, for her train to arrive. After two minutes, the light of the subway shone like a beacon through the darkened tunnel as the train made its approach to the platform. As the front of the train whisked by, Michelle peered inside its windows. She was surprised to see that there were many empty seats on the train, especially considering the sub-freezing temperature outside.

The subway noisily screeched to a halt and its doors opened. While most of the chilled people on the platform clamored into the fairly-crowded center cars of the train, Michelle and five others stepped into its almost-deserted last car, each of the new occupants finding an empty seat next to one of the double doors as they came to a close.

Michelle removed the brown leather glove from her right hand so that she could gain a better grip on the newspaper's pages, and turned to the back to read the football previews for the upcoming week. Page 102, the inside back page, contained articles on both New York area teams, the Jets and Giants, each of which was expected to lose their upcoming games. After glancing at these predictions, she rapidly flipped backward through the pages, intending to stop at the movie section. When she reached page 94, however, an article caught her eye and she stopped, staring intently at the page before her.

Brewers' Coach Pleads Guilty to Lesser Charge of Involuntary Manslaughter; Will Be Sentenced Next Week

November 17, 2013 (AP) (Milwaukee) - In a move that further shocked the baseball world, Milwaukee Brewers' coach Greg Bloom today pleaded guilty to involuntary manslaughter in connection with the mid-July murder of Brewers' outfielder Mike Jones. The plea agreement, apparently reached early yesterday morning, was shocking both for the admission of guilt and for the expediency with which it was reached.

The plea agreement also gained heightened praise for local and Wisconsin state authorities, who had been unable to identify a suspect in the Jones murder for almost four months, until Bloom's arrest on unrelated charges.

Bloom was arrested late Sunday night for purchasing narcotics, along with three current Milwaukee players, from an undercover police officer. One of the Brewers' players, Rob Patton, was later identified as having cooperated in the DEA's sting operation, and was released from custody later that evening. The other two players, Jerome Johnson and Jim Patterson, were released on bond and are expected to be charged with various drug-related offenses.

A subsequent search of Bloom's apartment uncovered various forms of drug paraphernalia, as well as evidence linking him to the Jones murder, including the murder weapon, a handgun that had been registered to Jones himself. The killing of the outfielder had baffled investigators since he was found dead almost four months earlier, and Bloom was indicted for the murder only one day following his arrest.

Sources inside of the Milwaukee prosecutor's office would not confirm nor deny rumors that Bloom had identified others who may have been involved in the murder. As of this time, it appears that Bloom's plea may prove an ending to the matter. One government source, who spoke on condition of anonymity, opined that it was likely that the investigation would be closed after Bloom's sentencing.

Sentencing is scheduled for next month. It is expected that Bloom will spend the first portion of any jail time in a drug rehabilitation center, as he has reportedly requested such counseling from local authorities. The same government source refused to speculate, however, on whether Jones' murder was drug-related. Spokesmen for major league baseball and the Brewers also refused comment.

Michelle sat, mouth agape, at the article and its contents. As the subway reached its intended destination, she tore the article from the newspaper, leaving the remainder on her seat as she exited to the platform, a gust of air smacking her in the face as a train whisked by in the other direction. She climbed a flight of stairs from the platform, and then walked to the giant escalator that would take her to the Columbus Circle station street level. The chill in her bones increased as she ascended to the top of the escalator, as the Columbus Circle winds whipped around with hurricane-type force. Again bowing her head forward to shield her face from the biting cold, she turned to her right and slowly made her way to her apartment building.

The article on Greg Bloom continued to haunt her during this two-block walk, however, as she clutched the torn article in the almost frost-bitten fingers of her left hand. Tears welled up within her eyes, as she thought back to the times that she and Jeff had spoken to Greg about his career, as well as the trip to Milwaukee when she and Jeff went to see the Brewers play the Yankees, complete with Greg's post-game locker room tour. The two cousins appeared so close at that time, and Greg had treated her as if she were a member of the family. It was shocking to her that Greg, who appeared to be such a decent

327

person during that visit and other occasions, could have been involved with drugs and the murder of another human being.

Deep in thought about Greg and the possibility of his going to jail, she thought nothing of the police car parked across the street from her building as she entered its front door and walked up the two flights to her apartment. Crossing the hallway to her front door, she unsteadily removed her keys from her pocketbook, as the warmth of the building's interior provided her body with a thawing effect. Her fingers, despite the leather gloves that she had worn to protect them, were beginning to tingle as the warm air provided some well-needed solace from the low temperatures of the street. She looked down at her shaking hands, failing to notice that she was not the only person in the hallway. As she unlocked the door, however, it became apparent that she was not alone as a deep voice came from her left.

"Michelle Stein?" the voice asked.

Frightened, she turned to her left, and found herself face to face with three men, two of whom were dressed in the dark blue uniform worn by New York City police officers. "Yes, Officers, I am Michelle Stein," she replied, her voice cracking with fear. "Is there a problem?"

The officer who had asked her name was standing closest to her. He motioned to his partner, standing directly to his left. "Ma'am, my name is Officer Casey, and this is Officer Brown. The other gentleman is Special Agent Matthews. May we have a word with you?"

Michelle began to tremble, a combination of thawing from the cold and fear. "Is it something serious, officers?" she asked, as a tear fell from her left eye. She wiped the tear from her cheek with her left glove. "I've always heard about how policemen go to people's homes to tell them that a loved one has died. Oh please, don't tell me that someone has died," she croaked, her soft voice continuing to strain with emotion. She began to tremble as more tears fell down her cheeks, and her bag dropped to the hallway floor.

"Nobody has died, ma'am, please calm down," the officer replied, placing his right hand on Michelle's shoulder in a reassuring fashion. "We are just here to speak to you about something. I don't feel comfortable talking about it out here in the hallway, though. May we speak to you in private?" Officer Casey asked, glancing to his right and then quickly to his left. He gestured to the apartment door, and then bent down to pick up Michelle's bag from the floor. "Perhaps we can come inside and speak to you over a cup of coffee. It would help to thaw all of us from this cold weather, don't you think?"

Michelle breathed a deep sigh of relief and gathered herself together, producing a crumpled tissue from her pocketbook and using it to wipe the remainder of the tears from her left cheek as her breathing slowed to a more normal rate. "Yes, please do come in, officers," she whispered, removing her key from the lock and pushing her apartment door open, "We can sit at my kitchen table. I hope you like decaffeinated coffee or, if you prefer, I can make tea."

CHAPTER 33

While his cousin remained behind bars in a Wisconsin holding cell, facing sentencing for the crimes to which he had confessed, Jeff retreated into a self-made prison of his own. For two days now, he had not left the confines of his apartment. Curtains drawn, he sat in the dark, fearful that the investigation surrounding his cousin would eventually lead federal authorities to his door. A thin corona of light peeked in from the edges of the drawn curtains, giving the left side of the room an eerie, albeit faint, glow.

The mere ringing of the telephone, like a shrill whistle piercing the silence, sent shivers up Jeff's spine and caused his heart to skip a beat. He would not answer either his home or cell phones, however, and both the answering machine and his cell phone were jammed with two days' worth of messages from concerned friends and family asking if he had heard the news about Greg Bloom and wondering how he was doing. The only call that he had returned was his parents', who had already called seven times and were threatening to call the police to check on him if he didn't call back immediately.

By his own admission to his father, he was not doing well. He told his father that he was extremely distraught over the accusations facing his cousin, but never told of his fears regarding his own actions and the actions that he and Greg had essentially taken together. Moreover, the lack of food and sleep over the past 48 hours had taken its toll not only on his body, but also on his mind. It wasn't just that he ignored the numerous phone calls and was fearful of stepping foot outside his apartment, no, it was much more than that. He was growing increasingly paranoid -- his fear of being swept up in the Jones investigation and being sent to jail consumed him, making him fear everyone and everything. He was unable to eat, he was unable to sleep, he was unable to do little more than sit in his apartment and stare at its walls, imagining how the world would look to

330

him if he was viewing it from the inside of a jail cell. He could not even use the telephone with the exception of the quick call to his parents, simply because he was unable to trust anyone. He could not tell anyone of what he had done; for fear that they would turn him in to the authorities.

He was fearful and distrustful of everyone, that is, with the exception of one person - the one person whom he longed to have in his life again. Last night he had listened to Michelle's voice on his answering machine, her second message of concern bringing tears to his eyes as he listened to it over and over again. "If you need me, just call," she said, her voice cracking, and the sincerity in her voice made Jeff believe her. He also believed, though he did not know why, that she was his only hope; that he could tell her the truth and she would understand. That she would be able to help him. That she could somehow make it all better and get him through. He did not stop to question why she was again calling him after months of avoiding his calls and attempts at reconciliation, except to reason that she had read about Greg and was concerned about him. She was worried about him, and she still loved him. He saw her calls as an extension of an olive branch to him; in his mind, all that he had to do was weather this storm and they could be together again.

As night began to fall and the penumbra of light around his shades began to fade, he decided that he would attempt to return her call. He reached for the telephone hesitatingly, and slowly, almost as if in a trance, punched out the digits of Michelle's phone number. Though he had not spoken to her for months, he remembered her number instantly. It was as if the numbers were emblazoned on his brain, permanently imprinted in his memory like ranchers brand their cattle.

One ring, two rings. On four he would hang up -- the last thing with which he wanted to deal was an answering machine. Third ring – "Hello?"

"Uh, hi, Michelle," he croaked, his quiet hesitancy masking the excitement of hearing her voice, "it's me."

"Jeff, is that you?" she answered. "You sound terrible. How are you?" she asked, making Jeff's emotions start to race even further. "Once I heard the news about Greg, I immediately called to check up on you. I couldn't believe what they were saying about him. I'm just so glad that you called me back."

Jeff unleashed an audible sigh. "You were always too good for me, you know," he muttered. His voice became a whisper, each word less audible that the prior one. He cleared his throat, the deep rumbling echoing through the receiver. "Look, it's not just about Greg and his problems. I'm in trouble, too. Do you think that you could come over?"

"What kind of trouble?" she asked.

His voice lowered. "I don't mean to be cryptic, but it's not something that we can discuss over the phone. Can you come over here?"

"I could be there in fifteen minutes," she replied.

"Wait, I have to clean up and get showered -- cleanliness has not exactly been a priority lately. Give me a half hour." The words were coming easier now, as the mere thought of seeing Michelle after all this time rejuvenated his spirit.

"Come on, Jeff, I know you well enough that you do not have to clean up. Remember, we dated for quite a long time. Or have you forgotten that time in your dorm room?" she asked, with just the faintest hint of laughter.

There was a memory that he had not thought of in a long time. They never did fix the furniture after they broke the bed and one of the chairs in his suite; they just exchanged them with furniture from someone else's room and left the others to pay for the damage. "Of course I remember. I remember all of the good times. Why do you think I'm calling?" he asked. "Why do you think that you are the only one that I trust?"

There was a pause. "Alright, Jeff," she answered after a few moments, "I will be there in a half an hour. Can I bring you something to eat?" she asked, to which he declined.

Jeff frantically straightened up the living room and kitchen of his apartment in anticipation of Michelle's visit. He threw all of the empty bottles, pizza boxes, and other evidences of foods consumed days and weeks earlier into the garbage, and picked up all of the newspapers which littered the apartment's floor. He then quickly showered, and had just finished getting dressed when he heard the ringing of the doorbell. It had been eerily quiet in the apartment for the past few minutes, as he had made sure to turn off the ever-present television sports channel in anticipation of Michelle's arrival. Certainly he could not have a game on, or highlights show, or any other sports programming, as that could anger Michelle as it had so often in the past.

When he opened the door and saw Michelle standing there, her body shivering under her olive overcoat, the top of her long, flowing hair tucked under a Yankees' wool cap, he could hardly restrain himself. All of the thoughts, all of the emotions that he had been bottling up inside of himself for the past couple of days, if not the past couple of months, suddenly overwhelmed him with a tremendous rush. These swelling emotions took the form of tears that glistened in Jeff's eyes, the moistness further accentuating the rivers of red that flowed outward from his hazel pupils. He reached out to Michelle to hug her, to finally have something, or somebody, to hold on to.

But she pulled away. Jeff's left hand barely grazed her right shoulder as she recoiled into the hallway, stumbling slightly as her feet passed over the diamond-shaped welcome mat. "I'm really concerned about you," she said firmly after regaining her balance, "on the phone you said that you were in some kind of trouble. What did you mean?"

"Come inside," he said, his eyes darting rapidly from side to side. She hesitated. When she did not move immediately, he repeated his request. "Seriously, come inside. I do not want to talk out here in the hallway."

She nodded and stepped into the apartment. He closed the door behind her, his nostrils filling with the delicate scent of her perfume as he passed through the doorway. It had been so long since he had smelled that scent, the very scent that had filled his days and nights so continuously for the years that they had spent together. Even after she would leave for the day, first when they would go to their classes and, later, to their respective occupations, her smell would linger behind as a reminder of her presence.

He sometimes wondered whether he left a similar imprint on her apartment. What would it be like on those days when he would stay in her dormitory room for the night and then leave for class in the morning while she slept in? Could she still feel his presence in the room even after he had physically left?

He always doubted it. He did not wear cologne, and the only smell that he thought he could leave behind would be a combination of deodorant and soap, with a measure of fresh minty toothpaste thrown in to complete the pharmaceutical smell.

None of that mattered now. The only important thing was that Michelle had come to see him. She was standing in his apartment, with only an arm's length separating him from her. She had called him, and therefore she still loved him. Suddenly, he was not as afraid as he had been only five minutes before. He reached out to touch her, but she again withdrew from his grasp, this time walking to the far end of the living room, pulling aside the blinds, and gazing out the window. She removed her overcoat and tossed it to the floor before turning back around to face Jeff. She was wearing a college sweatshirt – an F&M sweatshirt.

It was the first time that the blinds had been drawn in days, but while some light did enter the room, sunlight did not stream into the room as if the angels had suddenly decided to smile upon Jeff. Instead, it was cloudy and dank outside. Every so often a sunbeam would creep through the cloud cover, but the sky had clearly taken on a drab, grey persona.

The room itself, however, did seem brighter. Jeff wondered why Michelle's mere presence could lift his spirits so, but he had no answers. His perception of the room's brightness was heightened when he saw her sweatshirt, because surely she was wearing the sweatshirt of their alma mater because she wanted to reconcile with him. The answers that he could give were those that he was going to give Michelle -- the story, the true story, of why he was in such trouble. "Michelle, listen carefully to me," he stated hesitatingly, "I have something to explain to you, something that is not going to sound all that good."

"Yes, Jeff, what is it?" she answered in a clear, low voice. "You sounded awfully jumpy on the phone when you called before, and to be honest with you, not wanting to talk in the hallway just makes it scarier." She looked him over from head to toe as she spoke to him, gazing at his unshaven face, reddened eyes, and rumpled clothing. "Well, you were right about one thing," she added, "you do look terrible. Have you even slept in the last week?"

"It's about Greg," he said, ignoring her assessment of his condition.

"What's about Greg?" she asked.

"You know," he said, softly, as he turned away from her.

"I thought so," she whispered sympathetically, "I knew that you would take all of this hard. But what happens to Greg happens only to Greg. If what they are saying is true, he killed that ballplayer, not you." Now she turned, again facing the window, and shook her head from side to side. "Like I said before, I was really surprised to hear about the whole sordid tale. It didn't seem like it was really happening. But it was." She paused. "But it was happening to him, Jeff, not to you." She turned to face him, and then walked back to the window. "There's no trouble for you, though. It's not you who will be going to jail."

"But it is," he mumbled, the words barely audible.

Her long brown hair flew through the air as Michelle quickly turned back toward Jeff. Her mouth opened wide. "What?" she cried. "I don't understand. I could barely hear you."

Again Jeff turned away, now afraid to make eye contact with Michelle as he revealed his secrets. He paused, and slowly walked toward her, lowering his head as he spoke. "Greg murdered Mike Jones for me," he whispered.

"What?" she cried again, her eyes growing as big as baseballs. "I think I heard you say something, but I'm not sure because you were whispering."

"Greg killed Mike Jones after I asked him to make sure that Jones was forced out of the lineup," Jeff said, this time much more audibly. "The murder was an accident, but the whole reason that he started with Jones was for my benefit. I asked him to do something so that I could win the league. He went

336

over there to injure him, to have him pull a muscle or something, to make him stop playing. Greg said that they got into a fight and he ended up shooting him with his own gun. He thought that he had covered it up perfectly, but then the cops found all of the stuff in his apartment." Jeff explained.

"You're kidding, right? Please tell me that this is just some type of alcohol-induced craziness. Please tell me that you didn't ask your cousin to actually hurt someone for you," she pleaded, tears welling in her eyes.

"No, it is not craziness. Well, it is crazy, I guess, but it's true." He paused, searching her face in vain for any hint of sympathy. "Well, most of it is true … it is true that I asked him to hurt the guy." He again paused, as a tear ran down his cheek. After clearing his throat and taking a couple of deep breaths to better compose himself, he continued his confession. "And there is more," he explained, "I knew that he was going to have that accident with Juan Sanchez and he even dislocated that pitcher's shoulder for me in that brawl."

"What do you mean for you? What in the name of hell are you talking about?" Her voice was rising to a fevered pitch. "Why on earth would you want a person dead or injured?"

"It was all for the league. Remember the fantasy . . ."

She cut him off once she heard the word "fantasy" come from his mouth. "The fantasy baseball league? Are you out of your fucking mind? What the hell are you trying to tell me?" she yelled, the veins in her neck becoming more and more evident as the volume of her voice increased even louder.

Her tone and volume of her response caught Jeff by surprise. He had tried to anticipate what she would say when he revealed the story to her, but he had never heard her curse before, other than when she was enraged, such as the

337

last time that she had been in his apartment and she had fled when he took that phone call from Bob Fishman. And yet the word "fucking" came from her mouth comfortably, as if she had used it in everyday language for the past ten years. Jeff could not even remember ever hearing her say anything filthier than "heck" or "damn" in all of their time together, other than that time and maybe one or two other occasions. Michelle had always presented herself in a classy, non-profane way, he suspected to avoid stereotypes from her small-town roots, such that such foul language was just not a part of her mystique, her persona.

"The fantasy league," he said, as he sat down on the end of his leather sofa and buried his head in his hands, "I wanted to win so badly." He wiped his face, tried to compose himself, and looked her squarely in the eye. "A hundred and fifty thousand dollars was at stake. I knew that I could do well, but I needed help to win. I offered him thirty five if he would help me."

"You call all of this help? Killing and hurting people? That is how your cousin helped you to win? And he helped you for what, the possibility of winning thirty five thousand dollars? You're both a couple of idiots, you know that?" Her sarcastic intonation on the word "helped" belied her disbelief and disappointment with what Jeff was trying to explain to her.

"I needed to get one of my players into the starting lineup," he explained, slowly, in an attempt to calm Michelle, "so Greg gave me a hand. At first, it wasn't that bad; it was just going to be Jones, and, like I said before, I didn't know he was going to kill the guy. The shoulder thing with the Baltimore pitcher was actually an accident -- he only meant to bruise the guy's arm so that he would miss a week or two, not the whole rest of the season. As for Sanchez, that was actually Greg's idea. I didn't ask him to do that one. He did it because he was jealous that the kid was playing and he wasn't. He came to me with that one. I guess that the resentment was really the drugs talking. I knew that he

338

would do something, but I didn't know exactly what or to whom. I probably could have guessed, and I didn't try to talk him out of it. But to be honest," he added, running his hand along his chin, "it helped my team to have him out of the lineup."

Michelle looked at him incredulously. "I cannot believe what I am hearing. It wasn't that bad at first? Are you kidding me? A guy died, Jeff. He died!" She hesitated, placing her hands on her hips and shaking her head in obvious disbelief. She moved closer to Jeff, not letting his eyes escape her glare. "I just cannot believe the way that you are justifying this bullshit. He only meant to hurt one guy a little? He wanted to hurt the other guy so there was nothing that you would do to stop him because you didn't know who would be harmed? Do you even listen to yourself? Do you hear what you're saying to me?"

She approached Jeff, so that they were now standing toe to toe. "So I guess that it wasn't your fault?" She stepped backward and shook her head, her hair flowing from side to side. "You are out of your mind. Do ... do you think that these excuses make everything alright? A guy got killed? I suppose that you have some whopper of an excuse for that one."

"No," Jeff stammered, "it was an accident, but no, I know that it's not an excuse . . ."

"To think that I spent all of that time with you, and that at one time I actually thought that we would get married and spend the rest of our lives together." She brushed a tear from the corner of her right eye, rubbing her left hand slowly along the back of her tensed neck. "Well, obviously we made a good decision in not getting married. You really need some help." She moved forward to him, lowered her left arm, and smacked him on his right arm. "How can you live with yourself? How could I have lived with you?"

Jeff was stunned that Michelle struck him. He slowly rubbed his right arm with his left hand, and then took his hand and reached for her hand, which she again pulled away. "But I swear," he cried, "the Jones murder never should have happened. I wanted him sidelined, I can't deny that. He was hitting way too many homers, driving in too many runs, and stealing all of those damned bases. I couldn't win if he kept producing at that level. But I certainly didn't want him dead."

"Then why is he dead?" she shot back as her face turned an even brighter shade of crimson. "Tell me, Mr. wanna-be baseball owner, why is he dead?"

Jeff once again lowered his head, unable to maintain eye contact with his enraged ex-girlfriend, his enraged would-be savior. "He's dead because Greg has a drug problem, just like you've probably read about. I know that this revelation won't be a surprise to you after what you've been reading in the papers, but he has been a heavy cocaine user for some time now. Jones was another coke-head. One night, the two of them were freebasing. Greg was going to start a fight with Jones, and he was going to try to break Jones' leg, make him pull a muscle, something." Now he looked back at Michelle, looking again for even a scintilla of sympathy. Michelle remained stoic, however, her arms now crossed as she listened to Jeff's story. "It was all part of our plan. He thought that if Jones got hurt while they were doing drugs together the Brewers would bury the true cause of the injury, because they would want to keep the drug habits of its player and coach a secret. In that way, nobody, outside of those involved, would know the true story of what happened."

"You're telling me that the team would completely hide the way he got hurt? How would that be?" she asked, her arms still crossed over her chest defiantly.

He tried to explain. "It's really quite easy and more common than you would think, or even want to think. The Brewers would release a statement that Jones had fallen at home or something to that effect. Every so often a professional athlete will suffer a phantom injury at home -- and most of them can be tied directly to drug use. Do you really think that athletes stab themselves with forks or other kitchen utensils? No, they don't, but their wives and girlfriends to. All part of the cover-ups that go on."

"And how do you know this?"

"That's not important," he said, slumping into his leather arm chair, both his body and the chair making creaking noises as his rear end sank firmly into its seat. "Anyway, Jones somehow got hold of a gun. Greg wrestled him to the ground, and the gun went off. The bullet went right through Jones' stomach, and he bled to death right there on the floor. Greg didn't know what to do, especially since he didn't pull the trigger. He just panicked and tried to hide the body."

"I can't believe this. It can't be true." Michelle's voice was rising again, and she was growing more and more visibly upset. "How could you be a part of this? What were the two of you thinking? And why the hell would Greg sabotage his own baseball team, a *real* baseball team, place his job and professional career on the line, just for you?" She was shaking with anger as her face grew redder and redder. "Rather," she asked, "why would he do it for the good of some stupid game?"

"I already told you. For thirty five thousand dollars," Jeff answered, quietly. "That's what I promised him if he helped me win. Thirty five thousand dollars buys a decent supply of drugs, and Greg was pretty much blowing through his salary at a fast rate."

"For a game you offered to support your cousin's drug habit? Are you crazy?"

For the first time, Jeff thought that this was a possibility. "Am I crazy?" Jeff wondered. Maybe, but that didn't really matter now. All that mattered was that he was in a heap of trouble and there was little hope, if any, of escape. That one glimmer of hope, Jeff still reasoned, rested squarely on Michelle's lovely shoulders. Jeff had explained to Greg the importance of family. Jeff's parents kept telling him about how family could always help. But he did not want to turn to family now. He wanted, he needed, to turn to Michelle. She was the family that he wanted. He didn't know how, but somehow, some way, she would be the one to help him avoid the inevitable consequences of his and Greg's actions.

"Look, I ... I really need ... really need your help," he stammered, as Michelle continued to gaze outside at the street below. "How can I get out of this mess?"

"What do you want me to do?" she shot back sarcastically. "Do you want me to wave a magic wand and tell you that everything will be all better? Do some ancient tribal dance to spare those on the way to prison, if not to hell, for murder? Turn back time?"

Turn back time. That had a nice ring to it. He could start all over again. Not just with this damned baseball league, but his whole life. Especially with Michelle. This time, he could do everything right. He would not ignore her. He would be sensitive to her feelings. Most importantly, he would care more about her than the batting average of the Los Angeles Angels' shortstop. No more sneaking off to watch a ballgame when he was supposed to be with her, unless she wanted to watch with him. No more watching games until three o'clock in the morning, unless she wanted to watch with him. No more hour-long phone calls with other members of his fantasy league trying to pull the trigger on a trade between four players that most people had never even heard of, unless she was not there or was otherwise occupied. He would devote his time to her and her interests. Most of it, at least.

And this time he meant it. He would not break his promises this time. He had to tell her.

"I need you, Michelle. I always have. I've always loved you but I messed up. I really messed up, just like I messed up this baseball thing. You gotta believe me. If I get out of this shit, I'll change. Everything will be different between us. Better. Not like it was. I will pay attention. I will put you first. We can go to museums and art shows and all of the stuff that you like. I will even stop with the baseball league." He paused and began to cry softly. "I can do it," he croaked, "and I want to do it."

"Jeff, stop it." Michelle's eyes were again beginning to well up with tears, and her upper lip quivered nervously as she fought back the emotions obviously churning within her. "Don't say anything else. It can't work between us anymore."

"Yes it can, I know it can. I know that I promised to be better in the past, but this time I'll follow through." At this point, he wanted to reconcile with her so badly that he was willing to lie to her in order to win back her favor. "I'll give up the fantasy league. I just need for us to be together, and for you to help me through this." He reached out once more to embrace her, and this time was able to grab her before she could squirm away. He pressed his lips to hers, and kissed her like he had vowed he would if he ever got her back again. He pressed his body firmly against hers, feeling every curve of her body as if it was the first time that he had held her.

Suddenly, however, he felt something hard between her breasts. "What the hell is that?" he yelled, as she broke free of his embrace and again ran to the window and peered out from in between the shades, quietly tapping her hand against the window. The resulting silence was quickly broken, though, by a loud knock on the door.

"Open up, Jeff," the deep voice from the other side of the door commanded, "it's the police."

Jeff glanced over at Michelle, who sat curled up in the corner to the right of the window, her hands covering her face as she sobbed and turned away from Jeff. "How could you do this to me?" he asked, "how could you do this to me?" By now his voice was but a whisper, almost drowned out by the continuous, rhythmic knocking on the door.

"Are you O.K. in there, Michelle?" asked the officer on the other side of the closed door. "The game's over, Jeff. Let us in and nobody will get hurt."

Jeff opened the door and stepped back. Three uniformed police officers rushed into the room, two of them immediately taking Jeff into their grasps as the other ran to protect Michelle. Jeff listened as the first officer read him his Miranda rights and placed his hands behind his back. He grimaced as the cold steel of handcuffs being placed by another cop cut into his wrists. As the two policemen started to walk him out of the room, he turned to Michelle. "How could you do this to me?" he asked again, his voice trailing off as the officers led him outside into the hallway, and then downstairs to a waiting patrol car.

344

But this time Michelle did not hear him. She sat sprawled in the corner of the room, crying uncontrollably as the third officer, Officer Casey, placed his hand on her shoulder, just as he had the previous day, in a futile attempt to comfort her. Through choked sobs, the only words that she could manage to speak were, "I just wanted to help you," but Jeff had already been led out of the apartment and was not able to hear her voice.

She also shivered from the feeling of cold steel as a mini-microphone sat clipped to her bra, firmly between her heaving breasts, Jeff's admissions preserved on the tape that was strapped to her waist and on the remote tape nestled under a file on the front seat of the nearby patrol car.

CHAPTER 34

"We live in a fantasy world, a world of illusion. The great task in life is to find reality."

- Dame Iris Murdoch, Irish-born British author/philosopher

The sun hung lazily over the Stadium, its bright blue seats and glistening metal shining brightly in the midday sun. There was nary an empty seat in the house, with the capacity crowd preparing for the home team's half of the ninth inning. The scoreboard indicated that the visiting Bayonne Bombers were leading the host Golds in the final stanza of a 4-2 game. The crowd groaned when the first batter in the bottom of the ninth grounded out to the shortstop, but then roared in anticipation of the second hitter, the group trying desperately to provide additional motivation for their team to rally and emerge victorious.

"Now coming to bat for the Golds, right fielder, number 32, Reggie Jefferson, number 32," intoned the public address announcer, his voice barely registering above the din provided by the crowd's cheering. The pitcher, clearly tiring and seemingly rattled by the deafening crowd noise, ran the count to three balls and one strike before Jefferson stroked the horsehide for a single into shallow left field. Bombers manager Joe Spadola, sensing that his pitcher was in trouble, strode to the mound, motioning with his right hand for his ace reliever, Joey Williams. The new pitcher strode to the mound as a cascade of boos thundered throughout the stadium, and then calmly took some warm-up throws before indicating to the umpire that he was ready to face his first batter. The crowd roared anew as the home team's hulking designated hitter walked to the plate from his position in the on-deck circle.

"Now batting for the Bombers," boomed the smooth baritone voice of Bob Sheppard, "the designated hitter, number 34, Randy Garcia, number 34." Williams, intent on holding the runner at first, threw three attempted pick-off throws to the first baseman before his first offering to Garcia. He was equally cautious in his pitch selection, and the patient Garcia was walked on five pitches. The next batter was catcher Len Cooper, who made the second out of the inning by laying down a perfect bunt to sacrifice the runners to second and third.

The Golds were down to their last three strikes, with only one batter separating the visiting Bombers from the league championship. Second-year outfielder Phil Nicks was the next scheduled hitter, but an unfamiliar figure strode from the dugout, stopping briefly in the on-deck circle to rub pine tar on the handle of his bat.

"Now batting for Nicks," announced Sheppard, "number 48, the player-manager of the Golds, Jeff Goldstein, number 48." Jeff Goldstein strode to the plate with long, bold strides, and planted himself in anticipation of Williams' first offering.

Goldstein watched the first two pitches go by, without even taking the bat off of his shoulder. The first was called a strike by the umpire, and the second, despite being in the same location, was termed a ball. With the count even at 1-1, the noise reverberating from the stands increased, the cheering of the crowd rising still, as the pitcher reared back for his third pitch. "Williams checks the runners, rocks, and delivers the ball plateward," exclaimed an excited Mel Allen to the nationwide television audience. The center field camera showed the hitter's eyes widen as the spinning spheroid neared him, seeming to grow larger and larger as it approached the plate, eventually appearing to balloon to the size of a watermelon.

Jeff Goldstein swung, and with an enormous crack of the bat and high arc of the ball, the crowd immediately sensed that the ball was going to reach the seats in left field for a game-winning, and championship-clinching, home run. Jeff, believing in the same outcome, thrust his arm skyward in celebration, and as he reached the first base bag he slowed and began a slow, deliberate home run trot to victory. Those in the Golds' dugout rushed from the bench, and stood on the top step of the dugout, watching the ball as it arced gracefully into the bright blue sky, approaching the far reaches of the stadium.

Their celebration, however, was slightly premature.

As Allen called the play, "Goldstein swings, and lifts a deep shot to left-center field. That ball was hit a ton. It's going, going, and … wait a minute, caught above the fence by the center fielder! HOW ABOUT THAT! What a play by the center fielder, leaping almost three feet above the fence to rob Goldstein of a home run and preserve the pennant for the Bombers -- What a play by that kid in center field! What a play by Mike Jones!"

"I'll tell you," broadcast partner Russ Hodges added, "the team expects fine things from the young man out there in center field. And he just robbed Jeff Goldstein of his chance to play hero, of his chance to be a winner. Remember that name, folks -- Mike Jones."

Jeff, instead of watching the ball soar into the distance, had initially lowered his head and begun loping around the bases. As he passed first base, he started to slow his triumphant home run trot. Now looking toward the outfield to admire what he believed to be the winning hit, however, he was shocked to see Jones leap, reach above the outfield wall, and make a spectacular, game-saving catch to preserve victory, and the championship, for the Bayonne Bombers. Stunned, Jeff dropped to his knees on the dirt between first and second bases as the visiting team swarmed the field, engulfing its relief pitcher in a mountain of players a scant few feet from where Jeff knelt. The Bombers' fielders, including Mike Jones, rushed in from their positions to join the fray.

Jones carefully held his glove to his side, the ball used to make the final out tucked inside for safekeeping. As he passed the kneeling Goldstein, he glared in the opposing manager's direction and then smiled, not just gloating over his remarkable catch but also seeming like someone who had achieved some form of revenge or retribution for a prior incident. Jeff saw Jones' smirk and, feeling overcome by an indescribable wave of guilt, quickly turned away. After remaining on the infield dirt for a moment, he struggled to his feet and looked toward the pitcher's mound of his home stadium, watching the opposing team celebrate its victory. Unable to watch that scene unfold in front of him, he turned and looked into the seats behind the home team's dugout, where he could see his cousin, Greg Bloom, and former girlfriend, Michelle, standing and watching the proceedings.

Greg, dressed in blue jeans and a blue denim shirt, stood next to a uniformed policeman. He grinned, the steel of the handcuffs which encircled his wrists reflecting the light of the sun as he clapped his hands furiously. Chains ran from his handcuffs down his sides, their ends shackled to the bracelets which ran around the bottom of his pants legs. Michelle stood to Greg's left, clad in a familiar cream-colored sweater and navy blue shorts. Catching Jeff's stare, she shook her head slowly from side to side in disapproval. She ran the fingers of her right hand through her hair, and then began to clap in appreciation of Jones' heroic effort. As he stared in her direction, Jeff could not help but notice that her fingers were devoid of any jewelry; conspicuously absent was an engagement ring. Jeff lowered his head and walked slowly, dejectedly, back into the dugout and sat on its bench. He did not make any more eye contact with either Greg or Michelle as he neared his destination.

There were no other people in the dugout. Jeff buried his head in his hands and began to sob. As he did, the cheering of the crowd slowly subsided, and was replaced by an eerie silence. Jeff wiped the last tears from his eyes and, taking a deep breath, decided to stand up and walk into the clubhouse to apologize to his team for his failure to deliver the winning blast. As he stood, however, he realized that he was not in the dugout. He was not in a baseball stadium. Scanning the room through his reddened eyes, he realized that, much like every day for the past year, he was all alone. To his left was a sink and toilet instead of a bat rack. Behind him was the hard bed on which he had been sitting, instead of the dugout bench. The walls around him were all brick, and the only door to the room was covered with vertical steel bars.

Jeff caught a glimpse of himself in the small mirror that hung on the wall, and saw the white numbers and letters stenciled onto his brown state-issued prison jumpsuit. A small amount of light trickled in from the two-by-two mesh window. Suddenly he remembered that he was not in a Stadium, nor was he home in his apartment.

A handwritten sign was taped to the wall to the right of the mirror, located just above a picture of Michelle. Scrawled in pencil, it read "Only thirty days until Spring Training."

THE END

ALSO BY ANDREW WOLFENSON

"*People may hate lawyers but they love to read about them and this book proves why. **In His Own_Defense** is a realistic look at the human drama that surrounds a high-stakes criminal case. The pitch-perfect prose and provocative plot compel you to read on, late into the night. New Jersey's own Andy Wolfenson is a north-of-the-Mason-Dixon line answer to John Grisham.*" – Henry Klingeman, Esq., Criminal Defense attorney and former Assistant U.S. Attorney for the State of New Jersey.

What happens when an attorney is wrongfully accused of murdering a client's husband? Are conversations and interactions between the client and attorney protected by the Attorney-Client privilege, or is the attorney capable of defending himself against the false accusation, even if his actions prove damaging to the client?

Eric Goldberg is a New Jersey attorney who is first seduced, and then falsely accused of murder, by one of his clients. While testing the boundaries of the attorney-client privilege in conversations with the local police, he travels to Brazil to locate the one person who can clear his name. There, he gains the assistance of a transplanted American architect and his free-spirited girlfriend, who lead him through the streets and clubs of Sao Paulo searching for his accuser. All the while, American and Brazilian police are searching for him.

"In His Own Defense" is available on Amazon.com and for Kindle

www.ingramcontent.com/pod-product-compliance
Lightning Source LLC
Chambersburg PA
CBHW071043250626
47159CB00002B/351

* 9 7 8 0 6 1 5 9 7 1 6 3 6 *